"ALERT. WE HAVE INCOMING," PRICE SAID UNEXPECTEDLY

"Buy me some time," Tokaido said, leaning over the keyboard. "Five minutes, maybe less."

"Too late. There's a trace on your signal," Wethers reported. "The second HK is trying to find you. I strongly suggest breaking the connection."

"Almost done," Tokaido whispered hoarsely, every muscle tense. "Just a little bit more."

"Break the link. It bypassed the SETI station and is coming after us directly," Delahunt said urgently, then added, "It already knows we're in eastern North America."

"If the people controlling the HKs find this base..." Katz left the statement hanging, but moved his hand to a locked gangbar, ready to cut the power to the entire base to prevent identification.

Breathing heavily, Tokaido flicked his fingers over the keyboard. "Ah! I found a hidden file. God, the encryption is triple induced morphisms! No time to break through that. I'm going to burn out their hard drive and steal the buffer."

"There's no time!"

W9-AUK-128

DON PENDLETON'S

STONY

AMERICA'S ULTRA-COVERT INTELLIGENCE AGENCY

MAN®

SKY
KILLERS

A GOLD EAGLE BOOK FROM
WORLDWIDE®

TORONTO • NEW YORK • LONDON
AMSTERDAM • PARIS • SYDNEY • HAMBURG
STOCKHOLM • ATHENS • TOKYO • MILAN
MADRID • WARSAW • BUDAPEST • AUCKLAND

First edition February 2002

ISBN 0-373-61941-3

SKY KILLERS

Special thanks and acknowledgment to
Nick Pollotta for his contribution to this work.

Printed in U.S.A.

SKY KILLERS

PROLOGUE

The heavy steel door of the underground bunker was pushed aside by armed guards, and a slim, elderly man walked into the dimly lit room.

His pace was slow, almost stately, the metal tip of his walking stick tapping against the cold marble with mechanical regularity. The face of the man was neutral, hiding every thought, yet his eyes were sharp and alive. Many in the room recognized it as the face of a trained killer.

In odd counterpoint the cane was polished ebony and covered with an elaborate network of silver filigree. It was his only item of high fashion. The rest of his clothes were strictly utilitarian, a light silk suit and woven leather shoes to combat the terrible heat outside.

Set into the smooth perfection of the marble floor was an elaborate symbol of some kind, the borders edged with gold. The old man walked over the design as if it were no more than a decoration rather than the bloody seal of honor that bound their lives together. Nobody made a comment.

With satisfaction he noted in passing the computer-generated maps of the world that covered the walls, lights and coded symbols constantly changing on the displays to show updated information: airplanes in flight, satellites in orbit, troop movements, tropical storms and such.

Watching the slow approach of their commander from the center of the chamber was a group of hard-faced men sitting in plush chairs situated around a heavy wooden table. Many of the grim men were chain-smoking, a few fidgeted nervously but nobody was drinking.

Some of the soldiers were old, others young, but all proudly bore scars from battles hard fought and won. Only combat veterans sat on this council. No thirty-day wonders or military-academy graduates were allowed, bold teenagers who had yet to take a life with their bare hands. Every man here had the agonized screams of friends and foes echoing in his mind, the terrible memories fueling the fire of their resolve to win at any cost.

At a leisurely pace the old man accepted a chair at the front of the round table and laid aside his cane, then spent a minute smoothing out the neatly pressed seams of his spotless silk suit. Wordlessly the leader of the consortium looked over the great assembly of his colleagues. Their faces were taut, eager, but none dared be the first to ask.

"It has begun," he said softly.

Stolid expressions slit into smiles, shoulders relaxed and many gave a low laugh or muttered a brief prayer.

On the walls behind them, several of the lights started blinking rapidly and one winked into darkness. Then another, and yet another. Four, six more!

At long last the war was in progress, and the nations of the world didn't even know that they had already lost the first battle.

CHAPTER ONE

The banging noise came from nowhere.

Suddenly alert, Hector Alvarez stepped away from the moss-covered wall of the crack-cocaine lab to look sharply about at the jungle. Swinging a 9 mm Uzi submachine gun in front of him, the man wondered what could it be. The banging and clanging was getting steadily louder from the east—no, the north.

Stepping out of the cool shadow of the overhang, Alvarez snapped the bolt on his Uzi and craned his neck to study the grassy slope of the small hillock that fed a stream of clear mountain water to the hardsite. Something was cutting a swath through the plants, jumping and moving as straight as an arrow. If not for the metallic sounds, he would naturally have assumed it was merely an alligator or wild boar. The runoff water from the lab sometimes carried trace amounts of the cocaine, and some local animal would go insane and charge the compound.

Glancing up at the guard tower across the compound, Alvarez raised a questioning hand and saw a man with a mustache shrug elaborately as his partner leaned dangerously over the split-log railing of the tower. He was holding a pair of military field glasses to his face, trying to find the source of the disturbance.

Then the second guard burst into laughter, and Alvarez caught a flurry of motion out of the corner of his vision.

Spinning fast, the big man almost fired his weapon until he realized that it was an old rusted barrel wildly rolling down the hillside. The battered container bounced over the rain gullies to land with a loud crash and continued plowing over the network of thick vines that covered the ground like veins in the living green flesh of the ancient jungle.

Easing his stance, Alvarez smiled at the antics of the water barrel, then abruptly frowned when he realized it was coming straight through the open gates of the palisade wall. Coincidence maybe, but how the hell did a barrel get up the hill in the first place? All of the drums they used for water and gasoline for the Hummers and gunships were in the garage. Acting on impulse, Alvarez snapped the bolt on his Uzi and sprayed a couple of bursts from the stubby weapon. Mostly he hit dirt, but when he finally hit the rolling barrel, clear fluid sprayed into the air from the copper-jacketed Parabellum rounds.

Okay, it wasn't some kind of a rolling Molotov cocktail; the barrel was merely filled with water. But the nervous guard still moved away from the concrete bunker of the chemical lab where the coca leaves were reduced to the silvery white powder of pure quill cocaine. There was a staff of five chemists inside, along with ten armed guards and thirty naked girls from the local village. Their lack of clothing was very pleasing, and no girl was more than twenty years of age, but it also served to make sure nobody was stealing even the smallest amount of the white gold. Death and horrible torture seemed to make no difference to deter thieves. In spite of their state of undress, the guards daily checked the girls for any pilfering. It was one of the nicer perks of the job.

Now reduced to a whirligig, the barrel sprayed out streams of water from the bullet holes as it built speed and rolled across the compound to slam directly onto the corner of the concrete lab, the cheap steel container noisily wrapping itself around the corner as it instantly stopped, jammed tight into place.

Armed men appeared from a dozen small brick buildings across the compound at the crash, and as Alvarez took a step toward the drum, brilliant white light filled the universe and the guard was flying backward from a brutal concussion of hot air. As he hit the ground hard and lost his weapon, his hearing returned with a vengeance. The strident detonation of a massive C-4 explosion rumbled across the hardsite, rattling the trees for hundreds of yards, birds and monkeys screaming at the violent intrusion of warfare into their peaceful world.

As the roiling cloud of gray smoke cleared, Alvarez could see the thick concrete wall of the lab was smashed apart. The exposed lab was on fire, glass vials cracking every second from the heat. Beyond was the packing table, where the girls loaded the balloons and condoms for the mules to carry. Everything was coated with a fine white dust, a hundred million dollars of coke scattered to the winds.

Just then the door at the other end of the bunker was thrown open, and out rushed the workers, clutching armloads of their clothes. Screaming and weeping, the naked girls dashed pell-mell for the open gate of the palisade, heading for the safety of the trees. Dizzy from the blast, Alvarez tried to follow them to close the gate when he saw a group of armed men step out of the jungle.

Military helmets with tinted visors covered their faces, giving the invaders an unearthly appearance. Each wore a combat rig of ammo clips and grenades over a camouflage-colored military uniform, additional pieces of vines and leaves draping their bodies to complete the illusion. Two of the soldiers held large weapons Alvarez couldn't easily identify, and the rest carried submachine guns, the barrels tipped with sound suppressors.

Growling an obscenity, Alvarez fumbled for his weapon

only to find the Uzi gone, the strap torn loose from the violent explosion earlier. There had to have been a C-4 satchel charge hidden inside the rolling barrel. The trick hadn't been that the container was filled with gasoline, but that the real explosive was protected by deflecting water.

Searching frantically about on the ground, Alvarez dived for his weapon as the siren on top of the guard tower started to cut loose with a strident howl. Almost instantly a fiery dart stretched out from the jungle to detonate on the platform on top of tower, the two guards and the .50-caliber machine gun blanketed with chemical flame. The guards fell from their post, screaming human torches as the four support legs were blown apart by the underground blasts. The wave of hot shrapnel spread across the hardsite to tear apart a dozen more guards. Then the crippled tower leaned over and crashed onto the garage, crushing the only door and sealing the Hummers with their additional armament inside.

A sharp whistling sounded from above, closely followed by muffled thumps, and thick clouds of smoke began to fill the air. Struggling to free a clump of earth from his jammed Uzi, Alvarez heard the telltale rip of an AK-47 somewhere to the right. It was promptly answered by a flurry of machine guns, their sharp chatter completely different from the Chinese automatics used by the soldiers of the Colombian cartel. That wasn't an American M-16, but something else. Good. Maybe this was only a raid from a rival Bolivian cartel. Anything but the American DEA! A man could cut a deal with the drug lords of Bolivia, but not the rock-headed Yankee bastards. They had no sense for business at all.

In the middle of the compound, an Ashanti gunship started slowly rotating its blades preparing to lift off. From within the billowing smoke came rolling thunder, and the bulletproof Armorlite glass of the Italian helicopter shattered. The pilot was ripped from his seat and crushed the gunner against the other side of the craft. Then the thunder sounded once more, and the bright orange flames from the ruptured fuel tank rose high into the azure sky.

Finally freeing his machine gun, Alvarez looked for targets, then recoiled as something shot by horribly close. A crossbow bolt slammed into another guard, pinning his gun hand to his chest with a feathered steel shaft. Screaming in anger, the guard clumsily switched hands, and took another hit full in the throat.

That was when the palisade of bricks and barbed wire stridently blew apart in several different locations at the exact same moment. More smoke grenades landed, and to Alvarez it seemed as if the world were tearing itself apart. Machine-gun fire tore up the ground before his boots, and as he ran a hot rush of air hummed past his check, stinging the flesh. Somewhere in the murky clouds, a brilliant orange tongue lanced across the compound as a guard brought a flamethrower to bear on the invaders.

A split second later the thunder sounded again, and the fiery wash vanished to be replaced with a double explosion of the fuel tanks erupting. Screaming insanely, the burning human silhouette just stood there, consumed by the hungry flames.

Now gunfire was coming from every direction, and Alvarez dimly saw a group of the scientists stumbling away from the lab, their arms full of plastic bags of cocaine. The guard didn't care about them at the moment. He could get the precious drug back later, but first he had to secure the hardsite. Only where to make a stand? The lab was gone, the garage burning, the guard tower destroyed…the missile bunker! Yes, that would do.

Equipped with a plan, Hector Alvarez forced himself to move through the carnage, ignoring the rattle of machine guns and awkwardly stepping over the dead bodies. Dimly seen through the smoke, a squad of guards poured from the barracks carrying the electric Gatling gun. The battery-powered monster could hose out 8,000 rounds per minute. That would sweep the compound clear in only a few seconds. Moving with trained expertise, the guards got off a short burst before shells dropped from the sky to converge on the team, the triple blast destroying men and machine.

Zigzagging across the compound, Alvarez desperately raced for the lee of the low brick silo holding the incredibly expensive Stinger and Amsterdam missiles. The bank of high-tech killers had been purchased as protection against a possible attack from various antidrug squads.

More explosions shook the camp, and men were running about randomly, gunfire coming from every direction. Most of the voices he knew as friends, and he flinched as each dropped. Good God! What were they being attacked by, the entire U.S. Army?

Spotting the sprawled corpse of the commander of the jungle base, Alvarez knelt alongside and fired the AK-47 in a semicircle to buy him some time, then pawed the warm body to finally locate the officer's cell phone. Hitting the autodial button, he waited breathlessly for the string of beeps to finish dialing and connect him to every other cell phone in the hardsite, plus several more hundreds of miles away. Tense seconds passed as the device kept endlessly dialing, as if it were unable to reach any of the other phones. It had to be jammed. Angrily he threw away the cell phone and searched the corpse for any ammo clips.

Finding only a handgun, Alvarez tossed away the Kalashnikov and pulled out a stainless-steel .44 Ruger Blackhawk. Tears from the chemical smoke blurring his vision, the guard crawled along, still trying for the bunker, tracking the dark figures running through the billowing clouds.

As he stumbled toward sanctuary, the hot barrel of a machine gun was pressed to the side of Alvarez's neck.

"Move and you die, amigo," a gruff voice said from behind.

Too tired to care anymore, the guard spun, slapping aside the stubby SMG and firing his revolver twice. Incredibly nimble, the soldier dodged out of the way and the vented barrel of his machine gun flashed into a fiery blossom. Hot pain took Alvarez in the chest, closely followed by a numbing cold and slow fall toward the ground that be never finished, instead tumbling downward into infinite blackness.

RAISING THE VISOR on his helmet, David McCarter swung back the monocle attached to the minicomputer of the MR-1 and looked over the battlefield with his own eyes. The dead lay scattered about, wispy tendrils of smoke from the flash-bang grenades moving over the ground like ghostly snakes. McCarter listened intensely. This fight was over and they owned the base.

Just to make sure, McCarter placed two fingers in his mouth and gave a loud taxi whistle. A few seconds later the call was repeated four more times from different areas, his team members reporting in that each was in a cold zone with no visible combatants.

"Phoenix One to hatchlings," McCarter said, touching his throat mike. "I want a perimeter sweep of the compound, then rendezvous on me in five by the gate. Confirm."

"Roger that, Phoenix One," Gary Manning replied over the radio.

The other members of the assault force replied in kind, and McCarter walked slowly across the destruction of the hardsite, serving as the anchor while the rest of his soldiers made sure the base was secure with no living hostiles.

Dropping the partially empty clip from his HK MP-5, the former SAS commando slapped in a fresh magazine just as a badly bleeding hardman near the lab tried to swing an

AK-47 toward him. Without conscious thought McCarter fired his weapon once.

"Trouble?" Calvin James said over the radio.

"No problems here," McCarter replied, going over to make sure the guard was dead. He was. "Continue the sweep."

"Roger."

A few minutes later the rest of the team joined him.

"Battle zone is clear," Hawkins reported, the long tube of a 70 mm recoilless rifle resting on a shoulder. The weapon resembled a WWII bazooka, only smaller, slimmer and without the heavy blast shield to protect the operator's face. A bandolier of rounds for the portable artillery was draped across his chest, half of the loops conspicuously empty. In the expert hands of the former member of Delta Force, the weapon could lay down a barrage of hellfire almost as fast as a mortar and with far greater accuracy. Hawkins was the pointman for the team, an expert on high-tech weapons and the silent kill.

"Any casualties?" McCarter asked, looking over the group. They were dirty and splashed with blood, but nobody seemed to be limping or otherwise damaged.

"Just Rafe," Gary Manning replied. He gestured at the other member of Phoenix Force with his Barrett Light .50-caliber sniper rifle, the barrel visibly radiating waves of heat from the recent combat. "He caught some shrapnel from an exploding Hummer."

The Barrett carried a huge 10-shot magazine larger than a cigar box extending from its belly, and fired a foot-long bullet. The awesome rifle rounds penetrated most light-vehicle armor, and could blow holes in brick walls a mile away. The colossal Barrett was a deadly machine of distant termination, but only in the hands of an expert marksman.

Lifting up the cracked visor and pushing away the monocle for his own helmet computer, Rafael Encizo patted his chest to the sound of dull thuds. "My NATO vest stopped the worst of it. No bones busted this time."

"Good."

"Just bet you're sore as hell," Calvin James added with a chuckle while checking the suppressor on his Heckler & Koch MP-5 submachine gun. At some time or another, each member of Phoenix Force had been shot while wearing body armor, and while it saved a person's life, ribs could still be broken and there were always huge painful bruises that lasted for weeks. Nothing was free in life, especially life itself.

"Any civilians lost?" McCarter pressed, scanning the sky, then glancing at the burning Ashanti gunship. That had been their biggest worry—the wash of the blades would have cleared away the smoke, giving the guards a clear field of fire, and then the gunship could have cut loose with its 3.5 mm minirockets. But Manning and the Barrett made short work of the helicopter.

"Far as I can tell, all of the women got away," Hawkins said gruffly, shifting the 70 mm recoilless to a more comfortable position. "Want a BDH?"

"No need for a body count," McCarter stated firmly, glancing around. Charred wreckage was strewed everywhere, along with pieces of bodies. "There are no naked people in sight, so they must have gotten away."

"Hey, Gary, nice job on that water-barrel ploy," Encizo said, inspecting the lab with a cool eye.

"Just a standard Trojan horse." Manning smiled, easing back his cloth cap, the oversize Barrett held in one hand.

The little Cuban rubbed his chin. "Now, I thought the Trojan horse was full of men, not bombs."

"What soldier wouldn't have to be bombed out of his skull to hide in a wooden horse with fifty other sweaty grunts wearing full armor for overnight?"

"I see your point."

"Cut the chatter," McCarter grunted, lighting a Player's cigarette and enjoying his first smoke of the day. Hiding in the jungle since dawn, the warrior could not take a chance on the guards detecting the smell of the pungent smoke.

Softly in the background came the irregular staccato of ammunition cooking off from the burning Hummers trapped inside the inferno of the garage.

"Okay, break over," McCarter directed, grinding the glowing cigarette butt against the side of his combat boot and tucking it into a pocket. "Fire the guard's weapons at each other to confuse the fight, then cover our tracks. Get ready to move in five. Gary, prep the charges. Go."

As the team moved without hesitation, the big Canadian headed for the south section of the palisade. Before the attack, he had managed to place C-4 charges along most of the stout palisade surrounding the jungle camp, and blown them all except for one section. Phoenix Force would leave traveling past that last stretch of wall, then he would detonate the charge from a safe distance. The blast and rubble would cover their tracks completely, and the jungle would do the rest. In a few minutes nobody would ever know they had been there but the dead.

Going to the nearby corpse of an officer, Encizo reached into a blouse pocket and slid a thick wad of large-denomination Peruvian money under the riddled body.

"Doing a little spin doctor?" James noted.

Dusting off his hand, the little Cuban flashed a grin. "Can't hurt. The Colombians and the Peruvians hate each other already. Maybe we can get a little war going on down here and they'll wipe each other out."

"Not likely," Hawkins said, opening a plastic bag from his belt pouch and scattering a handful of spent brass. "But sure worth a try."

"Time," McCarter announced and started toward the south wall.

As the team spread out in a standard pattern to cover their retreat from any possible snipers or survivors hiding in the thick foliage of the jungle, McCarter spotted a cell phone lying on the ground.

Grabbing the instrument, he listened intently, but there was only the endless beeping tones of autodial trying to secure a live line. Relaxing, the Briton turned off the phone and broke it into pieces, then tossed the parts away.

Thank God it was broken. That had been his worst fear. One loyal guard with a working cell phone could have gotten off a call for help to the big bosses back in Bogotá, and soon there would have been a fleet of merc Apache gunships streaking in with SOTA weapon systems ablaze. Real trouble with those. The phone had to have picked up a ricochet somewhere, or been dropped hard.

As the covert assault team slipped into the shadows of the jungle, McCarter turned his mind to the details of reaching their hidden base camp without leaving any traces. He gave the matter no further consideration—until several hours later when static completely blocked the men from communicating with Stony Man Farm back in Virginia and for a couple of hours their Global Positioning Device—GPD—no longer seemed to be functioning.

CHAPTER TWO

Washington, D.C.

Trapped in a monumental traffic jam, Harold Brognola wasn't going anywhere for the moment.

Horns blaring, the convoy of diesel trucks inched through Washington, D.C., pumping black exhaust into the downtown air. One hundred angry drivers in expensive imported cars leaned on their horns to add to the general madness caused by the arrival of the President. Even the sidewalks were packed solid with a crowd of demonstrators, waving placards and chanting slogans. Exactly what they were for or against, the big Fed wasn't quite sure, but they certainly did sound intense on the matter.

Giving shrill toots on silver whistles, the D.C. police in their tailored blue-and-gray uniforms waved white gloves, creating a ballet of wordless commands. Somehow they managed to force apart the endless line of vehicles filling the street, then easily parted the boisterous mob of protesters and allowed the long black car to roll through and head for the country club.

Caught in the middle of lunch with his wife, Brognola had instantly known that something was wrong when the President sent a U.S. Marine as a messenger to summon him to this meeting instead of a simple phone call. It had to be critical if the Man didn't even trust the secure communication lines of Washington, D.C., to make a call to the Justice Department.

As Brognola slowed the vehicle at the closed iron gate of the country club, a swarm of Secret Service agents popped the hood and trunk, then used mirrors set on angled poles to check underneath the car for bombs, while others used proximity detectors on the tires. Nothing unusual there to Brognola; the inspection was just routine. Although the Secret Service agents did seem especially diligent. Was that the problem? Had there been an assassination attempt he didn't know about yet?

But that was hardly a national emergency. Since the days of Eisenhower, there had been at least one serious attempt to kill whoever was the president every single year. Good or bad, Democrat or Republican, it made no difference. Most of the attempts were never heard about by the news reporters or general public, as the failed assassin was sent to the city morgue for a quick burial listed as the nameless victim of an alley mugging. Members of the U.S. Secret Service were acknowledged as the best pistol shots in the world, and the agents specialized in head shots with their .357 Magnum pistols. Those pocket cannons left very little remaining for the news media to interview afterward.

But why the early-morning summons on a Sunday? The big Fed chewed over the possibilities while looking at the huge crowd of demonstrators gathered outside the Chevy Chase Country Club. The group of people was a complete mix: they were young, middle-aged and old, men and women, teens and kids of every race and background. A female construction worker in hardhat and steel-toed shoes stood shouting alongside a slim, almost dainty man in a thousand-dollar Armani suit.

Finally satisfied, the Secret Service agents asked Brognola for his ID card a second time, and checked the magnetic strip on a scanner that used a satellite relay to link the handheld device to the massive array of mainframes in the concrete belly of the Justice Department building. There had to have been something wrong with the scanner, because it took two tries to link to the nearby computer complex.

Finally the scanner gave a soft beep, and the Secret Service agents passed back the card and waved the vehicle through. Once past the gates, the big car rolled along the elegant gravel driveway of the country club, the angry voices of the chanting protesters quickly fading into the distance.

Armed with M-16 assault rifles, a cadre of U.S. Marines in class-A uniforms formed an outer perimeter around the driving tee and a group of several men and women, in the center of which was the President. Beaming a smile, the White House press secretary was chatting amiably with the TV news reporters, and White House aides ran about fetching coffee and passing out pamphlets about the charity golf game.

Stepping from his car, Brognola wondered what could be so important that he had to meet with the President here in the open. Maintaining a professional calm, he again waited while a Marine sergeant checked his photo ID badge, then the Marines parted and waved him through. These meetings went a lot faster and smoother in the Oval Office.

Standing in the background, Secret Service agents watched everything. Each man and woman was casually dressed to try to blend in with the elite membership of the billionaire club. And even though he knew it was there, it still took Brognola a moment to spot the flesh-colored earphone worn by each agent, the miniature radios linking the agents into a single homogeneous unit. Although they didn't seem to be using them much at the moment. How odd.

Standing strategically near the President, one agent was holding a drink of some kind, and another a golf bag bearing the seal of the White House, but neither man was using both hands to do anything. One of the primary rules for the body-guards was to always keep a gun hand free to defend the President.

Slowly Brognola advanced to the slim dapper man in golfing clothes at the first tee checking the swing of a seven iron.

"Good morning, sir," the big Fed said.

His face pensive, the President set a golf ball on the wooden tee, addressed the ball and swung. The swoosh of the club combined with the striking of the ball into a single long sound as the golf ball arched over the fairway and out of sight. Nobody commented on the excellence of the shot.

"Sorry about this, Hal," the President said, passing the club to his caddy. "But this is a charity game to raise money for the homeless, been set up for months. If I was to cancel, it would raise a lot of questions I don't want to answer right now."

"Understood, sir," Brognola said, walking alongside the chief executive. "And the matter is too important to wait until going back to the White House?"

"Yes."

"Accepted. What's wrong? Anything to do with the protesters outside?"

"Sweet Jesus, no," the President snorted, waving at the distant news reporters. "This is something new and potentially a lot worse. We lost a military recon satellite over the Caribbean this morning."

The conversation paused for a moment while the President found his ball near the rough and used a nine iron to chip back onto the fairway.

Staying close, Brognola said, "Define 'lost,' sir. Disabled or destroyed?"

"We have no idea. The satellite just vanished from radar. There's no response from the internal transceiver, and SAC confirms that nothing fell from the sky, so it didn't do a fiery reentry into the atmosphere."

"Curious. EM jamming? No, NORAD could compensate for that. Okay, it's destroyed," Brognola said grimly. "A lost sat is bad, but nothing serious. We have hundreds of communication and spy satellites in orbit. Nothing to get overly excited about—machines break, solar storms burn out solar cells, all sorts of things make satellites die."

"That's one of the reasons why we have so many," the President said brusquely. "Redundant relays, multiple back-ups on top of the reserves and replacements. This way no natural disaster could possibly knock America out of the sky."

Brognola didn't speak for a moment. "This isn't the only one missing."

The President paused at the green and removed a tuft of bird feathers from in front of the golf ball. "Not by a long shot. This is the twenty-fifth satellite that's been lost in the past day. The first was a Brazilian comsat over the Caribbean Sea eight hours ago. Then NASA lost a weather satellite over the Florida Keys. Next the NSA couldn't contact an Echelon over Chicago. Then it was an Air Force recon sat that went missing. At that point it was brought to my attention, and we've been losing satellites constantly ever since then. A couple every hour."

"Just communication and weather satellites so far?"

"To date, yes."

"All in the same orbit, sir?" Brognola queried.

The President took a putter, addressed the ball and put it in the hole to make par. The reporters applauded, and the Man stood to wave again.

"No, Hal," he continued, walking away. "The comsats were in different orbits, distances and sections of the globe. One was very old, two were modern."

"Nothing in common. Except that they all belong to

America.'' Brognola rubbed a hand across his face. "What do the Joint Chiefs say about this?''

Using his fingertips, the President rested the golf club on the perfect blue-green grass of the private course. "Career soldiers have very little to say about anything until the facts prove a conclusion,'' he stated. "But my advisers believed that this could be the preliminary strike to remove our eyes from the sky. Make the nation blind to an enemy missile launch. We still have ground radar, but that only gives a few minutes' warning.''

"Have you consulted the TDT?''

"The Theoretical Danger Team at the Pentagon thinks we're already in deep shit. And that's a direct quote.''

The civilian scientists at the TDT were about the only people in the nation authorized to speak that way to the President. The military dreamers were all paranoid, slightly insane and more often than not horribly correct.

Standing straight, the President accepted his drink from a Secret Service agent and took a small swallow. "As of this morning I placed the nation on DefCon Three,'' he said softly.

A chill ran down Brognola's spine at the calm pronouncement. Sweet Jesus, just one short step away from global war. This was becoming a nightmare.

In the far distance, a twosome played through the rough, and a lone man struggled to blast his way out of a sandtrap with a wedge while his caddy watched in despair.

"How many more satellites do we have in orbit?'' Brognola asked bluntly. This was no time for finesse.

"Legally nine constellations, over eight hundred sats,'' the President replied, tightening the leather glove on his right hand. "In truth over a thousand. Including six the CIA doesn't know I am aware of, and two that they don't know anything about.''

"Then we're a long way from being blind in space, sir.

Unless whatever is happening rapidly accelerates the process.''

"Agreed. However, just to cover the nation's ass, as of this morning I received permission from the prime minister of Canada to send troops north to guard our ground-based radar installations, from the new X-class superradar in Alaska to the old DEW Line up in Canada. In case terrorists attacked the ground radar to make us completely blind to enemy missiles and not just goddamn nearsighted.''

A smart move. The Man was way ahead of the big Fed.

"Then every installation in the DEW Line blew up.'' The President looked at the ground, his voice made of stone. "Over a thousand soldiers are dead from explosives that must have been buried in the ground for months. Possibly years.''

"Christ!'' Brognola cried, then forced himself silent before the reporters could notice his agitated state. My God, a full battalion ambushed. "Who did we lose?''

"Name it—Rangers, NCI, Delta Force, Black Berets and a lot of Navy SEALs. Everybody not killed has been positioned around the White House and will stay there until further notice.''

Just a dot in the sky, a low-flying plane hummed over the private golf course, and one of the Secret Service agents whispered into a throat mike. A split second later several Apache gunships rose into view to escort the wandering plane back on course.

"What does the media know?'' Brognola asked, glancing at the camera crews dotting the rolling green field of the golf course.

"They're in the dark and we're keeping them that way. What civilian knows where the DEW Line stations are located?'' the President snorted. "Hell, most folks don't even knew the things exist anymore.''

Sad, but true. "And the general population won't realize

what is happening in space until their phones stop working and lost jetliners start falling from the sky,'' Brognola said. The urgent need for a cigar presented itself, and if a panatela had been available, he would have lit up on the spot.

Mopping the sweat off his brow, the President tucked the cloth into a hip pocket. ''As a precaution I have most of the Navy sailing to form a picket line along our shores, and SAC has every AWACS we own airborne,'' he said, turning to speak directly for a moment. ''NORAD is going to co-ordinate the inboard ship radar as our emergency backup in case the last of the milsats vanish from space. But this is a hell of a complex job. At the best it would only give us a maximum warning of ten minutes, and it takes twelve to launch an ICBM from scratch.''

''And once the last satellite is gone, Russia, China, even Korea could go launch nukes and we wouldn't know about it until the warheads started falling from the sky,'' Brognola stated firmly.

''America would be completely destroyed before our subs could possibly send a retaliatory strike. Only they wouldn't know who sent the missiles without satellite confirmation. Should we launch at everybody? Choose an enemy at random?''

A cold breeze from the Potomac blew over the men, carrying along the smell of freshly cut grass and bus fumes. Civilization. For a brief second Brognola saw the same landscape after the bombs fell, an empty vista of burning sand and lakes of solidified glass that glowed in the endless dark of perpetual winter, the sky black from the ashes of the billion unburied dead.

Shaking off the dire thoughts, he straightened his shoulders. ''What can I do, sir?''

Somberly the President took him by the shoulder, then realized the press was watching and laughed as if telling the man a joke. Brognola forced himself to smile, and they started walking once more.

"I want Striker operating on this. The FBI is preparing for riots, the CIA is hunting down spies and militants but I want the Farm to handle known terrorists."

"No good on Striker, sir. He was last reported in Madagascar. Something about repaying an old debt. He isn't in contact with us at the moment."

Frowning, the president sighed. "So be it, then. But this is top priority. Put everybody you have behind this, and I mean right now. Find whoever is behind the matter and stop them at any cost. Terminate with extreme prejudice."

"We prefer the word *kill,* sir," Brognola replied gruffly. "If my people have to pull the trigger, then you can at least have the balls to say the goddamn word."

Inhaling sharply through his nose, the President of the United States glared at the director of the Sensitive Operations Group for a long minute.

"Accepted. Find the sons of bitches and kill them," he commanded. "Is that clear enough?"

"Yes, sir," Brognola said, and turned about to walk casually toward his car. He only hoped that the radio was still able to reach the eighty miles into the hills of Virginia and Stony Man Farm.

What a hell of a way to start a Sunday.

CHAPTER THREE

With paintballs smacking onto the cracked pavement, Carl "Ironman" Lyons sprinted across the old street of the abandoned city, a huge M-60 machine gun held tight in both hands.

Suddenly a figure moved to his right, and Lyons burped a short spray in that direction without conscious thought. A red light flashed from the shoulder of the startled police officer, and with a grimace the man lay down on the ground and played dead.

Lyons hit the wall alongside the busted window of a ramshackle store across the street, and Rosario "The Politician" Blancanales popped into view to cover fire with his Skorpion submachine gun. The gas suppressor attached to the end of the barrel gave the weapon a science-fiction appearance, but that was the only way the blowback bolt of the gas-operated SMG could function firing blank cartridges used during the war game.

Under Blancanales's adroit control, a stuttering wreath of noisy blanks and silent laser flashes peppered the police on top of the hotel on the distant corner. Spent brass cartridges arched into the air, and the crimson dot of the laser tracker taped under the sputtering barrel of the Skorpion touched two of the officers, wounding one in the leg and "blowing away" the other. The rest of the cops dived for cover and blindly returned fire with their oversize M-16 assault rifles.

Paintballs hit the outside of the ancient store like an angry hailstorm, exploding in a barrage of rainbow colors as Lyons leaped through the open window to escape from the open street. He hit the wooden floor hard and rolled into a sitting position, the huge M-60 sweeping for enemies in the dilapidated building.

"Nice move." Hermann "Gadgets" Schwarz chuckled, lowering his AK-47, the Russian assault rifle also sporting a gas suppressor at the end of the barrel. "Thought the cops had you there for a second."

"Ironman getting rusty?" Blancanales said with a smile, while firing at a suspicious shadow under a rusted car chassis. "Never."

Not amused, Lyons only grunted in reply, listening to the floorboards above them for the slightest sound of footsteps. This training mission with the Philadelphia police stopped being a cakewalk in the first few minutes. The Philly cops were dead serious in their antiterrorist tactics, and grimly determined to win this war game at any cost. One of the cops had tripped on a fellow "dead" officer while rushing through a doorway and lost his weapon. Trapped by Able Team's cross fire, the defenseless officer stood his ground to give cover to other cops so they could reach the hotel. Then he charged for the dropped weapon even as Lyons pulled out a .75 paintball gun and "executed" the cop with a round to the helmet.

This was only a game for training purposes, but it was still most impressive. Lyons had heard that the mayor of Philadelphia once boasted that, given proper air support, his downtown police could take Baghdad in twenty-four hours. Lyons was starting to become a believer. These were the toughest cops he had ever encountered.

And this test area was very well suited for urban battle tactics. Once long ago, it had been a thriving town of moonshiners. J. Edgar Hoover himself closed down the contraband distillery in the Roaring Twenties, and it had lain barren and unused since then, until taken over by the local PD as a training ground for infiltration tactics, antiterrorist and hostage negotiations.

Dropping an empty clip, Blancanales pulled out in a fresh magazine from his shoulder bag, pausing first to make sure the rounds were blanks and not live. The men of Able Team had an arsenal of weapons in their car, but that was safely parked on the other side of the exercise area. No live ammo was allowed in the test area, but mistakes happened. Always best to be sure, or else this game could become very serious in the flick of a trigger.

"Remind me again how we get into this nonsense?" Lyons demanded gruffly, then hawked and spit. A gob of blue struck the dusty planks of the ancient store.

"Well, over a poker game I joked that we're so good taking out terrorists we should teach a course," Schwarz said, moving to the back door to watch the weeds for any sign of movement. "Unfortunately Katz heard me, told Price and here we are."

"Enjoying yourself yet, Carl?" Blancanales asked, working the bolt on the Skorpion.

"I've had fun before," Lyons growled, "and this ain't it."

With a startled expression Schwarz turned about sharply to stare at the big man. "Carl, that was a joke! Did you hurt yourself?"

"Go screw a rolling doughnut."

"Hey, you're wounded," Blancanales said, pulling a small first-aid kit from his equipment bag and tossing it over.

Lyons glanced down and saw that one of the small pieces of jagged glass in the window frame had cut his right leg. The tiny wound was bleeding slightly, but overall it was less than an inch long.

"Forget it," he grunted. "I get worse shaving with co
water. Shit, incoming!"

Just then a soda can wrapped in red tape—signifying it
was a smoke grenade—bounded through the open window.
Holding his breath, Blancanales grabbed the can and threw
it back into the street while Schwarz fired a long burst from
his AK-47 at all of the buildings across the street to stop
any possible charge.

However, Lyons kicked over a rickety table and trained
his M-60 on the back door. A split second later it burst open,
and in charged a masked woman wearing combat body armor, the M-16 in her hands firing on full-auto. Paintballs
hit everywhere. As Blancanales and Schwarz returned fire
at the Plexiglas mask of the helmet to blind her, Lyons
kicked the table toward the cop. She jumped out of the way,
and Lyons raked her exposed legs with the M-60. The falling brass hit the floor in a musical tingling even as the alarm
on her belt sounded a minor wound. Obeying the rules, the
cop dropped to the floor and tried to give return fire when
the M-16 ran out of ammo.

Frantically the officer fumbled for another clip on her
belt, but the three men advanced, shooting her in the armpits, neck and groin, anywhere the body armor didn't cover.
The spent brass from their combined weapons filled the air
as the paintballs exploded.

"Aw, shit," the woman swore, dropping her useless
weapon as a red light flashed on her helmet, announcing a
clean kill.

When she removed her helmet, a wild array of fiery red
hair cascaded to her shoulders. Her skin was milky white
and covered with a dusting of freckles, and a slight slant to
her green eyes hinted at some Oriental blood mixed into the
obviously Irish ancestry.

"Damn, you guys are good," she stated. "No chance in

hell you're actually Boston PD. So what are you really, Delta Force?"

"Go fall down, corpse," Lyons ordered sternly, moving past her to check outside. Opening the door a crack, he saw a movement in the bushes and gave a short burst from the big machine gun. A handgun answered in reply, but he dodged the paintballs and slammed the door shut.

"The name's DeForest, Lieutenant Madison DeForest," the policewoman corrected, sitting down to rest her back against the splintery wall. "How did you know I was there? I'm not wearing any perfume, and I threw away the loose change in my pockets. Got eyes in the back of your head?"

"Instinct. It's what I would have done," Lyons said, moving the table over to block any further entry. The teams had switched sides since yesterday, when the police had played the terrorists. Able Team had successfully stopped them from ramming city hall with a truckload of C-4 plastique. Now they were cops again, and the officers were hot for revenge over yesterday's fiasco. The rules be damned; anything was kosher today.

"They're planning something again," Lyons said, listening to the silence from outside. "Probably going to try a fake negotiation while they get closer. Maybe set the store on fire."

"Then we better make our move," Blancanales agreed, heading up the rickety stairs. "Keep them busy while I go for the roof."

"On it," Schwarz replied, lurching into action. Gathering the "dead" woman's weapon, he reloaded it with a paintball clip taken from her belt. Then going to the open window, he emptied the M-16 at the sky outside, pointing almost straight upward. Moments later the paintballs rained down on the police crouching behind the rusted car across the street. Twice more alarms sounded telling of hits, but no deaths.

"Mother of God, those Arab bastards got the captain!" a voice shouted.

"Arabs? I thought they were IRA bastards this time," another said. "Or was that IRS?"

"How about liberals?"

"Sir, you will be avenged!" a third voice added dramatically, and a patrolman stood to aim an M-79 grenade launcher across the street.

Even as he started to launch the fat 40 mm paintball, the police officer jerked once and dropped the weapon as a spray of red blood formed a fountain into the air from the gaping hole in his chest. The cop stumbled backward a few feet before falling to the ground, warm life pumping onto the cracked dusty pavement.

"Officer down!" a lieutenant shouted, scrambling to the still man. Kneeling in the blood, he checked the throat for a pulse, then covered the wound with a bare hand to try to slow the bleeding. "He's still alive! Johnson, radio for an ambulance!"

The short cop made no reply, but simply sprinted for the equipment van parked outside the testing area.

"This exercise is over!" the captain roared, standing into view, his uniform shirt splashed with blue paint. "Now, what fucking asshole is carrying a live fucking gun? Your ass is mine, buddy!"

Snatching the first-aid kit off the floor, DeForest started for the door, but Lyons stopped her with a grim expression.

"Don't go," he ordered brusquely, staying low. "They're already here."

Scowling darkly, the woman strained to hear anything unusual. Yes, there was some kind of machine noise, faint but getting louder.

"Choppers?" she asked, glancing skyward.

"Not the kind you mean," Lyons corrected grimly, the muscles in his thick neck bunching in anger.

The sound of the engines quickly grew into a muted roar as a howling pack of leather-clad bikers raced around a street corner on chopped Harley-Davidson motorcycles, wildly firing MAC-10 assault pistols and shotguns in every direction.

"Kill 'em all!" a blond biker screamed, his long hair flailing in the wind as the Ingram steadily chattered.

The lieutenant kneeling alongside the wounded cop in the road took a full second to realize this wasn't some aspect of the war game, then clawed for the weapon holstered at his hip. At this range the paintballs would hurt like hell, and a round to the face would blind anybody not wearing goggles. There was no time to drag the wounded man away, and the officer was sure as hell not going to leave a wounded man alone. Maybe the punks were just razzing the cops.

But the handgun barely cleared the holster when the bikers converged on the two men. An iron chain took the standing cop across the face, sending him sprawling to the pavement, then several of the Harleys rolled over the cops, the sound of crunching bones horribly loud.

Instantly a dozen police officers stood into view and fired their oversize M-16 carbines, the barrage of paintballs knocking the bikers about. One cried out as the MAC-10 was knocked from his grip and went skittering along the pavement. Then wheeling about, the rest raked the cops with a fusillade of 9 mm rounds, and a fat woman covered in tattoos threw a Molotov cocktail. The rusty chassis of the old abandoned car whoofed into flames as the glass bottle shattered, the conflagration forcing the police to retreat into the safety of a two-story wooden bank.

Seconds later there was a thunderous detonation from outside town, and a roiling black cloud rose above the small collection of buildings, the explosion closely followed by an endless crackling of small-arms rounds.

"I saw it from the roof. They got the equipment van," Blancanales said from the stairs from the floor above. "Hit it with a Molotov. The fire is cooking off the ammo in the lockers."

"Great. Which means no radio, no ammo, no backup," DeForest snarled, pulling an illegal set of brass knuckles and can of pepper spray from her belt. "Some damn stool pigeon must have told the Morlocks when and where to find us. Catch us with our pants down."

Then she frowned. "But most of these punks are tagged with prison bracelets. They must have found some way to smash the radio transponders without alerting a react base."

"Solve that problem later," Lyons said, removing the ski mask and placing aside the M-60. Quickly he stripped himself of the extra batteries, helmet, goggles and gloves and other assorted protective gear needed for the war game. This wasn't a test anymore.

Doing the same, his teammates tossed away the test equipment. The sensors and such didn't weigh very much, but parts of it swung free and would throw off the stride of a run. That alone was enough to get a person killed.

Many pounds lighter, Lyons brushed back his short, military-cut blond hair and placed the M-60 out the window to start firing single rounds as fast as possible. Without the gas suppressor at the end of the barrel, it was impossible to rattle off a string of shots, but he hoped the loud noise of the machine rifle would be enough to draw the attention of the biker gang away from the unarmed police.

The ploy worked, and soon the battered storefront shuddered from the arrival of dozens of 9 mm bullets, a neat line of holes appearing in the flimsy door.

"How long before they realize we're firing blanks?" DeForest asked, holding up her helmet to use the visor as a mirror to sneak a glance over the windowsill.

In reply Schwarz reached into a pocket, pulled out a fountain pen, twisted the bottom and took careful aim out the window. There was a sharp bang from the pen, and a biker toppled over, his neck spurting crimson.

"Longer now," Blancanales stated, firing more rounds from the Skorpion.

Unexpectedly facing live ammo, the bikers scattered before the barking military weapon, several of them driving away. But Lyons knew they would be back soon. But from which direction would they attack, the rear or the roof?

Dumping the useless Skorpion, Blancanales yanked up a trouser leg to pull out a small .32 Remington automatic pistol from an ankle holster. Carrying a live weapon into the test had been strictly against the rules, but Blancanales was a survivor and never went anywhere unarmed.

Jacking the slide on the small gun, he stood and fired three times. A biker across the street cried out and fell to the ground, but his Harley continued onward for a dozen feet before tilting over and crashing noisily to the pavement. The bikers shouted in anger and raked the storefronts with a hail of assorted lead, Ingram MAC-10s and shotguns blazing away.

"Okay, who are these people?" Lyons demanded, standing in plain view and firing the M-60 as fast as he could. The linked belt of ammo was dangerously short, and to any trained observer it would be clear they were blank rounds. But Lyons was betting that the bikers didn't know military weapons that well, only Saturday Night street guns. "What did you call them before, lady, the Morlocks?"

"Yeah, pretty literate for a bunch of degenerates. They're a biker gang that lives in the swamps south of here," DeForest said. "We've been hunting the assholes for years. Bastards make initiates kill a hitchhiker and eat part of them to get in the gang."

"Cannibals, eh?" Blancanales grunted, firing once more

with extreme care. Three rounds remaining, with no reloads. He'd have to make every shot count.

In spite of himself, he was impressed with their psychological tactics. It was brainwashing in a way. Once a man had eaten human flesh, there would be a strong shame to stay with the gang forever and away from others who didn't share the secret sin.

"Son of a bitch," Schwarz growled, fiddling with a cell phone. "The damn thing is as dead as my com link, but I don't know why. Neither seems damaged."

"Out of range for the service?" DeForest asked.

"Not this phone, lady."

"Stay frosty," Lyons warned, working the bolt to clear a jam. Once it was free, he triggered more blanks as the pack of motorcycles roared by again, a flurry of machine-gun fire smashing windows and rattling doors. The bikers were having fun playing with the trapped cops, confident they were in complete control of the situation. That was a bad mistake.

Across the street a cop fired a grenade launcher, and the massive 40 mm paintball hit a biker in the face. The screaming man fell from a Harley, clawing at his eyes. From the alleyway a cop sprinted for the motorcycle, while another raced for the dropped machine pistol. A hail of gunfire from the other bikers forced the bold cops back into hiding, the wounded man in the street limping out of sight and leaving a trail of paint and blood on the dusty ground.

"No mercy!" a bald biker yelled, firing a sawed-off shotgun wildly into the air. "Kill 'em all!"

"Then we'll eat 'em!"

"Yeah!"

"Try it, punks," Lyons said softly.

Whooping like a madwoman, a female biker threw a Molotov onto the side of the old bank, the soapy gasoline clinging to the clapboards like a fiery leech. But the cops had been expecting that, and helmets full of dirt were thrown out the windows to extinguish the blaze.

Lyons could only scowl at the tactics of the Morlocks. This was moronic! The bikers were still shooting at anything that moved, wasting ammunition and precious time. Every tick of the clock gave the cops and Able Team a better chance to respond, even though the police SWAT armory truck was only a pile of smoking metal by now.

"Wish to Christ we had some live ammunition," DeForest said through clenched teeth. "This is our chance to end these bastards for good. Take them down in open combat with no crooked lawyers or rich bleeding hearts to set them free again in twenty-four hours."

The members of Able Team exchanged approving glances. Long ago they had once tried operating by the rules, and it damn near got them all killed. Hard and fast, the covert warriors had learned that street justice rarely had anything to do with obeying the law.

"We have weapons in a van parked in a ravine to the left of the tumbledown grain silo," Lyons said, yanking up the breech cover and dropping in his last belt of blank rounds. "The keypad on the back door opens with the code 9-7-6. Got that?"

DeForest repeated the code, an eager look replacing the frustration in her face.

"Clips are loaded and in the green metal box," Blancanales added, firing again. A bearded biker racing by on a Harley cried out and slapped his arm, but didn't fall. Damn.

"It's illegal to carry loaded weapons in a moving vehicle," the lady cop stated. "Gotta give you a ticket for that."

"Aw, but, Officer, it's my birthday," Schwarz muttered, tucking away the dead cell phone. There was a mobile communications system in the van. He could contact the local PD, or better, the local National Guard unit from there. Have an armed response within minutes. Damn odd about the phone, though.

Grabbing the AK-47, Schwarz removed the gas suppressor and worked the bolt. Now the weapon looked deadly, even though it wasn't, and would buy them a few seconds of running time to reach the van. It was better than nothing.

Unexpectedly the pager on his hip silently vibrated, and Schwarz stared at the device. Set only to receive messages, the pager was reserved for emergency recalls. Stony Man Farm wanted them to return right now? With a flick of his hand, Schwarz turned off the device. He'd tell the others later. Able Team was busy at the moment just trying to staying alive.

Just then the sound of the bikes got noticeably louder, and Schwarz got out of the way as the front door crashed aside and in rode a bare-chested biker on a roaring Harley, an Ingram machine pistol hosing the interior of the store. Spraying the Morlock in the face with her pepper spray, DeForest then gasped as a hot round buzzed past her cheek, tugging on her hair.

The biker screamed, and without hesitation Lyons threw the M-60 like a javelin directly into the rear wheel. The long barrel went straight into the spokes, jamming against the yoke. Instantly the chain snapped off, and the bike flipped over to crash on the floor. Caught under the Twin-V engine, the gang member was crushed.

"Next time wear a helmet," Lyons growled, pulling the Ingram from the dying man's grip.

Checking the clip, the Able Team leader sprayed a long burst out the window. Two bikers were hit, and the cops cheered from the roof of the bank. The Morlocks sprayed the hotel, and a bathtub came plummeting from a window to nearly crush a biker to death.

Trapped and without weapons, the cops were still in the fight. Turning away from the window, Lyons fought the urge to charge into battle, and knelt down to rummage through the bloody leather jacket of the Morlock for ammo clips. He found two additional magazines and a grenade, an old World War II pineapple, streaked with rust. DeForest pulled a Ruger .357 Magnum pistol from the dying man's belt and cracked the cylinder to check the load. Lyons approved. Only fools and amateurs trusted an unknown weapon. This woman was a lot more than just an ordinary street cop. SWAT maybe, or a ringer from the FBI. Then again maybe she was just a natural. He had received no special training back in L.A. and yet had managed to capture the elusive Mack Bolan alive, just before letting the man go.

Confiscating a huge bowie knife from the dead man's boot, Blancanales spun the blade in the air and caught it by the handle to test the balance. Good enough. Meanwhile Schwarz took the grenade and used a strap from the discarded body armor to attach a full clip of blank rounds to the explosive charge. The combined blast would send out a deadly halo of brass shrapnel. Not much in the way of artillery, but every little bit helped.

More bikes roared past the store, and there was a glint of reflected light outside the window. Lyons and DeForest both moved like lightning, the Ingram and Ruger booming in unison. A Molotov exploded outside the store, glass shards and a fiery rain washing onto the outside of the dilapidated building.

"Too damn close. Those creeps are mighty serious about killing some cops today," Blancanales growled, firing his last round. An answering hail of lead hit the burning windowsill, sending splinters everywhere.

"So let's give them something else to think about," Schwarz said, yanking open the front door and throwing the modified grenade.

The pineapple bounced along the cracked pavement and

thundered into a strident fireball, dust and dirt from the shattered pavement forming a cloud bank. Even before the concussion of the blast finished, Able Team and DeForest were sprinting through the billowing smoke for the distant van.

"Look at 'em run!" A burly woman biker laughed, dropping a clip from her weapon and slapping in a reload.

"Hey, they got a MAC. The bastards aced Charlie!"

"Run 'em down!" the blond man ordered, his face a feral mask of hatred.

As the Morlocks charged for the runners, a fusillade of blanks came from the bank and hotel, but the bikers seemed to know those were harmless and concentrated on their prey.

Reaching a rust-eaten mailbox, Lyons spun about and fired the Ingram at the oncoming Morlocks until it jammed. While the man fought to clear the mechanism, DeForest triggered the .357 Ruger pistol twice, blowing the tire on a Harley and sending a biker to a tumbling death under the spinning wheels of his fellow Morlocks.

Shouting for the bikers to surrender, the Philly cops poured from the bank, holding wooden tables ahead of them for protection. The Morlocks ignored the cops until Lyons leveled the Ingram and emptied the rest of the clip. The Morlocks broke ranks and spread out in a dozen directions, vanishing behind the old buildings.

"Trying to circle and cut us off," Lyons said, dropping the empty clip and reloading for the last time. "Move with a purpose, people!"

Weapons at the ready, Able Team charged for the fallen silo with DeForest only a heartbeat behind. The four reached the corroded shell of metal just as a lone biker coasted into view from around a partially burned-out warehouse. As the biker leveled his weapon, Blancanales jerked his hand at the man and the grinning Morlock dropped the shotgun, the handle of a knife jutting from his fat, tattoo-covered stomach. Then DeForest stood and fired. There was a loud ping, and the Harley whoofed into flames as fuel hosed from the ruptured gas tank onto the red-hot muffler.

"In!" Lyons ordered, spraying the open street with the Ingram while the others jumped into the shallow ravine.

Running along the cracked mosaic of the dried mud, Schwarz hit the electronic lock on his keychain, unlocking all of the doors of the van and turning off the security system. A heartbeat later the ravine flattened into a weedy field and the van came into sight.

"Clear," Blancanales announced, visually inspecting the ground for any tracks. The bikers hadn't discovered the van.

Schwarz went straight to the front of the vehicle to radio for assistance while the others yanked open the back doors and quickly armed themselves from the compact arsenal.

"Sweet Jesus," DeForest muttered, going for the familiar and taking an M-16 carbine. Every cop in North America was trained to handle those. Standard police training.

Removing the clip, she slapped it hard against the stock to prime the load, then slammed it back into the weapon and worked the bolt to chamber the first 5.56 mm round.

"Who are you guys?" the lady cop demanded, snicking off the safety with her thumb.

"Friends," Blancanales answered, inserting a big 40 mm round into the grenade launcher clamped underneath the barrel of his own M-16/M-203 assault combo.

"Sure as hell hope so," she grunted, stuffing extra clips into her pockets. Then the cop spied a Glock .45 and took that, too. It never hurt to have a reserve weapon.

"Okay, help is on the way," Schwarz said, joining them at the rear. He also grabbed an M-16/M-203 combo, and slung a bandolier of 40 mm shells over a shoulder.

"What took so long?" Blancanales demanded.

"Lots of static," Schwarz said, priming his own weapon. "Strangest thing I ever heard. Never encountered anything like it before."

"Talk later. Let's go," Lyons said, tucking a .357 Colt Python and an Ingram machine pistol into his belt and lifting a monstrous Atchisson assault shotgun from a heavily cushioned box. Flipping up the rear sights of the automatic weapon, he started hoofing it back toward the test area. Time to teach those Morlocks some respect for the law.

Skirting the grain silo, the four warriors peeked around the rusted metal framework. The cops were still fighting off the bikers, paintballs and hot lead flying everywhere. Then one of the Morlock bikers tossed a Molotov over the barricade of tables, and it landed amid the police, forcing them out of the protective circle.

A sergeant threw his shoes at a biker, the laces tied together to form a crude bolo. The footwear got a gang member by the throat, and he dropped a shotgun. Another cop retrieved the weapon and fired from the ground, only to find it empty.

"Fresh meat over here!" Lyons shouted, stepping into full view on the street.

As the surprised Morlocks spun, the Able Team leader cut loose with the Atchisson, ripping off its full load of seven rounds in under two seconds. The hellstorm of lead tore the front line of bikers apart, sending more than one of them straight to hell.

Yammering a steady song of death, Schwarz, Blancanales and DeForest added the unbridled fury of the their M-16s to the firefight, the incoming tumblers smacking wetly into the bikers or throwing off sparks as the 5.56 mm tumblers ricocheted off the steel frame of a Harley-Davidson.

Screaming in outrage, the Morlocks pulled their bikes into a defensive circle and fought back with every gun at their disposal. Even as he swiftly reloaded the Atchisson, Lyons heard a hum and felt a tug on his shirt. Glancing down for a second, he saw a new hole in the black cloth and knew a 9 mm slug had missed his guts by only a fraction of an inch.

"Shit," DeForest cursed, dropping her M-16. Blood trickling down her wounded left arm, the cop knelt on the pavement to steady herself and clumsily drew the Glock to start placing her shots. The big-bore .45 rounds hit with devastating results.

Riding the bucking autoshotgun into a tighter grouping, Lyons removed another four bikers from the thinning group, just as his teammates pulled the triggers on their grenade launchers. In a double thump twin charges of 40 mm high-explosive went whistling at the Morlocks to land right on their blond leader.

The two explosions sprayed chemical flame over the startled bikers, the concussions sending broken bodies and twisted machines flying. Scrambling to their feet, the few survivors tried running from the ambush that had suddenly gone so terribly wrong, firing their weapons in blind panic over their shoulders.

Without remorse Able Team tracked the gang, the M-16 assault rifles and shotgun removing them with deadly efficiency. Reaching the imagined safety of the bushes, the last two Morlocks dropped their shotguns and ran just as a grim-faced sergeant stumbled from the smoking ruin of the police van, his clothes charred, his face a blistered expanse of cracked, bleeding meat. But in his hands was a brace of Heckler & Koch MP-5 submachine guns, and he hosed the escaping cannibals at point-blank range. The barrage of 9 mm rounds sent the killers sprawling.

"You're all under arrest!" the cop bellowed, limping forward.

Then from the ground, a bald man managed to draw a sleek Beretta and get off a round at the badly burned police officer, catching him smack in the shoulder. Blood sprayed from the impact, and the cop staggered, then forced himself erect and walked toward the gang member with his rattling

HKs, hitting the biker in a grisly orchestration of meaty slaps.

Arriving seconds later, Lyons and the others added the fury of their weapons to the Heckler & Koch subguns. When the deafening noise finally stopped, nothing was moving.

"That settles a lot of debts," DeForest growled, holstering the Glock with its slide kicked back.

"Wish we could stay and help more, but we have to go," Schwarz said, shouldering his hot weapon. "We'll drop off the trauma packs from our van. The evac choppers from Franklin General Hospital should be here in ten minutes, maybe less."

"Why the rush?" Lyons demanded, his hands reloading the shotgun without conscious thought. The exercise was scheduled to last another day, and there were no other pressing matters for the team to handle that he was aware of.

"Soup's on," Schwarz said softly.

An emergency recall to the Farm? Blancanales recorded the information without changing his facial expression, and immediately started jogging to the van. Lyons merely grunted at the news, then pulled out his wallet and extracted a business card.

"Call this when you get the chance," he said, passing it over to the female cop.

Cradling her wounded arm, DeForest glanced at the card. It was laser printed on cheap microburst paper with only a telephone number on display. No name or address.

"This going win me a free trip to Walt Disney World?" she asked, tucking it into a pocket. "Or you asking me on a date?"

"Something a lot better than that," Lyons stated.

At that moment the Philadelphia cops began stumbling around the corner of the bank just as the van arrived with Blancanales behind the wheel. The worst of the wounded were taken care of first, with Blancanales directing the administration of pressure bandages and morphine. The street cops knew basic EM techniques, but the combat soldier had become quite a decent medic in Nam and never lost the skill over the years.

A short while later there came the telltale sound of helicopters in the air. Not one but several arched over the test area. In the lead was a sleek Bell 407 air ambulance, closely followed a Bell 203, and even a gigantic Huey medevac bus from the National Guard. Taking center stage, the 407 landed close to the smoking motorcycles, with the rest going to ground nearby on the broken street. Soon over a dozen paramedics were disgorged with stretchers, splints and full field-surgery kits.

Quietly allowing the medics to take over the tending of the wounded, the men of Able Team slipped back to their van and drove away from the war-torn town, heading for the nameless secondary road that eventually reached Interstate 95.

Memorizing the license number of the nondescript vehicle, DeForest waited until the van was out of sight before inspecting her borrowed Glock. As she had expected, the serial number was gone. Good job, too. It almost looked as if there had never been any serial number on the frame in the first place.

Ignoring her throbbing arm, the lieutenant easily located a spent shell from one of the M-16 assault rifles and checked the markings on the bottom of the brass casing. It was blank. Nothing there but the mark of the firing pin, and that was impossible. All bullets carried the name of the manufacturer, often lot and batch numbers. At the very least what caliber they were! Yet this shell was completely blank. Suddenly the cop knew she didn't have to check the hundreds of other shells to know that every round would be the same, blank and untraceable.

"Who the hell are you guys?" Lieutenant Madison DeForest muttered under her breath.

CHAPTER FOUR

Stony Man Farm, Virginia

Barbara Price, mission controller at Stony Man Farm, curtailed her walk of the Farm perimeter and hurried back to the farmhouse. A call to her cell phone revealed that Phoenix Force had been located and was on the way back to base. Able Team was already en route.

Price paused for a moment on the front porch to allow the electronic security to recognize her presence, then she proceeded swiftly to the door and tapped in the entry code on a small keypad. There was an answering beep, a green light flashed and Price walked inside without hesitation. Anybody not pausing on the front porch would receive enough voltage to stun a platoon, and then Chief Greene would arrive with squads of blacksuits carrying enough SOTA firepower to blow away a Russian tank battalion.

The bedrooms for the on-site house staff were located on the second level, and the third level was for storage and defense. From there the command staff could activate land mines, disguised machine-gun nests and launch the SAM batteries. New equipment was added every month to keep the government hardsite absolutely state-of-the-art.

As Price moved past the open doorway to the den, the sounds of a football game coming from the big-screen flat TV hung on the wall. The picture was mostly clear, but popcorn bursts of static constantly crackled over the game, obscuring most of the action.

"What the hell is wrong with this thing?" one of the off-duty security men demanded, rising from his chair to fiddle with the controls.

"Must be a problem with the satellite dish," a janitor commented. Scrunching his eyes, the maintenance man tried to figure out who was on what yardline. "Damnation, the squirrels must have made another nest in the uplink dish. I told them not to position it so close to the seed storage. Call somebody in communications, will ya?"

Suddenly the distorted crowd on the TV roared in dismay.

"And hurry!" he urged.

Price knew it was a logical explanation, but utterly incorrect. Yet she said nothing as she took the stairs down to the next level. So civilian channels were already being affected. Matters had gotten a lot worse, a lot faster, than anybody expected.

Reaching the basement level, she paused at an intersection as a tall lanky man stepped from the gun room. John Kissinger was a master gunsmith. He was in charge all firearms at the Farm, even going so far as to create some of the specialty weapons for both Able Team and Phoenix Force.

"Morning, Barbara," Kissinger said with a smile. "Look here, the new 10 mm automatics from NATO just arrived. Can't wait to see the ballistic reports on these. I'm happier than a chicken with a pecker."

"Morning, Cowboy, we found David," Price replied, and strode to the massive armored portal of the War Room.

The gunsmith nodded and tucked away the handgun to follow the mission controller. He had been trying to keep the conversation light until McCarter and the team had been found. Technically Kissinger had no authorization to be in the War Room, but the gunsmith liked to keep track of what was going on with the field teams in case they needed something unusual

Price tapped in a code, and the steel portal ponderously swung aside with the soft hiss of hydraulic pressure.

Inside the room a large wall screen was split in two, one side showing Carl Lyons and Able Team hunched forward, the bland decor of a national motel chain in the background. The right was filled with the sweaty visages of David McCarter and Calvin James.

Dense jungle foliage filled the scene behind the men, and the rest of the team stood close by, weapons held in callused hands. All of the members of Phoenix Force were dressed in camouflage and Army boots, their combat webbing loaded with survival equipment and a wide assortment of death dealers. But some of the loops and pouches were obviously empty, and while their weapons were clean, the men were dirty.

As Price entered the War Room, she was greeted by a craggy faced older man with a missing right arm, a bare steel hook resting on top of the computer console beside him. Yakov "Katz" Katzenelenbogen had at one time been the commander of Phoenix Force. Now the ex-Mossad agent functioned as the tactical adviser to the Farm, directing field maneuvers and analyzing the potential of enemy forces.

"That was fast," Katz said.

"Have to be—we're racing against the clock," Price replied.

Then she turned to the wall monitor. "Gentlemen, thank you for responding so quickly. Heads up, we have a situation brewing."

As if in response, both of the screens flickered, and the sound rose and fell at random.

"Bloody hell, Calvin, will you get rid of that hash?" McCarter ordered. Sweat ran off his face in rivulets, making his green eyes squint in a protective gesture. Cloth bands on his wrists were both black with the sweat from his forearms. A Heckler & Koch MP-5 submachine gun was slung at his right hip, and the skeleton brace of his favorite silent-kill crossbow crested over a wide shoulder.

"Best I can do," James stated with a grimace, turning a knob on the laptop. Off to the side, a dish antenna on a tripod changed its angle in perfect harmony to the dial. "We got interference up the ass. All kinds of crazy stuff."

"Arse," McCarter corrected, lighting a Player's cigarette. He drew in the dark smoke and let it out slowly. "It really gets on my nerves when you Yanks butcher the queen's English."

"Anyway, David, sorry to catch you in the middle of a mission," Price said abruptly. "I hope nobody was injured."

"Only the mucking drug smugglers," McCarter replied grimly. "Just before we departed, they got recycled."

"Lead in, garbage out," Manning said.

"Not all of them. Some escaped," James stated. "But enough of them for today."

"Then the lab is destroyed?" Katz asked.

"Burned to the ground," McCarter stated, exhaling a long stream of smoke from the side of his mouth.

"And the workers?" Kissinger asked.

"Just girls mostly, they're alive and running for the hills," Rafael Encizo said, clearing his throat, pretending to cough at the faint wisps of smoke coming from the Briton's cigarette.

Implacable, McCarter paid no attention to his teammate.

"Along with every weapon and ounce of cocaine they could steal before we blew up the place," the little Cuban added.

"Good," Price replied. "Did you get the information we wanted on the Bolivian drug contacts?"

"Sure, Massachusetts is the entry point," McCarter

growled around the burning cigarette. "We have the names of the local contacts. Now what the hell is going on, Barb?"

"Is Striker in trouble?" Blancanales asked, leaning closer to the screen. He owed his life to Bolan a hundred times over, and if the man asked, Blancanales would march straight into Hell carrying a can of jet fuel.

"To the best of our knowledge, he's fine," Price replied. "He's busy somewhere else, and can't assist on this mission."

Just then, a wave of static obscured both groups of warriors.

"Damnation," Lyons snapped, and hit something off-screen, making the view shake for a moment. "What the hell is wrong with the computer link?"

"Nothing I can fix," Schwarz stated flatly, fiddling with something off the screen. "Must be line trouble, maybe a down relay or solar flares."

"You sure it's plugged in?"

"Get stuffed."

"It's a lot worse than static," Price stated, pushing away from the console. "Some of our satellites are missing, civilian and military, and more are gone every hour." Briefly she recapped the conversation on the golf course.

"Good God," Schwarz whispered. "Every type of communications link we have is relayed over satellites. Television, radio, cell phones, the Internet... Hell, not even local pay phones are purely hardwired anymore!"

"Just the U.S.?" Lyons asked. "Or is anybody else losing sats?"

"Canada, Great Britain, France, Brazil are confirmed," she said. "To the best of our knowledge, it was a Brazilian weather satellite that was the very first destroyed. But then, even the friendly nations are reluctant to talk much about the matter, and China flatly denies any losses have occurred. But the CIA says they have quite a few milsats gone."

"Be easy pickings when the last satellite falls," Hawkins muttered. "Everybody will be able to launch at anybody they like, without fear of retaliation."

"This is not necessarily a military situation," Katz said. "The international banks will lose track of trillions of dollars when the com net falls. We may simply be facing incredibly clever thieves, nothing more."

"A financial crash like that would cause thousands of corporations to go bankrupt, putting millions out of work," Manning pointed out. "Within days there would be food riots in every major city of the world. The death toll would be staggering."

"What's our confidence?" McCarter asked.

"High," Price replied coldly.

"DefCon Three," Encizo said, crackling his knuckles. That meant about a hundred people had their fingers on the nuclear button, ready to go. Some gung-ho pencil pusher could start a war that nobody would win but the stones in the ground. "How come we're just hearing about this now?"

"It's been less than twenty-four hours since the first disappearance," Price said, crossing her arms. "We weren't called in until it was confirmed this was enemy action of some kind."

"Do we know what is happening to the satellites?" Schwarz demanded incredulously. "Ultra-high-altitude missiles, or maybe a ground-based laser like that Eye of the Dragon we handled in the Middle East?"

Katz shook his head. "Not a damn clue. NORAD, SAC and the White House assumed it was a natural problem, meteors or solar flares. Then the DEW Line exploded."

"How many died?" McCarter demanded.

"Over a thousand of our best troops have been eliminated," Price said bluntly, finally taking a chair.

Clearly startled, Kissinger stepped away from the wall he

had been leaning on. "That many?" he said in a hoarse whisper. "I didn't know."

As if in reply, the two video screens flickered and McCarter said something with an angry expression, but the vocal transmission only arrived as garbled static.

"Phoenix One, repeat please," Price said, picking up a microphone. "Stony One did not receive, Phoenix One. Please repeat message, we did not receive."

"We copy, Stony One. Okay, do we know who might be behind this?" McCarter said grimly, a hand resting on the wide strap of his deadly crossbow.

"No," Price said loudly, as more static cracked on the screen for a split second, and then was gone.

"Possibly we do," Katz corrected, sliding out a sheet of paper from the book he had been reading. "Aaron unleashed his electronic riders to comb the Internet for any clues, and Carmen ran across this interesting post. There's a group of half-assed militants that regularly claim responsibility for any terrorist problems in North America. Always been after the fact until yesterday. Around midnight they did a mass e-mailing about how they would soon be sweeping the skies clean of the hated ZOG eyes."

"ZOG?" James repeated, chewing a lip. "The Zionist Occupation Government. Shit, are we saying that the KKK has declared war on America?"

"Not the Ku Klux Klan, but the Nazis," Katz corrected with a frown. "Actually a splinter group of the American Nazi Party, a bunch of hardboys in Baltimore called Avalon 88. The ANP disavows any dealings with them, saying they are violent madmen, even though they still approve of the group's ultimate goal, destroying America and bringing back fascism."

"Avalon 88," Lyons mused. "Named after the German 88 mm cannons that damn near won the war, I suppose."

"That is our assumption, yes."

"This is bleeding Dublin all over again," McCarter growled.

"Katz, we better put Hunt or Akira on this," Price suggested. "See if we can crack the computer files of the ANP."

"Aaron is handling them personally," Katz replied. "Plus, Carmen and Hunt are already on-line, and Akira will join him as soon as he gets back. We recalled him from a rock concert in Richmond."

"This is bullshit," Lyons growled, his ice-blue eyes snapping with rage. "The American Nazi Party couldn't field a successful hike in the woods without blowing off a foot. How the hell could those idiots find some way to destroy satellites orbiting in space three hundred miles high?"

"Go find out," Price directed. "Infiltrate their headquarters on Charles Street and see what they know."

"And if this Avalon 88 group is actually causing the trouble?" Blancanales asked. "You want anybody alive for questioning?"

"No," Price said without a hint of emotion. "Just make sure you get the right people. Burn the rope if necessary."

Slipping into a loud sports jacket, Lyons said, "Consider it done."

"We can get to Rio this afternoon and take the first commercial 747 flight home," Hawkins announced, glancing at his watch. "It'll be a lot faster than the Hercules, and you folks might need some backup."

In the rear of the screen, Encizo and Manning were already folding up the camp and packing away equipment.

"Appreciate the offer. Glad to have you with us," Schwarz said, then couldn't help adding, "We'll chill a nice root beer for David."

A confirmed Coca-Cola drinker his whole life, McCarter arched an eyebrow, then shot the Able Team communications expert with a stiff finger.

"Do not use a commercial flight," Katz said gruffly. "You would have to leave behind your weapons, and the Farm might need to divert you to another location while en route. Nothing is certain yet, so until we have a definitive target to strike, we better keep you mobile."

"Hell, Brazil could be behind the whole thing," he added as an afterthought. "What better way to divert suspicion from yourself than by being the first country to lose a satellite? Who knows at this point?"

"So send Jack with a Lockheed jet transport," Manning said, slinging a pack over his shoulder. "Get us home in a couple of hours."

Lighting another cigarette, McCarter nodded at the suggestion. Sounded good. Grimaldi was the ace pilot for the Farm, able to fly anything with wings or rotors, including a NASA space shuttle. Most people felt safer flying with him at the controls of a plane than in a parked car. Risking more than just his life, Jack Grimaldi had turned against the Mafia capos to help Mack Bolan out of a tight spot and had been on the right side of justice ever since. When Bolan and Brognola created the Farm, Grimaldi was one of their very first recruits.

Hanging up a phone, Price spoke to the monitors. "Jack is already on a different aspect of this mission. As for transportation, use the Hercules or your backup plane, whichever is better. Your call."

"What bothers me the most," Kissinger said, "is that we've been under attack for almost a full day, and don't even know for sure who the hell it is that we're fighting."

STANDING BEFORE the huge picture window of the cool room, Major Sebastian Cole crossed his hands behind his back and breathed deeply, listening to the sound of the burning logs in the fieldstone fireplace. In the far distance, a steady stream of cars rolled along a highway cutting through the dense forest of the green hills, a faint fog of blue exhaust hanging over the roadway.

So far, everything was operating smoothly, and he didn't like that a bit. No battle plan in the history of the world ever survived first contact with the enemy. Alexander, Caesar, Hannibal, Napoleon, even Hitler knew this law to be true. So if nothing had gone wrong yet, that could only mean America hadn't yet acted upon the destruction of its satellites. That was bad. Their response had been expected and countermeasures already established. If the U.S. government didn't do the expected, this whole thing could rapidly turn into a royal disaster.

There was a quiet knock at the door, and Major Cole turned as a young man in a crisp uniform entered.

"The prisoner has arrived, sir," he reported.

"Take me to him," the major said, and followed the man down into the depths of the subbasement.

ICY COLD brutally hit the Marine like an electric shock, slamming him painfully back to consciousness. He struggled to understand where he was, a kaleidoscope of images filling his mind. The forest, an explosion that shook the world and then black chaos for an long period of time.

Slowly the soldier realized that he was in a dimly illuminated basement, the walls and ceiling beyond the cone of light cast by the single bare light bulb suspended above. Trying to rub his chin to check the beard growth, the Marine realized he was tied with stout ropes to a heavy wooden chair. He was also stripped to the waist, his supply belt gone. Even his shoes had been removed. Huge bruises covered his chest, and his left arm was swaddled in bloody bandages, a dull ache deep inside telling of a serious wound muffled by localized painkillers.

Twisting his good arm about, the Marine tried to force it

free, but the ropes were too well tied. He'd have to try something else.

"Ah, awake at last," a gravelly voice said from the darkness, and a large man walked out of the shadows. "I had hoped for an officer, but I suppose a corporal will do."

Breathing hard, the Marine stared at the stranger. The man stood well over six feet tall, with coal-black hair slicked down as if he just stepped out of the shower. His eyes were violet in color, oddly disturbing in a male. His skin was darker than tan, which meant the guy could be Arab, Italian, Greek, Turkish or a mutt like most Americans.

Blackie had recently shaved, but the face held the telltale blue cast of a heavy beard that could never truly be eliminated. However, there was a long pink scar, which started at the left cheek and went under the jaw to end on the right cheek. Somebody had tried very seriously to cut this man's throat and failed.

The uniform he wore was paramilitary, like those civilians who pretended they were soldiers on the weekends. Only the boots looked right, and a pistol in a flap holster expertly rode at an angle on some combat webbing. That was something soldiers learned but civvies never got right because it looked off balance, yet actually made for a faster draw.

A flesh-colored earpiece and wire ran down a small radio clipped to his belt, and a heavy watch rode on the left hand, the metal tinted blue to prevent reflected light from giving away his position in the night.

Suddenly the trapped Marine began to understand his situation, and felt a cold shiver of fear run down his spine. The last thing he remembered was racing for the bushes to take a leak when all of Canada seemed to erupt, the DEW Line radar base and a dozen of his buddies flying into the sky as flames reached for the stars. He had to have been far enough away to survive, but how could anybody have found him in the wreckage before a recon team arrived? Only one way possible—they were already there. This asshole had to be one of the terrorists who planted the bombs. Might even be their commander from the way he stood.

"Sloppy work on the neck," the Marine commented. "He forget to hold your head still, or did you twist away in time?"

In reply the stranger drew the pistol and fired.

The 9 mm slug slammed into the Marine's shoulder with sledgehammer force, and pain masked everything else for a brief eternity.

"That was done to remove any idea that I am bluffing," the man said, walking around the prisoner with the smoking pistol in his grip. "My name is Major Sebastian Cole, and here are the facts of the situation. You are my prisoner. You will never leave this room alive. I am the last person in the world you shall ever talk to or see. How easily or hard you die depends entirely on your ability to give me information."

The U.S. soldier knew that most of what the man was saying was total bullshit, just a ploy to soften him up before the real torture. The wise move would be to play to the freak, try to join the terrorists, say how much he hated America, but the soldier was too tired and in too much pain for such a sophisticated tactic.

"F-fuck you," the Marine choked, spittle dribbling from his mouth as blood flowed freely from the throbbing wound. "Knocklebaum, Eric, corporal, United States Marine Corps, serial number—"

Cole slapped the prisoner across the face with the pistol. "Cease that nonsense immediately!" he snarled, holstering the piece. "Who else will the government send against us? We already know about the FBI, CIA, the field agents of the NSA, Delta Force, Navy SEALs, Green Berets, Black

Berets." He made a vague gesture in the air. "Tell me something useful, Corporal."

"How about the Space Marines?" Corporal Knocklebaum offered, remembering an article he had read in *Newsweek*. The damn fool could find about them over the Internet, so why not buy some time to think by telling him things he could find out by himself?

"For every joke, pain," the major said, drawing the pistol once more. "For every lie, a penalty."

"No, sir, it's true," another voice said from the darkness. "The Marine Corps has a special division in Fort Bragg, South Carolina, that is trained for combat in space. They have an official name, but everybody just calls 'em the Space Marines."

"Are they a potential threat?" Cole asked, a touch of fear creeping into his voice.

So, not as tough as he pretended, was he? Knocklebaum smirked in the privacy of his head.

"No, sir," the second voice answered. "We have them covered."

"Good, and thank you for the cooperation, Corporal," Cole said. "You, there, put a pressure bandage on the gunshot wound, and you, give the soldier here some water."

In spite of himself, Knocklebaum flinched as a military trauma bandage was clumsily applied to his gore-streaked shoulder, but he greedily drained the tin cup of cool water. Christ, that tasted good, and it was probably the last good thing he would ever experience. It was obvious that he was in the control of lunatics and would never leave this room alive. Stinging tears filled his eyes, and for a moment the urge for life filled his mind. Why not tell this guy what he wanted to know? These people were amateurs and might just set him free. Probably not, but it was a chance. He should take it and try to stay alive. Live at any cost, no matter what.

But soon cold reason overwhelmed the raw emotions of survival, and a calm resolution seized the corporal. These stinking bastards had already killed a dozen Marines, maybe more. Any information he gave them would only mean more death. He would tell them nothing, lie to his last breath. Nobody would know of this fight, no songs would be sung, no parades held in his honor, no banners, no fireworks. But the corporal would hold his ground until the sweet release of death. No more Marines would die because he talked. God, unit, Corps, country, that was the code. Jesus already knew the soldier was coming. Now it was time to fulfill his obligation to the Corps. The rest was up to them.

Watching the prisoner, Major Cole saw the conflicting thoughts cross the bound man's face, and didn't like what he saw. Now there was something different about the soldier, something he had never seem before in all his years of torturing people to death in South Africa and Angola. Was this defiance? Impossible.

"Tell me another special operations group," Cole said in a friendly manner.

"Well, I read about this one guy named Remo," Corporal Knocklebaum said in a mock serious tone.

The major sharply inhaled, then grabbed the prisoner by the hair and viciously slapped him across the face until blood flowed freely from his nose and mouth.

"That all ya got, bitch?" Knocklebaum growled, and spit blood at the self-proclaimed major, making him step away for a moment.

But that single moment was all the Marine needed. The old veterans from Nam sometimes talked about desperate tricks to use in a case like this, and thank God he had paid attention. Summoning his resolve, the Marine snapped his head hard to the left, then sharply angled his neck.

Instantly realizing what was happening, Cole dived forward to grab the prisoner and wrap his arms around the corporal's head to stop him from completing the action and snapping his own neck. Outmaneuvered, the Marine tried to get the man off by burying his teeth into the muscular arm across his face. Cole only grunted at the attack, and hung on until other men lashed the corporal motionless with wide leather belts.

"I see we have a hero," the major panted, pulling a broken tooth from his forearm, red blood welling from the wound. "So be it. Get the electric drill and the pliers."

Pinned immobile by the straps around his head and chest, Knocklebaum could only thrash about while a surgical trolley was wheeled into the cone of light, and devices were plugged into a coverless wall outlet.

Soon the terrible screaming started for real, and lasted far into the lonely night.

CHAPTER FIVE

Moving at a steady seventy miles per second, the Echelon-class satellite stayed motionless above the North American continent in perfect synchronization with the rotating world below.

Great solar panels spread like shiny black wings from the top of the government orbiter, gathering a steady trickle of power from the raw sunlight and converting it into electricity for the inboard computer system, which in turn operated the high-tech spy satellite. Dish antennae covered its belly, and dutifully the computer listened to every cell-phone conversation along the western coast of America.

Any keyword strings heard would trigger a relay to a ground base in Atlanta, where a bank of Cray supercomputers would analyze the words for implied meanings. Such as, if "plastique" was mixed with "government building," or "coke" or "cocaine" mixed with the name of a known street gang or Mafia boss. If the Cray deemed it was a real conversation, the entire cell-phone conversation would be instantly passed to a human agent for further analysis. This was part of the actual job of the NSA, to monitor and protect the lines of communications for the U.S. However, since this always caused a major uproar whenever people discovered they were being monitored, the base of operations for the fleet of Echelon satellites was located in the picturesque English countryside at a top secret installation referred to only as Menwithhill. The land grant for the base was part of a sweetheart deal with MI-5, which did the exact same to London with their own Vortex spy sats from a secret base located somewhere amid the ten thousand lakes of rural Minnesota.

"Lots of chatter in L.A.," the NSA technician said, leaning backward in his chair and chewing on the stem of a cold briarwood pipe. Smoking was bad for the office computers, but the man just could not leave his pipe at home. Thankfully smoking wasn't as badly frowned on in Great Britain as back home.

"Stallone making a new movie?" the MI-5 courtesy agent asked, busy peeling an apple with a German Luftwaffe dagger his father brought home from the last world war. It sometimes troubled the military officer that he constantly found himself referring to WWII that way—the last world war. As if another were inevitable and already heading their way.

"No," the American said with a smile. "But Sharon Stone just got her dog a bikini wax."

"Fascinating," the British officer drawled, slicing off a section of the ripe apple and politely offering it to his shift mate.

"Thanks," the other said, accepting the fruit and starting to take a bite when he dropped it to the floor.

"What the hell," he whispered, removing his pipe and inadvertently dunking it into a cold cup of coffee. "It's gone. The damn thing is gone!"

"What's gone, old man?" the Briton asked, wiping his mouth clean on a handkerchief and rolling his chair closer. "Not another Echelon missing, is it? We've lost six bloody Vortex so far today. That meteor shower the boffins told us about must be a real hellbender up there."

"This was a Skywatch," the American said slowly, his hands pulling out a small keyboard and typing like mad.

"The damn thing was there on the screen right in front of me, and then it was just gone."

The English officer frowned. A Skywatch was an American nuclear alert satellite able to detect a missile launch or atomic-weapons labs buried underground or even underwater. As protection from enemy hunter-killer antisatellites, the hull was coated with ceramic armor plating, proof against a .50-caliber rifle round. What kind of a meteor shower could take out that?

"What was near it?" the MI-5 agent asked urgently. "A missile heat trail or a shuttle of some kind, perhaps?"

Still typing, the American leaned closer to the computer screen until his features were reflected in the glass. "Not a thing," he said angrily, puzzled. "There wasn't a single goddamn thing visible in space anywhere near the Skywatch before it just vanished."

"Impossible," the British operative said slowly, a touch of fear in his voice. Suddenly the antique German dagger in his hand seemed to be uncomfortably warm, and he tucked it into a belt sheath sticky with juice.

"Balderdash," he added, then took the American by the shoulder. "Show me the memory loop."

Nodding, the other agent started the autorecord and the two men scrutinized the CD playback five times before admitting defeat. The sat was on the screen, then it was gone, and that was all. No radiation, no heat flash.

Chewing a lip for a minute, the American made a decision and reached for a phone to start dialing NSA headquarters in Washington. That meteor-shower story was getting thin, and if something was now removing U.S. milsats, then the White House should be appraised of the matter immediately.

Then he paused. But what was there to report? There had been nothing near the Skywatch sat, no missiles, no meteors or anything. Space had been empty for a hundred miles in every possible direction.

So what the hell happened to the damn thing?

Brazil

LEAVING THE SLEEK concrete venue of the BR319 roadway, the battered old delivery truck bounced along the dirt road outside the city of Eirunepe, about fifty miles north of Rio de Janeiro.

Wearing civilian clothes, Hawkins was behind the wheel sucking on a lollipop. Sitting alongside was McCarter, looking as if he had stolen a hamper of clothes from a stranger and chosen items to wear at random.

Returning to their hotel, Phoenix Force had changed clothing so as not to attract attention when going to their plane at the Rio airport. But they never even got near the city.

Stopping off for gasoline at a grocery store, the team was surprised to find the locals so excited and trying to buy weapons. McCarter and James both spoke fluent Spanish, but Portuguese was the official language of Brazil, and it took them a while to piece together what was happening.

As best they could guess, the entire telephone system of the nation had collapsed a few hours earlier, and then some radio DJ joked that it had to be the work of rebels. The tiny radio station was much too poor to afford bandwidth on a satellite to relay its broadcasts nationwide, so it used old repeater towers dotting the hills to reach the countryside and as many people as possible.

But with hash and static steadily increasing on the rich stations, all of southern Brazil tuned in to the poor station and heard fictitious reports of noble rebels bringing freedom and justice to Brazil and destroying the hated government filled with corrupt politicians.

"Thank you, Orson Welles and 'The War of the Worlds,'" Encizo groaned. "Perfect timing."

"And they believed the joke," James said, shaking his head. "Same as the U.S. did back in 1940."

Moving fast, the government shut down the local broadcast, but by then it was too late. People everywhere were rallying in support of the imaginary freedom fighters, many of them drunk and starting to loot stores or set fires. As riots swept the nation, the Brazilian government unleashed armed troops to forcibly restore order, sealing off the railroads and closing airports to hunt down the unknown rebels. Rio was reported to be a madhouse, the international airport burning out of control, so Phoenix Force counted its waiting Hercules C-130 transport as a loss and wisely diverted to the secondary escape route of Eirunepe City.

Driving past the huge dockyard that handled most of the shipping traffic on the Amazon, Hawkins rolled the rattling truck through the center of the town.

Eirunepe resembled a ghost town. Every store was closed down tight, storm shutters or iron grates covering the windows. The streets were deserted, and only windblown rubbish marked the presence of life somewhere in the vicinity.

"Where is everybody?" Manning asked, holding back the canvas flap covering the rear of the truck.

"No bodies," James said grimly, loosening the 9 mm Beretta tucked under his flowery shirt. "That's a good sign."

Studying the cityscape, Encizo frowned deeply. "Not always, buddy."

"Kill the engine," McCarter said, raising a hand.

Immediately Hawkins braked to a halt and turned off the engine. Stopped in the middle of the street, the men listened carefully. Over the ticking of the cooling engine, they soon faintly heard the familiar sounds of warfare.

"That's from the east," Encizo said, twisting his head in that direction.

"The airport," Manning stated.

"We're a good a mile away!" James growled, watching

columns of dark smoke rise into the clear azure sky. Too dark for wood or fuel. It had to be burning tires. Somebody was trying to use the fumes to get close to the airport. Smart move, but not going to work in this stiff breeze.

"Drive to that hill," McCarter ordered, pointing to the south. "We need a recon before making any decisions."

The team hastily piled into the vehicle, and stomping the gas pedal, Hawkins threw the big rig into gear and pushed it to highway speed through the empty city until reaching the top of a low hill. National troops surrounded the airport, and angry farmers were throwing rocks at the armed soldiers, an ill-advised endeavor.

Out on the landing field, a lumbering 777 was struggling to lift off. Gunners in the crowd were firing at the plane, and the Brazilian troops instantly responded with a sweep of heavy machine-gun fire over their heads. The crowd broke and bolted for the trees and farmlands. But in less than a minute they started coming back, shouting louder than before.

Scanning the area with binoculars, McCarter found the DC-3 transport Barbara Price had reserved for them in case of trouble. The mission controller was as sharp as they came, but even she never saw this mess coming. On the side of a runway, the DC-3 was parked near a dull green hangar. The side hatch was open, and government troops were all over the airplane, hauling out weapons and ammunition boxes.

"They seized our backup ride," he said, lowering the glasses and passing them to somebody else.

"Great. Now they probably think we're part of the resistance," Hawkins drawled.

"Going to make getting it back damn near impossible," James commented.

"We could hire a boat," Encizo suggested, looking backward in the direction of the busy dockyard. "Only take us a week or so to reach Miami."

The vast expanse of the muddy Amazon stretched for over a mile at that point, the thick black water from the distant mountain runoff easily visible. The famous black water was mineral rich and was considered a healthy treat to drink by many. It was also too cold for piranha and several other species of aquatic life that savored human flesh. The ebony band was a slim safe zone meandering through the most deadly river in the world.

"Got a plan, David?" Encizo asked.

"Almost," McCarter said, looking at his wristwatch.

A Hummer bearing the flag of the Republic of Brazil and jammed full of armed soldiers turned the corner. Driving toward the distant airport, a gray-haired sergeant in the front noticed the group of tourists and scowled in displeasure until the driver took another corner.

"First thing, we better get off this hill," Encizo said in warning, lowering his field glasses. "We stand out too much."

Easing back the hammer on the Beretta 93-R behind his back, Hawkins motioned with his head. "There's a cantina down the road that looks open."

"Sounds good," McCarter stated, doing the same to his Browning. "Let's go."

THE BRAZILIAN TAVERN was cool but not quiet, full of men talking nonstop, some frightened, others angry and more than a couple scared. The few women there advertised their ancient profession with every furtive glance and sway of their round hips, but almost nobody was interested. The talk of war filled the room like heavy smoke.

There didn't seem to be a waiter, so while Manning went for drinks, James secured a table in the far corner by bodily removing a snoring drunk and walking him outside. As

McCarter and Encizo sat down to hold the table, a few burly stevedores from the dockyard tried to take the table and push them aside, but a single stern look from the Phoenix Force warriors made them consider otherwise. The dock workers walked away muttering under their breath about stinking bastard foreigners who thought they owned the world.

"Brazilian martinis for everybody," Manning announced, laying down a tray of tall, frosty cold bottles of beer.

"No waitress?" McCarter asked, taking a bottle and using a Swiss Army knife to pop the top.

"They all went home when the fighting started," Manning said.

"Not bad," Encizo agreed, popping the top on a second bottle. The dust from the long dirt roads was lining his throat, and he had been dying for a cold beer.

"Ain't Lone Star," Hawkins said with conviction, placing aside the first dead soldier. "But it'll do."

"Bah. This is horse piss in comparison to Hale's Pale Ale from Dublin," McCarter stated with conviction, wiping foam from his mouth.

Conversation stopped for a minute while a group of men staggered past the table on the way to the men's room. The covert ops now knew why only the drunk had been at this table, as the strong smell of urine came wafting over them every time the door swung open.

"Ah, that takes me back. South Chicago in the spring." James smiled, breathing deeply, then coughed. "If it catches on fire, I'll get positively homesick."

The men shared a laugh and clinked their bottles.

Still holding his beer, McCarter lit a cigarette and drew the strong smoke in deep. "Okay, to work. We got five hours until nightfall, and I want to be airborne by then."

"So what is the plan? No way we're getting anywhere near our DC-3," Manning started. "The military will be expecting that and probably have parts removed in case we try.''

''Not even going to try,'' McCarter replied, drawing a rough map on the damp wood with a fingertip. ''That is way too obvious a target. No, we hit the garage and find something, anything, that flies and roll it away into the night to avoid their searchlights.''

Wiping the foam from his mouth, Manning gave a snort. ''Hijack a plane on the ground with the airport crawling the federal troops.''

''Nobody would expect it.''

''Nobody sane,'' Hawkins shot back, then grinned. ''But that's why I like it.''

''We did pass some fallow fields north of here,'' James added thoughtfully. ''Those might do in a pinch.''

''Good enough,'' McCarter said. ''We're going to need a major diversion.''

''I'll handle that,'' Manning offered, adding to the outline on the table. ''The hotels all turn off the electricity at 9:00 p.m. A lot of citizens and small businesses, too. If I helped that along by, say, ten minutes, it would buy us a window.''

Grinding out the butt of his cigarette, McCarter grunted in agreement. ''Then we strike at nine. With luck they'll only assume it was the regular power down for the night.''

''If not,'' Encizo added, ''then we'll have the whole damn Brazilian army hot on our ass.''

''Then don't screw up.''

''That was my plan.''

''Anything special we might need?'' James asked, running a mental inventory of the truck outside.

''We're low on medical supplies,'' Manning said seriously. ''So try not to get shot.''

''That's always part of the plan,'' Hawkins stated, pushing away a full bottle of beer. He could drink these city boys under the table, but this wasn't the time or place for a demonstration.

"Senhor?" a young voice asked.

The men of Phoenix Force turned with hands resting on their belts.

Walking closer, a pair of boys carrying a wicker basket that contained some empty beer bottles offered to remove the rest. Wearing rags and no shoes, they probably lived off the return deposit. Clearing off the table, the team nearly filled the basket, and then added a generous tip. The boys were delighted, and before leaving the older child reached up and tugged on Encizo's collar to whisper something to the man. The Cuban nodded and thanked him, passing him some more coins.

"My Portuguese is rather weak," Encizo said to the others. "But it appears our friends from the docks are waiting outside near our truck to teach us a lesson."

"Everything we have is in there," Hawkins growled, glancing at the bar mirror to see the front door. "The kid say anything about weapons?"

"Machetes."

"No guns?"

"Not that he knew."

With a grim expression, Manning pushed back his chair and stood. "Too bad for them."

A few minutes later McCarter and Hawkins drunkenly stumbled from the cantina and immediately found themselves surrounded by the smiling stevedores tapping deadly machetes on the palms of their heavily callused hands.

"You beg now, Yankee," the big man said in broken English. "Beg like bitch girl."

Weaving about, Hawkins gave a fake hiccup, and McCarter twisted sideways to kick the first dockworker in the gut with the edge of his sandal. The air exploded from the man, and he dropped his weapon, wheezing for breath.

Moving like lightning, Hawkins snatched the fallen blade and flipped it over to strike another on the wrist with the dull side. The bones audibly broke, and the stevedore backed away weeping uncontrollably, holding his smashed hand high.

"Kill you!" the lead worker snarled, and swung at McCarter's throat. The warrior ducked out of the way, and swept the ground to grab some dirt to throw into his adversary's face.

Waving the blade wildly about, the stevedore cursed as he tried to wipe his face.

That was when the rest of Phoenix Force appeared from the growing shadows behind the bar and attacked.

Ramming his forearm against a falling arm, Encizo blocked a machete, then stabbed two stiff fingers forward in a kung fu move. The man's face turned pale with the shock of the fire racing along his chest from the crushed nerve. Encizo spun and slammed an elbow into the paralyzed man's face, and he dropped to the ground, mercifully unconscious.

In a karate high-low move, James lunged forward with one hand jabbing for a man's crotch and the other going for his eyes. Trying to jerk out of the way, the stevedore protected his eyes and doubled over as James crushed his testicles. Tears running down his face, the stevedore slashed the machete, and James deflected it with a slap to the side of the blade. The weapon went spinning away into the darkness, and James continued the motion to spin and launch a powerful backkick to the worker, his heel striking the man in the solar plexus. The street tough fell to the ground twitching but alive.

Grabbing a loose shirt, Hawkins flipped another over his hip in a judo move, and McCarter broke a nose with the edge of his hand. Now the fight spread, with dimly seen figures moving in the thickening night, curses and cries of pain echoing the meaty thumps of fists hitting flesh. Soon there were a dozen bleeding people on the ground, with Phoenix Force standing over the moaning dockworkers without a scratch in the group.

"*¡Alerta!*" McCarter said in smooth Spanish, hoping they would understand.

As the stevedores tried to focus their blurry vision, the covert teammates drew their handguns and dramatically jacked the slides. The battered workers recoiled at the sight, some of them begging for their lives as they struggled to crawl away, dragging broken limbs.

"Next time we shoot," the SAS paratrooper stated coldly, displaying the weapon. "Next time we kill. *¿Entienden?* Understand?"

The man nodded energetically, holding a bloody arm to his torn shirt.

Holstering the 9 mm Browning Hi-Power, McCarter waved a hand. "*¡Vaya rápidamente!*"

Helping one another to stand, the dockworkers made it to the middle of the road and lurched toward town, fearfully watching over their shoulders in case this was a trick of some kind.

"That was fun," Manning said, flexing his hands. The big man's breathing was even and regular, as if he had done nothing more strenuous than order a pizza over the phone.

"Waste of our damn time," James shot back, picking up a dropped machete and throwing it at the soil. The blade sank in all the way, then he kicked sideways and snapped off the handle completely.

"Enough. We have work to do," McCarter said, and the team quietly climbed on board the truck and drove away into the darkness.

In the curtainless window of a house near the tavern, an old television set showing the fight at the airport crackled with static, the picture rolling and becoming fuzzy as the relayed transmission became weaker and weaker.

CHAPTER SIX

High Earth Orbit Above the Pacific Ocean

Something flashed just outside her field of vision, and the NASA astronaut slowly turned away from the satellite she was working on and in that direction as quickly as possible. What the hell was that?

But nothing unusual was in sight. Three hundred seventeen miles above the blue-white majesty of Earth, Captain Sharon Waltham was floating effortlessly in space, about a hundred feet away from the shuttle *Enterprise.*

Keeping one glove on a stanchion, Captain Waltham floated freely in space with her spacesuit tethered to the silver cylinder of a NavStar satellite. The civilian orbiter was a complex communications relay combining a nationwide low-jack security signal, a cellular help line and a sophisticated GPD map locator for luxury cars. Apparently this was all very important stuff to a lot of rich people, but for a confirmed Chevy driver, Waltham thought the whole thing rather frivolous. However, a subprocessor in the NavStar had stopped correctly responding several months ago, and after a dozen attempts by technicians to fix the problem from the ground, the New York owners finally paid to have NASA do the necessary repairs. So it was her job to fix the machine.

"Have wrench, will travel," the woman muttered to herself, returning to the job at hand. She didn't want to delay the repairs for very long. It had taken an hour to remove the external hull from the orbiter, and now its delicate electronic guts were exposed to the harsh elements of space.

Placing a set of surgical long-finger probes securely on a patch of Velcro to keep them from drifting away, the astronaut peeled off a small powered screwdriver and started to remove some internal bolts. As each came loose, she carefully captured the item and placed it into a plastic bag that was also attached to the outer hull of the satellite with a piece of Velcro. Best thing NASA ever invented.

As the thermal plate came away, Waltham frowned. Luxury cars her ass. There were way too many circuit boards in here she couldn't fully identify. This bird also had to be doing a bit of spying for somebody. The CIA most likely. But then most satellites did that. Even these civilian orbiters. Big Brother was everywhere these days.

Running some brief tests, Waltham saw the problem seemed to be a short circuit in the power transformer. As she rotated her head to check on the solar wing array, there was another blur of sudden motion and she craned her neck about to what was happening. NASA personnel were always a bit spooked about odd things happening in space ever since the "dancing lights" reported by John Glenn in his Mercury capsule. Many weird things had been reported over the decades in space, but most of them had been easily explained as natural phenomena. But not all. That was the scary part. Heck, ever since they got up here, the Cape had been constantly asking if they saw anything out of the ordinary in high orbit.

"Something wrong, Captain?" a man's voice asked over the headphones of her helmet. "Your heart rate just jumped there."

That would be Major Pierre Falawn, the shuttle's French relief pilot.

"No problem, *Enterprise,*" Waltham responded into her throat mike, the thrusters on her EVA backpack spurting tiny jets of HO_44 gas to keep her relatively stable. "Just thought that I saw something move by really fast. Any meteorites on the radar?"

"Screen is clear, Captain."

"What is it, old buddy?" Com specialist Professor George Terhune chuckled. "Spot a speeding UFO?"

Now, that kind of a joke could follow her for years, but before the captain could retort a good zinger, there was the motion again, and then several more.

"Motherfu—" Waltham bit her lip to stop the curse word. The mission specialists were on an open frequency so the civilians of the world could follow their conversations. It made for good public relations, and sure cut down on the loose talk when you knew the big boss heard every word you said.

"Houston, we have a problem," she said clearly, watching another flurry of motion in the ebony darkness of space. "Possible meteor shower in our vicinity. Small objects, very fast, fifteen- maybe twenty-degree approach."

"Report, *Enterprise,*" a crisp voice said in the perpetual NASA calm. "Is the shuttle in danger?"

"Unknown, Houston. Radar shows nothing," Terhune reported crisply.

"Could it be debris?" the Houston technician asked urgently.

Waltham felt a rush of adrenaline into her guts. "Why debris?" she replied bluntly. "Has there been some kind of a collision or explosion in near space?"

"Go to channel alpha, red, ocean, bravo," a new voice said in her headphones. "Code Blue."

The security channel, she knew. Something was very definitely wrong up there.

But as the captain started pressing in the access code into

the miniature control panel on the forearm of her spacesuit, there was a tug on her leg and a loud whistling filled her suit. A wave of cold swept through her as the air pressure dropped as the liner swelled to seal off the puncture.

"Collision alert!" Waltham said calmly, her glove reaching for the emergency patch disks on her belt. "I have been hit. Repeat, I have been hit."

"Hit by what?" the new voice demanded. "Goddamn it, what is happening, Captain?"

"How should I know? Small, dark, fast, that's all I can tell."

A hooting siren interrupted the conversation and blocked any possible speech, until the volume thankfully dropped.

"We've been holed!" Terhune said, his words distorted from being too close to the microphone. "Internal damage to robot arm. I am closing shuttle-bay doors on emergency protocol."

"Captain Waltham, are you okay?" Houston demanded.

"Seals are holding," she reported, feeling the heaters of her spacesuit drive off the brief wash of cold. "I am abandoning the satellite and returning to the shuttle immediately."

A loud bang sounded, making her jerk in the spacesuit, the backpack struggling to compensate for the abrupt motion.

"We've been hit," Terhune snapped. "Damage to port wing, and aft vector three."

Static hissed for several long seconds.

"Can you still operate, *Enterprise?*" Houston demanded.

"Roger that," Major Falawn replied. "Sharon, get your ass on board because we are leaving right damn now."

"On my way," the captain replied, and hit full power on her backpack. Speed was her best bet now. Something was tearing through this section of space like a shotgun blast, and the longer they stayed the greater the chance of a serious hit. The astronaut felt naked and vulnerable protected only by her mobile suit, and the tiny air-lock door of the shuttle looked as if it were a million miles away.

Then there was another loud bang, followed by a couple more.

"What the fuck was that?" Falawn cried out. "Jesus Christ, we've been holed! Port-side window!"

There was a howl of escaping air that sounded like a hurricane in a phone booth.

"Find the patch kit!"

"Got it! Out of my damn way!"

"Emergency pressurization procedures!"

Even as Waltham raced toward the shuttle, she saw the steady white streams of escaping air forming above the armored hull of the spacecraft.

"Pilot to crew, secure all holdings!" Falawn shouted, his voice cracking from the low atmospheric pressure in the ship. "I'm rotating the shuttle now!"

The belly of the *Enterprise* was its strongest section, the thick layers of ceramic-fiber tiles over titanium ample proof to the temperature and fantastic pressure of a fiery reentry. A meteorite would have to be of uncommon size to damage the craft on the bottom. Fifty yards to go.

Waltham was only yards from the open air-lock door when a flurry of moving objects blurred her vision with their passage and the space shuttle was horribly punched through in a dozen areas, broken tiles spraying outward at each impact point. A ferruled rocket vector was torn off the rear engine assembly, a wide hole blasted through the port-side wing, fuel hosing into space like gore from a wound.

A voice screamed, man or woman it was impossible to tell, then the warbling noise cut off abruptly. The other astronauts inside the crippled vessel were all shouting at once, trying to effect repairs from the countless tiny hits. But air was leaking fast, and there were so many people speaking the voices blurred one another.

Another object slammed straight into the belly of the ship, denting the underhull and achieving total penetration, wreckage actually spewing out the roof of the craft from the belly strike.

"Seal that hatch!"

"Susan is hit in the stomach. There's blood everywhere!"

"Put pressure on that wound!"

"Get into your suits!"

"Full auxiliary power! We're leaving this vector now!"

"What about Waltham?"

"No time!"

"Oh my God, fire in the ship!"

Frantically reversing her course, Waltham could only watch as flames silently filled the cockpit window, fed by the oxygen-rich atmosphere of the leaking LOX fuel tanks. In a single moment the conflagration blazed utterly out of control. The screams of the dying people mixed with the dull thuds of small explosions until the blaze reached the fuel tanks and the space shuttle blew apart.

"*Enterprise,* are you there?" the voice from Houston Control demanded urgently over the radio. "Respond, *Enterprise!*"

Covering her faceplate with both arms, Captain Waltham desperately turned from the blast and braced herself for death to arrive as shrapnel. Slow long seconds passed before she dared to look over a shoulder, and there was nothing in space behind her anymore. The hundred-million-dollar vessel was gone, torn apart by its own detonating fuel cells. A terrible cold seized Waltham as the woman realized that she was now alone as few people had ever been in the history of the world. Abandoned in deep space, three hundred miles above the surface of the world and without a chance in hell of a rescue mission being mounted before her air ran out.

Then the bright solar light was eclipsed as something moved between the sun and the astronaut.

Tapping frantically into the forearm controls of her spacesuit, Waltham raced for her life from the oncoming shadow, the maneuvering jets puffing long and hard to shove her out of the way. But the terrible penumbra shadow followed her every move with machine precision.

"Houston, they are not meteors!" she shouted, as a swarm of barely visible objects shot close by and overwhelmed the NavStar.

As if it were made of paper, the satellite was torn apart, the solar wings shattering into black daggers and the tattered remains of annihilated hull spread out in a secondary death cloud of shrapnel. Her sleeve tugged and an ice stream spewed from her suit as the escaping air started whistling into the deadly vacuum of space.

Going to the belt kit, the captain fumbled for a repair disk and slapped it onto a jagged puncture in her suit when another tug shook on her leg, white hot pain exploding in her knee. Then something ricocheted off the control panel of her chest computer, making half of the instruments in her helmet wink out.

Her forehead gauges said the radio was still working, but she could no longer receive and her batteries were losing power fast. Waltham had no illusions; she was already dead. But there was still a job to do. Astronauts were mostly chosen from military personnel for exactly this kind of a situation.

Hitting full power on her EVA backpack, she threw herself at the cloudy planet below, trying to escape from the killer above and stay alive for just a few more minutes.

"I cannot hear you, so do not respond," Waltham shouted into her throat mike. Australia was directly below her, a small storm moving across New Zealand. "We have been attacked by an enemy shuttle of some kind. A god-damn armored shuttle.''

Just then another flurry covered the woman, tearing her suit apart and spinning her. Looking straight up, she saw the enemy at last, fully illuminated by the sun.

"Son of a bitch, it isn't a shuttle!" Waltham shouted, blood starting to spray out of her suit as red snow. A killing cold seized the astronaut, and she fought to speak against a sudden and terrible weariness.

There was one more flurry of motion, visible only from the stars momentarily blocked by the passage of the tiny objects.

"Not a shuttle!" she repeated, her vision dimming from the fog covering the inside of her visor. "Repeat, Houston, it is not a shuttle!"

Incredibly sharp pain dotted her body, and Waltham tried to shout a description as the faceplate shattered into pieces, cutting her face. Exposed to space, the dying woman strug-gled to shout her last report even as the breath was ripped from her lungs and ice began to form over her eyes. Then a soothing warmth replaced the pain, and Waltham com-pletely relaxed into a chaotic dreamlike state as everything went black.

6:00 P.M., Downtown Baltimore

THE SUN WAS STARTING to set, the purple sky filling with the reflected glow of the million neon signs from downtown Baltimore and the resplendent inner harbor.

But darkness already ruled in a garbage-filled alley, mask-ing a battered van with tinted windows standing near a gar-bage bin, its engine softly idling. Stumbling through the alley, a drunk in rags saw the vehicle and ignored it, unzip-ping his fly with unsteady fingers to relieve himself on a rear tire. When he was done, the fellow shuffled off, bumping against refuse until reaching the street and was gone.

"The drunk made us," Rosario Blancanales said with a grin. "I knew those tires were too new. Bet he only whizzes on cop cars like that."

"We'll wash them next time with diluted carbolic acid to age the shine off," Carl Lyons said. "But we should thank the bum. Now we really blend into the environment."

"Homeless, Carl. We call them homeless people now."

The ex-cop grunted. "'Homeless' means you have no home. If you like living in trash and drinking yourself to death, then you're a bum."

"Okay, heads up," Gadgets Schwarz announced from an equipment-covered workbench inside the cramped vehicle. "We have good news and bad news. The chemical sniffers can't find any traces of C-4, TNT, fulminating guncotton or any other high explosives in the Nazi headquarters across the street, so the place probably isn't mined. It should be safe to enter."

"Should?" Lyons asked with a scowl. The big ex-LAPD cop was crouching on his heels, a hand resting on the grip of his .357 Magnum Colt Python. This close to the Avalon 88 group, he was fully alert and wired for combat, even though this was only a recon.

Schwarz spread his hands. "The basement could be loaded with thermite for all I know. That registers only as ordinary cans of paint. There's no way to tell the difference."

"Why paint?" Blancanales asked, puzzled, leaning an arm across the rear of the driver's seat.

"Technical reasons," he answered, sidestepping a ten-minute-long explanation.

"Great. So what's the good news?"

"That was it. The bad news is that the damn wall is too thick," Schwarz replied, pushing aside a thermal probe. The device resembled a shotgun with a soup bowl on the front and carried a price tag of staggering proportions. "I can't get through."

On a nearby table, a small monitor showed a swirling rainbow-pattern picture of the Nazi building. Normally the thermoscopic scan would be able to literally see through the wall of the building by registering the minute temperature differences of everything inside: human bodies would be reddish outlines with yellow splotches for the bellies and neck; bubbling coffeepots a solid orange and a recently fired gun would be a dull red tinged with bright yellow. Even cars passing in the street would register as completely red, with orange tires and yellow-white engines.

Unfortunately the ancient concrete and heavy clay tiles of the converted meat warehouse were an effective barrier. Designed to keep in the cold, the tiles were too thick for the thermal scan to penetrate. Even the small windows were bricked over, the combination of brick and glass making the computer-generated images of the interior blurry and questionable at best.

"Try the UV," Lyons suggested.

Tapping a row of illuminated buttons, Schwarz turned off the machine. "I did already. It's no good."

"Then we go in," Blancanales stated simply, and slid on a cloth cap with the words Baker Delivery printed across the front.

Carefully laying a silenced Ingram machine pistol into an oblong flower box, Schwarz placed a collection of fresh roses on top of the weapon, fitted the thin cardboard lid and tied it shut with a red silk ribbon.

"Here ya go," he said, passing the box to his partner.

Blancanales passed back a pizza delivery box, which Schwarz accepted and then clipped a change maker to his belt.

"What are you, an ice cream man? Who pays for pizza

with coins?" Lyons asked, buttoning closed his Fenton Plumbing shirt.

"Nobody. But it adds a nice touch of realism."

"On Mars, maybe," Blancanales added with a snort. "This is the age of plastic and faxes."

"Not for much longer," Schwarz muttered, slipping on a CD to his belt and draping headphones around his neck.

The humor wasn't out of place. Infiltration was their specialty, and the men saw no possible problems arising from this assignment. They had smooth talked their way into a Mafia hardsite; this radical splinter of the American Nazi Party should be a cakewalk.

Then Lyons flashed back to a bloody day when he said those exact words once before, and felt a shiver touch his bones. Overconfidence got more soldiers shoveled into the ground than any weapon ever made.

"Take grenades," he said, adding another M-26 fragger to his toolbox next to the cloth-covered weapon.

The Stony Man urban commandos slipped from the rear of the van, their exit well hidden by the garbage bin. Walking casually, they moved through the crowds and traffic to reconvene behind the building across the street.

With his teammates flanking him, Lyons placed a contact stun gun against the cheap brass handle of the door and knocked with his free hand. There was a muffled noise from the other side, and the tiny beam of light coming through the peephole vanished.

"Yeah, and who the fuck are you?" a gruff voice demanded.

"*Heil* Hitler. Your door is unlocked," Lyons said urgently.

The light returned as the unseen man muttered a curse and rattled the doorjamb to see if that was true. Instantly Lyon pressed the button on the stun gun, and electric sparks crackled over the conductive surface in a pyrotechnic display of lights. A strangled cry was closely followed by the thud of a falling body.

Lyons cut the Taser and stepped aside for Schwarz to place a reverse-lens scope to the peephole and see inside.

"Nobody else in sight," he reported.

Kneeling on the dirty asphalt, Blancanales was already working on the lock. A minute passed, then another.

"What's wrong?" Lyons demanded brusquely.

The lock clicked loudly, and Blancanales pulled the door open. "Nothing," he said, sweeping the interior of the building with a hand tucked inside his box of flowers. "Just a good lock."

"It would have to be in this neighborhood."

Moving past the man sprawled on the linoleum floor, Lyons made sure the area was clear, then grabbed the guard by the belt buckle and carried him to the corner to drop him on a pile of dirty canvas. Blancanales entered and stepped to the left with his hand on the weapon in the flowerbox, ready in case of trouble. Schwarz closed the door behind them, then slipped a smooth tin key into the lock and twisted it hard. The cheap metal snapped off, completely jamming the lock. Now it was impossible for anybody to seal off their escape route.

Moving into the next room, the men found cardboard boxes full of hate pamphlets, and in a corner was a rickety table covered with a half-eaten sandwich and an open thermos of hot coffee that reeked of cheap whiskey. On a nearby chair was a paperback book laying facedown, its garishly yellow cover showing a mature naked woman tied helpless to a bed while several grinning Nazi soldiers undid their belts.

Lyons scowled at the porn and felt the hairs on his neck rise. This idiot was reading porn and drinking coffee after his group had sent a warning to the White House? That made absolutely no sense. Then he remembered the DEW

Line. These satellite killers liked traps. Maybe these men were a sacrifice to make invaders drop their guard for an ambush.

"If these are terrorists, then I'm a ballerina," Schwarz stated.

Lyons silenced him with a stern glance.

Proceeding deeper into the building, the Able Team commandos discovered more stacks of propaganda, a small Gestetner printing press in desperate need of a cleaning, a filthy bathroom, a kitchen crawling with cockroaches and not much else. The front door proved to be barricaded with a pile of cinder blocks. Obviously the Nazis discouraged casual visitors, and all business was handled out the back door.

Finding a stairwell going to the next level, the men walked carefully up the steps, keeping all of their weight on the extreme sides where the wood would be the strongest and thus least likely to squeak and betray their presence. They made it to the top without incident.

A door blocked the landing, and they could hear the flat, artificial sound of machine guns firing. Going to the keyhole, Schwarz used his lens again. Stripped to the waist, two bald men were lifting weights and drinking beer while watching a war movie on a big-screen television.

Blancanales tricked the lock in under a minute. As the door swung open, the men turned and Able Team shot them with Delta Force air guns, the feathered darts slamming into the hard pectoral muscles of the startled Nazis. Rolling his eyes, the first man simply dropped on the spot, but the second clawed at the dart and tried to lumber away, wheezing a shout as he headed for a battered wooden desk in the corner. As Schwarz closed the door, his teammates shot the man in the back, and the young giant finally succumbed to the drugs. Sighing deeply, he collapsed to the carpet and began to snore.

As Blancanales killed the television, Lyons opened the

desk to find a .22-caliber target pistol suitable for shooting tin cans and not much more. He checked the clip and smelled the barrel, but the weapon hadn't been fired recently.

"Not exactly Interpol headquarters," Blancanales whispered with a frown.

Pulling a thick plastic wand from his belt pouch, Schwarz ran the sniffer over the hands of the unconscious men. "These guys haven't touched C-4 in the last month," he stated confidently, tucking the device away. "But they might have worn gloves."

"Let's finish the sweep," Lyons ordered, easing past the open doorway. If this was the radical arm of the ANP, then America had nothing to fear from these people. This was a clubhouse where fools got drunk and talked big on the weekends, nothing more. Unless there were a few wolves mixed in with the sheep.

The next room was obviously where the men held their meetings. Folding tables were laid out in a swastika pattern and covered with flags. There were coffee-mug rings and food stains on the flags, showing their constant use and rare washing. A cheap gun rack on the wall held an assortment of shotguns and one bolt-action .475 Magnum hunting rifle. Overflowing ashtrays were everywhere, with a lot of ground-out butts on the floor, as well. A sweet smell wafted in the air, and it had nothing to do with tobacco.

Staying alert, the team kept moving. In the hallway a half flight of stairs led to a large open room with a fat guard snoozing in a chair, his grimy T-shirt riding up to expose his roll of stomach. Blancanales simply walked directly to the man and touched him with the stun gun. The sleeping Nazi awoke in a galvanized start as the twenty-thousand volts shot through his system, then he went limp. The door was open, and the team slipped inside only to find a large room full of equipment that was also deserted.

The air was hot and dusty, carrying the stale taste of ancient paper. Old black-and-white pictures from the Holocaust covered the walls, along with modern color shots of Nazi troops proudly marching down streets while crowds cheered. It looked liked Argentina, but it could also be Skokie, Illinois.

A homemade shelf of bricks and pine boards held a ragtag collection of military communications manuals, and Schwarz gave them only a brief survey. Each book was decades out of date; even the radios on the covers weren't manufactured anymore. A huge complex radio rested on a small stand, but it was only a shortwave set decades out of date. Most Third World countries had better than this junk.

This was bullshit, Schwarz realized. There wasn't enough equipment here to block a kid's crystal radio, much less a satellite in space.

Lyons stood guard while Blancanales went through a file cabinet, the lock on the drawers offering no resistance to his combat knife. After rifling the bottom drawer, Blancanales shook his head. Lyons did a sweep of the back of the closet while his teammate stood guard. Buckets and mops, and baseball bats with blood on them. There had been something going on here, but from the look of the bloodstains it was very long ago.

"Club initiation," Blancanales guessed.

Lyons shrugged and closed the door. Then he opened it again and knelt to examine the floor. Holstering his dart gun, he started to shift the contents out of the way. Scratch marks were discernible on the floor, forming a short arc. Running his hands along the sides of the closet, the big ex-cop easily found the hidden catch. With a loud click the back panel swung aside.

As his teammates watched the room, Lyons holstered the dart gun and pulled his Colt Python from under his shirt.

The massive weapon filled his hand as if it had been designed for no other purpose.

Pushing the fake panel aside with the toolbox he still carried, Lyons entered the hidden room with his handgun searching for targets.

The floor was clean carpeting, the walls wood paneling with no decorations of newspaper clippings or other nonsense. A large vaulted skylight crested the room, the frosted glass admitting a wealth of soft light. State-of-the-art radio communication systems filled a long table the length of one wall, and a bank of computers sat humming steadily. A large Nazi flag adorned the wall at the end, flanked by gun racks holding AK-47 assault rifles. Boxes of magazines and ammunition were stacked on the floor. In a corner were several plastic crates of thermite grenades, and on the wall was a five-foot-long Finnish 20 mm antitank gun resting on a polished mahogany frame. Bandoliers hung from wall pegs, the leather loops full of fat, oily shells of HE.

"Bingo," Lyons whispered, easing back the hammer on his Colt.

"Got to buy a tutu, Hermann," Blancanales said.

"At least I have the legs for it," Schwarz countered as he went to the radio and started to check the equipment.

Listening for any movements, Lyons and Blancanales swept the room, searching for guards, but the place was empty. A heavy curtain closed off the far end. Beyond it was a studio setup with a large bed bolted to the floor, video cameras and a lot of klieg lights. Chains were draped over the satin covers of the large bed, and on the walls was an assortment of whips and chains clearly designed for sexual acts with very small people. Tall bookcases were filled with identical rows of labeled cassettes with colorful covers whose titles left nothing to the imagination.

"A home video studio," Lyons cursed, looking over the

titles. "These assholes make chicken flicks to finance print-ing their leaflets."

"Kiddie porn," Blancanales said, wiping off his hand that touched the cassettes. "This place gets burned before we leave."

"Damn straight," Lyons agreed grimly.

"How many thermite grenades do we have, Pol?"

"Six. More than enough. This crap is highly flammable."

"Good."

Schwarz strode across the room and grabbed them both by a shoulder. "Do nothing," he whispered hoarsely. "This whole place is a trap. The ISP on those computers is wrong. Different than the ones used to post the message on the Web."

"Get hard," Lyons ordered, setting the toolbox on the floor and lifting the lid to withdraw a sawed-off M-16/ M-203 combo. The flash suppressor had been removed, along with the telescope/handle and the stock. It was a mod-ified special by Kissinger and some of his best work.

"Any chance they might have done that deliberately to hide their identity?" Blancanales asked, tucking away his dart gun and pulling out the 9 mm Ingram machine pistol from the flower box.

Holstering his own dart gun, Schwarz opened the pizza box and withdrew the MAC-10 machine pistol. "There are ways," the communications expert agreed, working the bolt and flicking off the safety. "But not this time. We've been suckered. The post was a fake."

Slapping a flip clip into the breech of his assault rifle, Lyons cursed under his breath. He had only one 40 mm round for the M-203, and here they were standing in the middle of another ambush. Only the computer skills of Her-mann Schwarz had blown the trap early and given them a fighting chance to live.

"No bombs in the basement," Blancanales said. "So they must have something else planned."

Far across the long room, the Nazi flag fluttered on the wall as if somebody were moving behind the material.

"And here it comes," Lyons growled, dropping into a defensive crouch and aiming his weapon.

CHAPTER SEVEN

Somewhere in the Swiss Alps

The strong mountain winds buffeted the old 747 back and forth, then the deck seemed to drop a foot, only to slam upward once more. Coffee cups crashed to the deck, loose papers went flying, passengers screamed in a chorus of assorted languages and the cockpit crew cursed as they fought for the life of the blind aircraft.

"Mayday! Mayday!" the pilot shouted into the hand mike while desperately holding on to the yoke and trying to maintain control. "Please respond, any airport or landing field. Anybody at all! Respond, goddamn it!"

Only swirling gray was visible outside the windows, the storm clouds and thick ground fog combining to form an impenetrable mist that seemed to blanket the world.

"Well?" the copilot demanded, madly flipping switches. As per regulations, he already primed the black box, and the stewards were helping the passengers to assume crash positions.

Distant thunder rumbled, and there was a faint flash of lightning. A storm, that was all they needed at the moment.

In disgust the navigator threw her headset to the deck. "There's nothing!" she shot back. "It must be a malfunction on our end, because how could every radio in Europe stop working at the exact same time!"

Everything had been perfectly fine on this flight until half the instrument board went suddenly dead, ILM, telemetry, GPD, the com links, airphones—even the radio was nothing but crackling hash. Trying to compensate, the inboard computer struggled to handle the overload of data, and then crashed. The crew was down to a magnetic compass. The vaunted inertial guidance system, part of the computerized navigation system, was presently as dead as the proverbial doornail.

"Maybe the satellite relays are gone," the captain grunted, fighting to control his bucking ship. The winds were strong.

"All of them?" the navigator asked. "Impossible. What meteor shower could do that?"

"Maybe it was a comet."

"Shut up!"

Unseen below the lumbering 747 were the yawning chasms and soaring peaks of the Alps. Trained professionals, the crew could almost feel the mountains around the aircraft. There were countless safe routes through the Alps, but the storm blocked any chance of dead reckoning, and without the GPD or satellite navigation they were helpless.

"What's our height?" the navigator demanded, inserting new fuses into the control board to no effect.

"Forty thousand feet."

"Sir, that's eight thousand above our flight plan!" the copilot admonished. "We could hit another jumbo jet at this height."

"And we'll hit a mountain if we dare fly any lower!" the older man retorted, his shoulders hunched as if expecting a blow. "We can't see a thing in this soup. So if you have a better idea, tell me now, because down is not an option!"

Suddenly the short-range radar began to wildly beep.

"Proximity alert!" the navigator shouted. "Hard ten degrees to port!"

Dropping the mike, the pilot fought the titanic craft, wrapping both arms around the yoke. Sluggishly the craft responded and began to angle to the left. Then a blast of wind shook the 747 and the copilot gasped as he clearly saw a craggy mountain peak directly ahead of the huge aircraft. At their current speed the small gap would be covered in only seconds! One wrong move, and they would be smashed to pieces.

The radar was sounding nonstop, when there appeared a break in the clouds. Sighing in relief, the crew saw only clear sky ahead and a peaceful snowy valley stretching underneath, with no dangerous peaks anywhere nearby.

"We made it!" the navigator shouted in triumph, raising clenched fists. "Who needs satellites!"

"Thank God," the copilot said, closing his eyes to touch the crucifix under his shirt.

Then from the starboard fog came the dark shape of another 747 jumbo jet heading straight for them. Both of the captains reacted instantly, but there simply wasn't enough time. The two aircraft hit, creating a fireball that illuminated the Alpine valley in hellish light.

Stony Man Farm, Virginia

BARBARA PRICE BURST into the Computer Room. "How many dead in Switzerland?" she demanded, going to the main console.

Yakov Katzenelenbogen glanced up from his keyboard, his face a mask of pain. "Over one thousand," he said, a tremor in his voice.

"Two commercial jetliners collided in midair, and the burning wreckage fell onto a small Alpine village. The last we heard, most of the village was on fire and the only bridge in or out had collapsed."

"Can we confirm any survivors?" Price demanded. "Through an Internet account, fax machines, anything?"

"There are no working cell phones in the valley," Akira Tokaido said, "and everything else is off-line. With the satellite relays gone, no radio signal can get out of the mountains. Most of what we know comes from a CIA Keyhole spy sat traveling over the section of the world."

"Can we talk to them?"

"Just barely. We have a shortwave radio here at the Farm, and I can send a signal to our geosynchronous comsat directly above and relay it to the Keyhole over southern Europe," the man said, then gave a shrug. "But what can we say that might be of any assistance?"

Good God. A shortwave transmission from Virginia to the eastern Alps. Tokaido might as well try shouting to the victims. Price tried not to imagine the trapped villagers, tons of wreckage falling from the sky, most of the city on fire and the wounded endlessly calling for help on radios that wouldn't reach outside of their valley, much less to anybody that could help. It could be hours, even days before somebody discovered the crash. She glanced at a medical-response stat map on the wall. And only a hundred miles away, there was a mountain rescue station over the border in France. Medical helicopters could reach the village in less than an hour.

"And nobody knows," she said grimly.

"Oh yes, the Italian government knows," Katz said grimly, gesturing at a military alert map of the Mediterranean with a coffee mug clamped tight in his hook. "We decoded a transmission about the crash from one of their northern military bases in the Po River valley."

"And they're not doing anything?" Price demanded, a cold rage filling her body.

"Nothing. They are afraid to reveal their lack of recon satellites and invite an attack from a foreign country."

"The bastards!"

"Absolutely. But understandable," Katz added. "After World War II, and then the Mafia, lots of folks don't like Italy and would love to plow the country under the dirt."

"Aaron, if we sent a call for help, could it be traced back here?" she asked quietly.

"Possibly," the head of the cyber team stated. "Under these circumstances there are simply too many variables for me to even hazard an intelligent guess."

"Akira, how long before the Keyhole is beyond the horizon and out of range?" Price demanded.

"Two minutes, thirty seconds," he replied instantly.

So it was now or never, then. "On my authority send a noncoded message to the French rescue team. Get those people some help!"

Without looking, Tokaido hit a button on his keyboard, and a sequence of commands flowed across his monitor. "Just waiting for your okay," he said.

She nodded. Good man.

"Good thing we're only talking about a theoretical broadcast," Kurtzman said, sliding a CD-ROM disk out of his console. He snapped the plastic into small pieces, before tossing the shards into the trash can. "With the nation at DefCon Three, revealing the location of the Farm would be considered an act of treason, you know."

"Punishable by fifty years in prison," Price said, walking back to the men and standing alongside them.

"At the very least," Katz added.

Reaching past the man, she picked up a couple of blank disks and broke them apart, sprinkling the bits into the trash can to mix with the other garbage. "Good thing we didn't do it, then."

"Absolutely."

"Rescue teams are on the way," Tokaido said, studying

his computer, then glanced up from the monitor and grinned. "Theoretically, that is."

Patting the young cyber expert on the back, Price took a seat and checked the message log. "No word from David yet?"

"Not yet," Katz answered, spooning some sugar into his coffee. "Or Able Team, for that matter, and they're only a hundred or so miles away."

She frowned. "Are things that bad already?"

"Not quite. They're just out of touch at the moment. We will be the last country to go off-line. America has a hell of a lot more satellites than Switzerland."

"Not for long," Price stated. Soon the entire world would be as blind and deaf as the Swiss Alps, and then all hell would break loose.

8:35 P.M., the City of Eirunepe, Brazil

TWILIGHT RULED the sky, and a new four-story brick tower downtown began to chime half past eight o'clock when a 70 mm rocket streaked in from nowhere and hit the brick wall surrounding the substation with thunderous force.

Bricks and concrete dust filled the air, then a second fiery explosion hit the exposed bus bars of the electrical substation. Sizzling blue flashes crawled like a creature possessed over every metallic surface, blowing transformers and safety circuits.

In the valley below, the streetlights went dark in orderly sections until blackness ruled the landscape. The only sources of light were the mayor's mansion, several police stations, a luxury hotel for tourists and the hospital. Thirty minutes before schedule, the city of Eirunepe was plunged in total darkness, along with the airport. Almost instantly alarms began to sound. Angry voices filled the night.

High on a nearby hill set between the power plant and

the city, T. J. Hawkins checked the alignment of some stones he had carefully placed on the ground, reloaded the recoilless rifle and fired again. Unlike a LAW, there was no fire trail from the rocket to track back to the soldier, and thus the rounds screamed in from out of nowhere according to the target. Maximum disorientation effect.

The first round slammed into the ground fifty yards from an APC at the front gate of the airport, throwing a ton of grass and dirt over the military transport. Caught by surprise, the startled troops inside immediately started to fire their .50-caliber machine guns, adding to the general confusion.

Double-checking to make sure the access road was clear, Hawkins laid down a neat line of shells around the main hangar, making it appear as if a major invasion force were trying to gain entrance. The paramilitary police force and the Brazilian regulars scrambled to counter the attack, and the sky above the airport was speckled with the crisscrossing lines of burning tracer rounds.

The troops clustered tighter around the DC-3, and Hawkins laid the crosshairs on the plane for a moment, then swung away with his finger off the trigger. He had no intention of slaughtering innocent troops. This wasn't a hard probe, but merely a diversion.

Just then a flash of light came twice from the woods outside the airport. Hawkins answered with a flashlight, and the signal came again. It was the all-clear from James. Now Hawkins placed an HE round directly into the main gasoline storage tank to the extreme south. The container had to have been only half-full, but the explosion rattled windows more than ten miles away, and the fireball that rose from the aviation fuel seemed to fill the sky.

At the far northern section of the airport, trucks full of troops raced toward the airfield battle zone, and Hawkins waited until the last JPX truck crossed a small bridge before laying down his last round and blowing the bridge to smithereens.

Suddenly sirens and flashing lights peeled away from the burning electrical substation and headed directly for the hill where he was hidden. Out of rounds, Hawkins muttered a curse as he removed the trigger assembly from the recoilless rifle. Somebody had to have spotted his answering flash of light and guessed what was actually happening. The troops at the airport were running around firing at nothing, but whoever was assigned to the power plant wasn't buying the scam.

Tossing away the exhausted weapon, the Phoenix Force commando climbed into a stolen compact car and hit the gas, racing down the steep side of the hill without headlights.

Huge fireflies filled the night, and Hawkins had to keep the wipers going constantly to push away the pulp of their crushed bodies. Cutting through a field, he followed the ruts to try to hide the tire tracks, then cut through a cow pasture that seemed to never end before coming out the other side onto a paved road once more. Savagely twisting the wheel, he took off down the road just as lights and sirens appeared from around a curve behind him. His pursuers were fast!

An amplified voice shouted out a warning in Portuguese that meant nothing to Hawkins. A few seconds later he recognized the sound of a British .30-caliber light machine gun, and something smacked into the trunk, blowing off the lid.

The moonlight bathed the world in a silvery hue, making the shadows under the trees edging the road seem impossibly black. A small stone bridge was roughly a mile directly ahead, and Hawkins tried to urge the little car to go faster and gain a few extra yards. The machine guns spoke again, tracers stabbing overhead.

"Gary, where the hell are you?" he muttered.

AS THE COMPACT CAR streaked over the stone bridge, Gary Manning stepped out from the bushes on the east side and slashed out with his knife. A taut rope stretching over the ravine parted under the sharp blade, and a tree branch on the west side swung forward like ramrod, slamming into a stack of wooden crates. The crates went flying and hit the road to smash apart, shattering their contents of beer bottles into a million sharp pieces of brown glass. Manning wore night-vision goggles. The landscape was brightly illuminated, and he could see without hindrance, although everything was the same color of green.

When the first military truck hit the field of glass, both tires were blown instantly. As the vehicle veered wildly out of control, the driver slammed on the brakes and fought the shuddering vehicle to a screeching halt.

A furious officer climbed down from the truck and stomped on the glass, cursing and swearing. But the other man in the front of the truck said nothing as he watched the shadows under the trees. Then he snapped on a searchlight attached to the side of the door and swept the dense foliage. The beam of white light just passed over Manning, and he flinched as the magnified light burned his eyes, then the automatic safety turned off the goggles.

Blinking tears from his eyes, Manning removed the goggles and waited for his vision to quickly return. While the overpowered lenses reactivated, Manning studied the slim man working the searchlight so efficiently. It was almost as if the guy had been looking for somebody wearing night-vision goggles.

The rumpled uniform gave no clues, but the guy was carrying a Glock .50 in a fancy shoulder rig. With an expensive, imported ceramic gun, he had to be S-2, Brazil's black ops team. Nobody else would carry such a weapon. Those men were the best in all of South America, just what Phoenix Force didn't want on the job.

Moments later the convoy of trucks and armored cars arrived and stopped a safe distance from the stalled truck. Climbing down, the S-2 agent shouted orders. The big JPX trucks started lumbering forward again to push the disabled truck out of the way so they could cross the bridge.

Perfect. Nimbly, Manning finished attaching the electrical wire to the small generator in his grip, then twisted the charging lever as hard as he could. Nothing happened. Damn it, a malfunction somewhere.

There was no time to try a repair, so Manning slid the Barrett off his shoulder, levered in a round and fired high. The thundering muzzle-flash lit up the bridge, startling the Brazilian troops, and gave him a perfectly clear view of the C-4 satchel strapped to the main support.

The S-2 agent started laying rounds in his direction, but Manning concentrated on the bridge and triggered the titanic rifle. A heartbeat later the bridge erupted, throwing stones and twisted steel everywhere. Something metallic rammed into the ground in front of Manning, and he quickly dived behind a tree for protection. Nearly killed by shrapnel from his own explosion—that kind of shit never happened in the movies.

As the billowing smoke began to clear, the Phoenix Force warrior slipped on the night-vision goggles and saw a ten-yard gap in the bridge, impossible to cross.

Just then a man's voice cried out, and from the other side of the ravine, machine guns raked the woods, bullets smacking into trees and knocking loose a wild flurry of torn leaves. Sprinting away from the berm, Manning slid down a muddy bank into a shallow creek and crossed the waist-deep water closely watched by an alligator eating some small animal. With a full belly, the gator bawled at the soldier but did nothing more. With the bore of the Barrett never leaving the reptile, Manning reach the other shore and sloshed his way back onto dry land.

Running silently through the darkness, Manning glanced at the stars overhead to keep on track and soon burst out of the trees onto a large field of soybeans.

The throaty purr of a plane engine barely disturbed the night, and Manning whistled sharply three times before heading that way. The thick Brazilian night slowly brightened to the vague outline of a small plane, with a man standing at the side door.

"A Cessna?" Manning growled in recognition. "Couldn't you find anything smaller, like a Sopwith Camel or a triplane?"

"Shut up and get in," McCarter growled from the pilot's seat, a hand adjusting the throttle on the single engine.

"Drop everything you can first," Hawkins added through the tiny passenger window of the plane. "We're way over the weight limit already."

Swinging open the curved door located underneath the top-mounted wing, Rafael Encizo flashed a grin. "Tighter than a crab's ass in here," he agreed from the rear cargo area. "We already yanked out the passenger seats to make room and lighten the load."

Shrugging out of his combat webbing, Manning dropped his backpack, then placed the Barrett on top.

"Everything," James said from the floor. "This box only holds four, and we're packing in five. We emptied the survival kit, and threw away the life raft. Every pound counts."

"Every ounce," McCarter corrected, adjusting the trim and thinning the mix. "Move it."

Manning scowled as he undid his ammo belt to drop the holster and pistol. Next went his knife and sheath, grenades and a few personal items that couldn't be traced back to the Farm.

"Shoes, too," James directed, wiggling his stocking feet.

"That tight, eh? Maybe I should try swimming home,"

Manning growled, slashing the laces with the knife and pulling them off.

"What was that?" Encizo asked pointedly.

"Oh, nothing, nothing important."

"No, what was that sound?" Hawkins demanded, glancing around.

In the distance machine-gun fire could be heard, sirens howling and the baying of dogs. A few miles away a dark shape moved above the city, and they could see it was a Helibras 360 gunship. Bad news. The helicopter was fully equipped with infrared scanners that could find the Cessna in a hot second. If it looked in the correct direction.

"No problems. We can fly under their radar," McCarter stated confidently. "Once I get this piece of toss off the ground."

"If you get it off the ground," Manning corrected, squeezing into the cramped compartment.

"Couldn't find anything smaller?" James asked, punctuating each word with a grunt as he fought to close the door on the packed mound of military muscle.

"Nothing that would still fly," Encizo replied, squashed against the rear firewall.

"Excuse me, but even the Brazilians are going to discover the trick soon and start looking for us along the other roads," Hawkins said tersely, over a shoulder. "Ya wanna close the freaking door there, pal?"

James finally slammed the door shut and worked the lock.

The purr of the engine rose to a roar as McCarter worked the ceiling slides and gave maximum fuel to their single engine. Awkwardly at first, the lightweight plane started to roll along the ground, bouncing and shaking at every irregularity and heading with increasing speed for what appeared in the moonlight to be a sheer cliff.

"Ravine," Manning warned, pointing ahead.

"Only a drainage ditch," Hawkins said, tightening his

seat belt. "Not more than forty feet deep. Shoot, boy, we dig barbecue pits deeper than that back in Texas."

"Nice to have a hobby."

Suddenly the Cessna was over the ditch and sailing into the air. The team relaxed, then the plane hit an air pocket and dropped a dozen feet before McCarter brought the little aircraft back on course and started to climb fast.

"We should be fine," McCarter said with a triumphant grin, leveling the wobbling wings. "As long as their coastal radar doesn't pick us up and shoot a Tamuz heatseeker up our ass."

"Do we have a reachable destination?" James asked. "Or are we going to try and fly this crackerbox back to Virginia?"

"Nearest U.S. base is in San Juan."

"Panama is closer."

"Too dangerous."

"And still too far," Hawkins said, scribbling fuel-ratio calculations on the folded flight chart. Since the GPD wasn't wholly reliable anymore, the charts were necessary for navigation and had been allowed to stay on the plane. But the clipboard had gone out the window. "I would estimate our maximum range is twelve hundred miles."

"We'll have to refuel to reach San Juan," Manning stated as a fact.

"I know where we can acquire some additional fuel," Encizo said, hugging his knees. "Maybe even get the loan of a larger plane. St. Vincent Island."

Hawkins raised an eyebrow. "That British SETI base?"

"That's the place," Encizo acknowledged. "Although the phrase 'loan us a plane' may be somewhat misleading."

"Steal. We're going to steal a plane."

"I prefer the term 'permanently borrow.'"

"Any armed guards?" Manning asked, trying to get comfortable on the vibrating metal floor.

Following the contours of the farmland, McCarter frowned as he gazed out the window onto the silver moonlight bathing the endless wheat fields that stretched to the horizon and the deadly morass of the Amazon jungle beyond.

"Sure as hell hope not," he muttered softly.

CHAPTER EIGHT

Oval Office, Washington, D.C.

It was always a surprise to the new staff members in the White House that the Oval Office was indeed oval, with the truncated corners blending into the curved outer wall with its five tall bay windows that overlooked the sculpted rose garden and tall Jefferson mounds. Facing away from the bulletproof windows was a massive hardwood desk, with two flags hanging from poles on either side: the right bearing the Great Seal of the President, the left, Old Glory.

Across the room was a working fireplace flanked by a pair of molded doors. Both of the portals were set flush against the wall and were discernible only by the thin crack of their outlines. The freshly whitewashed walls were spotless and mostly bare, with only a few small paintings on display, giving the room a just-moved-in feeling. In raised relief overhead was the Great Seal of the United States, a smaller version of which fronted the President's desk and was woven into the carpeting on the floor.

The room was immaculately clean: vacuumed, dusted and debugged daily by a housekeeping staff whose security credentials rivaled those of Pentagon generals. A faint smell of lemon polish scented the air, and the wooden tabletops felt oily smooth to the fidgety fingers of the waiting dignitaries.

However, this day the curtains had been drawn to block

any view of the decorative trees or distant Washington Monument. The temperature of the Oval Office was cool, but the atmosphere of the room was electric. Military officers and government officials filled the two couches set before the fireplace, their faces tense and unsmiling. Government aides, mostly young college graduates, scurried about delivering reports and relaying messages, while the White House kitchen staff brought in trays of coffee and sandwiches, first laying cushioned cloths over the antique Hoban drum tables before setting down their silver trays. Nobody made a move toward the vast array of food.

Hushed conversations stopped as the President entered from his private office set alongside the Oval Office. Dutifully the executive security council stood until the Man took his customary place at the high-topped leather chair behind the desk. The President looked a bit haggard.

"Okay, people, how long do we have?" the Man asked.

Perched uncomfortably on a divan, a general cleared his throat. "Roughly twenty-four hours. America will be blind in space by 9:00 a.m. tomorrow."

"Less than a day." The President sighed, scratching an unshaved cheek, his eyes red and puffy from lack of sleep.

"Sir?" a woman asked.

"Yes, Vicki?"

Miss Victoria Wells, chief of the U.S. Secret Service, stood as she always did when making a report. A result of being an Army brat and raised on military bases her whole life.

"As a precaution to civil unrest, as of 1700 hours today, I placed the White House on full alert. All tours have been suspended during the interim, all personnel not in a hospital sick have been recalled, and I have assigned fifty additional agents to the Stinger missile squads on top of the old Executive Building."

"What about the bunker?" he asked.

"Stocked and staffed," Wells reported crisply. "At your disposal, sir."

"May God grant we never need it," he added softly.

"Well, the city is in order," General Hal Overton stated, shifting his bulk in the dainty Kennedy chair, making it creak ominously. "The mayor has the local blues recalled, and the FBI and National Guard are moving into position."

When there was no reaction to his announcement, he continued. "Plus I have allotted an additional ten thousand troops from our Virginia and Maryland bases into the D.C. area to strengthen our present reserves."

"Macdonald Air Force Base is on alert with the everything they have ready to scramble in a second's notice," an Air Force general added. "And our Minute Man and HAWK missile bases are hot and ready to go."

As much as the President didn't want to prepare for warfare, it only made sense for them to be ready. America had a lot of enemies who would relish this golden opportunity to strike.

"Good enough," he said, then turned. "Admiral Sullivan?"

Leisurely the old seaman put aside his cup. "Roughly the same, sir," he said. "The naval defense grid has been activated with both coasts on emergency watch. Our sonar nets on the bottom of the ocean are fully operational. Our boomers have gone deep, and the picket line of ships along our two coasts is nearing completion. Say, another fourteen hours."

"Acceptable."

"The B-17 bombers are already deployed, sir," the Air Force general said grimly. "And our spy planes are patrolling the Pacific in shifts, three up at a time, three in refueling, two in reserve."

"With the combined resources of our air-based and ground installations, we still have a crude umbrella of radar working, sir,'' a NORAD general added, her long hair pulled back tight in a small bun. ''But since we are unable to link them together with satellite relays, there will be holes in the coverage.''

''And if we catch an incoming missile, what would be the response time?'' the President asked.

Several of the soldiers exchanged glances, and one finally spoke. ''Ten minutes, sir. Except in Alaska. With the new X-radar there, we have a full thirty-minute warning time.''

''So we're safe from Russia or China, unless they launch over the North Pole,'' the President said. ''Then we're screwed. By the time we see a missile, it's already too late.''

''Yes, sir. Best response time in our Nebraska silos is seventeen minutes from standby to launch,'' the NORAD general stated bluntly.

''Mr. Bailey, what is the status of our ABM bases?''

''Mr. President,'' the head of the CIA said slowly, glancing at the press secretary taking notes. ''Officially the antiballistic missile bases do not exist yet.''

The Man gave the spy a withering look. ''That wasn't my damn question. Can our antimissiles stop incoming ICBMs in time?''

''Yes and no, sir,'' Hal Brognola said, closing the outer office door. The big man walked across the office.

''Our ABM bases can stop a limited barrage, say from North Korea or Iraq. But if any major power hits us with, say, a hundred missiles, we'll be completely overwhelmed.''

''My interceptors will stop anything that gets through,'' an Air Force general stated firmly. ''By crashing their jets into the missiles, if necessary.''

''But about half will still get through,'' the President said in a flat tone. ''Correct?''

Using a pencil-tip mouse, an aide activated the monitor on a palm computer. ''Yes, sir, that is the estimate,'' he agreed. ''A fifty percent penetration.''

Still more than enough megatons to smash every major city into a glowing rubble. The death toll would be staggering, unimaginable. And then there was Wisconsin.

One of the greatest weak points in America had always been the dairy state of Wisconsin. A single dirty nuke to the extreme northern edge would pollute all five of the Great Lakes, ruining the watershed for half of the country. There were almost as many Minute Man missile bases built to protect the Wisconsin area as there were in the D.C. umbrella. Half of a war was winning, but the other half was surviving afterward.

"Enough on defense. I want this problem solved before the hammer falls," the President commanded, leaning forward in his chair.

"Well, sir, we have every radar dish and optical telescope scanning the sky," the NORAD general reported. "But no results yet. There just doesn't seem to be anything up there."

"But the satellites keep getting destroyed."

"Yes, sir."

"Could it be invisible?"

"Actually? No, sir. That is a scientific impossibility."

"Okay, then, some sort of a stealth device that is totally radar proof."

"That is much more likely, sir, but unfortunately..."

"How do we find it to know where to shoot?" the President growled, rubbing his temples. So this was what it was like for the rest of the world worrying about the undetectable American stealth bombers. Some damn fool had actually suggested firing a barrage of nuclear missiles into space and blanketing the outer atmosphere with atomic fire. That should destroy anything up there. Which it would, along with every satellite in the world and leaving enough radioactive isotopes floating in space to bar humanity from returning for a thousand years. Deep firewall wasn't an option.

"Talk to me, NASA," the Chief Executive ordered.

"We're doing what we can, sir. No positive results yet."

"Shift it into high gear, then. Get those shuttles flying. I want those ZGC Marines from Bragg deployed quickly. This is crunch time."

"Understood, sir."

"And what about our special people?" the President asked, looking directly at Brognola.

The big Fed faced the Man without flinching. "We've lost contact with some of them. We think they're on the trail of the enemy, and are burning the rope. But I can't be sure."

"Is—?" The President stopped himself from saying a name just in time.

Brognola understood and shook his head. "We have no idea, sir. His whereabouts are completely unknown."

"Damn." The President rose from his desk and turned to face the bulletproof windows, hands clasped behind his back as so many of his predecessors had done over similar decisions. In every chain of command, there was somebody to make the tough decisions. Right or wrong, it was his job to weigh the data and choose a course of action.

Sitting stiffly at attention in a nearby chair, an Air Force major held a steel briefcase on his lap, the handle handcuffed to his wrist. In Washington, D.C., slang, that was "the Football," the portable computer console to activate the hellish nuclear forces of the United States. The President looked at the officer, and the guard gave no visible response. His job was merely to carry the briefcase and guard it with his life. Nothing more.

"All right, send the vice-president to Cheyenne Mountain and the speaker of the house to Camp David. I want them as far apart as possible in case the balloon goes up on this. Understand?"

"Maintain the chain of command," Overton replied. "On it, sir."

"Good. I'll stay here in the White House, down in the bunker," the President stated. "Harrison, tell Congress what is happening, then activate the emergency broadcast system and warn the civilian population to be ready. Inform the Joint Chiefs of Staff of the contingency plans, prepare to go to DefCon Four. I want NORAD and SAC ready to launch every long-range bomber and short-range interceptor on my command. Then hold the planes at the outer markers. Do not encroach on anybody's sovereign airspace. But we will be ready. Is that understood, gentlemen and ladies?"

Murmured voices responded appropriately.

"And at the first sign of an enemy attack, regardless of the country of origin, we immediately go to DefCon Four and strike back with everything we have. No limited responses. Total annihilation."

Nobody spoke for several minutes. There was nothing to say.

"Here, take this, Hal," the President said, opening his desk and withdrawing a thick, cream-colored envelope.

Brognola accepted the packet and looked it over. The envelope paper was thick, almost a parchment. There was no name on the front, but the back was held closed with a wax seal of the Oval Office, a wafer top secret seal that would ignite the paper if opened incorrectly and the thick red ceramic seal of the United States of America.

"Those are for you to deliver, by hand and in person," the President said sternly. "In case of war, it directs your people what to do and to whom."

A kill list, or locations to defend? So this was it, the eve of nuclear war. The world would fall because of paranoia. Their unknown enemy didn't have to fire a single bullet; just remove America's eyes in the sky and humanity destroyed itself.

"There should be a Marine guard outside to escort you to a waiting helijet," the President added. "Consider the aircraft at your disposal until further notice. Deliver this message, then do as you wish."

Then the President stood and held out his hand. Stepping closer, Brognola took the Man's hand and they shook, a lot of unspoken thoughts being passed by the solid grip.

"You have my prayers. Good luck."

"You, too, sir. And sir?"

"Yes, Hal?"

"Life is not a chess game," Brognola said, then turned and left, the thick envelope he slipped into an inside pocket of his jacket seeming to weigh a ton.

The President nodded at the private joke, and sat back down in his chair and started placing calls on secure land-lines. Whatever happened tomorrow, America would be ready.

Avalon 88 Headquarters, Baltimore, Maryland

ON THE ROOFTOP of the old meat warehouse, six men removed their Peace Brigade red berets and stuffed them inside their shirts, then wrapped black scarves around their faces to mask their identities before accepting sleek G-11 assault rifles from their commander.

"Alive or wounded?" a disguised man asked, checking over the weapon.

"Neither," the commander replied, clicking off the safety on the 4.7 mm caseless rifle. The G-11 took minutes to reload, but was the fastest firing weapon on the planet, and he expected no trouble with the removal of this government team. Delta Force most probably, here to get some payback for their dead teammates. Too bad for them.

A barrel-chested man smiled behind his mask. "No prisoners, eh? Good. That's the way I like it." He chuckled and slipped the fire-selector lever from single to full-auto.

"Do we go after them?" a young man asked, wiping moist hands on his gray pants.

"No need," the commander snorted. "We wait for them to come to us." Taking a position behind a rotating air vent feed, he leveled the deadly rapid-fire weapon at the only door leading to the roof.

STAYING LOW, Able Team watched with weapons ready as the Nazi flag was pushed aside and out walked a large powerful man wearing casual clothes and carrying a cutdown cardboard box full of sandwiches and beer cans.

"Hope you bastards didn't start the movie without me," he called loudly, placing the box on the computer table.

Turning, he froze at the sight of the three armed men across the command center in the small film studio. They were wearing uniforms for delivery services, but the military weapons they expertly held told the truth.

"Cops!" He sneered, crossing his herculean arms to expose a wealth of tattoos. "So where is your search warrant or your writ? I want a lawyer. This is trespassing."

"We're not the police," Lyons said.

A flash of worry, then contempt, crossed the big man's face. "So the JDL finally got some hair on its balls, eh? Never thought the Jewish Defense League ever had the guts to strike back."

"Wrong again," Schwarz told him.

Now fear filled his eyes, and the man dived for the gun rack and grabbed an AK-47. But three dart guns coughed again and again until the man hit the wall and dropped the weapon, slowly sliding to the floor in a ball.

In standard one-on-one cover formation, Able Team swept forward fast and checked behind the flag to find a wooden door banded with iron straps. It was locked tight, with heavy bolts slid home on the inside.

There was no viewport or peephole, so Blancanales placed an ear to the door and listened carefully. Stepping away, he shook his head, then eased back the bolts. Beyond was a clean modern stairwell completely unlike the rickety wooden stairs they had found earlier. Clearly Avalon 88 kept the dilapidated meat warehouse as a front to disguise their real headquarters, a military hardsite hidden within the decaying building.

One flight up was a second door that led to the roof. Able Team stayed motionless in the doorway for several minutes until a muffled cough sounded from the other side.

"Clever fellows," Blancanales said, easing shut the door so they could talk freely. "They changed their MO."

"Last time there were bombs underground," Lyons said. "Now rooftop snipers."

"Standard police techniques would be to start in the cellar and work to the roof in order to trap a suspect high in the air with nowhere to run."

"So the satellite killers are waiting for us to come to them," Schwarz said, rubbing his jaw. "Unless it's just more Nazis looking at the moon or drinking beer. Could be anybody, really. We need target acquisition."

Crossing the room, Lyons went to the cardboard box and started counting. "Two six-packs of beer," he said softly. "But only five sandwiches."

"Five Nazis found so far," Blancanales said thoughtfully, then jerked his head. "That narrows it down some. But not enough for us to charge in with guns firing. Want to fire off a few rounds and see if they come charging down shooting?"

"Too smart for that old trick," Schwarz said, frowning at the stairwell door. "We need something to really catch their attention. Something that would make any innocent bystanders run for their lives. Got any ideas on how we flush out an enemy on the floor directly above us?''

"Yes," Lyons replied, shouldering his M-16/M-203 combo.

Walking to the gun rack, he took two of the AK-47 assault rifles. Then checking the clips, Lyons worked the bolts and cut loose with both weapons at the glass skylight overhead.

The noise was deafening in the enclosed command center, and the reinforced glass took more than a dozen rounds before finally shattering and blowing out a hellstorm of shards into the nighttime sky.

"Son of a bitch!" a man's shocked voice cried from above. "I'm covered with glass!"

"The building is surrounded!" Lyons boomed in his best policeman voice. "Surrender, and come out with your hands raised!"

"Bullshit! Cops don't shoot first," another cursed. "It's Delta Force again!"

Again? Ironman felt a rush of adrenaline. The White House had clamped down a complete news blackout on the Canadian slaughter. How could anybody know about the ambushed soldiers unless they had been there?

"Who cares? We killed 'em before!" a man yelled, stepping into view. "Let's do it again!" Then he raised an arm high to throw down a grenade.

Gotcha. Instantly Lyons emptied the two assault rifles through the opening, catching the unknown terrorist in the chest, the impacts of the 5.56 mm tumblers throwing him backward out of sight. A few seconds later the building shook with a tremendous explosion. Alarms started ringing throughout the structure, and water sprinklers gushed into action.

Dropping the spent Kalashnikovs, Lyons shook the water

from his face and burped his M-16 to keep the people on the roof busy.

Seconds later there was a splintery crash as Blancanales and Schwarz smashed through the stairwell door with their silenced guns firing sustained bursts.

Bleeding profusely, one of the hardmen grabbed his face and slumped to the ground as the others dived into the shadows under a tall water tower. Crouching behind the steel support legs, the terrorists returned fire with their G-11 rifles, the caseless weapons humming, the muffled noises combining into a deep rumbling sound. Across the rooftop the doorjamb exploded into splinters, the bricks breaking apart and throwing off sparks from the incoming hardball rounds.

Rolling with his MAC-10 in both hands, Schwarz fired off a few short bursts and kept going until he was behind the huge refrigeration unit that dominated the rear of the roof. Bright sparks flew as the caseless rounds raked both sides of the metal framework, as if expecting their target to break cover. Fat chance. Pulling a grenade from his belt, Schwarz ripped off the safety tape, dropped the spoon, then the bomb flew over the mammoth AC. The charge detonated in the air, and screams announced several hits from the deadly shrapnel.

Then the telltale chatter of an M-16 announced that Lyons had joined the battle. Weapons fire probed the darkness of the roof, distant windows shattering from rounds that missed their targets. That was the work of the terrorists; Able Team wouldn't fire without a clear avenue of attack. Their job was to save civilian lives, not use them as bullet stops.

A short break occurred in the battle as the enemy reloaded exhausted weapons. A muffled curse informed Blancanales that a terrorist was having trouble loading the tricky G-11 He ducked out from behind a dish antenna and sprayed the shadows under the water tower. A voice gurgled in pain and a weapon clattered to the old roof. Blancanales ducked out of sight a split second before return fire rattled his section of the darkness, the caseless rounds punching straight through a ventilation fan and smashing more bricks.

"Bo-jitsu, Los Angeles!" Lyons ordered, ramming in his only spare fresh clip. "Kung fu, New York!"

Swinging to the west side of the refrigeration unit, Schwarz cut loose, while Blancanales attacked from the east. Each man had been identified by his individual style of martial-arts training. Only a rank amateur would yell out instructions to the troops in plain English. Able Team had a thousand codes and dropped them after only one use; that way nobody could ever decipher their directions.

Momentarily trapped by the incoming fusillade, the terrorist dug in, waiting for a break. But stepping backward into the growing moonlight, Lyons discharged the stubby M-79, and the high water tank erupted, throwing out wooden planks in a hundred directions, its load of some fifty thousand gallons washing across the roof like a tidal wave.

"Jesus Christ!" the man screamed as the water slammed into him, throwing the man over the edge of the roof like a rag doll.

Still shooting the G-11, he sailed for yards before finally arching down to plummet toward the hard city streets below. The sound of his arrival was unheard by the living men on the top of the warehouse. Then car horns started blaring loudly, and voices were raised in angry shock.

Deathly quiet ruled the roof, broken only by the steady trickle of water flowing from the broken feeder pipe leading to the tank. Dripping wet, Able Team waited a few minutes before doing a sweep to make sure the area was secure. Only soaked dead men littered the rooftop, the blood washed away from the deluge of drinking water.

"Anybody hurt?" Blancanales asked, a runny smear of red on his hands gripping his weapon.

"No damage," Schwarz reported, carefully checking into the yawning pit of the busted skylight. Only brass shells and shattered glass were to be seen. Nobody had been flushed inside and survived.

Police sirens began to wail in the distance, and the team moved fast. Spotting a G-11, Schwarz shouldered the weapon while Lyons went to a corpse and took its watch and rings before going through the pockets. Meanwhile Blancanales pulled a slim leather case from his pocket, flipped it open and pressed the dead man's hand to the soft plastic. Folding down that page, he went to the next corpse and repeated the procedure. The device was something the U.S. Army had created for corpsman in a combat zone to use in helping to identify corpses of soldiers. Artillery often removed heads and thus dog tags. Sometimes a corpsman would find only an arm without an owner, but every member of the military had his or her fingerprints on record in the Pentagon.

Schwarz gave a sharp whistle from the corner of the roof. "Found a live one."

THE PAIN IN HIS LEG was incredible, and the Peace Brigade soldier knew that it was broken in several places. Sprawled on the roof of the next building over from the warehouse, the young man realized that he had to have been thrown over the alleyway to land there. It was a wonder every bone in his entire body wasn't broken!

Concentrating on listening, the wounded man couldn't hear the voices of any of his comrades, and then watched in horror as a trio of shadow figures appeared on the other building and stared directly at him. The soldier knew it was only the angle of the streetlights, but they seemed like giants from mythology.

Then two of them lifted a plank from the destroyed water

tank and started swinging it over the gap between the buildings to make a crossway.

"Easy or hard," a tall man said in a voice of stone, starting across. "You're coming with us."

For interrogation. Major Cole had already proved that any man could break in time, given enough pain. But he wouldn't surrender; the mission was far more important than a single life. Even his own. Visions of his girlfriend and fishing with his father came and went, then the young man was filled with a grim resolve.

"What we do," the man shouted, the words echoing strangely over the moonlight roof, "we do for the world!"

Then before Able Team could respond, he drew a handgun, shoved it into his mouth and fired.

CHAPTER NINE

Tanegashima Island, the Sea of Japan

Gleaming glass and shining steel, the Osaki launch site filled the eastern part of Tanegashima Island in the Sea of Japan. Gentle waves washed along the sloping shoreline, cresting playfully against the eight-foot-tall concrete lee edging the space port. An additional ten-foot fence rose from the sturdy lee, plastic strips interwoven into the strong wire to prevent any possible intrusion in either direction from the launch base.

Unlike so many other space facilities, the command bunker, assembly building and the two launch pads were set among low hills of lush greenery. Thick black industrial railroad tracks, eminently suitable for moving in shuttles and rocket cores, crisscrossed the beautiful spaceport.

At the southwestern side of the sprawling complex, in the four-story executive center, two old men were having a quiet test of wills. The passing ghost of an ancient samurai warrior would have approved of their grim determination, but would have been totally at a loss over the issues.

"No," Massaso Yanaga repeated, sitting behind the tidy desk. "There will be no launches for another six weeks because of the fishing season." The director of the Osaki facility was grimly polite, but his voice was strained with the urgency of his conviction.

"I do not care about frightening the fish so that they do not mate and the catch next year will be destroyed," Dr. Nubo Toda stated. The National Space Development Administration official seemed to radiate a cold fury. "The prime minister and NASDA demand immediate action on this matter. With the loss of our communications satellites, our nation could go bankrupt in less than a week. A single week!"

Unable to keep his hands still, he brushed a palm over his bald head. "You will launch within the hour."

A light flashed on the desktop, and Yanaga cut off the incoming message with a foot switch on the floor. "No, sir. Even if I received written authorization to override the Ministry of the Environment, it still could not be done."

"Could not?" Toda repeated, growing dark in his face. "Or will not?"

Yanaga gave a meaningful head bow. "My apologies. Cannot. There is no disrespect involved. You may as well ask our people to lift the oceans with their bare hands. The loss of the fish catch for a season would mean the total collapse of our local economy, thousands unemployed and most likely rioting."

"Well, then what about the Chinese?" Toda raged, pointing to the west. "Without constant surveillance they could send off troop ships and catch our shore batteries by surprise."

"They can anyway. Nothing has ever stopped them but fear of the American fleet in our harbors."

"But think of it—an invasion force of those filthy animals marching through the streets of Tokyo!"

Primly Yanaga leaned back in his chair. "I am sorry, but that is a military concern, and has nothing to do with the space ministry. A launch is impossible. I do not speak for just myself here. If I authorized a nonseasonal launch, the staff would rebel, and the on-site police could arrest us both for high treason.''

Toda went limp in the big cushioned chair. ''Then we are doomed.''

''That remains to be seen,'' Yanaga stated bluntly. ''Unless you wish to accept the direct responsibility of personally commanding an illegal launch?''

So be it. He had tried and failed. The nation knew the gamble it had taken building a launch facility directly in the middle of prime fishing grounds, but at the time it seemed a reasonable risk to be able to have the base on Japanese territory and under their direct command, not halfway around the world like the French.

Rising from his seat, the NASDA scientist walked heavily to the ocean window. Underlined by the foamy sea, the shiny perfection of the space shuttle *Tashehira* sat impotently on the Q launch site, its nose lost in artificial clouds of steam and fog from the fuel tanks. He certainly hoped the fish harvest was especially good this year. Because it just might have to feed the entire nation for a very long time.

The Annex, Stony Man Farm, Virginia

FOOTFALLS POUNDED down the tunnel, and an armed blacksuit sprinted into view, clutching a leather pouch.

Resting against the wall just in front of the Computer Room, a slim black man was smoking a briarwood pipe. He calmly watched as the blacksuit pelted along, coming straight toward him.

With his black hair frosted at the temples with silver, Professor Huntington Wethers seemed to be the very epitome of a distinguished university educator. In an electronic battle the former teacher of cybernetics was known to be as cool and ruthless as they came.

"As requested, sir," the blacksuit panted, thrusting a sealed pouch into the man's hand.

"How did you get this so quickly?" Wethers asked, tapping out the ashes of his pipe into a stainless-steel receptacle. "I thought the long-distance lines were so jammed with calls the faxes couldn't work efficiently anymore."

"F-15 Tomcat delivered it to Dulles from Houston Space Command," the blacksuit reported crisply, already recovering from his sprint. "I took over from there and got it here."

Inspecting the seals on the NASA pouch to make sure they were intact, Wethers crinkled his brow as he slit them open with a thumbnail. "You drove a car through D.C. traffic at this time of day?" he asked incredulously, pulling out some paper documents from the collection of CD disks. Instantly the paper turned red along the edge from the acid on his fingers.

"Harrier jump jet, sir."

"Smart move. Thank you so much," he stated, already deeply engrossed in the top secret report.

Returning to the Computer Room, Wethers wandered over to his workstation while Price and Katz held a hushed conversation in one corner. With them was Aaron Kurtzman, the chief of the Stony Man Farm cybernetics team.

The status monitors on the wall were flashing with lights, most of them going out, but other symbols were thickening along the borders of several of the larger nations. Troops massing to repel invaders, he sincerely hoped, and not the other way around.

"I have a copy of the NASA astronauts' final report before they went off-line," Wethers announced, sliding a CD-ROM into the waiting tray of his console. It slid in and started to load.

"Died," Akira Tokaido translated, gulping a soda while still typing with his free hand. "They died, Hunt."

"Their death is unknown for certain, merely a high probability," Wethers replied calmly. "But their inability to respond is an empirical fact."

Placing the recorded video of the last, chaotic moments of the space shuttle *Enterprise* on the main monitor, the crew watched the desperate acts of the escaping astronaut as the noble craft was torn apart.

"Not a shuttle," Hunt murmured around his pipe, repeating her words. In spite of the efficient air scrubbers and filtration systems, smoking was strictly forbidden in the Computer Room. The airborne particles were extremely bad for the delicate heat-sensitive circuits of the Cray SVG Mark IV supercomputers. However, the slim professor still liked to keep the briarwood in place to help him think.

"Could mean it was an ASL," Katz postulated, rubbing his hook.

Aaron Kurtzman resembled a librarian who lifted weights for a hobby. He rolled his wheelchair closer to review the screen capture from the CD that was on the main monitor. There was only a flicking shadow in space above the astronaut.

"Not a shuttle," Kurtzman said thoughtfully. "Yet any antisatellite laser powerful enough to reach that far from the ground would have lit up our warning system like Christmas during Mardi Gras."

"Same with a missile," Tokaido agreed.

"Maybe a stealth missile?" Price suggested.

Kurtzman shook his head. "No good. Rockets still use chemical fuels, and nothing large enough could hide that kind of heat exhaust."

"So what else can it be?"

He frowned. "Far too many things. An X-ray laser, ionic pulse charges, O'Neil rail gun, a new type of cosmic ray, even a purely natural phenomenon."

Scraping the bowl of his pipe clean, Hunt Wethers made

a face but withheld comment. The professor detested making guesses on such meager information.

Carmen Delahunt was bent over her console. A VR helmet covered her face, and one hand was tucked into a VR glove while the other typed on a keyboard at a furious pace.

"Success," she reported without any preamble. "I managed to access the AVI files of the inboard shuttle camera."

"An extra camera inside the craft?" Price asked, surprised.

"NASA redundancy. They always have a second camera to record everything."

Linking her console to his, Kurtzman grunted. "Comes in damn handy sometimes."

"Like now," Katz said, walking closer to watch over their shoulders. To the former Mossad agent, computers still had a fairly magical feel to them, and he never ceased to be impressed watching the technological wizards of the Farm in action.

"Nothing, damn it," Delahunt cursed, waving the glove in the air to close the link to the Houston database. "The camera was focused on the repair work of the satellite and stopped working almost before the astronaut turned from the work."

"Query," Wethers said, removing his pipe to inspect the tip for a moment. "Were there any other spacecraft in operation at the time that might have recorded the event?"

"Yes, a GMS-5 Holland oceanographic satellite," Kurtzman replied, checking a side monitor. "Same vector."

"On it," Tokaido said, hands flying at blinding speed. "Barbara, do you mind what I do to get their files?"

"No. You have carte blanche."

"Then let's rock and roll."

The wall clock blinked only three minutes before the young man cried out in victory.

"We're hot," Tokaido announced, flipping a gang bar on the control console. "Monitor three."

The large high-density liquid crystal monitor crackled with static for a moment, then settled down to an odd black-and-white view of space.

"No color?" Katz asked, blinking, as if the problem were with him.

"Too low a frequency," the young man replied. "I've got the signal relayed through weather sats, cell-phone stations and three spy satellites, one of which isn't ours. We're lucky we have any view at all."

"Everything is harmonics," Wethers corrected.

A sweeping vista of starry space moved above the colorless Earth, the moon in frame for only a second, then the Dutch video moved onward, angling lower, then higher.

"Freeze that frame," Kurtzman commanded, and the view stopped. "Increase pixel depth fifty percent."

The view became more detailed and vibrant. Something was blurring across the black background.

"That looks like rain," Price said.

"Computer enhance that," Kurtzman ordered.

"Little cubes," Delahunt said, still inside her VR helmet. "A swarm of tiny cubes."

"It's an O'Neil," Katz growled, slamming his flesh hand on the console. "Goddamn it, I told the Pentagon to slap a national-security label on the device. It's too damn easy to re-create!"

Price frowned deeply. An O'Neil linear accelerator. Invented by a professor from Rutgers College, the device used a simple series of electromagnets to pull a projectile along a straight track, rapidly accelerating the object to fantastic speeds in only seconds. God alone knew what the machines were capable of generating these days with computer guidance for the pulsating mag fields, she thought.

It sounded inoffensive, but when the projectiles struck

something, their massive kinetic force was instantly converted into caloric heat. The blast of a half-inch cube was equal to that of a 40 mm grenade. Most of the satellites in space were as lightweight as they could be made, so less fuel was need to get them into a higher orbit, where they could cover more area. Anything hitting with the force of a 40 mm shell would blow apart a conventional weather satellite. A dozen could tear a space shuttle into billion-dollar confetti.

"A rail gun in space," she muttered, then got hard. "So where the hell are they coming from?"

"I'm following the angle of descent backward," Tokaido explained, the view flowing smoothly along the initial course of the swarm.

Briefly something seemed wrong with the picture and the man moved onward, but then he paused and went back to the trouble area.

"No stars," he said softly. "Why are there no stars in that one area of space?"

"Maximum magnification," Kurtzman directed. "Now switch to the UV spectrum and overlay with the infrared and X-ray spectrum."

The screen swirled in wild colors, visible light tortured beyond endurance. Slowly a vague outline of something could be discerned, then the different frequencies overlapped and there was a silhouetted object as clear as day.

Moving with tremendous speed above the planet was an angular sphere, its surface covered with hundreds of flat interlocking tiles. The hull wasn't the usual silvery material, but a dull, reflectionless black that seemed to swallow light whole.

"So that's the bastard," Kurtzman muttered, adjusting the controls. "A stealth satellite."

"A stealth hunter-killer," Delahunt corrected grimly, behind her mask.

"Just another satellite," Price said confidently. "Fine. Now that we know how to locate the device, inform the Pentagon to send everything they have to that location and blow it to pieces."

"Already too late for that," Kurtzman stated. "This thing is in plain sight, but we still can't get a reading on radar, even the X-radar. It must be completely nonferrous. Radar passes through like light does glass."

"But the rail gun is magnetic," Katz stated.

"True," Wethers said, chewing the stem of his pipe and staring at the monitor. "However, lots of ceramics can convey magnetic fields."

"Ceramic mag cores," Price said, dimly recalling a government release on nuclear weapons with similarly designed solenoids. This thing was very high tech, and incredibly expensive. "Okay, it's armed like a battleship, so what about its hull?"

"The same," he said, pointing. "See where the sunlight glistens off the hull? We can get a mass spectrograph recording from that. The outer cover is a composite ceramic, like we use in stealth fighter planes. Very tough. Possibly even proof against its own weaponry."

Pulling out a chair, Price sat down heavily. "Then nothing we have already in space could dent this monster."

"I would say yes to that conclusion."

"What size is it?" Tokaido asked, both hands moving as he duplicated the known data and saved it to a disk.

Craning his neck, Kurtzman glanced at a sine-wave graphic rising and falling on a submonitor. "Roughly forty-two feet."

"Mighty small for a space capsule." Price frowned, drumming her fingers. "Must be only one man inside. Possibly even a trained chimpanzee."

"Pardon me, but I would postulate that it isn't a craft," Wethers said. "Robotics is much more likely the correct answer. Look at the diminished heat signature. No, there is nothing alive in that orbiter.''

"Which means more room for ammo," Katz said. "The more it holds, the longer it can attack."

A heavily armored stealth satellite packing the very latest in weapons technology. This was no rogue hunter-killer that got its computer fritzed and went amok. This was a carefully crafted high-altitude war machine, built to do only a single task—kill other satellites.

"'And a lion strode among the sheep,'" Price said in an angry whisper, "'until the ground was red and the very stones cried in pain.'"

"That's not from the Talmud," Katz replied. "But I recognize the quote."

"Armageddon," Kurtzman added. "Doomsday."

"Well, I can't find any external antennae or passive receivers," Delahunt announced, removing her helmet. "How can its builders control the thing?"

"My hypothesis is that it can't be controlled," Wethers said, running an analytical program on the composite on the armor hull. "The device is simply set loose in space until it has completed the assigned task."

"More importantly," Kurtzman said thoughtfully, "how the hell did anybody get that monster up there?"

"Gotta be a space shuttle," Price stated. "What else could carry such a payload? Five tons, maybe ten?"

"That doesn't matter. Whose space shuttle is the key to the problem," Katz said. Only five major nations possessed space shuttles, but parts were endlessly stolen, and there were other even more dangerous possibilities. So many options, so very few choices.

"However, we now have a way to find the thing," Price said, rising and going to a telephone. She only hoped it was still possible to reach across the country on a landline. "We can track it by its pattern of eclipsing known stars. With some luck that'll be enough for Jack.

"Hello, communications?" she said into the phone. "Get me Edwards Air Force Base pronto. Top priority."

Unexpectedly another milsat exploded in space on a side monitor. Puzzled over the event, Delahunt started checking the range and found that it was nowhere near the hunter-killer they were currently watching on the Dutch satellite. Perhaps the Australian milsat had been previously damaged and its self-destruct finally kicked in and finished the job. That was a possibility. She certainly hoped that was the reason.

Otherwise there was more than one of those lethal juggernauts in space, and the whole world was in much worse trouble than any of them had thought possible.

Above the Caribbean Sea

WITH THE MOON on its wings, the tiny Cessna plane skimmed the choppy waves of the Atlantic Ocean, barely clearing the foamy crests. A dolphin jumped from the briny depths, and arched high as if greeting the man-made artifact, then it dived back into the sea and disappeared.

A former Navy SEAL, Calvin James smiled on the antics of the mammal and took it as a good sign. St. Vincent Island had been very expensive, but uneventful. Phoenix Force had been able to top off the fuel tank, and even get a couple of extra cans of aviation fuel for about the cost of the Hope Diamond. But that wasn't out of the ordinary there. Prices always went high for outsiders in trouble, especially North Americans.

"Repeat please, Stony One," Hawkins said, turning up the gain on the dashboard radio, straining to hear the crackling message over the headphones. "Yes, roger that, Stony One. Confirmed. Over and out."

"Good news, I hope," McCarter said from behind the yoke of the Cessna. The man sat tense at the controls, rigidly alert. A pocket of warm water could create a thermal and toss the tiny airplane a dozen yards in any direction. But only fifty feet off the surface of the water to avoid any possible radar, one air pocket could send the team of commandos into a watery crash unless the Briton responded to any shift instantly.

"We rendezvous with a supply ship at East Caicos Island," Hawkins said, readjusting the crackling radio receiver. "They'll have another plane for us with full supplies."

"Distance?"

"Two hundred miles north by northeast."

"A stretch," McCarter said, checking their airspeed and fuel gauges. Then juggling a few numbers in his head, the man nodded. "But I think we can make it. If the weather holds."

"East Caicos—never heard of the place," James said, hugging his knees. "And I thought I knew the Caribbean."

"Just a deserted island that used to have a guano mine," Manning said, chewing on a candy bar.

"A bat-shit mine?" Encizo asked, smiling.

"Sure. Some of the older caves are hundreds of yards deep."

"Bat shit?"

"Cheap nitrates for military explosives," Manning explained, wiping his sticky hands clean on the blanket. "But then the market for that material dried up in the seventies, and with no deep-water harbor for cruise ships, the place died. Nothing there anymore but the ruins of the abandoned mining city and bats. Lots and lots of freaking smelly bats."

"So you've been there," Hawkins said, studying a compass they had purchased in St. Vincent.

Manning shrugged. "Yeah, once when I was with the SEALs. A total hole."

"Sounds like fun," Hawkins muttered, then pointed more to the left.

Slow and steady, McCarter made the course correction. The GPD was dead, and without telemetry from the airfields of St. Bart or Miami, they were reduced to a compass and the stars. And if the rain moved in, they would only have the compass.

"So after we get a real ship, where next?" James asked, resting his head against the firewall and closing his eyes. The first thing any soldier learned in boot camp was to catch a nap whenever possible, regardless of the adverse conditions.

"Barbara doesn't have a target for us yet," McCarter said, glancing enviously at the man. "But all of the action seems to be in the D.C. area."

The one-engine Cessna was too small for anybody to squeeze in and exchange positions with him, so the Briton was the pilot until landfall.

"Really?" James brightened. "Been a while since we handled an internal problem."

"At least we'll be able to order a drink in English," James added.

"Pirates," Manning said, looking out the port-side window.

"What about pirates?"

"Below us," Hawk said grimly, turning to see out the copilot's window. "Those are pirates, chasing a yacht!"

Trying not to tip the plane, the team managed to check the action on the port side in turns. Sure enough, there was a sleek old-style yacht with sails unfurled going hell-bent for leather. At the helm was a young woman in a bikini struggling to control the racing craft, while an older man at the stern was firing a shotgun, the fiery tongue of the scattergun reflecting off the waves.

Close on its wake was a large tramp steamer, thick plumes of smoke pouring from the twin stacks of the coal-burning motors, the water churning white from its aft props. The cargo ship was five times the size of the yacht, but its huge engines were making the difference and the steamer was steadily getting closer to the smaller vessel.

Suddenly the forecastle of the cargo carrier crackled with bright flashes as a large-caliber machine gun cut loose. On the yacht pieces of teakwood were torn from the deck, and the elderly man with the shotgun fell, dark red spreading on his flowery shirt. Dropping from the man's grip, the shotgun slid across the deck and disappeared over the side with hardly a splash. The woman turned and shouted something lost in the distance, while the pirates fired again, ripping a line of holes in the mainsail.

"Goddamn pirates are attacking tourists, and here we are unable to help," James said in cold fury. "A satchel charge would end that real fast."

"Poor folks in the yacht can't even call for the Coast Guard," McCarter agreed, slowing their speed slightly. "With all the trouble on the airwaves, the pirates are free to do what they want, to whomever they want, without fear of getting caught."

Already elements of society were staring to unravel. The criminals were getting bold. Unacceptable. The men in the Cessna became quiet, their minds racing with battle plans, each one critically flawed by the fact the Cessna carried no weapons.

The yacht was of no concern to them; the craft would be captured intact and receive a new registration to be sold again on the market, probably in Chile, or the Lesser Antilles. Far away from the site where the true owners had been murdered and tossed overboard like live chum. Unfortunately the fate of the young woman would be much worse than the simple death of her companion.

"Screw this. David, wanna show us just how good a pilot you really are?" Manning asked, drawing his ankle pistol and jacking the slide.

"I'm the best," McCarter stated, watching the oil pressure as he commenced a long slow descent. "Why, do you have a plan?"

"Yes."

"Then let's frag the blighters," McCarter growled, slipping to the left and starting a run on the colossal vessel.

ON BOARD THE TRAMP steamer a Jamaican sailor on the main deck threw back his tangle of dreadlocks to shout a warning while pointing at the sky. Lowering his binoculars, the bos'n didn't know what the man was indicating for a moment, then came the steady purr of a small plane passing by overhead.

"Police!" a German sailor roared, drawing the Webley .44 revolver from the belted waistband of his trousers. The holster rode directly in front of his stomach as protection, and a long machete hung from the side. The pistol was to clear the deck of a stolen ship, the machete reserved for slaying the crew after they surrendered.

"Even if it is, there's nothing they can do," the French bos'n said with a sneer, returning his attention to the fleeing yacht. The craft was worth a hundred thousand U.S. dollars easy, and if the crew didn't bruise the girl too much, the captain could fetch an excellent price for her on the slave market in Madagascar. With the crew getting their fair share of the loot. The rich old men down there enjoyed having an American chained in their playrooms, and went through the young women very quickly, so the demand was always high. As would be their price.

Just then a sailor in the crow's nest shouted a warning,

and the pitch of the little plane's engine changed as it dived at the huge steamer. Surprisingly they heard only the sound of several small-caliber handguns crackling.

Going to the balcony alongside the wheelhouse of the old cargo ship, the Dutch captain rubbed a greasy hand over his partially exposed belly and roared with laughter. Pistols at that range?

"Ahoy, the deck!" he shouted down to the crew. "Feed those morons to the fish!"

Situated in a sandbag nest roped tightly to the deck, a pair of beefy sailors swung the massive .50-caliber machine gun around and sent a hammering of copper-jacketed lead after the spiraling aircraft.

The pilot was doing an evasive maneuver? The captain felt a cold touch of fear at that military maneuver, but then relaxed when he realized there was nothing the crew of the plane could do with mere handguns. They'd need rockets and bombs to even damage the ship!

As if in defeat, the Cessna slowly moved off, and the pirates continued after the yacht. The woman at the helm was very young, her frightened face gleaming with sweat in the moonlight as she glanced over a shoulder. The sailors grinned lustfully and shared boasts of what they would do with her once that tiny bikini was removed. Meanwhile a young sailor with a deep, authoritarian bass voice boomed over a loudspeaker for the crew of the yacht to heave to for a routine maritime inspection. Few ship owners fell for the bald-faced lie, but it was always worth a try. New fools were born everyday.

"What's this?" a Spanish ensign commented, turning to look over a shoulder as the noise of the small aircraft began to increase again as it headed back for the steamer.

"Stupid." The captain sighed, shaking his head in disgust. They could have lived, but wanted to play at being heroes. What good did that do—how much coin did that put into a man's pocket? "Bernstein, blow that shitbox out of the sky!"

"Yes, sir!" a burly mate answered in a thick British accent. Going to a canvas-covered lump, the tattoo-covered man pulled away a stiff tarpaulin to reveal a 30 mm deck gun.

Spinning the transverse wheel, he rotated the weapon hard about and began cranking the double barrels across the stars to find his prey. A single burst would end this troublemaker forever.

Dangerously slowing its speed, the Cessna almost stalled its engine coasting leisurely over the main deck of the huge ship. The deck gun started to spit fire, and the airplane sharply banked along the keel, disappearing directly into the black fumes pouring from the twin smoke stacks amidships.

In brutal clarity the captain now understood the danger and grabbed the microphone on the wall, flipping switches to reach the engine room and order them to kill the furnaces. But it was already too late.

The side hatch of the Cessna was thrown open, and out came a rectangular shape that dropped neatly into the second flue of the ship with amazing accuracy. Almost instantly there was a tremendous explosion from below the deck, closely followed by a groaning roar and then a thunderous geyser of live steam erupted from the hold on the main deck, the blast throwing men overboard.

The bastards dropped a bomb and blew the feeder lines!

"Get that plane!" the captain screamed, lurching for the weapons locker and ripping the cabinet open to snatch a Russian RPG launcher.

As the fat man clumsily inserted a DL-3 rocket into the muzzle of the deadly antitank weapon, he was suddenly thrown to the deck as the entire ship violently shook. The steady throb of the engines felt through the deck ceased, and he knew there had to be a breach in the feeder lines that delivered seawater to the boilers and cold ocean had reached the red-hot furnace. It was only a matter of time now. His ship, his beautiful ship stopped dead in the water by a toy plane and a goddamn firecracker!

HIGH IN THE PURRING Cessna, Phoenix Force watched as the pirate ship rapidly fell behind the racing yacht, the gap between the hunter and the hunted widening with every moment.

Huddled in the wheelhouse, the older man was wrapped in bloody towels, and they couldn't tell if he was alive. But the young woman blew a kiss toward the tiny Cessna, then bent over the tiller and concentrated on leaving the area at best possible speed.

"Two ten-gallon cans of aviation fuel with five handguns strapped to the outside make a decent bomb," Encizo said, patting the empty holster on his belt.

"Shrapnel from the ammo made the difference," Manning agreed, watching the pirate vessel dwindling in their wake. "Once the feeder lines got damaged, it was all over."

Now black smoke poured from the tramp, and some portions of the deck seemed to be on fire. With nobody able to hear a call for help, the thieves were in a very bad situation. Turning away, the warrior completely dismissed the matter from his mind.

"Shrapnel might have missed," Encizo insisted.

Manning shrugged. "Then we would have tried something else."

"Such as?"

"Re-create the situation, and I'll tell you."

"Unfortunately we are now very low on fuel," McCarter interrupted, working the ceiling levers to thin the mix and easing out the airfoils. The cans had been their reserve, but it was the stunt flying that drained their tanks to the danger point.

"Will we make the rendezvous point?" James asked, observing the fuel gauge from his seat in the rear. He knew what was in the sea below, but saw no reason to mention the presence of the great whites. If the Cessna hit, there was nothing the men could do about them anyway.

"Gonna be a bit of the ol' nip and tuck," McCarter admitted, holding the yoke rock steady. "But we should reach land."

"Anything we can do to assist?" Hawkins asked. Ahead of them stretched a featureless vista of shimmering water. Not a ship or island marring the rippling expanse of the Atlantic.

McCarter shook his head. "Wish there was."

"Then wake me when we arrive," he said, rolling over in his seat.

AN HOUR LATER Hawkins snapped awake as the plane began to rapidly descend. On the eastern horizon was a small atoll without any lights in view.

"How's our fuel?" Encizo asked just as the engine coughed and died. Now the soft hush of the wind under their wings was the only sound to be heard.

"What fuel?" McCarter replied, fighting the shifting air currents. A veteran of a hundred night flights, the Briton ignored the negative aspects of the approach—irregular winds, plane badly overweight, his own exhaustion—and concentrated on making small moves with the yoke and letting gravity do the work for him. Just not too fast. Easy now, easy...

Craning his neck, Manning tried to see through the front windshield. "Where's the landing field?"

"Over there," McCarter said, jerking his chin. "Near the broken railroad tracks."

"That's a landing field?" the big Canadian demanded in disbelief. There was trash and debris everywhere, the ground littered with rusted machinery and smashed railroad carriages.

"It served PBYs in WWII, it'll take this kite," McCarter said, switching on the landing lights. Bright cones of white light washed over the junkyard, thinning some sort of fog covering the island.

"Hold on," McCarter growled, crushing the yoke in his hands. "No time for a pass, we're going in!"

The ocean flashed by the plane like a rippled mirror, there was a brief view of a wide beach filled with huge green turtles, then the Cessna was racing over dry land with bushes and trees everywhere.

A flight of bats flew by screaming at the intrusion of the plane, and the sagged ruin of the mining town rose on the horizon. Keeping his motions strong and smooth, McCarter banked into the wind to slow his speed. The rough landscape flashed by in a blur as the Cessna rose to clear the buckled railroad tracks. The corroded bands of steel arching high were a deadly trap for the landing wheels of the tiny plane.

Then it was past and the former SAS commando yanked a lever with all of his strength to drop the airfoils into place. The passengers were thrown about as the plane slammed backward from the impact of hitting the air, then a heartbeat later, the craft touched down on smooth rock. Bouncing a few times, the Cessna put its full weight on the ground and rolled along the sandy earth, jerking about. Easing on the brakes, McCarter rode the bucking airplane into a gentle stop, then locked the wheels and stalled the propeller. The wings wobbled some in the gusting ocean breeze, then settled into place.

"Any landing you can walk away from," McCarter said, releasing the yoke and flexing his hands. As the circulation returned, he turned off the controls, but left the lights on full. A weird moving fog lay over the island.

"There's our ride," James reported. "Four o'clock low."

A hundred yards away, a SeaHawk attack helicopter sat in the silvery moonlight, partially obscured by the island fog.

"Get ready to run," Manning warned, breathing deeply to charge his lungs with oxygen. From his expression the man appeared to be preparing for a dash through a minefield.

Holding the door latch, James stared at the other man. "What in hell would we run for?"

"We're going to be strafed," he replied, buttoning his sleeves and closing his shirt collar. "Ready?"

"Lead the way," James said, and yanked on the handle.

The instant the door swung open, in flowed the buzzing fog and the men were inundated with countless mosquitoes. Swatting every inch of their exposed skin, Phoenix Team did a dog trot for the helicopter, leaping over the debris and garbage until reaching the big gunship.

"Open the damn hatch!" McCarter ordered, slapping his face and neck.

His skin crawling with bugs, Encizo got the side hatch moved and the men piled inside, taking a black swarm of the insects along with them. Frantically the soldiers ripped open the waiting equipment packs until finding repellent. As they slathered on cream and sprayed chemicals into the air, the bugs departed and finally fell to the deck, twitching and dying.

"Where did all the mosquitoes come from?" James demanded, relaxing his muscles as the military cream eased the torturous itching from the dozens of bites.

"They live off the bat crap," Manning explained, spreading more cream over his neck and down into his shirt.

"Which comes from the bats who eat the mosquitoes," Hawkins snarled, opening his pants to rub cream on his legs. "Ah, the circle of life."

"You start singing," Encizo growled, brushing dead insects out of his black hair, "and I'll shoot you. That's a promise."

"Please," Hawkins said, scratching his neck vigorously with ointment-covered fingertips. "And make it soon, okay?"

McCarter moved into the pilot's seat of the spacious cockpit, reviewed the control systems, then soon had the twin GE power plants turning over smoothly. The rotors began to slowly turn, steadily building speed, and soon the wash cleared the area of the vampiric fog.

"Fuel tanks are full," he reported, pulling on headphones and flipping switches with expert ease. "We are fully armed with Penguin and Maverick missiles, and ready to leave at any time."

Taking the navigator's seat, Encizo flipped on the communications system and turned the radio to a specific frequency.

"Don't bother. It's too far for Stony Man to hear us," McCarter said. "We'll need a lot more altitude to reach a relay station on the mainland."

"No problem," Encizo said, pressing the transmit switch on the mike. "This is a local call."

TWO HUNDRED FEET above the calm Caribbean Sea, a U.S. Navy SeaSprite helicopter moved through the darkness. The steady throb of the heavy rotors could be felt in the teeth and bones of its two passengers from the *Yorktown* missile cruiser.

Touching his headphones, the pilot frowned. "Incoming message, sir," he said, flipping a switch to put the call on the squawk.

"Hello, supply ship," the radio speaker said in a deep voice. "Repeat, hello supply ship. This is the SeaHawk. Come in, please."

The captain of the USS *Yorktown* looked at the radio

receiver for a long moment, unsure if he should accept the call. Then curiosity got the better of him.

"Read you loud and clear, SeaHawk," he said, thumbing the transmit switch on the mike. "This is…the supply ship. What is your problem? Over."

There was a crackle of static. "There's a tramp steamer about fifty miles to south, southwest of here," the voice said. "They were shooting at a yacht and trying to board 'n' storm. You might want to check on them."

"Pirates?" the captain demanded, sitting straighter in the seat.

Following standing orders, the pilot of the SeaSprite released the safety interlocks on the complement of Hellfire missiles, then waited for authorization from his CO to arm the warheads.

"Roger," the nameless voice on the radio answered. "That would be our guess. We crippled the steamer, but stay alert, the tug has a functioning deck cannon and one serious mad on. Over."

"Wilco, SeaHawk," the captain replied, gesturing the pilot to proceed. "Anything else?"

"Double thanks for the bug spray, sir. Much appreciated."

"We thought that would come in handy. Our pleasure, SeaHawk. Over."

"Over and out," the voice replied, and the radio went silent.

"Now, how the hell could anybody damage a vessel a thousand times their size in a damn Cessna?" the captain muttered, a smile almost crossing his weathered features.

"Skipper, any idea who they are?" the pilot asked softly.

The captain frowned. "Who are you talking about, sailor?" he said, stressing the potential reduction in rank. "We were on patrol, I had a serious mechanical failure and had to ditch a fully armed SeaHawk. Luckily you were nearby in a SeaSprite to rescue me. Are we clear on that?''

"Aye, aye, sir," the pilot agreed woodenly. "A tragic loss of Navy property. Nobody here but us and the fish."

"Bloody heavily armed fish," the captain added, watching the brightly illuminated silhouette of his Ticonderoga-class warship crest the horizon.

Well, whatever the special men on East Caicos Island were involved in, he certainly wished them luck. Because some battlefield instinct told the veteran that they were soon going to need all the help they could find.

CHAPTER TEN

Edwards Air Force Base, California

The starry night was heavy in the California mountains, and a dust devil whirled about Jack Grimaldi's boots as he zippered closed his flight suit and strode across the flat concrete landing field of the military air base.

Armed security patrol guards formed a fence around a small building made of gray-painted cinder blocks, only the double-wide doors and massive exhaust fan in the roof clearly marking it as an airplane hangar. As Grimaldi approached, the SP guards only briefly glanced at the photo ID, obviously expecting him, and the Stony Man pilot went inside to claim his bird.

The interior of the building was brilliantly illuminated, and several nervous-looking technicians in lab coats and a couple of cocky young pilots in DeCamp flight suits stood waiting expectantly. But Grimaldi ignored the welcoming committee and went straight to the sleek fighter-bomber. The only vehicle in the hangar, the huge craft nearly filled the building, and he was pleased to see that both of the stubby clipped-Delta wings were full of sleek missiles and fat auxiliary fuel tanks. The candle was ready to go hunting for bear.

The oddly shaped cowling was already cycled up like the shell of a clam. Going to the left side, Grimaldi found a portable access ladder waiting for him and he climbed into the sleek, angular jetfighter.

"Sure you know what you're doing, sir?" an airman asked from the ground, clutching a clipboard to his chest.

The fellow had a chewed pencil stuck behind an ear, and his nails were chewed to the quick. Obviously the nervous type, Grimaldi noted, always worrying about filling out reports, and not enough fiber in his diet. Poor bastard.

"I've been in space before," Grimaldi said, settling into the pilot's seat of the ultrasleek fighter. The interior smelled of plastic wrapping, sweet resin and silicon polish, the craft was that new.

The flight manual he skimmed in his bumpy flight to Edwards riffled through his mind, and the chief pilot for Stony Man Farm started flipping switches and pressing buttons. Grimaldi knew the operations of the bird, but it never hurt to double-check before a mission. Especially one as last minute and dangerous as this.

Violating several treaties, the Pentagon had already tried the Star Lite laser system to bring down the enemy satellite, but the results had been zero. The high-power laser kept defusing from the clouds, dust and moisture in the air of Earth, and couldn't deliver enough joules of power to destroy a known satellite. But then, four hundred miles straight uphill was a long way to go for any weapons systems.

Naturally the Navy unleashed dozens of antisatellite missiles from their fleet of the Aegis-equipped warships, but the computers couldn't hit what they couldn't find. A stealth hunter-killer was something nobody had seriously theorized about, and the reality caught the whole world with its pants down.

Combining multiple phasing technologies, the Farm had found the enemy satellite in a static picture, but in combat there were too many variables endlessly changing, and the best missile-targeting computers were too slow to handle the massive flood of conflicting data. Grimaldi knew that he was going to have to find this hellish thing by simple vision. This mission was where the art of war took over and left the science behind. No machine could do this job; it required the intuitive mind of a living person.

Circuits warmed slowly, indicators glowed into life, meters swung alive and gauges lit up as the complex war machine sluggishly came to life under his adroit control.

"This isn't like anything that has ever flown before," a young pilot said loudly over the building engines. Then he hastily added, "Sir."

"She's got wings, right? That's good enough," Grimaldi replied, clipping on his seat harness, then attaching the life-support hose to his jumpsuit. That would keep him cool or warm, depending on what was needed, and feed the pilot pure oxygen as necessary to keep his heart pumping in crushing high-G combat turns.

"Sir, I know this bird better than anybody alive," a young Air Force pilot said firmly. "And if there is a mission to be flown, I should be at the stick."

"How many combat missions have you flown, son?" Grimaldi asked, running a quick test on the weapons systems. Everything was green for go, the four AMRAAM-ASM missiles and 20 mm Gatling gun were primed and ready. His bird was hot.

"Well, none," the man replied honestly. "I'm a test pilot, one of the best in the game."

Glancing over the cowling, Grimaldi flashed the man a smile. "And that's why I'm here, so get out of the way or go stand behind and toast marshmallows, because either way, this crate is going up."

As the other people moved to a safe distance, the young pilot got a very serious expression on his face and started breathing deeply. For a minute Grimaldi thought there was actually going to be trouble with the rocket jockey. Out of sight behind the cowling, he slipped a hand into his flight bag and clicked off the safety of a U.S. Army Colt .45 automatic.

Unfortunately the hangar was full of fuel and munitions. A single bad shot could set off a chain reaction that would vaporize the whole place, and a good section of the landing field outside too. There was too much at stake here, so if the hot shot gave Grimaldi no choice, he would be forced to do a clean kill, one round in the chest. Going for a wound in his leg or shoulder would just be too damn risky. Softly easing back the hammer with a thumb, he waited for the pilot to make his decision, the checkered grip of the heavy automatic heavy in his hand.

"Watch for when you use a missile. The door causes a hell of a drag," the pilot said, snapping a crisp salute. "The torque will send you into a tailspin if you're not careful."

"Thanks," Grimaldi said, easing down the hammer on the gun. "I'll remember that. She torques to the left when I port a missile. How bad? Worse than a World War I British Fokker with those Belgian clutches?"

"Almost," the test pilot replied, a faint grin appearing for an even briefer second. "You are a pilot, aren't you?"

"Watch and see. Clear!" Grimaldi ordered, and the ground staff moved away from the plane as he fed the twin Pratt & Whitney engines some fuel. A double wave of thundering fire blew from the aft vectors, the directional trims flexing and adjusting to the thermal wash.

Pulling on his helmet, Grimaldi slaved the optics to the control board, then eased off the brakes and started to roll forward. The hangar doors cycled open to the soft sigh of hydraulics, and the F-22 Raptor interceptor rolled into the pitch-black of the desert night.

The ultrasleek F-22 stealth fighter wasn't scheduled to go into production for another couple of years, and would start seeing service even later. But for this mission, Barbara Price pulled some major strings and got him the original prototype of the superfighter. To fight an invisible enemy, you needed an invisible sword. The Raptor was the best America had, also the only one of its kind, and worth a cool billion. Grimaldi was well aware that a lot more than his ass was riding on the outcome of this battle. Hopefully he really was as good as he always told people. Time to find out the truth.

On the horizon the California mountains were only vague purple shapes rising into the sky, their greatness lost in the sheer distance. A dry desert breeze blew listlessly across the military base, and a Gila lizard scuttled across the concrete apron, headed in the direction of the buildings and hangars of the base. The single tall brick-and-glass column of the flight tower rose high above the others.

Out in the desert, glistening white radar domes kept a vigilant watch above the top secret base, while black Hummers full of armed troops moved steadily by on a never-ending security patrol. There was no press in attendance, no civilians, no cameras of any kind. There was nothing recorded on paper, no files, and officially this flight wasn't even happening. The F-22 Raptor was locked safely in its hangar receiving some routine maintenance.

"Tower, I am ready to go," Grimaldi said into his throat microphone, checking the fuel mix and adjusting the temperature of his flight suit. "Any particular strip you want me to use?"

"Take your pick, Stone Bird One," came the prompt reply, a tiny figure waving an arm in the brightly lit glass booth at the top of the tower. "The field is yours. Godspeed."

"Roger. Do my best," Grimaldi said, feeding the engines more fuel. With the first pulse, the aft wash billowed dust across the field, blocking his sight of the hangar. Slowly at first, then with increasing speed, the Raptor began to creep forward.

Taxiing to the main runway, the craft built takeoff speed incredibly fast and was soon airborne. Then in a thunderous roar, the fighter lifted into the clear sky on pillions of fire, its departure rattling the windows of the entire base.

Folding back its clipped Delta wings, Grimaldi sent the aircraft into a steep climb. Then the Pratt & Whitney turbines hummed into silence as the afterburners erupted with volcanic fury. The G factor slammed the pilot against his heavily cushioned gel-pack seat as the Raptor took off almost straight up.

Since radar was useless, the U.S. had every major optical telescope observatory in the hemisphere probing space for any stars blotted out by the passing of the enemy satellite, and Grimaldi had the very latest positioning on the machine. But every passing second made the data more obsolete and risked turning the mission into a total fiasco.

The sky before the hurtling fighter was distorted by the sheer speed of the craft. But through his helmet visor, Grimaldi could see clear air in front of the vessel, a calm tunnel surrounded by misty turbulence. The phenomenon was called a velocity tube, but he had never achieved the effect so quickly before. Then the F-22 shook ever so slightly as it passed Mach 1 in under ninety-seven seconds.

Ten thousand feet, twelve, fifteen, the stealth fighter dropped its first external fuel tank and streaked through the cloud layer of the thinning atmosphere, leaving no contrails in its wake to mark a visual passage. Invisible to even the Pentagon's new X-radar, the composite hull radiated no heat and was nearly silent. Grimaldi watched the fuel gauges drop rapidly as the deadly fighter punched through the thirty-thousand mark, leaving behind the commercial traffic.

Nearing Mach 2, the craft reached forty thousand feet and the curve of the Earth began to become visible to Grimaldi; that was when the muted hush of the hull went completely silent. There was no longer enough air outside anymore to convey any sound.

Suddenly the twinkling stars went diamond bright and a wave of heat washed over the Raptor as it erupted from the atmosphere to be bathed in raw sunlight. Free at last from the clinging drag of Earth's dense air, Grimaldi kicked in the thrusters full force and the F-22 blasted forward in renewed velocity. The acceleration crushed the man against the gelatin seat, and his helmet automatically increased the flow of oxygen to his laboring lungs.

"I am on attack vector," Grimaldi subvocalized into the mike. The device was a necessary addendum to the usual communications equipment. Doing a ten-G turn at Mach 1.9, the pilot could shatter his own jaw trying talk normally.

Only static answered from the ground, then there came a brief message crisp and clear.

"Stone Bird is go. Situation is Blazing Skies. Repeat, Stone Bird is go for harvest."

More hash filled the radio, and Grimaldi lowered the volume of the link. The pilot was on his own. "Blazing Skies" meant the enemy was armed and near. He guessed "harvest" was the newest Air Force euphemism for "kill." Grimaldi frowned and tried to urge a few more mph out of the silently roaring turbojets. Harvest his ass. The Stony Man pilot was here to blow the thing to hell.

Checking the aft long-range radar gave only jumbled readings of scattered chaff in high orbit, and Grimaldi soon realized the debris was the flying remains of more smashed satellites. He would have to stay alert for that flotsam. At these speeds tumbling garbage could hit like bullets and damage the craft. The poor quality of the radio suddenly made sense. How Price had guessed so early in the crisis was utterly amazing, and one of the many reasons why she was the mission controller for Stony Man. Then again, maybe Price had just played the odds and prepared for the worst. That was fine, too. Smart was better than lucky any day.

Reaching the maximum altitude of twelve miles, Grimaldi strained his eyes to sweep the starry blackness, but saw nothing. Yet he knew the enemy was out there somewhere, two or three hundred miles above the Earth. Even the Raptor couldn't reach that far to dogfight the satellite, but this high up the AMRAAM Mach 5 missiles on board could cross that distance in only seconds. Personally he hoped he faced a living enemy and not a computer. People were always easier to defeat than machines.

The X-radar and Doppler-R were both silent, but the inboard proximity sensors gave a beep. Then the computer quickly confirmed the location of the bogey and plotted a course for missile interception. Show time. The hunter-killer had passed in front of a known star and given away its location for a split second. It was called eclipse tracking. It was nowhere near as exact as radar, but the AMRAAM missiles would do the rest. Two were low-yield chemical warheads, and the others were tactical nukes. This was the nation's best shot at the satellite, and Stony Man was pulling no punches.

"Stone Bird, one away," Grimaldi said for the flight recorder, and thumbed the fire button on the joystick.

A panel set flush to the outer hull of the Raptor swung aside and out leaped a massive AMRAAM antisatellite missile. Instantly the Raptor swerved from the drag of the open port, and Grimaldi fought to keep the jet on course.

Dropping safely away from the interceptor, the missile fell through space, then the chemical rockets flashed into life. The AMRAAM streaked away too fast to watch, leaving behind only the fading shock diamonds of its passage.

On his helmet the beeping of the missile approaching the enemy came louder and faster, then abruptly stopped and there was only the beeping of the outgoing missile.

"Negative on impact," Grimaldi stated, tightening his grip on the stick. "Target gave a ghost. Repeat, bogey gave a radar ghost. I will reengage."

Kicking in the emergency boosters, Grimaldi fought his silent beast even higher into the stratosphere, and started tapping new commands into the computer. On a small video screen, a silvery silhouette of the Raptor rose another eighty miles, reaching a low Earth orbit, a dogfighting posture, and something on the western horizon stared to race closer. The enemy had fallen for a radar ghost of his own. Perfect!

Not daring to miss this golden chance, Grimaldi launched a combination of chemical-warhead and nuclear AMRAAM missiles at the approaching satellite, saving the last nuke as an emergency reserve. Faster than sight, the ultrasonic missile darted forward on diverging courses and disappeared into the distance. Then the computer sounded a warning buzzer, and a vector graphic on the battle screen assembled an outline of the enemy hunter-killer.

But was that real, or another ghost? Grimaldi tried adjusting the attack computer, but the software couldn't give a true reading. Two enemy satellites, only one real. Which was which?

Almost in perfect synchronization, the two AMRAAM warheads flared on his screen, the brilliant flash of their detonations visible briefly through his polarized windshield and helmet visor before they went completely black. As his visor slowly cleared, the pilot scanned for the amount of wreckage, but the volume seemed too low. Then the optical scanner announced an eclipse event. Shitfire, it was still alive!

Then a flurry of objects streaked through his last position with unbelievable velocity, and the computer showed a vector graphic of the tiny cubes. Return fire from the O'Neil rail gun, and the projectiles moved even faster than the AMRAAMs. How was he supposed to fight that? Then the proximity alarm sounded and the computer screen filled with a second swarm coming right down his throat.

Banking into a tight turn, Grimaldi dived sharply into an evasive maneuver, then rolled over and looped under to rise once more, his hands arming the last AMRAAM missile. He had to move fast. The cubes were as small as pennies but were like bombs and could blow holes in even the hull armor of the Raptor. Wind shear would do the rest, ripping open the holes and tearing the interceptor and pilot apart in seconds.

Climb, baby, climb! Throwing out chaff, Grimaldi dropped flares, fired four more phantom radar missiles, cut in his scramblers, generated two ghosts of the Raptor and launched the AMRAAM antisatellite nuke.

Only a thousand yards away, the missile broke apart, then detonated, the fireball filling the sky in a nuclear dawn. The polarized windshield and visor darkened to solid black to protect his sight, but the pilot flipped the visor to check the computer screens. How much debris was there? Had he gotten a hit? Then warning lights flared as the Raptor lurched, and a monitor showed a small puncture on the starboard wing, the indicators showing a loss of oxygen along with amazing amounts of fuel.

The urge to stay was strong, but Grimaldi knew when to retreat and reluctantly turned tail. Blindly firing his 20 mm chain gun, Grimaldi straightened his airfoils to increase speed, then opened the weapon ports as if launching more missiles. The double drag slowed the Raptor so fast he almost broke the safety harness, and he felt a rib give. Ignoring the pain, Grimaldi closed one hatch and the torque threw the craft violently to the side. The combined pressure was too much, and the ace pilot blacked out for a few seconds from the G factor.

As he came to again, something flashed past the ship and the radar began to keen, the beeps were packed so close together. The hunter-killer was still on his tail! However, he was already miles away and could dive deeper into the safety of the atmosphere, while the satellite was a prisoner in space and could only chase the Raptor so far. He hoped. Okay, time to see what this billion-dollar kite really had under the hood.

Nosing into a sharp dive, Grimaldi alternated the missile ports to throw his craft randomly across the open sky, then completely turned off both of the massive engines.

Silent and cold, the F-22 stealth fighter fell through the thickening atmosphere, leaking precious resources. Then another swarm of tiny projectiles streaked after the departing fighter, punching new holes in the weakening armor of the red-hot hull.

CHAPTER ELEVEN

Stony Man Farm, Virginia

"Damn! We just lost contact with Jack," Kurtzman reported, looking up from his console. He was clearly angry at the failure. "I have already switched to another orbiting Keyhole satellite, but after the radiation wave the nuke dispersed, he was gone."

"Vaporized?" Price asked softly. Leaning against the wall, the woman stood with her arms crossed, braced for the bad news.

Leaning backward in his chair, Kurtzman shook his head. "I have no idea. The fight happened too quickly. But yes, that is a distinct possibility."

"And more bad news," Katz stated, tapping a pencil on the console for attention. "There's more than one hunter-killer. Figuring a similar swarm of a dozen cubes per each satellite known to have been destroyed, this thing would have run out of ammunition sixteen times already."

"So that's how they've done this much damage so quickly," Tokaido stated, sliding a new music CD into his stereo. "Spread out in waves and attacked on multiple orbits, the higher sniping the lower for added punch."

"Using gravity itself to boost their already considerable weaponry," Wethers said. "Ingenious."

"You mean deadly," Price corrected. At the rate the enemy was going, soon the Stony Man orbiter directly above them would go, and then the base would be helpless to fight in the coming war. That was unacceptable.

Turning toward Kurtzman, Price paused as she could see on his monitor the man was already positioning American and British hunter-killer satellites into new orbits near the Stony Man communications satellite for added protection. The Farm would stay on-line for as long as possible. Every second would have to count.

Okay, if Sigint wasn't delivering, maybe she should try Humint, but where to start? Every major space power had the ability to build such a device once it was conceived, but who would risk the nuclear wrath of the entire world on such a gamble?

Just then, everybody jumped as the door to the Computer Room opened and a blacksuit rushed in to give Katz a heavy journal marked top secret.

"Get me a number," Price demanded, rolling up her sleeves. "How many of these damn things are there in space?"

"At the rate we're losing satellites," Wethers stated, "I'd calculate a dozen, certainly no more than twenty maximum."

"Twenty!" Price exclaimed with a scowl. Then the Farm was facing an entire fleet of the stealth hunter-killer sats! She offered a private prayer for Jack Grimaldi, and wished the pilot well.

Sliding on her VR helmet, Carmen Delahunt linked to the mainframes and dived into the Net on a new search pattern. Building the hunter-killers had to have cost millions, maybe hundreds of millions. That was the way in—the ancient rule of follow the money. Closing files madly, the woman slipped into the jammed data stream of the transatlantic cable and entered the shaky European Net. Lots of cash for a secret project meant covert transactions from legitimate banks. Yet even in Switzerland there would be records. Not in the banks, of course, but in the e-mail of the employees to family and friends. Hints, clues, passing remarks about a busy day, that was all she needed. Somewhere in the infinite morass of casual chatter somebody knew the truth, unaware that he or she held the key to stopping the fall of civilization.

"Cash," Wethers said unexpectedly. "Carmen, have you considered—?"

"On it," she reported, her gloved hand opening and closing files with every gesture.

"Damn, nothing!" Katz growled, flipping pages in the journal. "What I want to know is how did they get the monster up there without us registering a dozen or so unauthorized launches?"

Steadily he went through the collection of telephoto views showing every known shuttle and high-orbit missile-launch facility in the world. "From underwater? Maybe near a volcano to mask the heat signature? No, ridiculous. The eruption tremors would topple any conceivable missile, much less a shuttle. Maybe near an artillery range to hide the shuttle exhaust as a bomb flash? Or a hidden base near a known base to time a double launch?"

Angrily the man tossed the journal aside. A perfectly timed double launch was flatly impossible. Not even Houdini could have pulled off that complex a magic trick. What was he missing? What was he overlooking?

"Armed satellites," Price said slowly, furrowing her brow. "Killing machines in space, destroying everything in sight."

She turned. "But they aren't destroying everything, are they? There must be some sort of an identification signal to stop them from blasting one another. If we can find that, duplicate and then broadcast it from our own sats, the hunter-killers would pass by harmlessly."

Startled, Tokaido glanced up from his work. "Stopped cold by their own codes? Yes, that might just work."

"Barb, you're brilliant," Kurtzman cried, shoving away his coffee mug. "Hunt, give me a global sweep, full spectrum. I want a record of every modulated signal in near space, EM, ionic, radiation, syncopated light, the works! I'll start building a filter program."

"Of course," the former professor replied calmly.

First and foremost Wethers would need some ears to listen in space, and he knew where to steal some. Flashing through a virtual reality of glowing cables, the man raced along interconnecting landlines until reaching the nearby state of Kentucky. Following the jumbled symbols of low-level government encryption, he found a few military bases, an ICBM silo and then located a university project operated by an old Cray Mark I. The computer was struggling to analyze the meager trickle of data coming from a bank of dish antennae listening intently to the endless crackle from deep space, electronic ears trying to find any recognizable signals.

It was a SETI project, the Search for Extraterrestrial Intelligence. The Kentucky university mainframe was operating seventeen fifty-foot radio dishes perfectly linked together into a single unit. Designed to plumb the depths of interstellar space, the electronic chatter of the orbiting satellites was actually filtered out of the probing sensors. But that could be easily fixed. Ninety seconds flat.

Wethers seized the university computer and made the changes in less than a minute. Now a flood of data poured into the Farm, the fiber-optic cables nearly overloading from the terabyte data flow. Binary-code sine waves flashed past his eyes in a blur, but the cyber expert rode the flow like a concert violinist listening to a hundred-piece orchestra and appreciating the beauty of the woodwinds even while catching the flat note from the brass. His mind raced, but his body was relaxed, almost limp.

Then a tiny crackle spurted into the glistening data stream, and Wethers instantly cut the abnormality from the barrage of noise for detailed inspection. It was irregular, nonrepetitive, not on the cold-hydrogen line and resembled a static discharge where none should be located. However, he had no doubt it was the sparking discharge of damaged electronic circuitry. But from what? Could be the international space station, or a partially destroyed shuttle. He pulled in two supercomputers to assist and eclipse tracking from Mt. Wilson Observatory matched the source. He had found one of the enemy satellites, and it was damaged.

Quickly linking with Tokaido at his console, Wethers shared the revelation and the two cyber warriors rode the EM beams of the SETI dishes and washed over the hull of the satellite searching for a way inside. Only there didn't seem to be any exterior antennae, receivers, solar cells or even radar arrays in use to gain entrance. How did the hunter-killer see, visual light? Simplistic and totally secure. There was no way for government hackers to enter through the eyes of the machine. A maser that big had yet to be constructed. EM security on the orbiter was excellent. Whatever else they were, the builders of the war machines hadn't been fools.

Studying the wealth of information from the passive sensors, Wethers narrowed the source of the short circuit until he had a lock. Bingo. A microthin crack in the ceramic armor exposed loose wires sparking from a damaged internal cable. Nothing more than a pinhole, but that was enough. He brought in Delahunt while Tokaido attacked with a dozen macros sequences and override codes. The war satellite resisted, and Tokaido boosted the data flow, sending out megabytes, then gigabytes of data from the SETI dishes, the barrage washing over the enemy satellite like water from a garden hose, trying to seep into that tiny little crack.

Then he was in, the signals locked, and the massive computers were linked to the bare metal of the minuscule opening. Instantly the autodefenses of the satellite threw up a firewall across the cables and tried to rotate away from the subterranean foe on the planet below. But Tokaido killed the retro jets, pinning it motionless even while accessing the subroutines of the machine. Delahunt's presence appeared on-line and together they forced a full diagnostic, then Tokaido expertly followed the command prefix as it went through all of the main sequence. The smiling intruder from the Farm rode deep into the heart of the machine, carried along by the very program designed to destroy any hostile invaders.

"Excuse me," Wethers said calmly, his hands flying across the keyboard, multiple screens flashing and scrolling. "I do believe that we have something."

"Go," Price commanded. The mission controller had known the cyber warriors were doing something big from the increased vibration from the mainframes.

"We have gained entry into one of the hunter-killers," he stated, bringing the rest of the room alert. "And Akira is trying to dump its core memory into one of our mainframes."

"How did you get in?" Kurtzman demanded, slaving his monitors to their flashing screens. Unknown circuitry strobed by at lightning speeds, one wild section in particular catching his attention. "A short circuit and crack in the hull, eh?"

"Not the garbage?" Price asked, trying to follow the electronic battle. But it was all happening so fast, how did they keep track of anything?

Linking in another mainframe, Kurtzman snorted in disdain. "Don't be ridiculous. Those are always much too heavily protected. Everybody guards against invasion that way. The ploy has been used in too many movies.''

"I don't like easy," Katz said with a scowl. "Could this be another trap?"

Headphones thumping, Tokaido snorted. "Possible, but I'm still going to steal everything I can before it gets rid of me. Our firewall will stop any possible counterattack.''

"Hopefully," Price said. Famous last words. She remembered a similar statement said just before Jared Quinlan blew the Farm apart a few years ago.

"Blast, that was a fake core," Tokaido muttered, savagely closing a file and denying a download. "Nothing but a virus to scram our link.''

"Careful," Wethers warned. "Try duping the carrier tone, slide in on a side band and seize a subroutine.''

Popping a stick of bubblegum into his mouth, the Japanese-American hacker nodded and closed his mind to everything but the silent, invisible battle for supremacy over a thousand miles away.

Flipping a latch, Kurtzman gave the young man every mainframe on the base, and an entire line of system monitors became alive. Tense minutes passed, only the power gauges and systems monitors showing that anything was happening.

"Okay, I'm in the core!" Tokaido cried in triumph, and in orderly procession the hunter-killer satellite began to turn over all of its controls to the man in the Computer Room of the Stony Man Farm. The hacker felt exhausted and sweaty, the computer systems of the satellite had proved as well armored as the hull was on the exterior. Tokaido felt as if he had just spent a week kicking a hole through a brick wall.

"These are German and Chinese boards," Kurtzman said, schematics crawling along a wall monitor. "I recognize that pattern. State-of-the-art. Good as anything we have here.''

"So it's Chinese?" Katz scowled.

The man in the wheelchair grunted. "Only some of the parts are. This is the twenty-first century. Not everything comes from Silicon Valley or Siberia Technics, you know."

"Alert. We have incoming," Price said unexpectedly, adjusting the controls on console. "You may have been found. Another satellite is dropping into an attack posture directly above the satellite you seized. Ninety degrees universal above the elliptic."

"Buy me some time," Tokaido said, leaning over the keyboard, his face inches away from the glowing monitor. "Five minutes, maybe less."

"Too late. There's a trace on your signal," Wethers reported, both hands busy. "The second hunter-killer satellite is trying to find you. I strongly suggest breaking the connection. Base security may soon be compromised."

"Almost done," Tokaido whispered hoarsely, every muscle tense. "Just a little bit more."

"Break the link. It bypassed the SETI station and is coming after us directly," Delahunt said urgently. Then she added, "It already knows we're in eastern North America."

"If the people controlling the satellites find this base…" Katz left the statement hanging, but moved his hand to a locked gang bar, ready to cut the power to the entire base to prevent identification.

Breathing heavily, Tokaido flicked his fingers over the keyboard. "Ah! I found a hidden file. God, the encryption is triple-induced morphisms! No time to break through that. Going to burn out their hard drive and steal the buffer."

"There's no time!"

"I can do it," he muttered, both hands typing smoothly over his keyboard. But then there was a small flash on the status board and the link went dead.

"The second satellite blew our captive to hell," Katz

growled in surprise. "Apparently our enemy is more afraid of us finding them than they wanted to get us."

"Damn, and we were so close." Delahunt sighed, brushing damp hair from her face.

"Closer than you know," Wethers said, tapping on the nonglare glass of his computer screen. Different views of the ocean jumped across the monitor, and soon a landmass filled the view. "After blowing the one we captured, the second just reported to base for further instructions."

"In the middle of a fight you were still recording EM transmissions in space?" Price asked.

"Of course."

"Did you catch the message?" Katz demanded, releasing his grip on the gang bar.

Pouring more coffee, Kurtzman sighed. "Not possible. It was a condensed data tone, hours of information in a single beep."

"However, I did record the location," Wethers reported primly. "Not that it will do us any good, I'm afraid."

"Give me precise latitude and longitude," Price said, lifting a telephone and starting to press buttons. "I'll have SAC bombers level the place and end this within the hour."

"The communiqué was sent to the southernmost tip of Barbados in the Caribbean Sea."

"Location is confirmed," Tokaido reported, blowing a bubble.

The slim honey blonde stopped hitting buttons and lowered the receiver. "Come again?" Price asked incredulously.

"Barbados, Caribbean Sea."

"The United States of America is being attacked by Barbados," Price said slowly, pronouncing the words carefully, as if she had to have heard them wrong. "Impossible. Where was the message then relayed to?"

"Unknown," Kurtzman said gruffly. "With so many satellites gone, it's difficult to trace foreign landline calls. But this is where it was received." He lifted a laser pointer and put a red dot on the wall map. "At the extreme southeast end of the island, near an old artillery field."

"Where?" Katz demanded, jerking his face in that direction. An old artillery field in Barbados?

"There used to be an American Navy base there in WWII."

"Maybe they have a plane in a hangar, or there's a ship in the port," Price said, thinking aloud.

"No, this is their base of operations," Katz declared, standing and staring at the map. "By God, they're using a HARP!"

Swiveling, Price looked at the man. "Gerald Bull's old space cannon?"

"Exactly!"

Kurtzman frowned deeply. "Could that antique still be functional?"

"Maybe," Price said, chewing a lip. Long ago she remembered hearing about the gunsmith Gerald Bull and how back in 1965 he built the HARP—High Altitude Research Project—cannon in Barbados. With a barrel of over a hundred feet in length, the gun was capable of putting a fifty-pound projectile into a low Earth orbit. Later cannons were used for different purposes, and she naturally supposed that the very first HARP was a rusted pile of trash by now. Salt air destroyed metal amazingly fast. But it was possible that somebody rebuilt the abandoned cannon to handle bigger loads and was launching these new hunter-killers into space.

"Can't work," Tokaido said, turning a palm-pilot computer for the others to see. "According to the *Encyclopedia Britannica,* the muzzle-flash of the original HARP was four hundred feet long and illuminated the entire island while the concussion shattered windows for miles. Houses had to be moved because of so many complaints. There is no way they could launch dozens of these machines without alerting every tourist for a hundred miles.''

"Rail gun,'' Price said, turning around sharply. "The hunter-killer is armed with a magnetic rail gun, why not launch the same way?''

"A rail gun?''

"Okay, a coil gun, then. Same thing.''

"Convert the existing steel barrel of the HARP cannon into an O'Neil magnetic coil gun,'' Kurtzman mused, rubbing his chin. "Cowboy would know about the feasibility of that better than us, but it sounds possible. The launches would then be silent, without any muzzle-flash, and the occasional boom of a launching orbiter breaking the sound barrier would merely be considered a distant storm or old munitions going off. The HARP was situated on a sea cliff beyond an abandoned artillery field for just that reason—nobody wanted the land and so Bull got it cheap.''

"Damn clever,'' Katz said. "If we had a working weather satellite, we could check for any unusual magnetic fluxes. But that's probably why they took out the Caribbean area satellites first thing, to mask their position.''

"Makes sense.''

"And if we sent in a spyplane from a HAWK station in the Florida Keys, that would only warn the terrorists operating the machines,'' he added grimly. "And we need them alive to turn these damn things off, or at least get us the enemy signature-recognition codes.''

Then it occurred to Price that Bull also designed the Babylon Supercannon for Iraq. That was ten times larger, the biggest functional cannon in the history of the world. It made the German Paris Gun look like a kid's cap pistol. They would need an invasion force to penetrate that deep into Iraq and take that monster out. Exactly the sort of action that would start the chain reaction leading to nuclear war.

Her face had to have revealed the dire thoughts, because

Katz loudly rapped the computer console to demand attention. "The Babylon Project was never finished before Bull died, and was one of our main objectives in the Gulf War," he said formally, as if reporting to a room full of high-ranking officers. "Our troops blew it to pieces and leveled the valley. Then on every flight across Iraq, the Air Force would drop a few more bombs just to seal the deal. It became a sort of game for the pilots at the end, to still find something standing to destroy. There's nothing there but sand and shrapnel."

"Good news," Price said, relaxing slightly. "But Hussein still has the blueprints. So for somebody else to build another is still a possibility."

"Sadly, yes. But it would be harder than hell to hide," he said, then thoughtfully added, "Unless the enemy built it underground, like Bull's first tests in Vermont."

Nobody in the room had a response to that.

Weighing the new information, Price asked, "Hunt, do the enemy know that you found the location?"

"Highly doubtful. Our circumnavigation was most adroit. I would say that disclosure was extremely unlikely."

Price frowned. This was no classroom exercise. In combat there was an ocean of blood between maybe and yes.

"All right, have communications try and reach our military base in Saudi Arabia. Have them do a flyby, and if they find anything, we'll have to get an okay to bomb it."

"That could start a war."

"Or stop one," Price stated grimly.

"Nothing on the Net," Tokaido said.

"I'll hack the Department of Defense computer files," Delahunt said, slipping on her VR helmet and glove. The banking aspect could wait. They had the tiger by the tail, and minutes counted. "Try and get us a download on the HARP cannon, schematics, structural blueprints and such."

"And the Canadian Department of Defense," Katz added. "Bull worked for them also."

"ASAP," Price ordered, already punching numbers into the console phone. They had a possible target; now it was time to send in Phoenix Force for a hard probe. This was exactly the sort of thing she had been holding them in reserve for.

As the communications officer came on the line, the mission controller gave the man detailed instructions on the matter, then added, "And get me a status report on Able Team. They're long overdue."

"Acknowledged," the officer said crisply. "But they have the com link turned off. Must still be undercover working the Avalon 88 headquarters."

After this long?

"Accepted," Price said, replacing the receiver. Great. The enemy was finally starting to reveal itself, and half of her field teams were missing. She only hoped they were still alive.

CHAPTER TWELVE

Launch Pad 4, Cape Canaveral, Florida

The winds were blowing mostly from the southwest, carrying away the wisps of steam from the main fuel tanks of the NASA space shuttle *Atlantis.* Dozens of ground crew rushed along the gantry attached to the spacecraft, sitting patiently on its pad waiting for the code to launch.

Frantically rushed through the assembly building with countless safety checks bypassed, the cargo bay of the shuttle was packed solid with nearly a hundred stripped-down replacement Keyhole and MilStar satellites, merchant and scientific orbiters bumped from the spaceship in the name of national security.

The crew worked with grim faces inside the vessel, running systems checks again and again. By now every nation in the world had lost satellites, and the fear was starting to spread. The Pentagon was hiding a full constellation of hunter-killer satellites in polar orbits to use as emergency reserves to protect the last precious milsats. This flight was rated as beyond top secret and considered more important than the lives of every man and women on the base. Half of America's orbiters were gone, civilization communication nets were beginning to fall and the defensive radar umbrella of the nation was breaking apart. Never in its tumultuous history had America ever stood on the threshold of such a double-edged disaster, enemies from without and financial ruin from within.

"Base, we are go for preignition," the commander of the *Atlantis* crisply reported into her throat mike.

"Roger, we confirm. You have authorization."

The commander counted down and flipped the latch with a thumb to press a large red button. The shuttle quivered ever so slightly, then steadily began to vibrate as the thousands of gallons of fuel were blown out the aft rocket vectors, thundering into the blast pit below the launch pad, the side tunnel venting off the pressure to prevent a blowback explosion.

"Full pressure," announced a technician monitoring the blast waves creating a chemical volcano under the small craft. "Internals green and steady."

"Confirm, base," the mission commander said with a grin, nodding to the pilot. "We are ready for liftoff!"

"Roger, *Atlantis*," Mission Control replied calmly. "Gantry is released. All lights green. Umbilicals are released. Status is still go. Switch to internal power."

"We're hot, Control," the commander said, tightening the neck ring of her helmet. "Computers are on-line."

The ship was shaking around the crew, the titanic engines fighting to be set free. Every unprotected item on the launch pad was metallic vapor by now; only the kilotons of seawater rushing through the brick-lined cooling vents kept the launch pad itself from breaking apart under the throbbing power of the main engines.

"Igniting boosters, *Atlantis*. Godspeed."

"Thank you, Control. We are green to go."

Now the solid-chemical booster rockets attached to each side of the main fuel tank gently pulsed into life, a reddish glow increasing into a hellish roar. The shuttle engines combined with the boosters into a deafening rumble, orange-yellow light bathing the concrete field, reflecting off the shimmering waves of the ocean and seeming to extend to the horizon.

"Jesus Christ!" a voice called over the earphones of the shuttle crew. "Kill the mains! We have an irregular firing pattern in the boosters!"

"Are you sure?" the commander demanded, feeling her heart beat louder than the rocket engines. Strapped into the acceleration couch, it felt as if the whole world were exploding around the vessel. Even the cockpit windows only showed billowing clouds of smoke and steam. "My board shows status nominal!"

"That's an order, *Atlantis!* Abort!"

With no choice the commander slid back the access panel of her couch and hit the kill button. It locked into place, and the shuttle engines instantly turned off.

But the strident rumbling around the crew only diminished and didn't cease entirely.

"*Atlantis,* we have a runaway!" Mission Control announced calmly. "Abandon the shuttle now!"

No further words were needed. The crew members snapped their release harnesses and expertly grabbed convenient stanchions to pull themselves from the couches. Moving like gymnasts through the vessel, the astronauts reached the air locks and a man hit the explosive bolts button. In a double explosion, both of the air lock panels blasted away from the hull, admitting a hellish vista of flame and toxic fumes.

Instantly the shuttle was filled with exhaust, visibility reduced to only inches. But months of hard practice in simulators led the crew blindly through the billowing fog, and they reached the gantry in perfect timing just as it returned. Horrific winds tore at the people, but they held on to specially textured handrails and forced themselves across the protected catwalk to reach the escape balcony.

Struggling to stay on her feet, the commander cursed bitterly. This was their own goddamn fault! NASA had by-passed too many safety checks, ignored too many procedures to meet the impossible schedule, and now the astronauts were paying the price.

Reaching up, each astronaut found a slim bar positioned overhead, the two-hand grip firmly attached to a sloping wire as thick as a soup can. One by one, the crew grabbed on to the grip and kicked off the gantry to slide away into the storming night.

Still locked into position, the *Atlantis* stood quivering, tiles shaking loose from its hull as the boosters continued to burn at full strength completely out of control.

Rapidly building speed, the crew left the gantry and shuttle behind, hurtling through the burning fumes until a hard jolt broke their hold, and each fell into a plane of blackness, a thick protective wall of steel-reinforced concrete blocking their view of the thundering booster. Then the world went abruptly silent as the crew splashed into a reservoir of water. They descended rapidly, and their boots gently tapped the cushioned bottom of the basin as the life-support systems on their spacesuits kicked on automatically.

Unable to communicate with one another underwater, the commander checked every crew member by hand, rapping old Morse code on their helmets with her gloved fist. They responded in turn, shaken but undamaged. She considered it a miracle. Created right after the *Apollo 8* disaster, the escape slide had been in existence for decades, melting away after each launch, only to be rebuilt again just it case it was ever needed. This was the first time the guy wire had ever been used, and it had worked perfectly. Thank God for that famous fanatical NASA attention to details. Even if the shuttle, the external fuel tank and the boosters all detonated in unison now, the crew would still survive the fireball.

However, their mission was a scrub. There would be no

launch tonight, and whatever resources America possessed in space was all there would be for quite a while.

The commander sincerely hoped it was enough.

South Main Street, Baltimore, Maryland

THE DARK STREETS WERE mostly empty, traffic in the heart of the city nearly nonexistent at that early hour. Somewhere in the night, a dog barked and a cat yowled in reply. A glass bottle clattered loudly as it rolled along a sidewalk, a car door slammed and a distant foghorn gave a deep moan from the city harbor, sounding like a lonely prehistoric beast rising from the deeps.

"Still there," Gadgets Schwarz said, peeking into the side-view mirror to see behind the moving van. Hookers on a street corner waved frantically at the passing vehicle, then vanished into the shadows of the night already forgotten.

"The people are good," Carl Lyons said, both hands on the steering wheel as they bounced through a shallow pothole. "Very good."

"Could be cops, or more Nazis," Blancanales muttered, easing a clip into his M-16/M-203 combo.

"That's not how I read it," Lyons said, loosening the Colt Python in the shoulder rig under his windbreaker.

After the fight on the rooftop of the Avalon 88 warehouse, Able Team slipped down the fire escape to avoid the coming police. However, in their wake, the commandos had jimmied open the secret door in the closet and even left a trail of videotapes scattered around for the cops to find. The rest they would leave to the capable hands of the police department.

When the unconscious members of the local Avalon 88 Nazi party finally awoke, they would be going away for a very long time. Whether or not the Nazis could survive a term in prison once the other inmates discovered what kind of porn the Nazis had made for a living was of no concern at all to the men of Able Team.

When Blancanales thought about such things, he considered it evolution in action, a thinning of the herd. To Schwarz it was a cosmic thing, the universe in balance, and Lyons just didn't give a damn. If the animals ate one another in their cages, that merely saved him the trouble of pulling the trigger. But there were always more beasts to replace the fallen, new predators born every day to stalk for fresh prey.

Identifying their rooftop attackers was going to prove to be very difficult. The ammo the gunmen had used couldn't be traced, as the Heckler & Koch rifles fired caseless rounds. The rifles might be traced, but that rarely worked with so many hot guns on the streets for sale. H&K even had a local Virginia plant, making the availability of the rifles even greater. The fingerprints Blancanales had gotten off the corpses led nowhere. Watches, jewelry and clothing labels were similarly useless in establishing the identity of the attackers. The gunmen could be from anyplace on the map. Able Team was fighting air on this mission.

But within only a few blocks, the men of Able Team realized they were being tailed by a plain sedan with muddy plates. To test the theory, Lyons tried a few simple tricks to shake a tail, suddenly reversing his course, driving through a closed car wash, and the sedan disappeared, only to be instantly replaced with a green compact car and then a rusty SUV.

As the blocks went by, the three vehicles expertly followed the van, no single car staying for more than a few minutes. But the combat veterans recognized a standard three-man rotating surveillance pattern when they saw it in action. Obviously this was the backup for the assault team on the roof. But whether these gunmen were out for revenge over the deaths of their comrades, or to track Able Team to where they lived was unknown.

Soon the sedan appeared without hubcaps to alter its appearance, then a man replaced the woman behind the wheel of the compact. Lyons didn't like that; these folks were professionals. Few people paid attention to the traffic around them; alter a few minor details and the vehicles became different cars over and over again. The tinted windows of the SUV hid the passengers inside, and the big ex-cop instinctively tagged it as the crew wagon, full of armed muscle.

"Think they know we've made them?" Blancanales asked, working the bolt on his M-16.

"Not yet," Lyons told him, the sawed-off M-16/M-203 cradled in his lap. Cowboy had done a superb job. The modified U.S. Army assault rifle worked so well, much better than a G3-Tiger, which was the same size but fired 9 mm rounds.

Maintaining a steady pace, Lyons passed the exit that would have taken them toward Stony Man Farm in nearby Virginia, and headed for downtown Baltimore to buy some time. If they drove about randomly for too long, the gunmen would get suspicious and back away, or attack right here in the middle of the city, neither of which Able Team wanted to happen just yet.

In less than a mile, the van went past the statue of Lord Baltimore and took a corner to cut through the inner-harbor area. Formerly a slum, the city spent millions to buy the land, razed it to the ground and then rebuilt twenty square blocks into the jewel of the state.

Even at this hour, traffic was heavy with a well-dressed crowd meandering along the walkway that cut through the waterfalls and flowering gardens separating the inner-harbor from the city proper. This drastically increased the danger to civilians, but Lyons was gambling the sedan wouldn't attack with so many cameras around. But when the hammer fell, they needed combat room, a long clear stretch of road where gunfire wouldn't result in civilian deaths, and he had to choose quickly. Lots of empty roads to the west, also lots of farmhouses with families. Couldn't go south, and the ocean filled the east.

Beyond the dancing waters was the glass-encased food court, its 122 restaurants alive with thousands of people. The mall alongside was closed this late at night, but still brightly lit with holiday-style lights. Searchlights from the planetarium swept the sky, and in the calm waters of the harbor, a Revolutionary War clipper floated serenely alongside the only known captured German U-boat. Then a crowd roared its approval from the aquarium as the evening dolphin show got into full swing.

Unexpectedly the shortwave radio buzzed for attention.

Startled by the intrusion, Schwarz picked up the earpiece and held a hushed conversation while working the controls.

"That was Price. Things are bad," he said succinctly, and quickly brought the others up to speed.

"Dozens of hunter-killer satellites?" Blancanales asked, arching an eyebrow.

"That was the number given."

The combat veteran whistled. "Christ, how big an organization are we facing?"

"More important," Lyons growled, waiting for a red light to turn green before merging with another lane, "how long have these bastards been running around free right under our freaking noses?"

Schwarz glanced at the side-view mirror as the compact took a corner and the sedan perfectly replaced it in the stream of traffic. "Who are you people?" he muttered.

"Time to find out," Lyons stated grimly, shifting gears. The green compact sat two cars away, the man at the wheel smoking a cigar and tapping his fingers to music on the radio. The very picture of innocence. That was, except for the telltale bulge under his right shoulder, where a handgun of some kind rode.

The big ex-cop frowned as he again upped his opinion of the faceless enemy. If they had the piles of cash to put satellites into space, then they had the jack to get the best mercs on the planet. He would assume the sedan was armored, possible the SUV also. Plus they could have the equipment needed to trace their shortwave broadcasts.

"Better kill the radio," Blancanales suggested, looking over a shoulder.

"Way ahead of you," Schwarz said, clicking off the shortwave and removing the fuses. A strong enough induction field could turn their own communications equipment against them, making the speakers into microphones and allowing others to listen on the conversation in the van. But not with it turned off. That trick had yet to be invented.

"Three cars," Lyons said, heading away from the harbor. "How smart do you think they are?"

"Very smart," Blancanales replied, rubbing a bruised hip from the rooftop fight. "But they don't seem very experienced. Maybe trained by a pro, but not veterans of anything but obstacle courses and field exercises."

Lyons and Schwarz listened carefully to the psych master think aloud. In matters like this, Rosario's gut feelings were almost always correct.

"The roadster," Blancanales stated suddenly, working the bolt on his weapon. "Their leader is in the armored sedan."

"The last place he should be," Lyons said, moving easily around a slow-moving truck full of used furniture. "We need some combat room to take the guy. Too crowded here."

Swiveling his chair, Schwarz worked the keyboard on the laptop attached to his workbench with Velcro. On the dashboard of the van, a submonitor glowed into life, displaying a network of roads and highways. Blancanales grunted at the choice, and Lyons agreed. Close enough not to rouse any suspicions, but empty of potential bystanders at this time of night.

"Gunpowder it is," Lyons said, hitting the turn signal and taking the next highway ramp.

Mixed into the sparse traffic, the three cars followed along and spread out across the highway, the SUV even speeding to go ahead of the van, trapping them in a moving box. An almost perfect surveillance pattern for long-distance trailing. Also a good formation for an attack. Lyons cursed under his breath. Just who was the hunter and the hunted here?

Schwarz pulled out night-vision goggles to look over the bumpers of the cars and saw small compact CB antennas. Gotcha. The cheap low-band radios wouldn't reach five miles, but that was enough to keep them in communication with one another. Smart.

The northern hills of Maryland rose on the horizon as the four vehicles raced toward Gunpowder Bridge. Taking Route 95, Lyons headed north, steadily building speed while the other men slipped on combat gear and got ready for open warfare. There would be no suicides this time. They were coming back with prisoners. End of discussion.

"CONFIRM, SIR. We attack on Gunpowder Bridge," Lieutenant Banyon said into the mike of a CB radio under the dashboard.

"And take one alive for questioning," Major Cole ordered.

"Roger, sir. Consider it done."

"Also, the hostage is no longer needed. Remove him from the equation."

"Confirm," the lieutenant replied, hanging the mike on a clip and then tuning to the next channel as they did after every conversation. It seriously hindered outsiders from following their conversations.

Tied with layers of rope, the drunken homeless man from the Baltimore alley sat like a trussed turkey in the back seat of the sedan. There was a faint bathroom stink around the prisoner that hadn't been there when he was first captured.

"Karl, set him free," Banyon ordered from the front.

Nodding his understanding, a burly man with short-cropped blond hair removed the drunk's gag.

"Bless you," he wheezed, gulping in fresh air. "I'm sorry, for whatever I did I am truly, honestly sorry, and it'll never happen again, sir."

"Yes, I know," Karl said, drawing a knife.

Pinned against the car door, the drunk tried to scream as the man slid the knife very slowly into his chest, his face contorting into a feral expression until the blade reached the drunk's beating heart. Then Karl twisted the blade and the homeless man slumped over, exhaling a last long breath.

"Stinking bum," he said with a sneer, shoving the warm corpse to the floor.

"Don't remove the blade," Banyon ordered. "They still bleed for a while."

"I've done this before, sir," the man replied, pulling another blade from a hidden sheath on his calf and tucking it into the empty sheath on his belt. The old man had been no challenge at all, not like that Marine. He had lasted for hours.

"Took you long enough," another man taunted, elbowing the killer. "Getting old?"

"Must have hit a rib."

"Should we toss him out?" a man grunted, swinging a 9 mm Sten machine gun from his shoulder and jacking the bolt.

"Later," the lieutenant said, working the bolt on a Browning Automatic Rifle and sliding a clip of steel-tipped rounds into the open breech. "First we handle these cops, then we make room for our new friends."

"Yeah," Karl added, "what we do, we do for all humanity."

Grim-faced, the members of the Peace Brigade nodded in understanding and prepared all of their weapons for battle.

"LOOK! THEY KNOW!" Blancanales stated angrily. "They're driving differently, no longer trying to hide."

"Probably going to try to force us off the road."

"Then we give them something else to think about," Schwarz said, pressing a series of buttons on a device the size of a shoebox. The device gave no indication that anything was happening, but he knew that every CB radio in the area was now effectively dead, every channel filled with a strident squealing.

An elderly driver of a brand-new station wagon and a yawning blonde in a sleek but badly dented Lotus gave no reactions. However, the armed men in the sedan and the compact violently jerked, then lurched forward to fiddle with something under the dashboards. If anything was happening behind the tinted glass of the SUV, it was impossible to tell.

"They look mighty pissed," Blancanales said with a grin.

"Good, that means they're amateurs, not pros," Lyons stated, checking the fuel gauge. Half a tank, more than enough.

"So much for a coordinated attack," Schwarz said.

"Still three to one." Lyons loosened the strap over the Colt Python on his shoulder rig. "And the element of surprise is gone."

"Then we attack first." Blancanales rolled down his window.

The cool ocean wind rushed in as he leveled his M-16/M-203 and cut loose with the M-16, the flash suppressor making the muzzle-flash resemble a fiery flower. A neat line of holes punched through the fiberglass body of the compact, and the wounded driver slammed on the brakes, quickly dropping behind the van trying to get out of the way.

But the bleeding man couldn't control the wheels. The vehicle sharply banked and promptly flipped over, rolling wildly along the roadway with doors flapping, glass shattering and bodies flying across the ribbon of black asphalt.

"Goddamn it, we didn't want them dead," Schwarz stormed, lowering his own M-16.

Just then, the side of the van dented, its thin armor bowing under the furious assault of incoming rounds.

"Don't worry, there are more," Lyons retorted, and started fishtailing the van to throw off the enemy's aim. The side-view mirror shattered, leaving only the burnished metal frame and a few sparkling shards.

Now the sedan and the SUV pulled away from the gray van, widening the gap. Far behind them, the compact burst into flames, sealing off the highway to any further civilian traffic from that direction. That gave Able Team valuable combat range, but would also bring the police and a host of rescuers. In a single instant time was now against them.

"Here they come," Lyons said, drawing his revolver and driving with one hand.

Aiming at the tires of the SUV ahead of them, Blancanales emptied the M-16 out his window, spent brass bounding everywhere inside the van. Pistols fired in reply from the passenger window of the recreational vehicle, hitting nothing.

Then the men in the sedan behind Able Team stuck Sten guns and BARs out of both sides of the vehicle and started firing. A rifle round hit and penetrated the body of the van, leaving a hole large as a thumb.

Ignoring the incoming AP rounds, Schwarz snapped a

safety belt dangling from his belt onto a roof hook, and kicked open the rear doors to cut loose with the M-16 directly at the oncoming sedan. But the 5.56 mm tumblers peppered the black body and ricocheted off, barely leaving a mark. Then rifles spoke again, and the shortwave radio burst apart from a direct hit.

The handguns still shooting, the SUV in front of the Able Team van tried to match the side-to-side weaving of the vehicle and failed. Then the rear hatch was thrown open and a bearded man in a crimson beret leveled an X-18 grenade launcher.

Lyons twisted the wheel hard just as the weapon fired, and the 30 mm shell streaked by sizzling with yellow light. A magnesium round! Then the gunman fired again, and a barrage of lead pellets pounded the window of the van, sending out a score of tiny spiderweb cracks, but failing to break the resistant glass. However, with sixteen more rounds, Lyons knew it was only a matter of time before the gunman hit them with something that would rip the van apart.

Without further thought, he flicked on the high beams. The gunman covered his face for a second, and Lyons drew his Colt and started firing at the already weakened windshield. The hardball Magnum ammo shattered the glass, giving the Able Team leader a clear view, and he emptied the revolver into the rear hatch of the SUV. The heavy-duty combat slugs punched through the chassis as if it were cardboard. Recoiling with pain, the man with the launcher tumbled out, the weapon smashing into pieces as it hit the highway. The gunman clawed for the bumper, missed and landed with similar results.

Thrusting on sunglasses against the wind, Lyons could see the SUV was packed with men and weapons. He had been right; the damn thing was a rolling arsenal! Slapping in a fresh clip, Blancanales raked the vehicle with tumblers and the rear hatch flopped down, ammo boxes, grenades and a LAW tumbling away.

Swerving hard, Lyons avoided the rocket launcher and saw it spin away like a cheerleader's baton into the night.

With a cry the gunman with the Sten dropped the weapon, his hand a bloody mess. Dropping his spent clip, Schwarz slapped in a fresh magazine as the sedan stopped firing for a moment. Realizing what they were going to try, Schwarz held on for dear life as the armored car accelerated and rammed the van hard. Everything loose in the vehicle went flying, and the collision tore his hands free. Helpless, Gadgets fell towards the open doorway, only to stop from going through by the jerk of the safety line. As the sedan retreated to ram again, he fought to keep his footing and wildly fired the M-16, then used the M-203 almost straight down. The 40 mm shell hit the road as they zoomed past and violently detonated, the blast throwing him back safely inside the van, his flak jacket protecting him from the deadly shrapnel. The sedan rolled past the explosion completely unharmed, the BARs speaking again, the triburst blowing out a taillight and shattering the glass in the swinging rear door.

Kicking out a large chunk of the ruined shortwave radio at the black roadster, Schwarz quickly checked himself for damage, but there was no moisture on his clothes marking a hit.

"We got trouble!" the electronics expert shouted, casting aside the spent M-16/M-203 and snatching up an Uzi machine pistol. The stream of 9 mm slugs hit the sedan and stayed there, flattened lumps of hot gray lead. No penetration.

Shitfire, that thing was a goddamn tank! The weapons trunk held a LAW and a Stinger, both of which would reduce the sedan to scrap metal in a thundering heartbeat. Unfortunately neither could be used from inside the van.

The fiery backblast of the launching rockets would blow the vehicle apart like a soda can with a firecracker inside.

"No, they do!" Lyons growled, holstering the spent Colt and reaching into a canvas bag on the floor to grab the silenced Ingram from the warehouse. He hosed the SUV and got another man, then noticed several small spheres bouncing along the road coming their way.

Grenades! Lyons instantly stomped on the gas pedal, and the van charged forward, the big Detroit power plant screaming as it ferociously built speed. The grenades went right underneath the vehicle, and the warrior waited for a long two-count until the military charges exploded in their wake, covering the roadway with the billowing flames of white phosphorus.

With spent shells and screwdrivers rolling madly across the floor of the weaving van, Schwarz covered his face and backed away from the inferno. Then he saw the sedan roll through the chemical fire untouched. Armored below, too. Okay, he had an answer for that! He started to grab a satchel charge, then paused, remembering they wanted prisoners, not corpses. Reluctantly the man placed the canvas bag of C-4 to one side and grabbed a fresh clip for the Uzi, concentrating his aim on the tires. The slugs hit and went in, but nothing else. Had to be self-sealing, exactly like the tires on the van. Who were these guys?

"Heads up!" Blancanales shouted over the wind roaring through the open ended van. "Gunpowder Bridge straight ahead!"

Straight ahead of them was the long bridge brightly illuminated by a double row of halogen streetlights. The flat expanse of concrete stretched across Gunpowder Ravine and the rocky river hundreds of feet below.

Lyons had been planning to start this fight on the other side, where the highway cut through the hill, both sides of the road sharply rising rock walls. But the bridge would have to do now. The mists from the river below lay like gray cotton across the span, hiding the gentle curve in the middle. That was where the SUV would have to slow down to take the curve, and Able Team could pounce.

Dropping a spent clip, Blancanales inserted a fresh magazine and fired the M-16 ahead, then pumped a 40 mm grenade behind.

"I can't keep this up much longer," Blancanales shouted over the weapon's discharge, his wavy salt-and-pepper hair ruffling wildly from the driving wind.

"Won't have to. Gadgets, use the Armbrust!" Lyons shouted, speeding and slowing to throw off the aim of the gunmen while steadily burping the Ingram.

"In the van?" Schwarz demanded, thinking the man was crazy. Then understanding brightened his face. The tolerance factor was slim, but the tactic should work. There was no way they could fight both vehicles while hampered by the necessity of trying to take some prisoners alive for questioning. The solution was obvious. Remove one of the other cars. But which, the one with armor, or the other full of heavily armed men? That was an easy choice.

Racing to the weapons trunk, he shoved aside the LAW and Stinger to free an Armbrust from its cushioned nest. Checking the weapon, he zeroed the aft port, and went to the front of the van. Rocking back and forth to the shifting of the racing vehicle, Schwarz took a stance between the front seats, shoved the aft end of the launcher through the broken windshield and aimed out the rear doors. Only there was nothing in sight but empty highway and some thickening tendrils of river fog.

"Go left!" Blancanales shouted, watching the sedan in the remaining side-view mirror.

Lyons shifted the wheel, and for a split second the black roadster came into view. Schwarz fired.

A hushed blizzard of frozen nitrogen flakes vomited from

the aft end of the launcher, the icy backblast crossing the fifteen feet separating the two vehicles and filling the SUV with an explosion of bitter snow. Temporarily blind and deaf, the gunmen screamed, accidentally fired their weapons at one another, adding to the chaos. Out of control, the vehicle brutally slammed into the center divider of the highway, sparks spraying out as the fenders scraped along the rough concrete at sixty miles per hour.

In the same moment the stealth antitank rocket launched from the front of the tube and flew down the length of the van on the initial pulse, then exited. Its compressed gas rocket kicked into action fifteen feet outside the van.

Transfixed with horror at the sight of the incoming rocket, the driver of the black sedan couldn't force himself to move. Shouting obscenities, the gunman in the passenger seat reached out to grab the wheel to try to dodge the Armbrust, but it was too little, too late. The rocket crashed into the bulletproof windshield, but the glass offered insufficient resistance to activate the warhead. Continuing onward, the projectile plowed through a gunman and rammed into the rear seat, where it hit the steel chassis and finally detonated.

A fireball engulfed the sedan, lifting it off the road and spraying out flaming debris, weapons and body parts flying everywhere.

As the Able Team van rocked to the concussion, the SUV in front of them suddenly flipped over and landed with a crash, sliding sideways across the highway and blocking every lane.

Instantly Lyons stomped on the brake pedal with all of his strength. The frame shook, brakes squealed, tires smoked and their speed dropped fast, but not enough. The van still hurtled onward at the creaking SUV packed full of high explosives.

Desperate, Lyons pulled the lever for the emergency brake to no noticeable effect. With no other choice, he pushed Schwarz out of the way and abruptly threw the transmission of the roaring van into full reverse.

The Stony Man operatives were nearly torn from their seats as the vehicle violently shuddered and lowered its speed by half. Then the floor between the front seats erupted as the transmission broke apart, gears and bands tearing through the floor and then the roof like a mechanical shotgun blast.

Still standing on the brakes, Lyons fought to keep the van under control as every warning light on the dashboard came alive. Jerking and bouncing, pumping out boiling fluids from under the hood, the van finally came to a groaning halt just as the rear axle snapped and sent a wheel careering away.

Struggling out of the tilted Chevy, Lyons reached the roadway and started forward, with his teammates close behind.

"Thanks for saving my ass," Schwarz said, snapping the bolt on the retrieved Uzi. "But you can never borrow my car again."

Ingram and Colt Python at the ready, the Able Team leader made no reply, his full attention on the teetering wreck of the SUV.

But as they got near, a blond man rose from the ruin of the vehicle, firing a shaky handgun. Ruthlessly Lyons stitched the man across the legs with the Ingram, hoping to take him alive. The gunman fell, but then rolled over with something shiny held triumphantly in his hand. Crippled and possibly dying, the man still smiled as if in victory.

"Grenade ring!" Schwarz cursed and dived for distance.

Lyons and Blancanales did the same and hit the concrete only seconds before a deafening roar split the night and the bridge faintly shook as the six ounces of plastique sent out a lethal halo of plastic shrapnel. The divider crackled from countless hits, and both of the smashed vehicles rattled as if caught in a bad hailstorm.

As the echoing concussion faded away, the three men stiffly rose and hobbled closer to check the rest of the gunmen in the SUV, but the antipersonnel grenade had done its job well. There were only corpses inside.

"Strip 'em," Lyons ordered brusquely.

Shouldering their weapons, the two men went through the riddled bodies removing wallets, wristwatches, clothing labels, wedding rings and anything else they could find that might shed some light on the owners.

Standing guard, Lyons studied the burning wreckage of the sedan down the road. He didn't like this. What was so important to these people that they would commit suicide?

"Damn fanatics," Blancanales muttered, pulling on the drawstring on the canvas bag. "Think it's another jihad, a religious war?"

"'What we do, we do for all humanity,'" Lyons repeated. "That's what the kid on the roof said."

"Sure as hell sounds fanatical to me," Schwarz agreed, pressing an armless hand to a sheet of the FBI paper. Then he tossed the lump of flesh away and carefully tucked the sheet of paper into a pocket with several others. No prisoners, but hopefully they had still obtained what they needed, some sort of a clue to the nature of this new faceless enemy who dared to challenge the world.

The sounds of sirens reached them from the distance. Quickly gathering their weapons along with the heavy bag of personal effects, the Able Team warriors melted into the darkness, the river mists swallowing them whole.

CHAPTER THIRTEEN

Sriharikota Island, India

Below the equator another great island was covered with people and machinery. Sriharikota Island was covered with four huge launch sites, edging its shore along the eastern coast facing the Bay of Bengal. The endless flat expanse of rock and hard-packed sand was crisscrossed with paved roads and railroad tracks set in thick beds of concrete. The facility wasn't pretty, but highly functional. And the few blast craters made from missile failures were easily concealed among the natural irregularity of the land.

Humming along, electric forklifts scurried about everywhere, and people in lab coats marched in serious groups from building to building. But the four launch pads were clear of any vehicles, and two of the gantries were currently in the process of undergoing periodic maintenance painting.

Set far back from the deserted launch pads, safe behind a triple-thick brick wall, was the massive Vikram Sarabhai Space Center, crested with an array of dish antennae linking the underground mainframes to the orbiting weather and communication satellites. On the top floor of the structure, the head of the India Space Research Organization was talking on the telephone directly to the prime minister.

"No, sir, there is no chance.... Yes, the ISRO could get

up a manned capsule, or perhaps even a shuttle in time. We have that lovely new one recently purchased from America only six months ago, the *Yarma*."

The man was speaking quickly, fighting a neverending battle with the low-caste idiots in charge of his base. "But in my professional opinion, there is no chance that India can make any difference up there. We have launched three new satellites already, and all have been destroyed within hours. As much as you do not wish to hear the facts, we simply do not have more satellites!"

Leaning backward in his hard chair, he placed woven leather shoes on top of the polished expanse of his spotless desk. "Eh?" he replied loud enough for his secretary to hear through the partially closed door of his office. "That's non-sense, sir. And even if true, our own radar shows nothing up there. How can we attack something we cannot find? No, sir, I have no idea how the Americans or the British are tracking the enemy. Whatever it is. Maybe by stellar eclipse, but we do not have the technology to do so. Not on our budget. Yes, sir, raising food is more important, I agree. So why are you calling, then? We would only waste money and lives in the attempt, and quite possibly make ourselves fools before the world."

That last argument did it, of course. No politician in India would suffer ignominy for anything. The man on the other end of the telephone gushed apologies and hung up.

Placing his sandals on the carpeted floor, the head of ISRO replaced the telephone receiver and pressed a button summoning his secretary. Now he could get on with much more important and pressing matters at hand.

If war came, so be it. Death was part of the cycle of life. Karma ruled them all. But personally, down deep inside, he prayed hard that his faith wouldn't be tested today. Some other day perhaps, please, not today.

The Island of Barbados

DRIVING A RENTED Honda along the stretch of highway, Gary Manning found no exits or ramps to leave the new road, so he parked the car on the loose gravel of the berm, then slashed the front tire with his Tanto combat knife so that it appeared he had merely stopped to fix a flat and then wandered off.

Slinging an equipment bag across his back, the Phoenix Force warrior climbed over the brightly painted guardrail and hoofed it through the thick forest, the wild mix of trees giving the story of the tropical island: palm trees, cherry blossom and now mahogany. To anybody knowing the history of Barbados, that said everything—first they were free, then slaves of England and now independent once more.

As silent as a deer, Manning raced through the dense woods, keeping his course by the dimming stars overhead. Dawn was coming soon, not good. A distant murmur slowly became the sound of the crashing surf, so he paused in a dark grove to slide the bag off his back and get dressed for battle.

Back on East Caicos Island, to avoid being eaten alive by the endless mosquitoes, the team had lived inside the SeaHawk until receiving a transmission from the Farm. Only a few hundred miles from mainland America, they naturally were ordered to reverse their course and head almost back to the coast of Brazil, and the tiny island nation of Barbados. A HARP, didn't that just beat all.

His face painted, fully armed and ready, Manning did a final check by patting his web harness without looking to make sure everything was in the proper place. Fumbling for a weapon in battle got you killed fast.

Double-checking the grenades on his chest, and the long Barrett slung across his back, the big Canadian took off again.

Moving through the foliage, Manning listened to the chattering monkeys awaken as the predawn light lightened the

sky. The island was pulsating with life. Stopping occasion-
ally, he took a leafy stick from the ground and tucked it
into the webbing of his combat rig to aid camouflage.

Then the man froze and drew his Desert Eagle pistol as
he spied hurricane fencing cut through the forest, the stout
fence topped with shiny coils of concertina wire. There was
no insulation marking it as electrified, so using the tip of
his knife, Manning tapped the metal and it rang musically.
New. This was definitely not left over from the 1960s and
the HARP Project.

Following the fence to the north, Manning stayed in the
shadows as much as possible. Soon the trees thinned to a
grassy field with only the vaguest suggestion of a dirt road
in the surface, and set into the fence was a wide gate, as
solid as the rest of the barrier. Only the lack of concertina
wire on top marked its location. There was no latch on this
side, but there was a small hatch at head level for talking.
The faint smell of cigarette smoke indicated the presence of
a guard.

Wary of land mines or trip wires, Manning reached the
gate and paused to screw a fat sound suppressor onto his
.357 Desert Eagle. This was another Cowboy Kissinger special, but was only good for one or two rounds before the
full-throated roar of the Magnum was unleashed. He would
have to make every shot count.

Softly tapping on the gate with the pistol, he waited a
few minutes, then knocked loudly with his hand.

"Private property," a man's voice said from the other
side. "Go away or you'll be arrested."

"Ah, but mister," Manning said, pleading, "the wife and
I really wanted to see the ruins of the HARP gun."

"Scram!"

"I'll pay big bucks," the Phoenix Force warrior whined,
easing back the hammer on his piece. "How about five dollars American?"

The other man snorted a laugh, and the small hatch in the door swung open, showing the unshaved face of an amused man in gray clothes who carried an AK-47 over his shoulder. There was no mistaking that barrel. Formerly British owned, the Barbados Defense Force carried a 9 mm Sterling Bullpup, and weapons of any sort were totally forbidden to anybody else. The Kalashnikov alone showed this man wasn't a member of the Royal Police Force, or a Barbadian soldier. Fair game, then.

"Five bucks?" the man snorted. "Go kiss a monkey."

Then he gasped at the sight of Manning covered with weapons, and swung the AK-47 toward the man. With his pistol rock steady, Manning flipped the Tanto knife forward and the guard gurgled, dropping his weapon to clutch his bloody neck with both hands.

Reaching through the hatch, Manning opened the gate and kicked it aside, sweeping past with the Desert Eagle searching for viable targets. Caught by surprise, a second guard was smoking a cigarette, another was sleeping against the fence, his Kalashnikov resting in his lap. Without hesitation, Manning fired and both men went down, the soft chugs of the silenced Desert Eagle perfectly matching a crashing wave on the nearby shore.

Quickly removing the now useless suppressor and reclaiming his knife, Manning checked the corpses for a radio. The man at the gate carried a Kenwood 400 megahertz portable radio, but it was code locked and useless. With an alphanumeric keypad, the combination possibilities reached into the millions. Impossible to solve in the field. Turning the volume to its lowest setting, Manning stuffed the military transponder into a pocket to monitor the traffic, even if he couldn't understand what was said. A trained ear might be able to learn a lot just from the tones of voice.

Dragging the bodies outside the fence, he put them in the

tall grass and covered the still forms with some camouflage cloth to hide them from a casual search.

Locking the gate behind him, Manning crawled to the edge of the hillock overlooking the Foul Bay Valley, and the old HARP test site. Below him the lush valley spread wide and smooth, the rolling hills on each side resembling a reclining woman. Wild grass and bushes covered the land, with large pieces of rusting machinery and some huge cannons lying impotent on the soil just in front of an escarpment that extended over the churning Caribbean Sea.

The water was crystal clear, the beach composed of glistening white sand. The shoals were filled with black stone columns of irregular shapes, a touch of primordial ugly that only served to heighten the serene beauty of the Barbadian shoreline. Made a hell of a postcard. However, there were no breakers to buttress the island from the raw power of the sea, and the waves rolling in were easily over twenty feet tall, forming the type of tubes that made surfers drool.

Nearby the hillock stood a rusty army air corps pillbox on a thick bed of stained and cracked concrete. The door was lolling open wide, clearly deserted. Manning found nothing inside, no hot soup simmering over a sterno can, not even some MRE packs or a folding canvas chair. Mighty hard digs for the troops. He'd known better in rice paddies during an air strike.

Leaving the antique pillbox, Manning chose a thick clump of grass and lay down to thread a fat coffee-can suppressor into the barrel of his Barrett .50-caliber rifle. Not even Kissinger was able to tinker something that could muffle more than a single thundering round from the sniper rifle. But that was better than nothing.

Levering a round into the chamber, Manning settled down to focus the telescopic sights and adjust for windage and drop. Any moment now all hell was going to break loose. He needed to be ready.

SWIMMING OUT of the murky depths of the Caribbean Sea, four figures slowed as the sound and pull of the surf above made themselves known. The men of Phoenix Force knew they had to be very close to the shoreline to feel the currents so strongly.

Patiently giving Manning enough time to get into position, the team floated in the darkness. They were equipped with strong halogen wands, but those would have given away their position as well as firing off a flare gun.

Heavily burdened with watertight equipment bags, each man was strapped to a SEAL rebreather so there would be no air bubbles rising to betray his location. The team was also wearing what civilians incorrectly called an underwater radio, but what the Navy referred to as a Gertrude, the origin of the feminine nickname lost in the annals of time. The device was actually a modified sonar device, altered to handle the spectrum of human voices for underwater communication. But that wasn't its purpose on this mission. Any such communication could instantly reveal their presence. However, the Gertrude also served to mark the presence of active sonar emplacements searching for invaders. So far, nothing. But they stayed alert; the surf could only cover their presence just so much.

That far from land, jagged piles of limestone and banks of sharp coral filled the shoals. Combined with the hammering impact of the waves on the surface and the riptide, invading from the sea was nearly impossible. But doing the impossible was the team's specialty.

Timing himself to the rhythm of the crashing swells, Encizo kicked to the surface and lifted a compact digital camera out of the water, angling it about, then quickly descended again. Replaying on a swing-out monitor only the size of a matchbook, Phoenix Force briefly reviewed the island launch site.

Old concrete barricades lined the churning shore just

above the tide mark, then there was sheer rock for fifty feet that finally crested with a jutting escarpment that led to the valley beyond. A tough climb.

On both sides of the sloping valley were swells of ground that rose to modest hillocks. Large limestone caves with deep tunnels worn away by the sea over the centuries had been the inexpensive workshops for Gerald Bull and his crew of scientists while they struggled to build the HARP space cannon. A laudable enough idea, even if its use had been eventually perverted by greed and foolish pride.

Bits of wreckage and rusted machinery were strewed across the landscape, the ownership of the defunct equipment legally unclear and politically unwanted, so it was abandoned to nature. Once the very pinnacle of scientific technology, the space cannons were now covered with weeds and bird droppings. Ignored and forgotten.

But not by everybody. There were also a few good views of armed men wearing gray uniforms and carrying AK-47 assault rifles. At last the antiterrorist team could see the face of the enemy. Gray uniforms and Kalashnikovs. For some reason the combination seemed familiar to Encizo, but the man couldn't quite pinpoint where he had seen the combination before. Bosnia maybe, or could be South Africa.

Glancing at his watch, Encizo tapped McCarter, and the Briton started to swim toward the shoreline. Show time.

Hugging the sandy bottom, the team easily maneuvered around the limestone columns and coral only to discover countless unexploded ordnance and core charges from the Martlet projectiles used by SRC and Bull. The scientists had to have just dumped the misfires into the sea, expecting the ocean to consume the nitro-based propellants over time. Bad idea.

Most of the ordnance was rusted through, no more than metal cakes with loose ignition wires swaying like the tendrils of a jellyfish. But others appeared intact, and the team wasted minutes giving those a wide berth. Old bombs were the land mines of the sea, exploding when they felt like it, and there was no predicting what would set them off. Between the limestone, coral and the decaying explosive charges, the mix of science and nature formed a nearly impassable maze, the best of its kind the team had ever traversed.

As the surface waves crashed, the piledriver force pushed them to the bottom, and the divers had to fight the fierce riptide. But as the tide eased for another wave to swell, there was a short span of relative peace and the team used that to race across the intervening distance, only to be battered by another giant wave and forced to repeat the cycle over and over, sometimes only gaining feet.

Slowly the shoals rose below them, and the team turned away from the launch base and continued along the shore until reaching a turbulent patch of white water. Putting their backs to the rock wall, they slipped sideways past the hammering downpour and found relative peace in the lee of a waterfall.

That had been their goal from the start. There was no way to reach the launch site from the sea without being seen, so the team decided to stay submerged all the way. The Foul Bay waterfall was wide and gentle in comparison to most others, splashing off green rocks and several vine-covered ledges in a beautiful display before reaching the warm ocean. The cascading fall also offered a perfect access to the land above. McCarter and the team could only hope the terrorists hadn't discovered the chink in their armor and were prepared for this tactic.

Although hampered by the weight of their rebreathers, the men needed them for the next leg of the journey, and took the additional pounding from the waterfall as they stubbornly found handholds in the rough stone and started climbing the hidden face of the river, masked by the roiling mist. Onward they climbed, but soon the rocks became slick with moss. Time and again they had to scrape the vegetation away to obtain a sure grip, but always managed to stayed submerged and out of sight from the armed guards on the nearby escarpment.

Reaching the middle of the river where the water was the deepest, McCarter was startled and almost lost his footing as a fish slammed onto his shoulder from above. Then James pulled out a piece of stone as he tried to use it for leverage and nearly went tumbling down. But the ex-SEAL stabbed his Randall survival knife into the exposed crack and kept going, carrying the broken chunk until there was nobody below and it was safe to let the rock plummet into the Caribbean.

Shifting from stream to stream, Phoenix Force eventually reached the top, where the force of the river was noticeably lessened and they eased over the crest of the falls. Now the team fought to swim against the currents of the riverbed, arching around the jumbled boulders and tree trunks, until reaching deeper and slower waters.

Once more, Encizo used the digital camera to record the shoreline, and they swam farther upstream until finding a secluded area to leave the river. Wading through the rushes, the men reached dry land and spit out the plastic mouthpieces to turn off their rebreathers. Poised and alert, Hawkins pulled a silenced 9 mm Beretta from a sealed plastic bag and stood guard while the others opened the watertight equipment bags and retrieved their weapons.

Among the many supplies dropped off by the crew of the USS *Yorktown,* aside from the helicopter itself, were some new weapons. Removing a new MR-1 assault rifle, McCarter eased in an ammo clip and then nimbly attached a coaxial cable from the stock of the weapon to his helmet. He tapped on the push-button controls of the assault rifle, and a clear monocle flipped out from the side of his helmet in front of his right eye and became alive with a stark black-and-white picture of the forest, a crosshair centered in the view. As he moved the MR-1, the picture on the monocle changed to whatever the telescopic sight of the weapon was aiming at. McCarter hit another button, and the UV view became the mottled red of infrared, then he tried Starlite. The view became a muted green, with everything basically only a black outline in an emerald field. Everything seemed to be in working condition, no damage incurred from the swim and climb.

Aside from the visual augmentation, this computerized weapon also allowed the soldiers to literally shoot around a corner without exposing any more of themselves than a hand. A bloody great idea if he ever heard one.

In a clearing Hawkins already had assembled the repeater radio, its silver dish antenna unfolded and pointing at the northern stars.

McCarter grunted. That was fast work. If the microwave transmitter was working, then the crew at Stony Man Farm should be able to watch everything seen through the crosshair scope of the MR-1 and record the events. However, with the decreasing number of satellites, McCarter seriously doubted Price and the crew were in silent attendance. He wouldn't depend on any external assistance from the Farm. His team was on its own as usual.

Going deeper into the bushes, the men got ready for battle by removing their flippers and donning black sneakers, then pulled on combat webbing before streaking their faces with night camouflage paint.

"Silent penetration," McCarter directed in a hushed whisper, finding a comfortable grip on the new weapon. "Five-yard spread. Kill on sight."

In a tight formation, the Phoenix Force warriors swept out of the trees, running low to the ground as they crossed the swell of the low hills, then down the other side to reach the valley.

On the point position, Encizo froze and indicated a trip wire running through the weeds. Watching their step, the men went over the obstacle and spread out.

Chatting softly, two guards were standing in the middle of a field. Hawkins moved to the left, and James went to the right. Their silenced guns coughed in the darkness, and the guards slumped to the ground. Kneeling by a groaning man on the ground, James stabbed him directly behind the ear and twisted the blade. The man went limp instantly, not even his last breath sighing as he died. Slice the ganglia, and it was like turning off a light switch. Instant death.

Going to the escarpment, McCarter stayed low in the tufts of weeds, looking for possible danger zones. The limestone caves were clearly visible in the pale starlight, the left tunnel slightly higher than the other, indicating they were a natural formation. Sandbags blocked the entrance on the right, with only a narrow passage for people to get through. The tunnel on the left was blocked solid to waist level. That was the hardsite; any trouble would start from right there.

McCarter froze as a guard walked into view for a moment, then turned and walked back inside only to reappear in less than a minute. A sentry on patrol. With a finger on the trigger, the Briton checked the man's profile in the scope of the MR-1, then slipped into the night. Not yet. But soon.

Spread over the valley was an assortment of different cannons pointing out to sea. In the download from the Farm, the team learned that the five- and seven-inch cannons had been the first built by SRC to test the feasibility of the project. Those were merely Navy ship guns with the barrels cut smooth. Nothing special.

The real space cannon were the sixteen-inchers, one still standing straight upward in its cradle of steel and concrete, and then the big brute lying on the ground. Originally only

400 mm, this version was much larger, and the length of the colossal space cannon was ringed with ferruled supports to reinforce the thick steel to handle the titanic pressures of firing an object hundreds of miles into space. The question was, could it actually do the job, or was this merely another trap from the nameless killers?

A soft grunt in the darkness told of another guard removed by the team. McCarter continued his inspection. Logically enough, the main barrel was in segments, each smaller than the one before, the top division attached with four additional support stanchions to help ride out the muzzle-blast. Hydraulic rods supported the cannon on four sides, and the base rested on wide railroad tracks, to handle the incredible recoil when it originally used conventional chemical propellant. McCarter couldn't imagine what this monster had sounded like in operation. It had to have been louder than the creation of hell.

Thick power cables lined the ground like exposed veins, and McCarter followed those to reach the motor assemblies. Checking the gear housing to move it skyward, his fingers found thick grease and smooth patches. Placing his watch next to the barrel, the magnetic-proof timepiece stopped moving. If the residual field was that strong, there could be no doubt this was the real thing, an O'Neil rail gun launcher. This weapon was no dummy on display—it was live and ready to fire, hidden in plain view for the whole world not to notice.

"We have a bingo," he murmured into his throat mike. "Begin cleaning house."

"Hey! You there, get away from that," a gruff voice snapped, steps coming his way over the grass and loose gravel.

Leveling his MR-1, McCarter stitched the guard across the chest with a burst of 5.56 mm tumblers. But the man only staggered under the impacts, then stood to shout a warning as he clawed to swing around a G-11 caseless rifle slung over his shoulder.

Bloody hell, these buggers weren't just wearing body armor, the Briton observed. It was NATO body armor! He recognized the muffled ting of hardball ammo deflected off the Kevlar-and-titanium sheathing. Nothing Phoenix Force was carrying would penetrate that.

Lowering his sights, McCarter raked the man across the legs with the MR-1 assault rifle. He fell screaming, exposing his throat, and McCarter fired once more, ending the noise.

"Head shots only," the Briton said into his radio. "Repeat, they have Cristat armor. Head shots only. NATO Crisis Status body armor."

Across the way, a guard bent over to fumble with his AK-47, then inhaled sharply and collapsed, his exposed armpit darkly red.

"Armpits are good, too," James said from the darkness. "Kills just as fast."

"Take a knife fighter to know that," Hawkins said from somewhere.

Suddenly bright lights came on from halogen clusters on the side of the hillock, filling the entire valley with deadly illumination.

Caught by the glare, Encizo and Hawkins cut loose with their assault rifles, the rounds shattering the bulbs and returning a blanket of darkness. But then came the familiar sound of a Kalashnikov on full-auto, and the unnerving stuttering hiss of a G-11 caseless rifle. Ricochets crackled off the eight-inch cannon like firecrackers, and the little Cuban popped into view to heave a grenade, and the G-11 stopped. But the AK-47 continued its chatter, several more added their firepower to the defenders and now an alarm started to howl.

From the left tunnel, a man appeared carrying an electric Gatling minigun with a huge ammo reservoir pack strapped to his back and shoulders. The man strode out boldly hosing the area with a barrage of flaming lead, chewing up bushes and cutting down small trees. The spent brass from the ejector port formed a solid line of twinkling gold in the air, arching yards away.

The Phoenix Force warriors hit the dirt and rolled for cover, firing on the move. Releasing the firing handle, the gunman turned around for another sweep with the Gatling, but his head exploded off his neck in a horrid spray of brains and bones. A split second later a rumbling boom rolled down from the hills above.

"Nice shot," McCarter said, working the bolt on his MR-1 to free a jam. The light fifty was on the job.

"On your nine!" Manning commanded calmly in his earphone.

Releasing the assault rifle, McCarter rolled over, shooting with his Browning Hi-Power and a guard fell back with most of his face removed.

"Thanks again," he panted, reclaiming the MR-1. The breech was clear now and back in operation. In spite of the amazing computer enhancements, the MR-1 was still only a modified M-16 with all of the weapon's inherent flaws.

Darting out of hiding, a guard rushed across the grass going for the fallen minigun. James and Hawkins tore the fool apart with cross fire, and the Barrett boomed once more, the power pack of the Gatling splattering into a million pieces, instantly making it as dead as its operator.

"So buy me a beer and we're even," Manning said over a crackle of static.

"American or British?"

"Your choice."

"Done."

Dropping a spent clip from the MR-1, Encizo caught a motion and fired his .38 Walther PPK from the hip. Ten yards away, a man with a G-11 jerked as the stock was hit, then was torn apart as the internal caseless ammo block detonated. Slapping in a fresh magazine of brass, he moved on, shooting in controlled bursts. He never had liked those caseless guns and now he knew why.

"Alert, trouble in the cave," Hawkins said, emptying his MR-1 at the limestone tunnels.

From their various locations, Phoenix Force saw several men wheel something large up to the sandbag wall, and they ripped off a tarpaulin to expose a Vulcan 40 mm minigun. An enclosed Niagara feed trailed from the breech to out of sight below the defensive wall.

James cursed. The Vulcan was what the Army used to clear landing fields out of the jungle, and it could mow this valley down to bedrock in only seconds. With this kind of weaponry, Foul Bay had to be the main base for the terrorists. The last trace of doubt was gone from his mind.

"Hit the cave!" McCarter ordered, firing the Browning while he used his Gerber knife to slowly saw through a hydraulic hose of the gear housing of the space cannon. Even if they died, this thing wasn't going to be launching any more satellites for quite a while.

Suddenly an outcropping shattered in front of the tunnel, followed by the noise of the Barrett. Another huge bullet smashed the rocky ground in front, but the angle was wrong, and Manning simply couldn't reach inside.

Hoisting a dead man across his back as cover, Encizo raced toward the cave, threw something and dropped. The guards peppered the corpse with return fire when the HE charge bounced off the limestone wall and a fireball exploded in the air, knocking over the sandbag wall, the Vulcan and the guards. Their clothes and hair burning, the guards hit the slope outside and tumbled away.

Then the Vulcan ignited, spitting out a stream of 40 mm shells that lanced across the valley and out to sea for only a heartbeat before detonating, the blast collapsing the front of the limestone cave.

Electrical cables parted, and the siren stopped working. More lights flickered into operation, only to be smashed as quickly as the first set. Gunfire strobed in the darkness, ricochets off the machinery and cannons zinging everywhere. His face a blank mask, a guard walked by with his left arm completely gone, but still firing his AK-47 even as his life poured onto the Barbadian soil. Hawkins wasted a round on the soldier, then James fell, hit in the chest with shrapnel. McCarter's weapon jammed again, and another grenade thundered, throwing out a geyser of dirt. A man screamed, and the true chaos of battle filled the night, the dead and the wounded mixing into a nightmare vision of flame and blood.

Computer Room, Stony Man Farm

LURCHING CONSTANTLY, the crosshair view of the battle was showing on a monitor in the Computer Room.

"We have them on the run," Kurtzman said confidently. "This'll be over in a few minutes."

Hunched forward, as if in the thick of the combat himself, Katz scowled deeply. "Replay that last sequence," he requested urgently. "Now, please!"

"Certainly," Kurtzman said, running ran his hands across the keyboard.

A submonitor rewound the scene to a garble of reversed voices and backward rifle shots, while the main monitor continued with the live feed. In only a few more minutes the terrorists would either be dead, or in custody. The Stony Man team was winning; what could possibly be wrong?

"Freeze right there," Katz ordered, pointing at the picture. "Now check the aperture."

"On it," Tokaido said, fiddling with his console. Moving a cursor, he ran the green outline of a vector graphic around a fallen Kalashnikov rifle, then moved the outline into the muzzle of the huge space cannon to measure the size. Without a known value to measure the barrel against, it was impossible to accurately check the scale.

"That's a regular AK-47, not a carbine," the hacker muttered, playing a duplicate image of the rifle standing on top of itself several times. "So we get a rough diameter of ten feet."

"Ten feet?" Price repeated. "But the hunter-killer satellites we've seen are forty feet across."

"Christ, the aperture is too small," Brognola stated, pushing aside the notes he had been jotting down for the President. "There's no way a cannon that size could have launched the hunters."

"Any chance they sent up pieces and assembled the machines in space?" Tokaido asked hopefully. Machinery wasn't his field.

"None," Price stated flatly. "Nobody has that kind of technology yet. This isn't the real launch facility."

"Oh, yes, it is," Katz declared forcibly. "Check the size of that big limestone stone, the one with the smooth walls."

"Exactly forty feet," Kurtzman answered softly, staring at the video monitor. "The tunnel is the rail gun?"

"Apparently so."

"Can it launch sideways?"

"Yes," Brognola said, feeling his heart pound in his chest. Which meant that Phoenix Force was fighting hard to gain entrance into the muzzle of the biggest gun in existence.

"Patch me through," Price ordered, grabbing a microphone. "Direct transmission, full power."

"That'll reveal our satellite to the enemy," Kurtzman reminded her, establishing the link.

"Can't be helped. Save those men," Brognola ordered,

taking a step toward the monitor as if he could physically help the team.

Tokaido flipped some switches and nodded at Kurtzman. "Go!" the man said, pushing the volume all the way to maximum, but lowering the gain. The transmission might be garbled slightly, but her message should get through.

Knowing only pieces of what she said might get through, Price cut to the gist of the matter. Details could come later. "Phoenix One, this is Stony Base. Retreat, retreat, retreat! The base is a trap! Repeat, the base is a trap!"

That was close enough to the truth to do the job. But as she started to repeat the message, the feed from the battle winked into blackness, as if the outgoing signal had been interrupted by a fantastically powerful magnetic field.

HARP Launch Facility, Barbados

THE MURKY AIR WAS thick with the stink of high explosives and death. Even with the sea breeze, bitter smoke wafted over the burning bodies and blast craters, and the ground was littered with spent brass.

Their weapons still chattering, but far less often, the last of the men in gray were rallying before the limestone hillock. Then the terrorists broke ranks and ran into the large, left-side tunnel, frantically scrambling over the low sandbag wall.

Going to the side of the opening, Hawkins and Encizo put long bursts down the smooth tunnel, the rounds skittering off the walls in a random pattern. A terrorist cried out from a hit, but kept moving.

As the sound of running boots faded quickly, McCarter paused at the sandbags and halted the rest of Phoenix Force from entering. Staying low, he switched the MR-1 to infrared and passed it over the canvas wall. Then he tried UV, but couldn't spot the enemy anywhere in the darkness.

Weird. How could they be running so fast now, when they had been limping on entering the tunnel. It was almost as if they wanted the team to follow, and the Briton was forcibly reminded of the Canadian DEW Line.

"Sniffer," McCarter commanded, pushing the coaxial cable of his weapon out of the way. These new rifles had their uses, but were rather cumbersome. He much preferred the simple reliability of a 9 mm Heckler & Koch MP-5.

Shouldering his MR-1, James pulled out the chemical probe and worked the simple controls.

"Clear," he announced, tucking it away once more.

Before he could respond, McCarter suddenly went blind in his right eye, and it took the man a moment to realize his video link with the MR-1 was no longer working. Yanking the cable loose, he tossed the computerized helmet away. That was when he noticed the rest of the team was doing the same thing. The short hairs on his nape rose at the sight of everybody's computer crashing at the exact same instant.

Suspicious, McCarter glanced at his watch and saw the liquid crystal face was blank, exactly as it had been near the space cannon. A major magnetic field was in effect, and the tunnel seemed to swell in his field of vision as the awful truth hit the soldier like a heat-seeking missile.

"This is the launcher!" McCarter shouted, knowing the radio would be as useless as the rifle computers near a charging rail gun.

The dire words galvanized the team members into a swift retreat, but they only got a few yards before a silent explosion of sand blasted into them with jackhammer force, painfully throwing the men to the ground. Loose wreckage and spent brass billowing in the air, a powerful wind pulled more than pushed them across the valley toward the escarpment. Rolling helplessly, the Phoenix Force warriors dropped their rifles and grabbed for the power cables snaking through the shaking grass. More than once they were hit by windblown trash, but the men hung on tight and rode out the howling hurricane, their bodies lifted up and suspended off the eroding soil.

His hair whipping about in stinging force, McCarter faced the sea and saw a dark spot disappear into the distance, steadily rising as the world rotated out from under the flat trajectory of what resembled a hurtling sphere.

"Son of a bitch," Hawkins gasped as the wind began to ease and they dropped to the ground. "Son of a bitch!"

"That was a hunter!" James added, panting for breath.

Releasing his grip on a power line, McCarter was forced to agree. No wonder nobody had ever spotted a launch. The rail gun generated so much speed the satellite had to go supersonic before leaving the end of the barrel. That would explain why there was no sonic boom as it crossed the threshold of Mach 1. The terrorists could launch the armored satellites during a parade and, aside from the brief wind, unless a person was looking in the correct direction, nobody would ever be the wiser.

"Rafe, go back to the river and get the reserve satchel charges!" McCarter commanded, climbing shakily to his feet. "We're going to blow the launcher apart!"

"Check," the stocky man replied, and started to head out when shots rang out.

Phoenix Force pulled out handguns as two men in gray appeared on top of the limestone hillock and pointed assault rifles at them. With no possible cover available, the men were sitting targets.

But even as McCarter swung his Browning upward, the chest of the first terrorist exploded outward, the grisly debris knocking the other guard off the hill. Yelling, he fell until landing sideways across the rusty barrel of the ancient HARP cannon, the crunch of the impact removing any possibility he might survive.

Close by, the freshly cropped weeds still vibrated from the violent passage of the armored satellite.

Waving a thanks to Manning on the distant cliff, McCarter next pointed at him, then at the cave. He knew the sniper would understand. Now with Manning covering the hill from afar, the team members recovered their weapons and brought back the satchel charges. After gathering fingerprints and some personal items from the corpses, McCarter and Hawkins filled the openings with gunfire to discourage any more action by the terrorists while James and Encizo armed the C-4 and tossed the canvas packs into the damaged cave and the disguised launcher. Then they added a mixed bag of grenades and ran for safety.

Quickly retreating over the low hill, the team barely dropped out of sight when the satchel charges detonated, the multiple explosions finishing the job started by the detonating Vulcan. Then secondary blasts began from underground, and the entire valley shook as the hill collapsed in upon itself, spewing out a great cloud of swirling dust.

After waiting to make sure the destruction of the facility was complete, Phoenix Force started up the hill to rendezvous with Manning and drive the rental car back to the airport. The SeaHawk was waiting for them in a private hangar.

However, the victory carried the taste of ashes, and their next move was unclear. Without a working radio link to Stony Man Farm, there was no way for the men to know if this action had put an end to the matter. Were the hunter-killers still attacking in space or not? Was this the main headquarters for the terrorists or just a secondary base?

Only time would tell.

CHAPTER FOURTEEN

The Atlantic Ocean

The bridge of the U.S. Navy aircraft carrier *Kitty Hawk* was in turmoil with officers shouting orders while the colossal warship steamed for South Carolina at her best speed.

A stiff wind was blowing, throwing whitecaps at the armored bow of the carrier. But pushed by four propellers as large as houses, the three-foot-thick hull smashed the ocean aside as if the crashing waves were only ripples on a pond.

A hundred feet below the bridge, ratings struggled on the mist-slick main deck to get battle ready, tying down loose hoses and manhandling an F-18 Hornet onto the port-side elevator to get the jetfighter safely into the hangar below.

On the bridge a low bank of controls edged the windows, and ratings working the controls in hushed whispers. Moving steadily, a dozen wipers kept a clear view of the main deck of the Navy leviathan and the surrounding ocean.

"So, is anything working?" Captain Randolph Mac-Pherson demanded, pushing back his duty cap.

"Every onboard system, aye, sir," a sailor replied from a complex console, the blinking lights covering the man in a rainbow of information. "Radar is working, sonar is A-1, main computer is go, internal phone lines and radios are green. We just don't have any working links to any of our satellites."

"How is that possible?" Cos Fontaine, the executive officer, demanded. The man actually seemed to radiate an aura of fury and impatience.

"Unknown, sir," the sailor replied crisply. "I ran a dozen diagnostics and everything seems fine, mechanics and electronics. They're, well, just not there, sir."

Holding on to the chart table with both hands, MacPherson frowned deeply. No link to Atlantic Command, or even the Pentagon. No orbital recon photos, or even a goddamn weather report. What the hell was happening in space? Even the cell phones weren't responding, and those were civilian channels. He already had a double team of techs working on the battery of Tomahawk and cruise missiles so that they could function without trying to autolink to the Navy's navigation satellites for global positioning readings. Without the GPDs working, his ICBMs probably wouldn't be worth a damn over any distance longer than a thousand miles, but with the SeaSparrow armed and ready, by God his ship would at least be able to defend itself if nothing else.

"You there, bos'n," the captain said, reaching into his pocket and withdrawing a ring of keys. He selected one and passed it to the waiting man. "Go to my cabin. In my closet you'll find a rosewood box. There's a sextant inside—bring it here on the double."

"A sextant, sir?" the sailor asked askance, then saw the expression on the captain's and saluted. "Yes, sir! Right away, sir. Five minutes."

As the sailor dashed from the bridge, the XO scowled. "Is that really necessary, Captain? We can compensate for the drift factor on our charts."

"Not for long," MacPherson replied, glowering at the chart table. "After a few days we'll start to lose our bearings. Even a two percent drift every fifty nautical miles will compound in a few days."

"Do you remember how to operate a sextant, Randy?" the executive officer whispered, stepping closer to his friend. "It's been a million years since the academy."

"Going to find out soon enough," MacPherson replied, tightening the hands behind his back. "We have to know where the hell we are. Sky is clear enough to shoot the sun. Why shouldn't it work?"

The XO could only shake his head in reply. The *Kitty Hawk* cost half a billion dollars and had taken five years to build, she held a crew of five thousand men and five hundred women. The ship was so big it had six private TV channels, a bowling alley and movie theater, ninety-six jet-fighters, and she carried enough nuclear firepower to challenge any nation on Earth. She even had a dozen gas vapor devices on board, the nonnuclear GV superbombs that could level Beijing or Tehran to bare ground in ten seconds. And yet this technological marvel of the twenty-first century was now reduced to a five hundred-year-old, hand-operated optical instrument that Columbus used to get lost and discover America. Swell. Go Navy.

Suddenly a radar operator glanced up from his glowing screen. "Sir! I think we have an incoming plane!"

Puzzled, MacPherson glanced out the windows of the tower. "Think?" he repeated in a dangerous voice. "You don't know for sure?"

"No, sir. I can't see the plane, but I have a good lock on its exhaust," the sailor said, then added. "Well, something is behind it. Could be a major fuel leak."

That was bad for any aircraft. "Can't be one of ours," the captain stated. "We don't have anything flying at the moment. Duty officer!"

"Nothing that I know of, sir," the lieutenant replied crisply, checking the flight status board. All of the lights were red or yellow, no green for a live flight. "Should I check with the air boss?"

"What's its origin?" Fontaine demanded, looking over the shoulder of the radar operator.

"Unknown, sir," the man replied, stroking the screen controls. The luminous arm of the main radar swept the grid of the monitor, leaving a clear field, then an irregular wiggle appeared. Tiny letters and cryptic numbers appeared around the moving dot, giving angle and speed. "I can't see the craft, sir, but yes, that is a fuel-loss trail and a big one! Whatever the craft is, it's coming in hot!"

MacPherson sighed. Shit. A damaged aircraft of unknown origin. This day was just getting better ever minute.

Going to the starboard window, the XO grabbed a pair of field glasses from a convenient stanchion and swept the sky in the designated approach zone. "Found it, skipper," he announced calmly, then excitedly added, "Jesus H. Christ, that's an F-22!"

At the chart table, MacPherson glanced over a shoulder. "A Raptor? Impossible!"

The XO passed over the Navy glasses and the captain adjusted the focus for a moment until finding the correct range on the tiny dot. Good God, it was a Raptor. Those weren't supposed to go on-line for years. Where had it come from? The craft was also in bad shape. Most of the fuselage was covered with burn marks, the canopy seemed to be cracked and something was leaking out the dead port engine vector. Fuel, oil, made no difference, the aircraft had been in some sort of a battle and gotten its ass kicked. Just amazing that it was still airborne.

"Tell the pilot to circle for another approach," MacPherson snapped, lowering the glasses. "The landing area isn't clear. We have Hornets on deck."

"No fuel, sir," a radio operator said, a hand holding part of a set of headphones to his ear. "There's a lot of static. He says he has to land now, or will have to scuttle. Pilot requests the immediate insertion of a SEAL team to attempt a rescue.''

Underwater? In that condition that fighter would sink faster than a free anchor. No way the SEALs could reach and extract the pilot before he dropped so deep the water pressure reached killing levels.

"Tell him to eject," Fontaine ordered.

"Malfunction, sir. He's already tried. Battle damage."

That settled the matter. "Sound the alarm," MacPherson ordered grimly. "Clear the deck. Emergency crash procedures, now!"

Sirens began to howl on the flight deck, warning of an incoming craft in critical shape.

SHOUTING DIRECTIONS on his throat mike, the air boss had ratings scramble off the flight deck while a Hummer roared into action and slammed into the side of an F-18 Hornet. The ten-million-dollar fighter crumpled like tin from the impact, the hull buckling and ripping apart as the Hummer brutally shoved the aircraft sideways across the deck with tires squealing. At the safety line, the Hummer stopped and the destroyed Hornet kept going to tumble over the side and down ten stories before hitting the ocean with a tremendous splash.

As the F-18 started to sink, an MP set the fuse on a satchel charge and tossed over the plastique. The canvas charge landed on a wing, and the impact set off the blocks of C-4, the blast ripping the Hornet apart. That was standard procedure to make sure the weapons and technology in the fighter craft couldn't be recovered by anybody else.

Two other F-18s successfully made it to the elevators and dropped from the sight, but an F-16 Falcon also went over the side, pushed there by the Hummer and bare hands.

By now the Raptor was visible in the sky with bare eyes,

and the interceptor was clearly struggling to keep an even keel as it did a final approach for the pitching deck.

"Landing area is clear!" a bos'n announced breathlessly. "Nets are raised, fire crews ready with foam, medics from sick bay are on the way."

"Better be worth it," the air boss growled, covering his throat mike with a hand to mask his comments. "That was twenty million dollars of taxpayers' money that just went into the drink, and it's my ass if this is a joke by the Marine Corps or something."

Dropping from the sky, the Raptor went out of sight below the main deck, then rose again, one wing dangerously tilted. It was obvious to the trained deck crew that the airfoils weren't working properly. Plus the single engine was sputtering and waning, oil mixing with the fuel and clogging the injectors. If the pilot lowered his speed enough to land, the engine would choke and possibly catch on fire. If not, he wouldn't be able to safely land on the 120 feet of available space on the deck. Too fast and he might go through the crash net and right over the end to his death.

"Come on, baby," a rating called out, gesturing the craft closer. "You can do it!"

As the craft slowly came closer, matching pitch and yaw with the *Kitty Hawk*, the crew clenched fists and several started to pray. The winds were pushing the F-22 away, and the craft itself was fighting the pilot's control. But the man stubbornly fought the weather and gained another few yards. The pilot was either a master aviator or the luckiest son of a bitch on Earth just to get this far.

"He's not going to make it," the air boss roared into his throat mike. "Flight Control, activate the PAL, mode one!"

"We already tried, sir," a woman replied brusquely. "But our equipment isn't configured for the craft. Technically the thing doesn't exist yet."

"Shit!"

"Our feelings exactly, sir."

A thousand feet away, a SeaHawk helicopter lifted off the secondary landing deck near the M-60 cannons, the SEALs sitting on the side already dressed in full scuba gear ready to make a try in case the plane hit the water.

Then in a rush of power, the Raptor darted forward against the wind and hovered for a split second above the listing deck. The ocean lifted the ship slightly, closing the gap between the two crafts, and the pilot simply turned off his engine.

Powerless, gravity reclaimed the metal, and the stealth fighter dropped ten feet to the deck onto a thick bed of flame-retardant foam. In spite of the cushioning, the Raptor hit hard, the undercarriage snapped off, both wings buckled and a thousand ceramic tiles sprinkled from the damaged hull.

Instantly rescue crews in silvery fireproof suits swarmed over the craft, hosing every inch with more foam while ratings slammed a ladder onto the fuselage alongside the cowling and crudely used crowbars to rip the canopy away.

"Are you okay, sir?" a rating asked, throwing a silvery fire blanket over the pilot and helping him down onto the slippery deck.

"Sure," Jack Grimaldi said, pushing off the blanket and removing his dented helmet. There was no danger of an explosion from the Raptor. He had been riding on fumes for the last hundred miles. "Give her a good wash, rotate the tires and fill it with unleaded. You take American Express, right?"

"Pilots," the air boss muttered in exasperation as the Raptor disappeared under a rising mountain of foam "They're all crazier than Alabama bedbugs in June."

"Hey, boss! Where's your CO?" Grimaldi demanded walking stiffly across the deck. The gel-pack seat and

DeCamp pressure suit had taken the brunt of the damage from the gravity pulls, but he still felt bruised to the bone.

"Right here," Captain MacPherson said, rising into view on an elevator. "Now, who the hell are you and what are you doing on my ship!"

"Sorry, sir. But you're not cleared to know what I'm doing here," Grimaldi said quickly. "However, what I need is another plane to continue my journey."

"Another plane," the captain said, his only external reaction to the statement the slow raising of an eyebrow.

"Sir, with the present communications situation, you have only two choices," Grimaldi said, looking the man in the eye. "First, I honestly am on a mission of the utmost urgency. Or secondly, I am the worst thief in the history of the world."

"Come again?" MacPherson grunted.

"I want to trade an experimental prototype stealth jet worth an easy hundred million dollars for anything you got that can carry enough fuel to get me to Gitmo. Maybe an F-14 Tomcat, no missiles or bombs, just fuel pods. Hell, an F-101 Delta Dagger would do if you happen to have one in mothballs."

"Guantánamo Bay, Cuba?"

Wiping foam off his flight suit, Grimaldi shrugged. "Bad weather made me miss NASA Space Center in Florida. I figure Gitmo is close enough to use as a refuel point to get me—" He stopped talking. The Stony Man pilot was tired, but not that much.

"Where?" the captain demanded, fists resting on hips.

Grimaldi shook his head. He had been tempted to say Walt Disney World, but this naval officer obviously possessed no sense of humor. Had to be an academy graduate.

"Cut the crap, son. You want to tell me what is really going on?" MacPherson demanded gruffly.

"Sure do, but can't," Grimaldi said honestly. "But I can

tell you this—you're helping to fix the problem. How's that?''

In spite of a gut feeling to trust the bold pilot, Mac-Pherson titled back his cap. "Sorry, but that is nowhere near good enough," he growled, and motioned a finger at the air boss.

The man nodded and touched his throat mike. A hundred feet away, two Marines in full combat rig started forward with a grim stride, each with an M-16 carbine and a holstered PDW on his hip. But just then from the base of the conning tower, a communications technician burst onto the deck and dashed past the armed guards at a full run, one hand holding on to his cover for dear life. Lose that hat and it came out of his pay.

"Okay, listen up, hotshot," MacPherson growled. "Since I don't know what or who you really are, the brig isn't an option. But you aren't getting another bird to leave the ship unless the President orders me to do that personally. You got that, mister?''

"Captain! Sir!" the rating shouted over the low wind and saluted with the hand holding a folded piece of paper, then quickly thrust it at the officer. "Here, sir. Top priority from Atlantic Command!''

"Something got through?" the captain said in amazement, unfolding the paper. "It was a tight beam from a SkyWatch, relayed from D.C.''

The officer tried not to show that he was stunned. D.C. sent him a message through a SkyWatch? What was it, the end of the world? Ripping open the red seal on the security envelope, the captain read the transmission twice, even though once had been enough. The message was terse and left absolutely nothing to the imagination or personal interpretation.

Looking up, the CO waved off the guards, who stopped

exactly where they were and waited, poised and ready in case the skipper changed his mind. From this range, even with the rolling of the deck, both Marines knew for a fact they could drop the stranger with a single round should it be necessary. This was a maneuver the security teams practiced often. Fighting on dry motionless land was child's play compared to a gun battle at sea.

"Well, Admiral Stone," Captain MacPherson said slowly, stuffing the paper angrily into his pants pocket, "exactly what kind of a bird would you like for me to provide for you, sir?"

Arizona

APACHE GUNSHIPS rose over the horizon and swept the deserted testing field of the Yuma Proving Ground in Arizona. Securing the area from above with electric Vulcan miniguns, paratroopers descended on lines and hit the ground running, their MR-1 carbines locked and loaded in less than a heartbeat.

Spreading out in a standard recon pattern, the men found nothing at the weedy HARP site, only sagging buildings, an empty lab and a rusted cannon no longer mounted vertically, its corroded barrel filled with mice droppings and beer bottles.

Again and again the scenario repeated itself across the nation as Army Reservists and police SWAT teams investigated every known location of Gerald Bull HARP cannons, from Livermore Base in California to Wollop Island, Florida. Although ready for more traps, instead they found nothing at all, and dutifully reported the lack of information to FBI agents who went away to relay the information to the Justice Department.

Where the data went from there was anybody's guess.

Stony Man Farm, Virginia

STROLLING DOWN the corridor, Katz met John Kissinger. The gunsmith was heavily armed, wearing a combat rig of two shoulder holsters attached to a belt of ammo clips. The checkered grips of a long-barrel revolver and a large automatic jutted low and loose for fast access. Damn, the Farm had to be on full alert. Something important had to have happened in the past few minutes.

"Hal's here," Kissinger said as a greeting. "He's with Barbara in the office. Came with some sort of sealed orders from the White House."

"War orders, probably," Katz said. "Any word on Able Team yet?"

"They faxed in some serial numbers and fingerprints about ten minutes ago," he replied, heading for the tunnel that led to the Annex. "Bear is running them personally."

"Good. Do they know about the corpse?"

Kissinger stopped and frowned. "I sure don't. Who's dead?"

"The report came in a little while ago. They found a Marine corporal from the DEW Line. The Potomac River patrol found the body floating in a sewer. He had been tortured by somebody who knew what he was doing. A real pro."

Kissinger knew that the Marine had to have talked. Anybody would, given enough pain.

"How old was the corpse?" the big Texan asked, the muscles in his jaw ticking from his controlled rage.

"Hours, a day at the most."

"Then the bastards are local," Kissinger said, feeling a rush of adrenaline.

"Looks likely," Katz agreed.

Yeah, there was no way a corpse could have floated from Thunder Bay, Ontario, down to the D.C. area in a day. Or ever, for that matter. There was no direct waterway to the sea. The soldier had been brought down here for an interrogation, and then dumped afterward.

Footsteps sounded on the stairs and Tokaido came into view, chewing bubblegum and riffling through a stack of rock music CDs with garish covers.

"Hi. We found them," he said, ambling past.

Katz took the young man by the arm. "Found whom?" he demanded.

"Them, the terrorists," Tokaido said calmly, as if this were old news. "Carmen crunched the data from Able Team and found that several of the men listed sizable donations to the Peace Brigade on their income taxes."

"The Peace Brigade is destroying the satellites?" Kissinger said slowly, crossing his arms. "They're just some environmental group."

Katz said, "Sure you don't mean the Soldiers of Earth? They're the militant group."

"Nope. I handled the field data from Phoenix Force. The Kalashnikovs were listed as stolen, the credit cards were fakes, but all of the men they fought in Barbados were already registered as dead. Been dead for years, real black-bag stuff. So I hacked their income-tax records and there it was again, donations to the Peace Brigade. Several were even listed as members."

"Well, I'll be damned," Katz said softly.

The cyber expert tilted his head. "We didn't need to run a statistical-probability program to know that was bull. The brigade is much too small for this to be a coincidence. They're not freaking Greenpeace with tens of millions of registered members around the world. Statistically these two groups both having members in the brigade was flatly impossible."

"Unless the group was involved somehow," Kissinger finished for him.

"Yep. So now we know."

Then the young man frowned. "Several of them also have extensive military training. Not all of it here."

"Mercs?"

"South Africa mostly. Departed when Mandela became president."

The two men were silent for a moment.

"Mercenaries that fled South Africa when it became a democracy," Katz said aloud in growing concern.

Was Stony Man facing members of the infamous Johannesburg secret-police death squads? The forensic report did say that the Marine corporal had been tortured by experts. That was what the South African termination units specialized in, unspeakable acts of torture and mass murder. Every one of them was under a standing international death warrant for countless war crimes.

"Christ, the Peace Brigade is staffed with a death squad," Kissinger muttered. "Our people may need some backup with these bastards."

"We have the blacksuits stationed here for just this reason," Katz said grimly. "How far away is the headquarters of the brigade?"

Tokaido shrugged. "Some skyscraper in Delaware," he said. "Able Team is already on its way to talk to the person in charge."

"A man named Major Sebastian Cole."

CHAPTER FIFTEEN

Compose Base, off the Northern Coast of Brazil

On the sunny sandy coast of northern Brazil was a small isolated patch of grass where once jungle ruled supreme. A wide assortment of brick buildings dotted the smooth landscape of Compose Base, and along the shoreline were three launch pads, simply gantry-and-concrete-pad affairs. Two were occupied by conventional rockets, prior experiments momentarily forgotten to accommodate the great white shuttle filling the middle position. The *Olinda* stood waiting impatiently on its array of solid-fuel and booster rockets, wisps of steam and frozen air escaped from the umbilical cords of the stout craft as they were released and tank pressures hastily equalized. Time was of the essence, and safety checks were being conducted with all of the care the brutal launch schedule allowed. Minutes were tight, but Launch Control assured everybody that they had more than enough.

Ahead of the base, a school of flying fish broke the surface of the ocean, their wings sparkling like jewels in the sun. Behind the largest of the brick structures, towering above the jungle growth in the distance, could be seen an imposing line of huge dish antennae. Some spun about wildly on their posts scanning the horizon for dangers. However, a few seemed frozen in a vertical position, their powerful radar beams locked on the distant sky above. A fortune to be made and lives to be saved were a powerful combination that the Brazilian space administration couldn't allow to be ignored.

"Shuttle, you are ready for liftoff," a voice said in the ear mikes of the six crew members on board the gleaming craft.

"On internal power," Dr. Henretta Montenegro announced. Her trained hands flipped switches above, in front and alongside her position in the cockpit.

The voice spoke again. "Begin preflight sequence now."

Adjusting dials and checking endless meters, Colonel Adolfo Lars, the pilot, responded, "Affirmative, base. On the mark of five...four...three..." The great ship trembled slightly in accompaniment to a soft rumble, the sound of twenty-five gallons of cryogenic fuel burning per second.

"We have main engine started," the captain stated calmly. "In three...two...one...ignition!"

Thundering flame washed from beneath the shuttle, pressure increased toward the millions of tons and the gantry safeties released. Pressurized fuel hoses cut their flow and snapped away to be disintegrated in the fiery wash. The guy wire parted like a gossamer thread, and like a graceful tiled dove, the *Olinda* and her booster tanks lifted majestically off the concrete launch pad.

"Shuttle, you are clear of the tower," a faceless tech reported to the crew.

"Confirmed, base," Dr. Montenegro acknowledged, crushed flat into the acceleration couch. "Beginning roll."

But the craft traversed only a few meters before Klaxons sounded in the underground control booth, the noise oddly echoing over the earphones of the shuttle crew.

"Alert! Abort! Shuttle abort!" a technician screamed over the radio. "Main boosters have broken loose!"

"It's too late to abort!" The captain cursed, flipping

switches with a hand that seemed to weigh a ton. "Blow the seals and we'll head to sea!"

There was no reply as frantic technicians at control boards reacted with lightning speed to free the shuttle, but a vibrating booster slammed into the main cluster of aft vectors, knocking a pump off-line. The underheated liquid oxygen pooled for a microsecond, which choked the combustion chamber solid.

A heartbeat later a fireball engulfed the South American base with disastrous results. The blast lit up the sky for miles, and shrapnel peppered into the Atlantic Ocean clear to the horizon, slaughtering hundreds of parrots and monkeys in the mainland jungle.

To many of the local inhabitants and tourists, the explosion sounded like the end of the world.

Stony Man Farm, Virginia

"WELL, I'LL BE damned," Hal Brognola said, finally lowering the sheet of computer printout.

Reclining in her office chair, Barbara Price agreed and crossed her legs at the ankles. "Hunt found it on a hidden Web site on the Internet. It is the manifesto of the Peace Brigade. Their real one, not that flowers-are-nice-please-stop-littering crap they post on their public site. This is for members only. It took Hunt an hour to gain access."

"Their encryption is that good?"

The woman nodded. "Best he's seen since Shatterstop. Very advanced stuff. There were lots of other things there, too, such as basic gun handling and how to make thermite bombs, then hide them from sniffers by using cans of metal-based paint."

Just what the world needed, the big Fed thought, another Web site packed with details on how to be a terrorist. He truly believed in the First Amendment. Freedom of speech was one of America's greatest liberties. But he personally considered such Web sites as this the equivalent of yelling "Fire" in a crowded theater. Being able to speak your mind, and deliberately inciting murder were two very different things. Why couldn't Congress see that and shut these bloody sites down?

Brognola glanced at the crumpled sheet of paper in his fist again. The incredible part was that these high-orbit attacks may very well be conducted by the Peace Brigade. The gist of their rambling lunacy was that the group were technophobes who hated machines and wanted to return the world to a simpler way of life. They firmly believed that humanity would soon completely destroy itself in a nuclear war, so the members had taken a blood oath to bring the war early, before the military was fully ready, and thus make sure some small percentage of humanity lived through the coming holocaust.

This Major Sebastian Cole and his mercs were the heart of the brigade, but the whole organization was composed of fanatics on a holy mission, using the very technology they detested to get the dirty job done.

"Where did they get the financing for all of this?" Brognola demanded, crumpling the sheet and throwing it into the trash bin. "Mercs, weapons, armored satellites. I've seen their 1040 forms. They're poorer than church mice after Lent. So are they running drugs or guns?"

"They buy guns, not sell them," Price corrected. "Carmen is already working on the bank records for the brigade, and for Cole personally. Nothing yet, but who knows? Maybe a member won the state lottery and turned it over to the group. Stranger things have happened."

"Not lately," Brognola replied, running stiff fingers through his hair. "Keep her on it day and night."

"I don't think I could stop her if I wanted to," Price stated. "When was the last time you got some sleep?"

"Seems like last year." The man sighed from his soul.

Standing, Price took his arm and herded her friend toward the couch. "Grab an hour. I'll let you know if anything happens."

Brognola sat and found the cushions remarkably comfortable. But then, he would probably enjoy napping on a slab of cold marble at that point.

"Thirty minutes," Brognola said, loosening his necktie. "No more."

"Forty-five."

"Deal."

Just then, the intercom squawked, and Price returned to the desk and hit a button.

"Price here," she said, placing both hands on the desk to lean over the device.

"Hey, Barb," Kurtzman said, a crinkling noise in the background as the man unwrapped something in plastic. "I'm the Computer Room, and we found the rail gun cannon."

"You mean the launcher for the satellites?" Brognola demanded, wearily standing. His posture slowly straightened as strength seemed to flow back into his form by sheer force of will.

"Affirmative. Big mother, too."

"On our way," Price said, and released the switch.

A few moments later the pair entered the Computer Room and stopped. Every wall monitor was showing a fast-moving series of jerky views of the ocean from various angles. The effect was extremely disorienting, and they turned their faces away from the wild kaleidoscope of pictures.

"Sorry," Kurtzman said, hitting a switch and freezing the monitors. "I forget that bothers some people. Anyway, I was reviewing the video feed from Phoenix Force, when I noticed this."

A monitor shifted to a view of the space cannon pointing

out to sea, then the body of the dead guard fell onto the barrel with grisly results.

"The weeds," Price said angrily. "The damn weeds are shaking!"

"No way that could be unless this was the first satellite they launched," Brognola stated. "Damnation, we've been tricked again. This isn't their main launch facility, just a dummy to divert us away from the real rail gun."

Once more Kurtzman worked the controls. "That was my opinion. Now, earlier today Yakov had suggested that from a tactical standpoint, the best location would be here," the man said, moving a laser pen and a circle of white appeared around the Caribbean Sea and northeastern South America. "This was the initial strike zone. With the least number of operating spy satellites in the sky, that zone would have the lowest chance of anybody finding them."

"Makes sense," Brognola said, going to the coffee station to pour himself a mug of coffee. "Also near the equator, which makes for an easier launch. Less distance to space."

Tokaido blinked in surprise, then looked at the Justice Department executive with new respect. Most impressive.

"That's still a lot of area to search," Price said in an exhausted tone.

"Bet your ass it is," Kurtzman agreed, moving the laser pen about. "Anyway, it occurred to me that the brigade must have spent a fortune on the fake site, so I decided to try something unusual."

"So where is the real rail gun?" she asked.

"I'm getting there—just want to see if you agree with my conclusion," Kurtzman said.

"Accepted. Go."

"Well, first I removed any high-density locations, known friendly military bases." The circle became splotchy with marked-out zones, most of the remaining open area was at sea.

"So it is in the general area of Barbados," Brognola said, sipping the scalding brew. "Maybe we were just on the wrong island. Lots of them there."

"No, I believe that's a dead end. I went through every inch of the video recorded by the MR-1 rifles of Phoenix Force and found nothing else of importance in the background." He paused. "On the land, that is."

"A ship?" Price said in disbelief. "You thought they might have been watching the fight?"

"Why not a ship? A magnetic rail gun has no recoil, and the brigade can't communicate with each other over the horizon any more than the rest of the world. If they tried to relay a signal off one of their hunters, we'd blow the damn satellite out of space and then nuke them in minutes. Secrecy is the only real armor they have."

"They were there," Brognola said as a fact. "Arrogant bastards."

"It was a critical mistake of judgment," Kurtzman agreed, twirling a dial. A picture from the scope of an assault rifle in motion appeared on a monitor. The crosshairs were sweeping away from a man with a spray of blood frozen in midair, his face only starting to register the hit. Behind him was the beach and a lot of empty ocean.

"What's the resolution?" Price asked, squinting. She was unable to see anything important, yet it must be there or the Farm's cyber team wouldn't have called her and Brognola in to see.

"One for one," Kurtzman said, adjusting the controls. "Now take a look at five hundred to one."

The scene blurred and now showed only discolored squares that vaguely resembled the horizon of the sea with some sort of dark blob in the middle.

"Hunt and I ran some enhancement software, added a

few million pixels and got this," the man announced, and the view clarified into a picture of a cruise liner moving along the horizon.

"So?" Brognola demanded, placing aside the cup. "There are hundreds of those near Barbados. It's one of the top vacation spots in the world."

"Number seventeen, I checked," Kurtzman stated, using the laser pen again to frame the bow of the vessel. That swelled to fill the monitor, and the view blurred once more into a string of letters only barely readable.

"The ship is the *Terra Nova*," he announced. "Built and registered out of Havana, Cuba. And it stopped accepting reservations from tourists over five years ago."

"New Earth," Brognola translated from the Latin, feeling a sudden chill in the room. "Okay, now you have my full attention. This is one hell of a coincidence, but it still proves nothing."

"Really? Then watch this," Kurtzman replied, and gestured at Tokaido. "I pulled the blueprints for the ship from the Cuban naval registry and got this."

Chewing his gum steadily, the young hacker typed in some commands on his keyboard and the monitor split in two, the new division showing only solid blue with white lines precisely detailing the construction design for a cruise ship.

"And?" Price demanded, then came alert. "The smokestacks!"

"There are only two in the blueprints," Brognola said excitedly, jerking his head toward the view from the Phoenix Force assault rifle. "But there it has three!"

"With no thermal pattern. In fact it registers as cold."

"The rail gun," Price said softly, her hands clawing the top of the computer console.

Kurtzman nodded. "We can arrive at no other possible function."

"No way Castro and his bunch are behind this," Brognola stated. "This is another blind end."

Kurtzman grinned. "Smart man. The ship was built ten years ago in Cuba, but the vessel operates out of Miami and is owned by the Tansnadar Corporation, home office Johannesburg, South Africa. The CEO is a Mr. Umbata Ziferra."

Then Kurtzman wheeled his chair around to see their faces. "But according to the *Wall Street Journal,* the chief stockholder of the Tansnadar Corporation is one Major Sebastian Cole, formerly of the South African special forces. Now retired."

Bolting from her seat, Price moved to the nearest console and hit the intercom. "Communications!" she barked. "Tell Able Team we have target acquisition. Sebastian Cole is the man behind the attacks. Get him and those nonfiring ID codes at any cost!"

"Don't know if I can, Barbara," the man replied. "The shortwave radio is jammed with as much traffic as the landlines."

The woman glanced at the ceiling. "Then use our satellite for a direct beam down to the D.C. area. Then contact Phoenix and tell them to find that ship and seize control of the hunters. If that isn't possible, then just sink it. Cruisers can't move very fast, so it must still be in the general area."

"Confirmed," the man replied and was gone.

"That will reveal the location of our comsat," Brognola said. "Once the brigade discovers they missed one that big, they'll be over it like white on rice."

The woman turned, her face a hard mask. "Good. Then just for once we'll have them right where we want them."

Suddenly several of the submonitors on the console flickered and went out, the glow of the screens fading into darkness.

"The Internet just collapsed," Tokaido announced, removing his hands from the useless keyboard.

"ISP and LAN?" Kurtzman demanded.

Wordlessly Tokaido gestured at the deactivated screen.

Damn, too many relays were gone. Now Stony Man was down to a single communications satellite, and the more they used it, the greater the danger. "So we're blind," Katz stated.

"But not deaf and dumb," Tokaido replied. "Well, not yet."

"How much longer before the U.S. is blind?" Price demanded, a hand still on the intercom. "Before the superpowers start launching missiles?"

"Several hours," Kurtzman said, saving a few files before terminating the link to the Web. "Maybe less."

"Then everything depends on Carl and David," Katz growled. "At least we have the best on our side."

"Always did," Brognola stated, going back for another cup of the powerful coffee. Dawn would arrive soon, and it was going to be either a very long or a deadly short morning today.

Roughly Two Thousand Feet Above Wilmington, Delaware

DAWN WAS JUST BEGINNING to lighten the eastern sky, the sun warming the world as it had for a hundred billion years. But just for this morning, Able Team wished the thing would go away and give them another precious hour of darkness.

With the wind whispering under its wings, the colossal C-130 Hercules was gliding across the brightening sky, its four enormous engines turned off and the props locked to stop any possible noise. A hundred feet away, the rear hatch was fully lowered, offering a splendid view of the city to the three Stony Man warriors as they carefully checked their bundles, packs and weapons. Their fatigues were mottled black and gray, city-style camouflage, their faces striped with the same mix of colors.

Since Grimaldi was somewhere at sea, the team had rendezvoused with another pilot from the Farm in Arlington and raced to Delaware. The flight had been insanity over Washington, D.C., with countless jetliners desperately searching for Dulles Airport so they could land. The ILM and UHF of the control tower were functioning perfectly, but the pilots had to find the airport visually without the GPD working, and that was proving to be a bigger problem than the FAA had ever anticipated.

Sticking his head into view from the cockpit doorway, the pilot looked down the stairs and across the long length of the military cargo plane.

"You folks ready?" the blacksuit called loudly.

"Check!" Lyons shouted over the rushing wind, giving a thumbs-up.

The pilot nodded and leveled the plane, fighting the thermal currents that rose from the sleeping town. Concrete and asphalt made excellent heat traps, and every major city in the world was a trouble spot for airplanes. Especially gliders.

"Wait for it," Schwarz said, checking the rushing cityscape with binoculars, marking landmarks. "Ready... now!"

In unison, the three Stony Man warriors stepped from the plane and hurtled from the sky. Spreading their arms, the men angled away from one another just as they reached the thousand-foot mark, and their backpacks broke apart, huge black silk wings snapping into position.

Using both hands to adjust the guide ropes, the Able Team commandos directed their parawings into a Delta formation and headed across the metropolis toward the rooftop of one particular skyscraper in the middle of town. The Peace Brigade had several storefront operations, mostly for passing out pamphlets and recruiting new members, but the Chester R. Dow Building at Fourteenth and Main was registered as their main office at the IRS, Environmental Safety Council and the state Better Business Bureau.

"That must be it," Schwarz said over a throat mike, pointing with a hand. Their battlefield radios were short range but didn't require satellite relays, which hopefully gave them a major tactical advantage.

"No garden around the middle," Lyons corrected, and released a guide rope to indicate a different skyscraper to their right. "Over there."

"Roger," Blancanales said, and shifted his wing into a gentler angle. In spite of the thermals, they were dropping toward the city with tremendous speed. But that was always the problem with parawing gliders; you wanted to be fast enough to avoid detection, but slow enough to survive the landing.

"Okay, students, don't forget to cross your ankles," Schwarz suggested over the link. "It cushions the force of the landing, and helps to make your skydiving experience a thrill for the whole family."

"Thanks, teach," Lyons snapped, a trace of humor in his voice.

Blancanales grunted a laugh, but then the men went quiet, concentrating on their task. The flight path seemed to be off by several blocks, and a pair of fifty-story buildings rose before them like a medieval barbican, with the rest of the city sanctioned safely beyond.

"Try to bank around!" Blancanales ordered urgently. "The wind shear between those two will tear our wings to pieces!"

"No time," Lyons said, feeling the adrenaline flow. "We're going through!"

Swooping down between the structures, the men saw their distorted reflections in the tinted windows, then the currents hit, buffeting the gliding warriors back and forth. Blancanales lost his grip on the guide ropes, going wild for a few seconds until he reclaimed the lashing rope and fought the wing stable once more.

Then Lyon's wing buckled and he banked hard in the opposite direction, sending himself hurtling toward the mirrored surface until the wing straightened with a snap. Only now the skyscraper rushed toward him like a wall of silver, and the man tasted fear. At this speed even a glancing blow would crush his body to pulp. Pulling both of the ropes hard, he dived downward at maximum angle to build momentum. The wind was shoving him toward the skyscraper, and the big ex-cop fought the deadly drift, knowing that one wrong tug on the trembling ropes and the weakened wing would fold again, leaving him helpless.

The tinted windows of the building filled his view, and for a split instant he could see inside, a pretty redhead yawning and making coffee, then he was past the curve of the structure and riding the open sky once more.

"Target is due south five hundred yards," Schwarz said crisply, as if nothing important had happened. Then added, "That was pretty slick, Carl."

"I like redheads," he growled wearily in reply.

Twilight still covered most of the sleeping city, and the three men dropped into shadow as they sailed closer to the target skyscraper. Details soon became discernible, and the men circled the building a few times to slow their speed, then finally swung down onto the grass-covered roof and arrived standing, running a few yards to stabilize their inertia before collapsing the wings and gathering the material into balls.

Twenty stories below, the concrete maze of Wilmington was alive with car horns, flashing police lights and several small fires. The criminal element of the city had to have discovered that burglar alarms no longer worked and was taking advantage of the situation. Watching the looting through field glasses, Carl Lyons for once approved of crime. It was a perfect diversion to cover their own activities this morning.

Rolling the wings into tight bundles, Able Team stashed them under some of the decorative bushes of the executive garden, then checked the restaurant for any witnesses to their arrival. It was empty, the stoves as cold as the austere customers.

Satisfied for the moment, Able Team pulled out pneumatic guns and loaded them with lengths of flanged steel. Schwarz kicked away the thin covering of dark earth to reach the plastic liner covering the actual roof, while Blancanales slashed the tough plastic exposing the bare concrete underneath. Checking a compass built into his wristwatch, Lyons indicated which side they should use, and the others started sinking pitons into the concrete and expertly attaching long ropes.

This probe had to be fast but quiet. The Peace Brigade was on the fourteenth floor of the Dow Building, but sixty other companies also rented offices here, including Greenpeace. If Major Cole and the brigade had mined their rooms, the potential blast could cut the building in two, sending tons of masonry hurtling at the city. The death toll would be staggering. On top of which, the brigade would be ready for them this time. The mission was dangerous, but there was no other choice. The numbers were falling, and America needed the nonattack codes as fast as possible to stop the hunter-killer satellites in space.

Suddenly Blancanales dived forward and rolled across the garden to stand with a tiny can in his hand. As the video camera swung toward the others, he reached from underneath and covered the lens with black paint.

"That wasn't listed in the building files," Schwarz said, his silenced 9 mm Beretta out and searching for any other surveillance devices. However, the rooftop restaurant seemed to be clear.

"Still don't like it. Double time," Lyons spit, holstering his Colt Python.

Checking the knots on the ropes, the big man slipped one through the climbing harness around his chest and cinched it tight. Then, easing over the edge of the roof, he swiftly descended with one hand holding the rope above to guide the speed, the other below to control the lash of the loose end. Seconds later his teammates followed, the shape of their bodies distorted by the heavy profusion of equipment.

At the fourteenth floor, the trio stopped alongside a carefully chosen window. While Lyons and Blancanales kept watch, Schwarz went to work. Reaching into a pocket on his thigh, he produced a slim cylinder topped with a plastic hose that ended with a long needle.

Still keeping a grip on the ropes, each member of Able Team pulled masks from inside their shirts and placed the filters over their faces. Once done, Schwarz gently pushed the thin needle through the silicon caulking that edged the unbreakable Plexiglas window. According to the federal building codes, any building higher than a few stories had to use Plexiglas, not ordinary glass, in the windows. Not only to resist breakage from storms, but also to prevent somebody from tripping and going through to fall to their death. A simple safety precaution that also seriously hindered burglars. Without using explosives, Able Team needed the window opened from the inside.

As the needle came out the other side, Schwarz turned the valve on top of the canister and a greenish liquid squirted out, quickly spreading into a fine mist before touching the thick carpeting. Rapidly the mist dispersed into an invisible gas, and spread along the corridor, carried by the ventilation system of the building. Room by room the vapor seeped past closed doors with no reactions at first.

Military V-4 or NRX nerve gas could have killed every living thing in the whole building in under five minutes, but that was exactly what the team didn't want. Sleep gas would knock out anybody on the floor, but that also rendered them useless for questioning, as it took hours to wear off. If Major Cole and his mercs were here, Able Team needed them alive and conscious. So they decided to risk trying something brand-new.

This gas tactic was an invention of Schwarz, and he was anxious to see how well it worked in the field. As a child he had learned that cooking gas used in stoves and furnaces was odorless and very deadly, so the gas company mixed another chemical with the fuel to make it reek something awful so customers could instantly smell a leak and run for help. Then one day it occurred to Schwarz if he simply took the pungent chemical and mixed it with plain air, there would be no danger of an explosion, but anybody smelling that famous stink would run far and fast to get clear.

Or to the nearest window to get some fresh air.

When the bottle vented clear, Schwarz tucked the dead container away and settled in to wait. Should be any second now. Another minute passed in silence, then cries of shock began to be heard. Soon a man rushed from a doorway to unlock the window and threw it open, gasping for breath. His face was pale and sweaty, but the man was dressed in gray, with a red beret, and a very illegal Kalashnikov assault rifle slung over a shoulder.

"Hi, there!" Schwarz said from the left side.

Startled, the guard stared at the hanging man, then grabbed for the AK-47 machine gun. Behind him, Lyons slammed the Plexiglas window hard against his head, knocking off the beret. The unconscious guard dropped the weapon and slumped to the floor. With the warming breeze tugging at their fatigues, Able Team slipped into the building and closed the window tight.

Quickly the men adjusted their face masks. The reek in the air was so thick it could actually be tasted, but their masks removed most of the putrid smell. Most but not all.

After binding the wrists of the fallen guard with disposable police handcuffs, the Stony Man warriors moved into the first office to find a dozen guards hanging out of windows fighting to breathe. Startled by the invasion of armed strangers, most of the Peace Brigade started to draw weapons, then realized in horror that a single muzzle-flash could ignite the very air, killing everybody.

Before the guards could decide if that was acceptable or not, Able Team clubbed them down, disarmed the men and bound their hands with more of the plastic handcuffs. Their AK-47 rifles were disassembled and thrown down the garbage chute. Lining the men up in the corridor, Schwarz stood guard while Lyons and Blancanales went into the next office, and then the next. The collection of prisoners grew to almost twenty before Blancanales pulled open the door to the copier room and four guards armed with combat knives rushed out to attack. With no choice he gunned them down with a short burst from his M-16 assault rifle.

The gunfire had a very sobering effect on the others, and the rest of the sullen brigade soldiers offered little resistance as they were herded into the hallway to join the others. Now Lyons stood guard while Schwarz searched the prisoners for any hidden weapons and found a small arsenal of derringers, switchblades and brass knuckles. Street junk, but still deadly. He tossed the concealed weapons into a humming refrigerator full of beer.

"Hey, does that use freon, or EPA-approved ammonia?" Schwarz asked casually, reclaiming his M-16/M-203 from Lyons.

But none of the prisoners rose to the bait, and stiffly stood at attention as if on review, staring hatefully at Able Team.

Looking over their faces, Lyons remembered the driver's-license photo of Sebastian Cole and was disappointed that none of the men even vaguely resembled the leader of the Peace Brigade. It had been only a slim chance they would find him here, but hope springs eternal.

"That's every room," Blancanales said through his mask, stepping into view from a doorway down the hall. "There's nobody else here."

"Bathroom, air vents?" Lyons probed, the words muffled slightly.

"All clear. Also opened some windows."

"Check."

Soon there was a steady breeze blowing through the offices, and the prisoners stood and breathed easier.

"You're not cops or Navy SEALs," a big man stated as a fact. His face was still red from holding his breath against the fake gas, which brought out a network of white scars across his face and throat.

"Smart man," Schwarz stated, making it sound like a bad thing to be.

"So who the fuck are you?"

Lyons gestured with the Atchisson. "In charge," he stated, settling the matter immediately.

The brigade soldier started to answer, then the nearest soldier nudged him with an elbow, and he went back to attention.

With the M-16 steady at his waist, Blancanales studied the line of brigade members, watching their expressions and body language. This was going to be a tough sell. These were fanatics and would never willingly assist them. Able Team had sodium pentathol, the so-called truth drug, but that only worked on frightened people, and then again only about half the time, the befuddled patient often merely giving wild stories without a grain of truth. And these soldiers weren't frightened, but angry and determined. Using the sodium pentathol here would only waste time and accomplish nothing.

Schwarz caught his attention, and Blancanales shook his head. Blast. The team was authorized to use torture, but that was literally the absolute last resort. There were a few tricks to use before the extreme was reached. But not many, and the combat veteran braced himself for the dirty job ahead. Millions would die unless these men talked. That's all there was to the matter.

Lyons fired a round at the ceiling to startle the prisoners, then shoved the hot barrel under the smooth chin of the youngest person there. "Where's Major Cole?" he demanded in a chilling whisper.

For a brief second the teen flicked his eyes at the hallway door in concern, then he got tough. "Somewhere you'll never find him!" he said proudly.

"So you know," Lyons said, shoving the muzzle in just a hair more. "Mr. G, take this terrorist into the next room and get the pliers."

Schwarz started forward.

"No," the teen said softly, going pale with the memory of what he had seen done to the U.S. Marine. "I'll...I'll talk. Please, don't hurt me!"

"Coward!" one of his comrades snarled, the words raspy from the aftereffects of the poisoned air.

The teenager turned to speak, and the red beret spun, kicking the fellow toward Able Team. Caught off guard by the tactic, Lyons instinctively fired at the rushing man, the thunderous discharge of the Atchisson autoshotgun nearly cutting the teenager in two at that range.

"Ask him again," the bound hardman said, sneering, and the others grinned in triumph.

Grabbing his med kit, Blancanales rushed to the fallen man, but it was too late.

Moving around the corpse, a furious Lyons slapped the

handcuffed troublemaker across the face with the stubby barrel of the Atchisson. Staggering from the blow, but not falling, the defiant man stood at attention with a broken nose and spit at the Stony Man operative.

"Come on," he urged, coughing from the trickle of blood in his mouth. "Do it, traitor. Shoot us all. See what that gets ya!"

"Traitors to what?" Lyons demanded, ramming the man in the belly with the Atchisson.

"Traitors to humanity!" the prisoner shouted. "We will fix the world!"

"By killing billions of people?" Blancanales asked in an innocent, almost hurt voice. Good cop, bad cop—if done right, it worked almost every time. All they had needed was an opening, and the death of the young man had given them that.

"Polluters!" the Peace Brigade member snarled in disdain, almost foaming at the mouth. "Rapers of their own Mother Earth! We'll cauterize her wounds with nuclear fire. Billions will die so millions may live!"

"Environmentalists who want to nuke the planet," Schwarz said, shaking his head in disbelief. "Bit of a mix there, don't you think?"

"We kill only to save!" another man added.

Then a different soldier called out, "What we do, we do for the world!"

As if that was a cue, all of the prisoners rushed forward at the same instant.

Retreating from the surge, the Able Team warriors put their backs to the opposite wall and fired some warning shots. However, the brigade members continued to charge the armed men, bound hands clawing for the weapons. Suddenly fighting for their lives, the Able Team warriors waded into the crowd slamming the stocks of their weapons into faces, trying to beat the terrorists into submission. But th brigade fought like madmen, biting and kicking, and the team soon was forced to start shooting.

Even then, the living used the dead as clumsy shields and slammed Lyons against refrigerator and tried to wrestle the Atchisson shotgun from his grip. Utilizing all of his strength, the Able Team leader barely managed to flip the selector lever to full-auto and fire. In a nonstop roar, the shotgun spewed forth its full load of shells in only heart-beats, the rebelling prisoners jerking like mad puppets from the hellstorm of lead. The battle was instantly ended.

"Clear?" Blancanales asked, the double barrels of the M-16/M-203 combo sweeping the floor for targets.

Grimacing, Lyons nodded, "Clear, damn it." With the abrupt turn of events, the team no longer had anybody to question. This mission was turning sour just as fast as the previous one. These weren't soldiers, or even guards, but kamikazes.

"Shit. We better not take any more of these guys alive," Schwarz said through his mask. "Until we find Cole, I say we kill on sight."

"No argument here."

After Lyons quickly reloaded, the covert operatives performed the grisly task of searching the corpses for any signs of life, then for scraps of paper, ID cards to gain entry into a secure location or anything that might be useful. But there wasn't even lint in their pockets.

"Okay, sweep the other rooms. Standard search pattern, one on two," Lyons commanded, and the team swung into action.

Unfortunately the other offices proved equally useless. Glancing at a window, Lyons could see that dawn had arrived and tried not think about the panic that was starting to set in across the nation as millions discovered what had happened during the night. He sent a silent prayer to every cop on duty that they lived to the end of shift. For many it would be unlikely.

"The computer is clear," Schwarz reported, returning from the office a few minutes later.

"Nothing useful?" Blancanales asked, wiping off his hands.

"Nothing at all. The hard drive has been erased, filled with junk, then erased again. It's called a burn. No way even Akira could recover anything. It's simply not there anymore."

"Carl, did you notice the guy they killed?" Blancanales asked, glancing at the dead men. "He looked at the hallway door before answering you."

Schwarz nodded. "Yeah, the traitor, they called him. Could be a trap. Or maybe he just wanted to get out of here."

"Let's go see."

Leaving the office, the armed men stood for a while studying the hallway. There was a turn with more doors, and at the far end was an elevator bank, with the metal door for the stairs conveniently alongside in case of fire.

"Seal that," Lyons ordered, sliding fresh shells into the Atchisson. Out here the stink of the fake gas leak was much more tolerable, and the Able Team leader thankfully removed his filtration mask.

Doing the same, Schwarz went to the elevator buttons and used a screwdriver to remove the plate, then shorted out the controls, killing the elevator. In the stairwell Blancanales pulled the ring from a canister of BZ gas and tossed it down to the next level. The stable hallucinogenic gas could incapacitate a dozen men without real harm, and there was no way a building this size could carry a larger security force than that.

As they returned, Lyons jerked his head toward the turn in the hall. "It's over there," he said out loud. From the first use of the thundering Atchisson, silence was no longer necessary. If Cole was hidden here somewhere, the man already knew they were coming.

Around the corner was a water fountain and several more doors—an accounting firm, an Internet company and corner office with pebbled glass on either side of a mahogany door with gold lettering across the front: Terra Nova Cruise Lines.

"Bingo," Schwarz whispered. "The name of the ship."

Going to the office, his teammates took up firing positions, and Schwarz checked the door for traps or alarms. Nothing could be discovered, but that didn't mean it was clear. The lock was easy, and the man began to slowly push the portal aside when he heard the sound of panting and saw several things move in the darkness. Guard dogs! He pulled the door shut fast. Something hit the door hard from the other side as he shut it, and the warrior knew he had just escaped having his wrist bitten off.

Stepping back, Schwarz peppered the door at knee level with 5.56 mm rounds. The glass shattered, wood splintered and the animals howled in pain. His teammates added their own weapons to the attack, then stepped through the jagged opening of the empty frame to track the wounded Dobermans as they tried to escape. The men had no choice in the matter, or else the dogs would constantly be in the way, or worse, try to attack again. The Dobermans had to be removed, and it was accomplished as painlessly and efficiently as possible.

When the dirty job was done, one at a time Able Team dropped clips and reloaded, surveying the bloody room. This was obviously a waiting room for clients, with comfortable sofas, oil paintings of people frolicking on the beach, a reception desk and neat stacks of magazines on an end table, most of which dealt with tropical vacations and scuba diving. Nothing on politics or pollution.

While Schwarz searched the secretary's computer and telephone, Lyons stood guard and Blancanales checked the double wooden doors to the main office.

The lock was a joke, which made the man wary, and as the mechanism yielded with a soft click, a shot rang out and a neat hole appeared in the door less than an inch away from him. He dived out of the way as Lyons sent a round from the Atchisson across the top of the doorway. If Cole was in there, he didn't want the man injured for any reason. Not yet, anyway. First and foremost, they wanted those codes.

"Major Cole, we have the building surrounded!" Schwarz shouted, giving a shrug to the other men. What the hell, it might work. "Come out with your hands raised!"

As if in response, the doors exploded into splinters and Able Team dropped as the return gunfire tore the heavy wood apart. The warriors fired back from the carpeting, probing for the gunman even as they crawled backward out of range. But the barrage continued unabated, and in a matter of seconds the hinges were gone and what remained of the doors collapsed to the carpeting. Exposed was a plush executive's office, a row of file cabinets and a Stoner light machine gun sitting on a tripod on top of a wide mahogany desk. There was a complex box attached to the trigger of the Stoner with a blinking red light on the side and a fast spinning dish antenna. Nobody was in the office, and no other doors in sight.

Even as Able Team watched, the weapon tracked downward and fired at them, the heavy slug ripping up the carpet. The men quickly rolled out of the way and made it around the door frame just in time to prevent being riddled.

"Remington AutoSentry," Schwarz said over the com link, dropping a clip and reloading. "The sensors track o motion and body heat. No way to get by that till it runs out of ammo.''

''Pretty high tech for these back-to-the-soil, boys,'' Lyons said into his throat mike.

''Cole is no fool. This is good design for a trap,'' Blancanales grudgingly admitted, plucking a painful wooden splinter from his arm. Over two inches long, the tip was covered with his blood, but the wound was minor and not worth bandaging right then. ''If we had come here first, we'd have been caught between the Sentry and the brigade guards. Sitting ducks.''

Swinging around the jamb, Lyons fired a triburst of shells at the Sentry and ducked back as the robotic weapon responded. ''Damn thing's fast,'' he grunted, looking at a hole in the leg of his fatigue pants.

''Well, the major certainly isn't here,'' Blancanales said, sounding annoyed. There was a short burst of static. ''So the question is, do we try for the files, or are they only bait in the trap?''

Lyons pulled a grenade, then put it back. That would destroy the Sentry gun, but also the files. They needed a third option.

''Can we turn off the power?'' he asked.

''Uses a battery pack,'' Schwarz stated. ''Good for weeks.''

Just then, a soft puff noise came from inside the office, closely followed by the smell of something burning.

Reaching into a pocket of his fatigues, Schwarz pulled out a plastic mirror and checked around the jamb. The closed file cabinets behind the Sentry were trickling smoke.

''The files are burning,'' he reported on the link.

Aiming at the ceiling of the office, Blancanales raised his M-16 and triggered a long spray. Sluggishly, the ceiling sensor reacted to the muzzle-flash and the fire alarm sounded, then the sprinklers cut loose. In moments everything in the room was drenched, and the smoke dwindled from the cabinet to finally stop.

"Now let's get that damn machine," he said, rising to a kneeling position.

Twice the men tried to rush into the office and twice the AutoSentry forced them back under heavy fire.

"Let's see, a Stoner weapons system with a standard munitions case," Blancanales said, thinking out loud. "So I would guess maybe six hundred rounds of 5.56 ammo, so it should be out of rounds in about an hour at this rate."

"Sooner or later the cops or more brigade gunners will arrive," Schwarz added, "and then we have a whole new fight."

"Any chance the water will cause a short circuit?"

"None. It was invented for jungle warfare."

With a growl Lyons reached out with the Atchisson to measure the width of the doorway. Then he did the same to the reception desk. Tight, but workable.

"Lend a hand," he said, standing to lift the end of the desk, papers, pens and other loose items sliding off to the floor.

Shouldering their weapons, the rest of Able Team found something to grip under the desk and rushed into the raining office. The Sentry pounded the furniture with lead, but the men crossed the few yards before it cut through the wood and rammed the machine off the desktop. Still firing, the Stoner landed with a splash on the soaked carpet and they slammed the battered reception desk on top of the control box. The machine gun fired off one last round, and the Sentry unit made angry whirring noises before Schwarz reached underneath and yanked the plug from the power pack. The smashed sensor dish stopped trying to twirl and went still.

"Where guile fails, brute force prevails," he commented, ripping out some more wires and then opening the breech lock of the Stoner. The linked ammo belt slid free and he removed the ammo box completely.

A sweep of the wet office discovered no other booby traps, but also nothing of interest. The hard drive was missing from the desk computer, and while the files in the cabinet were waterlogged and burned, the papers were still readable. But they only seemed involve fuel prices, import fees, cargo manifests and tourist reservations on the ocean liner. However, several large files were clearly missing.

"Damn!" Blancanales cursed, slamming a drawer shut and sending out a spray of droplets. "I have a feeling this place was cleaned out long before the first comsat was destroyed."

"Agreed," Lyons said, standing in the deluge wiping water off his face. "Major Cole has been ahead of us every step of the way. We need to think of something he forgot to do."

"Or couldn't do," Schwarz corrected, returning to the waiting room and retrieving the dropped telephone. Lifting the receiver, he listened for a dial tone.

"Waste of time." Lyons frowned impatiently. "That's got to be dead."

"Let's hope so," the electronics expert said, pulling out a U.S. Army laptop from his equipment bag. Shielding the computer from the water, he attached the computer to the telephone and hit Redial, but there was only a single tone. So Major Cole knew that trick, eh? To prevent anybody from redialing your last call, simply hit the operator button when you were done. It was an old CIA trick probably invented the day after redial was released as an option. However, had Cole thought of also doing the saved numbers? Why should they since the phones would be inoperative? Just a waste of time.

Tapping each of the saved numbers on the list, Schwarz got twenty musical sequences and two blanks. He had the laptop convert the tones into telephone numbers, then activated a search program. The portable computer held every telephone book for North America in its ample memory, and it soon brought up eighteen addresses for the listed numbers.

"We have the maintenance department for this building, some lawyer across town, a sandwich shop around the corner," he said, reading off the glowing screen. "Crap, nothing. Maybe this wasn't such a great idea. There does not seem to be anything here."

Then he looked up. "Except that the two telephone numbers are unlisted."

"Not much we can do with that," Blancanales noted, straightening his sodden cap. "The area code is the same for the whole state."

"It's a small state," Schwarz agreed.

Going to the smashed reception desk, Lyons started yanking open drawers until he found the local business directory. Returning to the waiting room, he flipped pages, checking for a certain address. Getting out of the downpour, his teammates joined him.

"Good thing it is a small state. The phone company is only nine blocks away," Lyons said, tossing away the book. "They'll have hard copies of the address for any unlisted phone numbers."

"Locked in a vault, an actual vault," Blancanales said, then patted a damp satchel charge of C-4 plastique. "But I think we can find some way inside that."

"Got to, it's all we have," Schwarz said, carefully packing away the laptop. The metal case had a small dent in it from a ricochet, but that's why he chose the Army model with a titanium lid. Costly, but durable. "Any idea what we do if these numbers don't lead us anywhere? If they're only Greenpeace, weekly lottery numbers or something like that?"

"Yes, we check them anyway," Lyons said bluntly.

"Even if it's a pizza shop or the public library. Somewhere, somebody knows where Cole is hiding, and we are going to find him."

Then turning on a heel, the big man left the office heading for the waiting ropes outside. Sloshing as they walked, the rest of Able Team was close behind.

CHAPTER SIXTEEN

Yukon Territory, Canada

The placid field of tall grass stretched out of sight, the imposing majesty of the MacKenzie Palisades rising on the western horizon.

Near a lush copse of spruce trees, a doe was lapping water from a crystal-clear stream that cut across the gently sloping landscape. Then the animal went stiff, both ears pricked up, searching for danger. Ever so slightly the nettles of the tress trembled, and the young female deer bolted into the forest even as the ground began to shake, then break apart.

There were no horns, no bells, no Klaxons as the layer of sod slid off the metal plates as they were pushed aside by tremendous hydraulic pistols. Wisps of smoke and steam rose from underground, masking the interior of the circular pit until dissipating to expose the glistening tip of a Redstone missile.

More steam hissed from vents, the shaking increased, then the missile lifted from its silo on military thunder, the fiery column pushing the modified ICBM into the air, then streaking high into the sky heading for space.

The Canadian Department of Defense had spent a fortune on altering the Redstone to remove the hunters from orbit. Normally armed with a fifty-megaton nuclear device, the ballistic rocket was now equipped with an EMP warhead, an electrical device whose explosive magnetic field had a far greater range than the natural electromagnetic pulse of a detonating nuke. There was no doubt that the device could overload and destroy even the shielded circuits of the hunter-killer satellites if the weapons could get close enough.

Huge and cumbersome, the EMP bomb had taken long hours to install into the rocket, since it was normally carried in a truck and driven to its destination. This way the devices could be used anywhere along the coastline to attack ships at sea, or driven to a point under an incoming flight of bombers to strike from below. One weapon with a dozen uses. Deadly and very cost efficient. The Bedlow EMP 4 was absolutely state-of-the-art in the north.

Naturally the CIA claimed to have a briefcase version that could be plugged into the wall and blanket a city block, but nobody believed them. The standard joke of the world intelligence community was that the CIA should move to Hollywood, they were all such amazing storytellers.

Tendrils of chilled atmosphere still clinging to the rotating hull of the Redstone, the missile crested the outer atmosphere of the planet and began to charge the accumulators of EMP preparing to strike when there was a blur of motion from the stars.

Seconds later the cubes arrived and ripped the Redstone apart, its massive fuel reserve detonating into a staggering fireball and annihilating the Bedlow before it could reach full power. Stretching out from the heart of the roiling explosion came a weak and feeble EMP field that reached only a few dozen miles, almost a hundred short of the nearest hunter-killer satellite.

At different locations across the planet, other countries launched similar attacks, some stubbornly trying again and again. But whether it was a single missile or a dozen, a combination swarm or a staggered array, each attack ended the same—in total destruction.

Firmly entrenched in the ultimate high ground, the hunter-killers of the Peace Brigade drifted through space and continued the destruction of every known satellite, completely safe from the furious military of the world below.

High Above the Atlantic Ocean

THE SURFACE of the ocean was smooth for miles, glistening in the rosy light of the rising sun.

"Where the hell is it?" Jack Grimaldi muttered as he sat in the cockpit of the F-18 Super Hornet.

With the arrival of dawn, four wings of Hornets had been dispatched from the *Kitty Hawk,* each wing sent on a widening angle of flight so that the fighters could cover as much ocean as possible. A simple passenger liner, the *Terra Nova* was designed to be as comfortable as a hotel, and thus the fat, bottom-heavy craft possessed no real speed. Even half a day after it had been first identified near Barbados, the possible search vector for the ship was less than a thousand square miles.

There was also a SeaWolf submarine somewhere in the immediate vicinity. But aside from blowing the *Terra Nova* apart with a nuclear torpedo, there wasn't much the boomer could do in this situation. If it was even here yet. And the destruction of the cruise ship was the very last thing Stony Man wanted at the moment.

The flock of Hornets departed from the *Kitty Hawk* only minutes after Grimaldi received the transmission from the Pentagon identifying the enemy. Reading the message with one hand while a doctor taped his bruised ribs into place, the Stony Man pilot knew what an incredible chance the Farm had taken forging the authorization codes of the Pentagon and Atlantic Command. With the nation at DefCon

Four, that was technically an act of treason and Captain MacPherson would have the legal right to execute the pilot on the spot. But there had been no time to go through proper channels, and Tokaido had performed at his usual level of excellence. The Navy cyber experts accepted the message as legitimate.

Flying with only his right hand, Grimaldi rested the aching left arm across his lap, and looked out the windows of the cockpit to study the featureless expanse of the shimmering ocean below. Still nothing in sight. Where could the damn thing be?

"Red Dog to Leader," a man announced crisply over the pilot's headphones. The long-range radios of the jetfighters were dead with satellite relays, but the short-range links to one another worked perfectly. Thank God for that.

"Go, Red Dog," Grimaldi stated.

"Sir, we have visual on a bogey at three-o'clock low," Red Dog announced calmly, without a trace of excitement. "Strike zone Alpha Zulu."

"There's nothing on radar," Grimaldi replied, tapping the screen with a gloved finger. The glowing monitor stayed the same, only the seven Hornets moving as bright triangles in a tight Delta formation.

"Sir, the QRD indicates localized jamming," the Navy aviator said, now a trifle impatient.

Grimaldi fumbled with the counterjamming unit, and it suddenly lit up with warning lights. Hot damn.

"Lead the way, Red Dog," the Stony Man pilot commanded, arming the weapon systems on the F-18.

The jets slipped sideways across the brightening sky, and soon there was a small dark object on the horizon, twin plumes of smoke rising from its three blue-and-gold funnels. That had to be the *Terra Nova*.

"Roger on that bogey," Grimaldi said. "Good call, Red Dog."

"Confirmed, sir. Request permission to do a flyby and confirm target ident."

"Negative on that. We hold and wait," Grimaldi demanded. "Attention, Longeyes, try and contact the Sea-Hawk, give them our new position."

Flying high above the fighter wing was a stripped-down F-16 Eagle, its greater altitude doubling the range of its radio and radar. Their own private relay point in the unfriendly skies.

"Roger on that, Admiral Stone, this is Longeyes," a young pilot reported. "I have an ident on a friendly at fifty miles. Have contacted and a Big Mac is on the way. ETA twenty minutes."

Big Mac? That had to be McCarter. But twenty minutes was a long time to wait. At any second the brigade could spot the fighter wing and start burning files and erasing computer files.

"Roger that, Longeyes," Grimaldi said, placing his left arm on the joystick and testing his strength. It hurt like fire, but was stiff yet. "Wing commander, prepare to execute an attack run on my command. We're going to keep that ship's attention on us for the next twenty minutes. I want them too busy dealing with us to stop and crap in fear."

"For twenty minutes? Sir, we don't have the fuel to fight that long," a new voice stated. "Check your gauge, sir. We're almost at Ponder now."

Ponder, or PONR, was the Point Of No Return, after which the Hornets wouldn't be able to reach the *Hawk* and safely land. Also the *Nova* was still steaming into the distance, steadily increasing the lag.

"Understood," Grimaldi said grimly. "Sure hope you guys can swim."

There were a few seconds of radio silence.

"We're naval aviators, sir," Red Dog stated calmly "You just tell us when and where."

God, he loved the Navy. The ships were steel, but the balls were pure brass.

"Confirm that, Red Dog, and thanks. Longeyes, fall back from combat zone and go to maximum height. Try and reach the *Kitty Hawk*. We have found the target and I am requesting the captain prepare, stress that, merely prepare a nuclear strike for this area. But do not launch without my authorization."

If the worst came, at least the Peace Brigade wouldn't be able to launch any more hunters into space. But getting the self-destruct codes to destroy the satellites already in space was the primary mission objective. Afterward the floating shitbox would be turned into an actual nova from naval gunfire.

"Roger, sir," the pilot of the Eagle said. "Wilco."

"Sir, is the situation really that high?" a young voice asked. "High" was aviator slang for "bad." Grimaldi flew along for a moment in thought, then made a decision. These men were about to go into battle, and unless the brigade were fools, that ship would have some sort of defenses. Maybe good ones.

"Roger that, Tigershark. These are the people destroying the satellites."

"I knew it!" Double Jet growled in a deep bass. "Okay, boys, lets show these sons of bitches what the Navy can do!"

"Negative, negative," Grimaldi said hurriedly as the other fighters started flying forward, coming into view through his side windows. "That is not the battle plan. I am the leader and you will follow me in. That is a direct order!"

"With all respect, Admiral," Ironbird said, stressing the last word, "you're as Navy as a bucketful of kittens. You didn't know what a JOC was, or that we call our hats a 'cover.' Now, the skipper says you're the man, and that's good enough for us. However, you also look like the loser in a baseball fight. One more bruise and you could start to internally hemorrhage. Be dead in minutes. You couldn't take the Gs to lead an air strike onto Candyland.''

That was true, but Grimaldi wouldn't relinquish his command. There was a job to do, and he wouldn't let the Farm down.

''You want to spend the next century in the brig, son?'' Grimaldi said forcibly, his attention on the tiny black ship on the horizon. ''Do you have any idea who I am?''

''Yes, sir,'' the Navy aviator replied. ''You're the civilian who got us here. Now get out of the way and let us do our job. Wing, I am assuming the position as attack leader. We will follow the admiral's plan, but I want formation C as in Charlie.''

''Roger, Obi Wan, wilco. Formation Charlie.''

''I'm on the leader,'' another said.

''The force is strong in this one,'' somebody else added.

There was a smattering of chuckles, then the airwaves went dead silent, as the young pilots of the Hornets folded out their wings and dropped in speed even as they hurtled lower in height, diving like blue lightning toward the luxury cruise liner.

''Here comes hell,'' Tigershark muttered.

Streaking low over the horizon at fantastic speed, the sleek fighters widened their wings, dropped from Mach and broke formation to circle once high around the *Terra Nova,* computerized video cameras checking for any signs of offensive or defensive weapons systems, or of any civilians who might be trapped on board as human shields used to protect the terrorists.

Dropping lower, they circled once more, hoping to draw fire and establish the status of the vessel. Instantly several lifeboats flipped over, exposing a Phalanx gun on each side of the vessel. The electric Gatlings automatically swung about tracking on the incoming jets and cut loose, the

20 mm electric cannons ripping 8,000 rounds per minute into the sky. The rounds were so close, the Navy pilots could see the dark lines swing after them through the rosy light of dawn. But the barrage was always a heartbeat behind the spinning Hornets and never came close.

"All clear!" Grimaldi said, itching to join the fray, but wise enough to give the Navy room to maneuver. Those Gatlings couldn't see the jets, which left only the human gunners to contend with.

The Stony Man pilot knew that he could fly damn near anything that existed, and a lot of these young men could only operate a Hornet. However, this specialization gave them an edge with the jets he could never obtain. Grimaldi was good, one of the best, but these boys were magnificent.

Nearly obscured from sight by the smoke of the other two funnels, the middle stack stood cold and open. Then there was a sudden blur that flashed into the sky, and the thick smoke shifted directions to streak upward for a few moments before thickening again and returning to flow behind the luxury liner.

"Sons of bitches are still launching!" Red Dog growled, twisting away so low his afterburners churned the surface of the water.

"Not for long," Tigershark spit, banking into another approach.

Now the Hornets spread out, racing away from the ship only to return from different vectors and retaliate with a flurry of Sidewinder missiles. A dozen crisscrossing contrails streaked past the liner from every direction. Yet even though the F-18s were less than a mile away, point-blank range, every missile failed to strike the huge steel ship and knifed past to plunge into the Atlantic and throw up plumes of water from their detonating warheads.

By now tiny figures were rushing madly about on the ship, men in gray clothing and red berets carrying long tubes with a skeleton metal box attached to the side of the barrel. The Hornets zoomed past as Stinger missiles climbed for height, chasing the nimble jets. Spiraling away, the Navy pilots dropped chaff and flares, and the heatseekers exploded like fireworks in the early-morning sky.

Now Red Dog veered directly for the luxury liner and dropped something large from under its belly into the sea. A few seconds later there was motion under the waves as a torpedo kicked into action and headed straight for the bow of the huge ship. The strongest part of the vessel.

The brigade soldiers on deck threw down a wall of Stingers and LAW rockets into the water before the rushing torpedo hit, shaking the entire vessel with its lightweight warhead and failing to achieving penetration.

The radar in his Hornet sounded an alarm, and Grimaldi flipped sideways to let a LAW rocket streak by. Somebody down there was a damn fine shot, but not quite good enough. Slipping into an easy angle, Grimaldi sent off a twin salvo of AIM-7 and AIM-9 Sidewinders, churning the water behind the gigantic craft. The Navy pilots had lots more missiles, but how long would it be before the brigade realized the Navy was hitting everything it aimed at and that this was only a diversion? Time to up the stakes.

Switching to their cannons, the F-18s skimmed the water, peppering the sides of the great ship, hammering it hard and shattering a dozen portholes and nothing much else.

"Longeyes, how long till Big Mac?" Grimaldi demanded, waiting until a section of the deck was empty of people before raking it with his own nose cannon. The heavy rounds threw off sparks from the deck and chewed apart teakwood chairs and the shuffleboard court.

"ETA ninety seconds, sir!" the high-flying pilot replied from the clouds.

"Keep up the pressure, Navy!" Grimaldi grunted, trying not to wince as he pulled away in an escape pattern. The thrust pressed hard on his bruised ribs until he grit his teeth to keep from crying out with the pain. "We gotta buy a few more minutes!"

"Roger, sir!" Double Jet called in his booming bass.

Just then the Phalanx cannons went silent for a moment as the human gunners frantically reloaded, and the Hornets raked the emplacements with their guns, tearing the men apart and smashing the useless radar array on top of the Gatlings.

"That's put the fear of God into the bastards!"

"Amen to that, brother."

Now folding back its wings for speed, an F-18 flashed along the full length of the ocean liner and banked away sharply, actually flipping upside down to get clear fast. A moment later the main radio mast that stood a hundred feet about the forecastle violently exploded in the middle from a well-placed bomb. Fire and shrapnel rained upon the bridge, and the ship abruptly turned into the currents and floundered for a few moments before going back on course.

"Bull's-eye, Stingray," Red Dog said, sending off another perfectly misaimed missile. "That sure scared the piss out of them."

"Mayday! I'm caught in a tailspin," Stingray replied, his words tense. "Can't get loose…"

"Use full power!" Double Jet yelled, knifing past the other Hornet as cover.

"No go. Main engine flameout!" Stingray shouted, his radio transmission suddenly distorted. "I'm going down!"

"Eject, man, eject!"

The canopy blew off the jet, and the pilot in his chair was blown clear of the fighter, soaring high and far away from the streaking Hornet. Then the built-in parachute blossomed wide and the pilot began to drift down as the powerless fighter flashed seaward to smash against the water, shattering into a million pieces before erupting in a fiery detonation.

The crew of the *Terra Nova* cheered in victory, then the starboard Phalanx roared alive once more, the stuttering line of 20 mm shells moving across the descending pilot trapped in his parachute. The dangling body and chair were blown apart, only ragged pieces falling into the waves below. Firing pistols and machine guns into the air, the Peace Brigade soldiers cheered even louder over the cowardly slaughter.

"Dirty motherfuckers will pay for that," Ironbird snarled, lifting on his afterburners and swinging about for a full-speed attack run.

"Belay that shit!" Red Dog commanded harshly, a tremor in his voice announcing the release of a pair of missiles. "We'll blow 'em out of the water when the times comes. But for now, keeping hitting nothing. That's a direct order."

"Roger, wing leader, confirmed. Wilco."

"Alert! Incoming friendlies," Longeyes reported calmly. "Seven-o'clock high."

"The second wave of Hornets?" Grimaldi demanded wearily. The pain in his chest was draining his strength, but until the next wing of fighters arrived, they had to keep attacking. And missing. The Navy was losing a lot of men and planes today—this damn plan better work.

"No, sir, Admiral!" Longeyes stated with an almost audible grin. "It's the SeaHawk!"

Craning his neck, Grimaldi spied the combat helicopter high above the *Terra Nova*. Just then there was a blur from the middle funnel and the smoke shot skyward again. Seconds later the Hornets visibly shifted positions as the vacuum trail caused by the passage of the launching satellite formed a perfect expanding circle about the colossal liner.

That was when five men jumped from the side hatch of the helicopter. Assuming a HALO formation with parachutes closed, the figures plummeted like stones toward the war-torn vessel.

"Godspeed, boys," Grimaldi whispered, frantically dodging another Stinger, then returning to the fight.

CHAPTER SEVENTEEN

United Nations Building, New York City

In an early-morning emergency meeting of the United Nations Security Council, the representatives of the superpowers hurriedly discussed the coming communications blackout but ended in a heated deadlock, unable to decide on any action to fix the problem. Very few of the diplomats believed that a handful of terrorists could possibly have created and launched the new class of hunter satellites. The rest of the politicians openly suspected that America was behind the mass destruction in space. Possibly it was some sort of a profit-making scheme by the money-mad Yankees.

The ambassador of the United States stayed for as long as she could, then grimly departed. Canada, Great Britain, Australia, Russia and Japan soon followed, leaving the rest to squabble among themselves.

Meanwhile IMF and NATO forces had gone to full-combat status and activated their counterstrike teams.

In space, Beijing Command sent one of its own hunter-killer satellites to destroy a Russian milsat and pave the way for invasion. The Kremlin Space Defense found and killed the Chinese satellite, but it required two of its own smaller hunter-killers to stop the Chinese monster. China immediately went to Angry Dragon status, and Russia went to Flag Four, the equivalent of the American DefCon Four.

Slowly building strength, German troops began to mass on the border of France. Open warfare erupted in the streets of Bosnia. In Africa and South America, several small wars started, Communist guerrillas in the democratic countries and freedom fighters in the Communist dictatorships each seizing this golden opportunity to achieve their cherished goals.

As more communication links fell, in the War Room of Cheyenne Mountain, supreme headquarters for NORAD and SAC, the Joint Chiefs of Staff formulated battle plans to launch swarms of ICBMS and protect the U.S. from annihilation by striking at their enemies first and thus surviving the coming worldwide blackout. The generals still needed the authorization of the President, but they stood ready to instantly attack. The silos were open, the missiles fully fueled. All that was required was the press of a button.

Oddly in the mounting confusion and madness, nobody seemed to notice that everything was peaceful and calm in the Middle East.

Delmarva Peninsula, Delaware

THEIR FACES WERE still streaked with black-and-gray stripes, but now Able Team was dressed in the mottled greens and browns of jungle camouflage, their weapons masked in similar cloth knotted about the barrel and stock.

In a field of young corn outside of the small town of Bearton, Delaware, Able Team lay motionless amid the tall green stalks and knew that something was terribly wrong here as they studied the empty streets and still houses of the rural farming community. There was no sound of human voices, no smell of breakfast cooking or even coffee brewing. Yet this was a farming town where the people awoke at dawn to start their long day of work, and it was already past nine o'clock.

Through the crosshairs of their M-16 rifle scopes, the

commandos could see only empty gravel streets, the few pickup trucks still parked in driveways. Then Lyons spied a bloody hand lying in the doorway of a garage, a trickle of red reaching the street. Across the town there was a smudged crimson handprint on the inside of a window at the post office, and flies buzzed thick around an idling car stopped in the middle of the only intersection, the driver's-side window smashed open.

Bearton, Delaware, population 150. This had been the home address of Major Sebastian Cole, but not anymore. This was now a city of the dead.

The staff at the Delaware Telephone Company had raised no objections to the masked men with big guns who wanted access to the unlisted telephone number files in the basement vault. The first phone number had been a bust, a cell phone with the bills paid over the Internet. Useless. But the second yielded gold; it was for the home of Sebastian R. Cole, 19 Colonial Way, Bearton, Delaware.

Routing a landline call from the phone company to the Farm took much longer than expected, a bad indication on the status of the crumbling communications system. But Schwarz finally got through and arranged for a blacksuit to deliver a replacement van at a nearby shopping mall. The more traffic the better to disguise the transaction. Afterward the men securely locked the phone company staff in an office and departed. The employees would be much safer behind closed doors then on the streets. Bad wasn't here, but it was coming soon.

Stealing a car from the parking lot, Able Team started for the mall, but apparently the expected rioting had started early, and National Guard helicopters were already patrolling the skies above the city, ordering the crowds to disperse, while police cars and ambulances screamed along sidewalks to get past the traffic jams blocking every street.

Using the threat of their handguns when necessary to

clear a path, the team finally arrived at the mall, but several men armed with crowbars were trying to break into the van. A blacksuit dressed in casual clothes lay dead on the pavement, the rear of his head gory pulp. His face was known to Able Team, and the warriors struck without mercy, gunning down the carjackers where they stood. One fired back with the blacksuit's pistol and was ruthlessly torn apart by Able Team's assault rifles. Badly wounded, the last man pleaded for his life, but Lyons executed the murderer with a precise thundering round from his Colt Python to the left temple. Death was instantaneous, and probably arrived with much less pain than it had came to the ambushed blacksuit.

"Kevin Davis," Blancanales said, shaking his head. "Due to rotate out in two weeks."

Rolling Davis over to face the warm sun, Able Team returned the stolen pistol to his shoulder holster, covered him with a blanket from the van and drove away. Buck Greene, who was in charge of the blacksuits, would be able to reclaim the body from the city morgue and give the fallen man a proper military funeral. That was, if the coming war didn't destroy the world.

Driving out of the city, Able Team lost precious time stopping several assaults on the outnumbered police with short bursts from their M-16 assault rifles. But unless a life was at stake, the Stony Man warriors did nothing to stop the looters and vandals. They had a mission to accomplish, and the numbers were falling fast.

As expected the highways were madness, and there was no police or military presence to direct the drunks and the frightened. Cars zigzagged across the lanes at ninety miles per hour, and more than once Able Team passed a burning wreck flipped over in the grassy median. The foolish drivers learned the hard way that speed limits weren't set arbitrarily, but as safety precautions. They killed themselves desperately racing to nowhere.

"'Behold, evolution in action,'" Lyons quoted as they rolled by the crackling funeral pyres of twisted steel.

Racing their van along southbound Route 95, they turned onto State Highway 13. Eventually the traffic became sparse, and Able Team had the road to itself. The rush of the wind and the hum of the tires on the concrete gave the world a quiet, peaceful feeling that beguiled the violent war being conducted high in space. But the air of the van seemed to be electrically charged with the import of finding and stopping the Peace Brigade, and the mission never left their thoughts for a moment.

An hour later Able Team turned off Highway 13 onto a two-lane asphalt road and started into the lower peninsula of Delaware. Soon the landscape was farms and vast empty fields, only the occasional isolated farmhouse dotting the flat vista.

Turning off the concrete ribbon, Blancanales directed the van onto Route 285, which was scarcely paved, and rolled along until a small rural town came into view.

"That has to be it," Schwarz said, checking the map. "There isn't another town around here for miles."

"Then stop here," Lyons directed.

Tapping the brakes a few time to pretend engine trouble in case they were under observation, Blancanales pulled over to the side of the road and went onto the grass and parked the van. Leaving the vehicle, Schwarz raised the hood and prodded around for a few minutes to make it seem they really had stopped for a repair. Surreptitiously, he poured some brake fluid on the radiator and stepped back as gray smoke rose.

Satisfied the van looked disabled, he joined the others already in the back of the van getting into their jungle camos with full weapons packs.

"Soft probe, right?" Blancanales asked, using his thumb to test the edge on a Gerber knife.

"Until we know better," Lyons stated, closing the lid on the case that held his Atchisson, and instead taking a silenced Ingram SMG again. In open warfare he preferred the autoshotgun, but for room-to-room fighting, the Ingram worked better. Sometimes silence was better than firepower.

Slipping out the side door, the men crawled into the nearby weeds and traversed a dry creek to reach some farmland. Running low and fast, they covered the acres of green corn, always watching the ground for any suspicious humps or depressions. A few such irregularities were discovered and expertly avoided. The marks might have only been rabbit burrows—or freshly buried land mines. There was no time to check. Speed was of the essence now.

Reaching the end of the field, Able Team was momentarily in open view while Blancanales snipped a hole in the wire fence. Then the team wiggled through and crawled into the weedy drainage ditch edging the farmland.

The thick silence was the first abnormality they noticed. This was morning in farm country. Where was the clatter of pots and pans, the smell of bacon and coffee? Then using their telescopic gunsights, the team found the blood and the flies.

Using sign language, Blancanales asked a question, Schwarz offered a suggestion and Lyons approved. Whether this was another trap or not, they were going in.

Moving as silently as shadows, the recon team slipped out of the drainage ditch into the some bushes, moving from garden to hedges to keep out of sight. Any possible cover ceased as they reached the town proper. Staying behind parked pickup trucks and station wagons, Able Team saw that the stores and diner were closed, with nobody visible through the windows. Even the hardware store was deserted. On a weekday? Easing back to the rows of houses, Lyons chose one at random, and Schwarz quietly jimmied the lock to gain entry.

A telltale coppery smell was thick in the air, red smears on the floorboards, and they found the corpses in their beds. A man and a woman lying side by side as if only sleeping. But the sheets were sticky with blood. Shot in the kitchen and dragged to the bedroom.

"Why?" Schwarz asked, checking the closet, but finding only old clothes that would never be worn again by their owners.

"It's a stage setting," Blancanales told him. "Anybody glancing through a window wouldn't notice anything odd."

"Next house, on the double," Lyons directed, heading for the side door.

The team moved through a dozen houses and always found the same thing until they reached the conclusion that everybody in town was dead. The entire population, man, woman and child, had been executed by professionals, then laid out in bed to hide the murders. Oddly the adults with children often had badly mangled hands.

"They tried to save the kids by attacking the armed men with only their bare hands," Lyons said. "I have got me a serious hard-on to kill these bastards."

"Take a number," Schwarz growled, his eyes glaring with rage. Even if Cole surrendered, he was going down anyway.

"They're near," Blancanales said. "Have to be. The brigade burned the town for only one possibly reason. The people here might have seen something important. So they must be close."

At a small noise, Lyons swung about, the Ingram ready to fire. Then a cat walked into the room and meowed for attention.

"Anything nearby?" the Able Team leader asked, rubbing the animal behind the ears.

Digging out his laptop, Schwarz pulled up a map of Delaware, then zoomed in for the area between Route 285 and

Highway 301. "Mostly farms and swamps," he said slowly, then added, "And the canal."

"Canal? Not the C&D canal?" Blancanales asked.

"That's the one."

"What is it?" Lyons asked. The former West Coast cop knew L.A. like the back of his hand, but was still learning the details of the east side of America.

"Chesapeake and Delaware Canal goes all the way through the Delmarva Peninsula," Schwarz explained, closing the laptop. An old girlfriend had been an avid biker and talked of the scenic bike route along the canal constantly. "It connects the Chesapeake Bay to the Delaware River. Cuts two hundred nautical miles off the route going from Baltimore to Philly."

"It's one of the busiest canals in the world," Blancanales stated. "Yachts, speedboats, tankers and even freighters to use."

"Deep enough draw for even a cruise liner?" Lyons asked, feeling a tingle course down his spine.

"Bet your ass it is. The sons of bitches have been right out in the open all the while where anybody could see."

"That's usually the best way. Skulk around and people notice. Walk boldly and they ignore you."

"How far are we away from the water?"

"About a mile, maybe less. Due south."

"Too close for killing like this," Lyons said, standing upright. "The base must be on the other side of the canal."

"Map has there's nothing there," Schwarz replied, patting the cat. "Just some private homes."

"Big ones, I'll bet. Estates on acres of land."

"Exactly."

"The perfect location for a megalomaniac to build a base and contact the *Terra Nova* as it sails by," the warrior said grimly. "Back to the van. I got a feeling we're going to need some help to reach Major Cole."

RETURNING TO their van, the Able Team commandos crossed the wide canal on the Highway 301 suspension bridge. With Blancanales driving at exactly the speed limit, his teammates used the elevated location to scan the shore to their right with high-powered field glasses. They found the target immediately.

Situated alongside the muddy canal was a sprawling estate completely encased by a high stone wall that had to have been a yard thick. The mansion was four stories tall, and not a soul was in sight on the grounds; the estate was a quiet as a cemetery.

"A mobile launch site at sea, with their headquarters a thousand miles away," Lyons said grimly. "Real pros."

Recording the view on a digital camera, Schwarz enlarged the pictures while Blancanales followed the gravel roads through the countryside, trying to reach inland. If the brigade was expecting trouble, it should logically come from the canal. The exact opposite direction was hopefully their best bet for a surprise attack. Unless Cole had anticipated that maneuver and they were driving into another trap. He had to admit that Cole was sharp, one of the smartest enemies America had ever faced.

"What a hardsite. Look at this," Schwarz said, passing the expanded-view photos forward. "Aside from the wall itself, see those canvas mounds outside the estate? Those inflate to confuse the terrain memory files on a cruise missile and make it pass by without detonating."

"Impressive. The wall is topped with concertina wire, and that's a dog run on the inside," Lyons told them, flipping through the views. "There, see that silver sheen in the trees? I'd say those were titanium nets to catch man-portable missiles and slow down an APC or Hummers."

"How much you want to bet there's a sonar net in the canal itself, and the shore is lined with AP mines?"

The man shook his head. "No bet. This guy covers every possibility."

"Which means clusters of land mines," Schwarz said. "Mantraps, pitfalls, poison gas, maybe even a missile bank to handle planes and ships."

"Where would be the best location to hide it?" Lyons asked, studying the digital photographs. "Flower garden, yes, that's where it is. We hit there first thing."

"Sounds good."

"Well, nobody should be able to spot us here," Blancanales said, taking an access road and slowing to a halt near a huge pile of loose gravel. He had been looking for this exact location. Delaware got winters just as bad as D.C., but this deep into farming country, nobody sane was going to salt the roads. Which meant a lot of gravel for the ice, especially for the bridge.

"Sounds like the Farm," Lyons said, frowning. As much as he hated to admit it, somebody else seemed to have come up with the same idea. The idea of trying to blow their way into the enemy's equivalent of the Farm without some serious air support wasn't pleasant.

"Looks clear," Schwarz announced from the rear windows, his M-16/M-203 balanced in both hands.

Double-checking the area around the van just to be sure, the team loaded up with some heavy armament, then clambered from the vehicle, leaving the doors unlocked in case they came back in a hurry.

"We'll use the top of the gravel as our base," Lyons directed. "Mark your targets before shooting. There might be one or two civilians still here to be used as shields."

"Gets tougher every time," Blancanales said, adjusting his backpack of rockets.

"I hear you," Schwarz muttered, loaded down with a bulky canvas bag.

Just then Lyons raised a clenched fist, and the others

froze. Pointing with his weapon, the Able Team warrior directed their attention to a stack of plastic bags full of fertilizer, the topmost bag broken open and exposed to the air.

This was a trap! Schwarz inhaled through his teeth at the sight and lowered the bag gently so as to not harm its contents. Turning around fast, Blancanales scanned the ridges of machinery and mounds of gravel, searching for the direction of the attack. There was no conceivable reason for a gravel pit to have a supply of fertilizer. Especially ammonia-based fertilizer, the kind used by terrorists to mask the presence of the natural trace ammonia in human sweat from the chemical sniffers of the FBI.

That was when the ground shifted under their boots and Able Team fell sideways as hands grabbed them from underneath the soil and yanked hard. The team members hit the ground, losing their weapons as more brigade soldiers crawled out of the disguised hole like corpses escaping the grave.

CHAPTER EIGHTEEN

Stony Man Farm, Virginia

"Fools," Brognola muttered, watching the radar screen relayed via the Stony Man satellite. Great Britain and Australia both had just launched dozens of antisatellite missiles. The sleek destroyers spread out upon reaching space, and detonated the instant they cleared the atmosphere. The random explosions filled hundreds of squares miles with hot shrapnel.

"Shooting blind," Price said. "Good idea if it works."

"But one miss and the radioactive fallout could land on a populated area and kill millions," Brognola said, angrily walking closer to the screen. The view of the flickering nuclear explosions was hypnotic, almost as if watching a video game, flashing lights and pretty colors that seemed to have no relationship to the atomic fury blanketing space.

"Unfortunately those nukes are nowhere near the hunters," Kurtzman reported, marking orbits on a white board. The colorful arcs crossed most of the world already. "Mt. Palomer Observatory reports no eclipse motion in the target area."

"So where are they?" Brognola demanded.

"Above the north pole, clearing away our secondary Skywatch and Peacemakers." The man sighed and leaned back in his wheelchair. "Also, SimComs, HERMES, SPOT, Vortex, Cosmos, Hughes and damn near everything else. Three MIRALL satellites attacked a lone brigade hunter and did nothing. Might as well be spitting at the damn things for all the good those antisatellite shotgun charges are doing.''

''Our hunter-killers are armed to stop satellites with sheet-metal hulls and glass solar-panel wings,'' Price reminded him sadly. ''Not a flying bank vault built to withstand Mach 5 launch velocities.''

''Yeah, well, if we get the chance,'' Brognola stated, returning to the main console, ''we'll fix that on the next generation of milsats.''

A bright flash on the wall monitor showed the destruction of a French military orbiter, and then a Norwegian.

''If we get the chance,'' he repeated softly.

Chewing steadily, Akira Tokaido blew a large pink bubble and chewed it back into his mouth. ''I have a crazy idea,'' he said slowly. ''Carmen, any chance you still have that ground line to the SETI array?''

''Yes, of course. I've been keeping it open in case of trouble,'' the redhead replied, swiveling in her chair. There was a brief glimpse of black lace until she crossed her legs once more. ''Going to try a straight invasion?''

''Why not? Only thing we haven't tried yet,'' he said, changing the CD in his stereo. He needed something that really rocked for this. The cyber warrior didn't find that peace of mind came from peace and quiet. ''An EM transmission is the same as any other. Why shouldn't they obey us, rather than the brigade?''

''Can you do that?'' Brognola demanded. ''Seize control of a hunter and turn its rail gun against the other brigade satellites?''

''Certainly. That's what we almost did last time, just didn't go far enough. Now we will,'' Kurtzman growled, nimble fingers linking the four computer consoles together. Now the hackers could cover each other. ''Carmen, keep that line open no matter what. Akira, you lead the charge. I'll run defense. Any antivirus or CI program that tries to stop you, ignore it, that's my job. Hunt, handle support and firewall. Go!''

Atlantic Ocean

THE ONLY NOISE in the control room of the USS *Connecticut* were the soft pings of the active sonar and the ever present hush of the turbines under the deck of the SeaWolf-class attack submarine. The officers and ratings stood tense at their posts, endlessly adjusting the complex array of machinery that kept both the crew and submarine alive and in fighting trim.

"Captain on com," an ensign said smartly as the older man strode into view.

Ducking his head to get through the hatchway, Captain Richard Maitlin nodded at his XO and went straight to the waiting periscope.

"Damn me twice," the captain muttered, both arms resting on the steering posts of the column. "How long has this been going on?"

"About fifteen minutes, sir," the XO replied, brushing a hand over his bald head. "Sonar caught the first debris hitting the water, so we backtracked and found this."

"F-18s pounding the shit out of a passenger liner," Captain Maitlin stated, stepping from the periscope. "Craziest thing I have ever seen. Have we contacted the pilots yet?"

"Negative, sir," a sailor replied from the communications board. "They do not respond to our hail."

"Any chatter?"

"Lots," the XO said, glancing upward. "The pilots are talking often, but the channel is scrambled and we don't have that code key."

"Got a positive ident on those American planes?"

"Aye, sir. U.S. Navy Hornets and Super Hornets. Those are our jets, sir."

"Doesn't mean the pilots are," Maitlin replied, tugging thoughtfully on his collar. The Hornets shouldn't be strafing a civilian ship. On the other hand the naval aviators certainly were missing a lot at point-blank range, and that civilian luxury liner had a hell of a lot of state-of-the-art weaponry. The situation seemed clear, but he had to confirm before taking independent action. Maybe badly trained enemy pilots were doing a sneak attack with stolen Hornets, and the *Terra Nova* was a covert Navy warship fighting for its life. Anything was possible.

"Talk to me, Ears," the captain said as an order.

The sonar operator glanced from his board. "There's only us in the area, skipper," he reported with eyes focused on nothing, his mind deep in the waters around the submarine. "We're blue and clear."

The captain grunted acknowledgment. "Just the same, we better play it safe. Helm, stay this course and hold our distance." Then going to an intercom, he hit a switch. "Forward weapons bay, load tubes one through six with heavy torpedoes."

"Aye, sir," the intercom squawked.

"But do not flood until my command."

"Aye, aye, sir!"

"We're going to join the attack?" the XO asked, frowning. "Okay, skip. Which do we try for, the birds or the boat?"

"Neither yet, Charlie. But I want to be ready," Maitlin said grimly.

Late the previous night, or very early that morning depending, the *Connecticut* received a broken message about terrorists in the area, but it had stopped before giving the mandatory identification suffix to show the transmission was from Atlantic Command. According to regs, he should ignore any partial orders, but with this bizarre communications breakdown the officer knew he would have to deal with this by gut feeling.

Rubbing his stomach for inspiration, Maitlin hit another button on the intercom. "Arms master, unlock the vault and prepare a nuclear torpedo."

"Ah, right away, Captain," the intercom squawked.

Then Maitlin raised his hand and depressed another before the man could respond further. "Forward weapons bay, this is a correction. Remove the MK 48 heavy torpedoes from one through four and load with class D specials. Also, keep tube five standard, and load six with the nuke."

"Sir?" a voice asked in shock. "Please repeat."

"That order is confirmed. Load with specials and a nuclear charge in tube six. Repeat, in tube six only."

"Aye, aye, sir!"

"XO, plot me a shooting solution," Maitlin said, cracking his knuckles. "I want a full broadside programmed to hit across the port side of that vessel in unison."

The executive officer didn't reply with words, but his face registered concern as he crossed the perforated steel deck to join a sailor already typing on a keyboard and feeding information into the onboard targeting computer.

Maitlin nodded in approval. "Data," Sherlock Holmes had once said. "Data, Watson! I cannot make bricks without clay." Damn straight. Maitlin needed to know what was really happening on the surface, and if the Hornets wouldn't talk, then he would just have to get everybody's attention the hard way.

As the PILOTLESS SeaHawk ran on a straight course out to sea, Phoenix Force fell toward the moving cruise liner, rapidly building speed in a HALO formation. A high-altitude low-open jump was a dangerous parachute maneuver, but it gave them minimum exposure time in the air to be found by enemy gunners.

"How much longer?" Manning asked into his throat mike, the wind riffling his hair. He was holding tight onto the forearms of Hawkins and James.

"Ninety-three seconds!" Encizo replied loudly, doing the same thing to McCarter and Hawkins. "That is, if we have the launch sequence right."

"Damn well better hope so!" he shot back.

Holding on to the wrists of Encizo and James to maintain the HALO circle, McCarter merely grunted in reply. From this position, it was obvious that there wasn't enough space in the launcher to fit the five parachutes in unison. But there was an answer for that.

Scattered gunfire sounded from the top deck of the vessel coming their way, but by now it was too late. Releasing one another, the men staggered their positions. Then they yanked on rip cords, and their backpacks erupted into silk chutes. The team was jerked skyward, their swift descent brutally slowed.

The mouth of the middle tunnel loomed below the paratroopers, the forty-foot opening suddenly seeming too small and much too large at the exact same time. Everything depended on timing right now. If the rail gun launched a hunter while they were in the cannon, it would smash through the men like a steel bullet hitting grapes with roughly the same results.

"Shift!" McCarter ordered, and slapped the release harness on his chest.

Instantly his body harness released and he flexed his shoulders to slip free and drop a few yards before grabbing on to Encizo. With the weight double, the two men dropped that much faster down into the narrow funnel as the wind shear carried the empty parachute away.

Manning set his chute loose and dropped for Hawkins.

but a sudden gust of smoke from the forward funnel yanked Hawkins outside the mouth of the black funnel. He saw his teammate fighting desperately to get the chute back on course when Manning entered the launcher and was swallowed by the shadows.

Panic hit the soldier for a split second before strong hands snagged his trailing safety cord and Manning slammed into James, the impact knocking the breath out of both men.

Clawing for a hold on the straps of the harness, Manning grabbed the other man and clung for dear life, then a strong arm offered him support and he managed to gain a better grip, hugging the taller man with both arms.

"Does this mean we're going steady?" James asked, chuckling.

"Only…if you…put out on the…first date," Manning gasped as his vision started to become adjusted to the darkness.

Vaguely he could see silvery rings set only inches apart along the entire length of the funnel. Those would be the EM coils that moved the satellites. However, the bottom of the funnel was still an unknown. Could be a closed breech, possibly even processing machinery that loaded the hunters into position, the exposed gears grinding the soldiers into hamburger.

"Phoenix One to Phoenix Four," McCarter said into the com link. "Come in!"

There was only static.

"T.J., do you read? Over!"

"Can't hear you," Encizo said. "These walls are magnetic steel. Nothing we carry is going to get a radio signal out of this thing."

"Bloody hell!"

Just then, there was a loud clatter of machinery from below and the warriors drew weapons, ready for combat, but also braced for horrible death.

NOW A PERFECT TARGET in the sky above the cruise liner, Hawkins drifted toward the top deck. Nobody was in sight, but the man knew armed troops were already on the way to capture him alive. No way that was going to happen.

Bunching his ropes, he compacted his chute and dropped faster for the deck. Then at the very last moment, he opened it wide to be pulled to the port side and managed to avoid the fake grass covering the steel deck and hit the swimming pool instead. Bracing himself, the contact with the water was hard, the shock traveling up his legs and hips as if he had hit wet concrete.

He went deep and started swimming for the surface even before stopping. Reaching air, the drenched warrior pulled in a deep breath as the world went completely white. The parachute had arrived, and now the sodden material draped over him in deadly clinging folds that anchored his arms.

Slapping the release on his chest harness, Hawkins got free and dived for the bottom of the pool again, this time heading under the dive board. If he had hit that on his landing, this would have been his last jump.

Blanketing the whole area, the parachute lay over the diving board, and he emerged into the pocket underneath the board to fill his aching lungs with air. Suddenly there came the sound of machine guns and wet smacks as bullets hit the silk-covered pool, probing for him. Drawing his pistol, Hawkins shook the excess water from the weapon and fired blindly, hoping for a lucky hit.

More AK-47 assault rifles cut loose. Hawkins pulled a grenade, determined to die fighting when there was a deafeningly loud sustained roar from above and the wet parachute was yanked away and fluttered after the backwash of an F-18 Hornet skimming low over the pool, the afterburners of the fighter hitting the brigade soldiers like a sideways hurricane. Several splashed into the pool, but most were bowled over, toppling off the elevated deck to disappear over the side.

Using the diving board for support, Hawkins crawled onto the deck and sent a mental thanks to the hotshot pilot who had pulled off that suicide move. It had to have been Grimaldi; he didn't know of anybody else crazy enough to try the stunt.

Shadows on the deck caught his attention, and Hawkins dodged and fired, the Beretta catching two of the gunners. Okay, he was still alive, but trapped alone on a ship with a thousand enemies who wanted him dead. Only one option. Go deeper and rejoin the team.

Skirting a line of cabanas and wicker chairs, he caught two brigade soldiers hiding between two of the canvas changing tents, ready to ambush the warrior as he ran by. Pitiful.

"Hey," Hawkins said softly.

As the men turned, Hawkins worked the bolt on his weapon and mowed them down on the spot. Taking their assault rifles, he moved on. Prisoners would have been preferable—he was a soldier not an assassin—but only a fool put aside violence when it was the only logical option.

Going to a wide staircase, the Phoenix Force commando raked the bushes on either side of the faux marble steps, and brigade soldiers tumbled into view dropping their weapons. Staying on the banister in case of land mines, Hawkins slid off the end and tucked into a ball to hit the carpet rolling. The man landed on his feet near some ornamental bushes shaped like animals that completely closed off a stained-glass skylight, the wide panels larger than a yard across.

That was when he saw a red blinking light in the shadows under the bushes and the arming wires leading from the remote trigger to the thick line of C-4 plastique edging every pane of the enormous skylight. Whatever it was, he knew instinctively it was trouble for Phoenix Force and reached to yank the red wire.

Suddenly the bushes shook hard. A round smacked into the thick trunk of an elephant-shaped bush, cutting the stem in two. Exposed, the warrior dived from the cover, wildly firing both of his acquired Kalashnikovs. Men in red berets fell down the stairs, leaving a crimson trail, but more hardmen were on the upper deck, spent brass spraying out from the tattoo of their weapons.

Still firing, Hawkins sprinted along the line of hedge, hoping the soldiers would hesitate to shoot at the plastique. It had to have been there for an important reason. Hopefully more so than killing him.

As the first AK-47 emptied, Hawkins tossed it over the side railing and heard it clank on a lower deck. Perfect. Turning the remaining Kalashnikov on the colorful glass of the skylight for a diversion, Hawkins backed toward the railing and only got a few yards before the whole ship seemed to explode.

The concussion of the blast shoved him into the railing as the plastique went off and a billion tinkling rainbow shards blew for the stars. The thick topiary bushes directed most of the colored glass upward, but some of the slivers tore through and covered the deck like a shotgun blast, smashing on contact. A brigade soldier running down the stairs was torn apart, and Hawkins put his back to the explosion and kicked over a glass-topped canasta table. The table shattered from the incoming glass daggers, but the collision destroyed the high-velocity shards and only small pieces pounded into the equipment pack on his back.

As the concussion faded out to sea, and Hawkins forced himself to stand, sharp stings on his thigh and ear announced small cuts, but nothing life threatening. Heading for the access ladder to reach the next deck, he heard a hushed rumble that was horribly familiar to him. Hawkins spun about, firing the AK-47 as the angular body of a Harrier jump jet rose from the ragged hole where the stained-glass skylight had once been. Then another Harrier lifted into view, then a third, each moving out of the way to allow access for the one following.

Goddamn, the brigade had to have been holding these as their escape vehicles! Clever bastards, but now the British fighters would mean serious trouble for the Hornets circling the liner. The F-18s had to be low on fuel by now and in no condition to tackle a fully fueled wing of jump jets and fresh pilots.

Supported on its VTOL belly jets, the fifth warbird floated motionless above the gaping hole, then turned slowly toward the port side, its rapid-fire cannon raking the deck and railing, spewing out gouts of shattered wood trying for the lone warrior.

As the AK-47 jerked empty, he dropped the weapon and threw his Heckler & Koch MP-5 submachine gun at the left intake of the jump jet. The weapon was sucked directly into the ramjet. The protective impeller blades started to shred the weapon, but designed only for large flying birds, the blades jammed on the Virginia steel and the backlash of torque twisted the shaft with the force of a bomb. The ramjet shuddered, then the ammo in the MP-5 detonated from the impact of the turbine smashing into the loaded clip. A dozen rounds sparkled fire in the mouth of the struggling engine, then the blade shattered, the spinning shrapnel tearing the inner housing apart. Fuel gushed out in a stream and promptly ignited before the automatic cutoff valves could activate.

With one jet on fire, the fifth Harrier tilted sideways and spun in a circle, completely out of control, its missiles and cannons firing randomly. The barrage caught a second jump jet, and the machine thunderously disappeared off the starboard bow. Now the damaged Harrier started to spin into the lower deck, and the other jets slipped away from the area as fast as possible.

Knowing what was coming, Hawkins hopped over the railing and crawled down to hang suspended over the edge of the deck a heartbeat before a colossal explosion shook the ship and hot shrapnel blew out to the sea, carrying along the hedges, tables and corpses.

The blast tore at Hawkins's exposed fingers, and the man lost his hold to fall several decks, landing partly through the canvas awning of a covered walkway. Kicking a larger hole in the brightly striped material with his combat boots, he dropped through to land sprawling on a teakwood deck, momentarily stunned.

Then an angry voice yelled, and Hawkins pulled his Beretta to see the familiar staggered barrel of an AK-47 come around a corner. Clicking back the hammer, he waited until the brigade gunner came into view, then shot the man in the left eye, killing him instantly. Stumbling closer, he found his ankle was badly twisted. The pain was strong but controllable. Best to ignore it, then. Retrieving the dropped assault rifle, Hawkins slipped away from the corpse and entered the double doors the man had just exited.

Inside was a spacious ballroom, thick carpeting surrounding a wooden dance floor, now dotted with smashed crystal chandeliers that had just been ripped from the ceiling by the violent detonation above. Several brigade hardmen were on the bandstand opening cases of U.S. Army Stinger missiles, and Hawkins took them out as he raced across the room. Rearming with a Kalashnikov from another corpse, he took an ammo bag of loaded clips from an officer draped over a Stinger carrying case. The Phoenix Force commando used a full clip on the missiles, precisely shooting them to render the weapons useless, but not igniting the solid fuel engine or warhead.

Kicking the radar box off the last live Stinger, he slung

it over a shoulder and knelt to aim for the elevator banks far across the spacious ballroom. A volcano of fire gushed behind him as the rocket streaked away to blow apart the line of elevators, doors spinning away like flying disks.

Dropping the spent launcher, Hawkins limped forward to find the first two shafts were empty. The third was blocked solid with the smashed cage jammed in place. However, the fourth and fifth showed clear, intact shafts and taut cables.

Grabbing a ragged piece of the soft carpeting, the commando wrapped it around the well-greased cable of the farthermost shaft, then slid out of sight down into the bowels of the huge vessel.

Down he went, deck after deck passing with increasing speed. The carpeting was getting almost to hot to hold, smoke beginning to rise from the material when he spotted the elevator cage. Squeezing hard, he ignored the pain and managed to slow his descent and cushion the landing for his ankle.

Then, yanking open the rooftop hatch, Hawkins saw the startled faces of a dozen men wearing red berets, and he emptied the AK-47 into the enclosed area. The brigade hardmen died screaming, their weapons still slung over their shoulders, not a shot fired in return.

Easing himself into the corpse-filled cage, Hawkins tossed away the spent Kalashnikov and took two fresh assault rifles, checking the clips and working the bolts. Armed and still alive for the moment, he pressed the button for the lowest level shown on the control panel. Logically the satellite launcher would have to be attached to the keel of the vessel to keep it stable from the ocean storms. With luck there would be an access hatch that he could use to follow the power cables for the magnetic rail gun and rejoin Phoenix Force. Alone in this floating fortress, he stood about as much chance as a virgin in a Hong Kong whorehouse on double-coupon day.

Luxuriating in the peaceful moment, Hawkins dug in his med kit for a shot of morphine and found only smashed vials from the earlier explosion. Loosening the laces on his boot, he tied them again as tight as possible to help support his ankle. Then he got ready as the elevator lights approached the last indicator and the cage began to slow.

With a musical ding, the elevator doors opened and Hawkins raced out, bent low and firing in every direction with both weapons crossed at his forearms. Again caught by surprise, more brigade hardmen fell twisting away from the stuttering assault rifles. Then one of the assault rifles jammed. Cursing softly, he cast it away and took another from one of the dead men just as he heard the barking of guard dogs.

With his ankle hurting so much he could barely stand on it, Hawkins was in no shape to fight dogs and men. Choosing a door at random, he jimmied the lock with his Ranger knife and slipped inside a luxurious stateroom clearly for the big-money clients. Everything was richly decorated and trimmed in tassels or monogrammed with the logo of the *Terra Nova.*

As the sounds of men and dogs moved past the broken door, Hawkins crossed the palatial suite and threw a chair at the large curtained windows. No tiny portholes on this big a boat. As the sea wind rushed inside, books fluttered on the shelves and Hawkins noticed that most of the leather-bound volumes had titles written in what appeared to be Arabic. He didn't know a word of the language.

Glass crackling loudly under his boots, he moved to the window and looked about, but there was only open sea outside and the smooth hull of the ship reaching into the foamy water. Damnation, he was below all of the other exposed decks on the liner! There was no place to go but into the sea.

Just for a single moment, Hawkins considered that option

then turned his back on the possible escape route. He wouldn't leave the others in the middle of a mission any more than they would leave him behind. Dumas had said it right years ago. All for one, or one for all—that was the only way to stay alive in a firefight. Without buddies at his back, a soldier almost always found himself dropped into a meat grinder.

Yanking open the courtesy bar, Hawkins grabbed a brandy and took a long swig for the pain. Then, placing an ear to the door, he listened carefully as he reloaded both of the Kalashnikovs from the ammo bag and got ready to try for the stairwell at the end of the hallway.

"READY TO LOAD!" a brigade technician called out, working the latch on the breech of the O'Neil launcher. The hatch weighed two tons, but the counterweights made moving it easy enough to be accomplished by a single man.

"Just a tick," a second tech replied, shutting off the flow of gel into the interior of a hunter.

An armored section of the hull was supported by four telescoping steel rods away from the satellite, the opening allowing easy access to the filling port. Removing the pressurized hose, the tech waved a magnetic key over a sensor, and the gel port irised shut, then the outer section of the hull was pulled back into place to lock and seal.

The gelatin had been the biggest problem in creating the hunter-killers. The rail guns could launch a satellite into space easily enough, but the staggering acceleration smashed any equipment inside the machine no matter how much cushioning was applied. Then they created a nonflammable, nonconductive gelatin to fill the sphere and evenly distribute the colossal pressure. In one stroke the impossible became practical.

Snaking the hose out of the way, another tech started the

conveyor belt under the satellite, and the first man swung aside the ponderous breech of the cannon.

Machine-gun fire riddled the brigade technician, and the Phoenix Force warriors climbed out of the funnel with their weapons ablaze.

The others shouted in shock and went for the holstered weapons on their tool belts. Too little, too late—the Stony Man team took the terrorists out until the immediate vicinity was empty of viable human targets. James was the last to leave and placed a Light Gear Harness bag in the launch chamber. If things went bad, they might desperately need the LGH to get off this floating hardsite.

As the warriors spread out, a rifle rang out and a slug ricocheted off the metal deck. Encizo fired his MP-5 from the hip, the spray of 9 mm rounds rattling the catwalk that circled the wall of the room. Dying men fell over the railing and hit the deck.

"Clear?" McCarter said over the com link, dropping a clip and slapping in a fresh magazine.

"Clear," Manning replied, using only one hand to awkwardly work the bolt on his weapon to clear a jam. Several fingers on his right hand had been sprained catching Encizo when he fell, but the minor damage didn't lower his accuracy with the submachine gun.

With weapon in hand, James boosted his com link to maximum power and turned, sweeping the walls. "T.J., can you hear me? T.J., come in, please." But there was no response. The steel deck did just as good a job blocking their transmission as the barrel of the rail gun.

"Gary on the catwalk, check for survivors," McCarter ordered, approaching the conveyor belt. "Rafe, lock the doors. Cal, mine the airshaft. We're digging in. Any minute the brigade is going to try very hard to get us out of here and we're not moving an inch until we have those codes."

Nobody replied. They just did it.

Walking past a control panel, McCarter stared with open hatred at the line of huge black spheres on the conveyor belt. Each was a dull ebony in color, light seeming to fall into the surface and simply disappear. Some damn boffin's trick. He wasn't impressed by the optical illusion.

Going to a control panel, McCarter ripped off the cover and yanked out handfuls of wiring. The conveyor belt stopped quivering with power and went still. Tracking the length, he could see that it reached completely around the entire room and once had to have held dozens, maybe even a hundred of the giant war machines. Six remained.

He glanced at his watch. "Our numbers are falling, gentlemen! How are we doing?"

"Nearly done!" Encizo stated, dogging a watertight hatch shut, then shoving a wrench into the spokes of the handle to hold it closed. "Hey, Gary, how many men do you think the brigade has on board?"

"Can't say for sure," Manning replied, turning over the dead with his combat boot. A few showed faint signs of life, but those faded before he could administer first aid. "I'd say two thousand troops."

"But that's exactly how many rounds of ammo we have," James said, wiring a Claymore to a floor vent.

"Then don't bloody well miss anybody, mate," McCarter commanded gruffly into the com link. "Are we sealed yet?"

"Tight as a crab's ass," Encizo replied, thumping a screwdriver firmly into the locking mechanism. "Nobody's going to get this open without high explosives. It'd be easier to come through the walls."

"They just may," the leader of Phoenix Force growled. "Okay, standard defense positions. Shoot on sight. Cal, breach one of these things and get the hard drive out. That'll have the self-destruct codes."

Faintly the whole ship shook from a distant explosion, and somebody tried the handle on the locked door. Then something heavy began pounding on the steel hatchway, trying to gain entrance.

"And hurry it along," McCarter added, taking a defensive position behind a coiled pile of chains. He started laying out his supply of clips and grenades.

"On it," James said, wheeling a sloped ladder to the nearest hunter. The forty-foot sphere towered over the man, and as he climbed, he expertly ran his hands over the armored hull, searching for some way inside the machine.

CHAPTER NINETEEN

Gravel Pile, Delmarva Peninsula

Dropping the Atchisson, Lyons hit the ground with both hands splayed and sharply exhaled as if he were catching the world like a basketball to cushion the fall. Curling one leg, he flipped over and kicked out with the heel of his combat boot, ramming it between the legs of his attacker.

Covered with dirt and camouflage netting, the brigade hardman groaned to the ground, and Lyons rolled over to shove a knuckled fist into the knee of the nearest man. The fellow fell, yowling in pain, both hands grabbing his shattered kneecap.

Rolling to his feet, the Able Team leader almost drew his Colt but thought better of the action. With the two groups mixed together, he couldn't use a gun out of the fear of hitting his own people. Which was probably the exact reason why every brigade member was armed with a knife and something else—a police baton, a Tanto—the Japanese short sword—a hand ax or a cattle prod. That was the really dangerous device, and Lyons took a stunning blow from the police baton on his forearm to kick the cattle prod away. Schwarz smashed it to pieces under a grinding bootheel.

Releasing his ammo pack, Blancanales swept his arm along the ground to bring down a brigade hardman, then shoved his own knife into the man's armpit. Ignoring the screaming man, he scrambled to his feet and ducked under an ax to chop the edge of his hand across another gunner's throat, smashing the Adam's apple. Gasping for breath, the brigade hardman lurched forward, and Blancanales threw him over a hip against the side of the van. The man hit so hard the glass windows shattered and he fell in a lifeless tangle of broken limbs.

Trying to appear frightened, Schwarz lifted both arms as if surrendering. His grinning adversary raised a foot-long bowie knife, and the Able Team warrior kicked and stepped as one smooth motion. The man jerked back with his teeth flying away. Nimbly Schwarz landed on the balls of his feet, and spun into a backkick, taking out the next man even as the Tanto sliced through the air.

Stepping over his fallen comrade, the next brigade hardman grinned as he flipped a U.S. Marine combat knife around so that the back of the blade rested on his forearm, then raised his other stiff hand, assuming the cat stance. Remembering the DEW Line, Schwarz could guess the origin of the knife, and also knew he was now facing a fellow black belt. But he had a possible answer for that problem.

When first deciding to study the martial arts, the electronics wizard knew that he wasn't tall or lean, and thus everybody would assume a beefy man would learn judo or karate. Strong arms meant strong-arm techniques. But certainly not monkey kung fu. He was completely wrong, not the body type at all. Naturally that was what Schwarz chose. In battle, he gave nothing away.

Throwing himself to the ground, the Able Team commando assumed the crab position to get under the knife and shattered the man's left shin in a hook-and-kick. The hardman screamed and fell to his knees. Few people in the world realized that a master of kung fu was more deadly lying on the ground than standing. A common mistake that filled many graves with eager fools. Slapping with both hands,

Schwarz clapped his enemy on the sides of the head and burst the eardrums. The pain had to have been excruciating, yet the man didn't grab his head, but only pulled backward to draw a derringer and fire. Twisting out of the way, Schwarz saw the hot flame wash over his shirt, but felt no impact. At this range that .44 round would go through his body armor as if it weren't there.

Wasting no more strength on disabling techniques, Schwarz lunged forward with all of his body weight in a double leopard strike and buried his knuckled fists in the vulnerable nerve center just to the right of the heart. It was a risky move, a quarter-inch either way and nothing would happen. Except that he would get his head blown off.

Shuddering all over, the brigade gunner went limp and toppled sideways, dark blood gushing from his slack mouth.

Pulling his own knife, Schwarz turned fast, searching for the next attacker. But only his teammates were standing amid the dead and the dying.

"This is a damn Pathfinder trick," Lyons said, easing his combat stance and drawing a silenced Ingram machine pistol. "David told me about this when we went fishing once."

"Pathfinders?" Blancanales asked, pulling in air as drew his own silenced weapon.

"British SAS special ops group," Lyons explained, walking along carefully, checking the maintenance area for any further hidden pits. "Most secret, Queen's eyes only sort of group."

Retrieving his M-16/M-203, Schwarz slung it over a shoulder. "Pretty slick, too. Almost worked," he grunted, flexing his aching hands.

"Which translates into they're dead," Blancanales stated, firing his silenced 9 mm Beretta pistol at any smooth areas of soil. "And we're not."

"Damn straight, brother."

For the next few minutes, Able Team did a full recon of

the area, spent brass flying as they probed the ground with hot lead. Several more disguised holes were discovered, but the only other nest of brigade hardmen they found was located under the front wheels of the parked van, the men underground crushed lifeless by the weight of the vehicle. They died without making a sound rather than reveal their location and destroy any chance the other nest had to kill the invaders.

"Fanatics," Lyons growled, inserting a fresh clip and jacking the slide to chamber a round for immediate use. "Come on, let's get the M-224 set up and start paving the road."

"Just hope they didn't hear us," Schwarz said, shouldering his heavy load and heading for the mountain of gravel. "These guys are very high tech."

"Got it covered," Blancanales answered, digging about in his fatigue blouse pocket and pulling out a butane cigarette lighter.

DEEP WITHIN the Cole mansion, a young soldier fine-tuned the controls on an extensive control panel. The radar and sonar showed clear, but he had briefly caught something that sounded like muffled gunfire in the vicinity. Or perhaps only a car backfiring—it was hard to tell sometimes. As he twirled a dial on the control panel, a dish microphone on the roof minutely altered its direction trying to zero in on the disturbance.

"Sir," he said hesitantly. "I'm not sure, but there may have just been weapons fire nearby."

"From the shore of the canal?" a lieutenant asked from a console covered with small television screens. On a set program, the monitors constantly changed views: from the front gate, to the gravel road, the garage, the sky above and a blurred, watery scene of fish and fat blue crab from the bottom of the C&D canal.

"No, sir, it was from the…" The technician scowled, then laughed. "Aw, hell, its just firecrackers, sir. Now I can clearly hear the fuse hissing amid all the banging. Must be some kids messing about."

"During school hours, at this time of the day, in farm country?" Major Cole said from the doorway, several armed soldiers standing close behind. "Bullshit. It's a diversion. Check the radio."

"Yes, sir!" the lieutenant said with a salute.

Reaching high on the console, the private flipped a switch and a monitor displayed scrambled sine waves on an oscillator screen, the pattern meaningless to the uneducated.

"Local police channels are clear," the technician answered. "CB is jammed worse than shortwave. Only thing on the air is the FM jazz station over in Goose Point. They're so low-powered, the idiots probably don't even knew there is a communications blackout yet."

"Then the firecrackers are cover for government troops," the lieutenant muttered, biting a lip. "Damn, they found us fast."

"But not soon enough. Get the Claymores and Bettys online," Major Cole commanded, digging into his pocket and pulling out a small notebook. Flicking a butane lighter, he applied the flame to the item and the chemically treated paper vanished in a flash.

There, that removed the self-destruct commands for the hunters. Not even he could stop them now. All that remained was the backup copy in the wall safe of his office. He would have to destroy that personally.

"Mines are active, sir!" the tech announced.

"Good. Lieutenant, release the dogs, activate the AutoSentries and arm the SAM bunker. Delta Force may have close air support."

"Be damn fools if they didn't," he added softly, checking he Desert Eagle at his hip. It was fully loaded with Glaser

Sure-Kill cartridges and Talon armor-piercing slugs. Let them come.

"Yes, sir!" the lieutenant said, sitting down to assist the crew at the defense control board.

On the consoles red lights turned green and meters swung to full power as the front gate locked and high-voltage electricity began to flow silently through the barbed wire encircling the top of the wall and the roof of the mansion. Land mines in the front and backyard of the estate pulsed on the status board. Hidden underground and hung in the trees, the Claymores were ready to detonate if they were jostled, or at the touch of a button.

Major Cole smiled in satisfaction at the display of formidable weaponry. In spite of the technology, the real defense of the mansion was that the government troops would want to take him alive, and that meant they would have to try to infiltrate the mansion. There was no way they would risk a direct attack and take a chance of killing him without obtaining the codes first. However, his own troops would have no such problems shooting down the paper tigers of the hated Americans.

"Sound red alert," Cole ordered, grinding his boot into the ashes, destroying any chance of the pages being reconstructed. "Have the troops kill anybody they don't instantly recognize. It's better to lose some of our people than let the command codes get into the hands of the government traitors."

"Yes, sir!"

"What we do," a brigade gunner said, solemnly working the bolt on his AK-47 assault rifle, "we do for humanity!"

Stopping in the doorway, Cole gave the man an emotionless expression, his face blank of any emotions.

"Of course," the leader of the Peace Brigade said smoothly.

Just then the technician gestured for their attention. "Sir.

I'm hearing an odd whistling,'' he said slowly, one hand holding a headphone in place, the other adjusting the controls on the console. "It sounds rather like a tea kettle building a head of steam.''

"A car on the Route 13 bridge could be overheating,'' the lieutenant suggested, his face furrowed in concern.

"No, I don't think so,'' the technician replied with a frown. "There's no rush of boiling water. This is sharper, cleaner. Unlike anything I have ever heard before. Getting pretty loud, too.''

"No,'' Cole whispered, glancing at the ceiling in fear. "It's impossible. Th-they wouldn't dare! They want the codes!''

"Do what, sir?'' the lieutenant asked, staring at the console in worry. The radar and sonar were still clear.

That was when the video screens showed a silent explosion on the front lawn, and the major ran out the door, his cadre of bodyguards following at his heels.

SHRIEKING DOWN from a clear sky, mortar shells arched over the wall and hit in the front path, blasting a yard-deep hole in the soil. Armed guards vanished in the strident explosion. The next impacted in the garden with hellish fury, the greenhouse shattering to reveal the concrete shape of a missile bunker.

More 60 mm shells arrived in a flurry, the blasts overlapping one another and creating fireballs that grew in size and heat, destroying anything nearby. In only moments the SAM bunker erupted as the combined thermite charges blazed with intense heat that stole the very oxygen from the air. Screaming men fried, the concrete walls crumbled and the warheads in the SAMs detonated, adding their fiery, destructive power to the mounting inferno. His body covered with flames, a dying man insanely fired his AK-47 at the roaring blaze before the ammo in the weapon cooked off and removed his destroyed hands at the charred wrists.

Now shells plummeted onto the wall, throwing away chunks of masonry. Brigade gunners hustled to defend the vulnerable opening, and in perfect synchronization, more rounds fell onto the massed guards, removing them from the face of the Earth.

Then puffs of smoke appeared from the top of the gravel pile over two miles way, and seconds later HAFLA rockets streaked in to hit the garage, reducing the Hummers and armored sedans into twisted wrecks of flesh and steel. Somehow still alive, the lone guard outside the main gate stared at the bright red laser dot jiggling on the barrier, then started to run. But a heartbeat later a LAW rocket arrived and blew the gate apart. Iron shrapnel and the brigade hardman hurtled everywhere.

ON THE CREST of the distant gravel pile, Carl Lyons studied the wreckage of the outer wall around the Cole mansion through field glasses.

"Two more degrees to the left," he said into a throat mike. "Then up six."

"Roger that," Schwarz replied into the com link, altering the cant of the M-224 light field mortar. Preparing another round, he dropped the fat shell down the smooth barrel of the mortar, and it blew skyward, sailing over the gravel pile to arch downward toward the estate, the air whistling from the sheer speed of its final approach. The 60 mm shell slammed into the rear gate, setting off a string of Claymore mines that obliterated the concrete walk going all the way to the shore of the canal.

"Bull's-eye," Blancanales said, casting away a spent LAW tube and preparing his last spare. "Send some more thermite into the orchard. I'll finish the wall."

Grunting in reply, Schwarz busily unwrapped the safety

tape from another round for the mortar. Sweeping across the estate, he gave the land around the mansion another a good pounding, setting off more land mines. Stumbling about in the acrid smoke, brigade hardmen were firing their Kalashnikovs wildly, doing more damage to one another than to the Stony Man team safe behind the distant pile of gravel.

Releasing the field glasses to dangle around his neck, Lyons picked up an Armbrust and placed the hard plastic tube on his shoulder. He pulled the trigger, and a blizzard of nitrogen snow shot out backward as the antipersonnel round streaked straight toward the mansion. The round burst in midair, showering the bushes and trees alongside the building with a hellstorm of fléchette slivers. Uniforms in tatters, the brigade gunners fell into view chewed to pieces by the antipersonnel charge.

"Got the feed ready?" Lyons asked over their com link, reloading the Armbrust.

"Say when," Schwarz said, placing one more 60 mm charge into a feeder slot alongside the machine. This was another of Cowboy Kissinger's modifications, and he sure as hell hoped it worked as it was supposed to.

Lyons launched his last projectile from the Armbrust and Blancanales did the same with a HAFLA from the other side of the loose stone pile. The country estate thundered under the double strike, debris thrown high and wide.

"Now," he commanded, dropping the weapon and starting down the loose gravel.

Nodding, Schwarz flipped a switch, and the box alongside the M-224 dropped a shell into the mortar. The live round thumped and launched for the estate as another shell cycled into the hot barrel. With built-in whistles, these rounds shrilly screamed down from the sky and hit the roof of the mansion to spew out tremendous volumes of thick green smoke.

The odd color was deliberate; the hue confused any ultraviolet scanners that might be in operation, and most people were hesitant to enter what looked like poison gas. With the heat from the rampaging firestorm in the orchard and garden confounding any working infrared scanners, and the land mines safely removed, the headquarters of the Peace Brigade was now ready for a hard probe.

Keening loudly, the barrage of shells seemed to last forever, HE rounds pounding the lawn, thermite and white phosphorus burning the orchard and garden into ashes, and a few airbursts to pound the open landscape with hot shrapnel.

The 60 mm rounds were still falling when the Able Team van came charging along the dirt road to the estate and the shelling stopped as they crossed the rubble of the fallen wall. As the vehicle jounced through the steaming blast craters heading for the mansion, three figures leaped from the moving vehicle and stealthily separated in the drifting clouds of chemical smoke.

Rushing from the mansion, a brigade soldier armed with an M-79 grenade launcher sent a 40 mm grenade straight at the racing van. The vehicle was blown off the ground and the burning chassis rolled sideways to crash into the side of the garage, smashing the door and exposing several police cars parked inside.

Running across the churned soil, Lyons unleashed the Atchisson in the direction of the gunman and moved on, quickly reloading. Nothing alive remained in the area of the grass from the ripping hellstorm of lead and steel shotgun cartridges.

Their weapons constantly firing, the Able Team commandos moved through the noise and chaos, implacable as a hunter-killer. If Peace Brigade soldiers came into view, they died, completely outgunned by the sharp-eyed marksmen from the Farm.

This was the biggest gamble the commandos had ever

taken, so much more than just their own lives riding on the outcome. But they had faith in Blancanales's psych call for Major Cole. The South African officer was the former head of a death squad, the deposed commander of the secret police and now the absolute commander of the paramilitary Peace Brigade. This wasn't the type of man who led troops into battle. Cole should be buried as deep as possible in the most secure location in the mansion. Most probably deep underground. Which meant anybody they met on the ground floor was a viable target. Blancanales could be wrong; he had been once or twice in the past. But there was no time for a recon first. The team had to go in now, and that meant taking chances.

Bracing against the recoil of his grenade launcher, Blancanales pumped a few 30 mm napalm rounds up and onto the roof of the mansion, then sent an HE round into the wide smokestack of the fireplace. The brick column blew apart, then swayed from the building and crashed to the ground, leaving gaping holes where the hearths were located.

Blowing open the front door with a grenade, Able Team waited a few seconds for the enemy to recover, then rolled in more grenades. Antipersonnel spheres cut loose, and the windows shattered from the blast of steel shards. Conventional military grenades used plastic shrapnel so the enemy doctors couldn't find the shrapnel and had to dig around to stop the internal bleeding. The "mercy" grenades left many terrorists alive to continue fighting, so Kissinger had fixed that, giving the Stony Man grenades coiled steel and a larger C-4 charge. Almost nothing survived the new AP grenades.

Using a standard one-on-one cover formation, Able Team charged into the mansion, firing into the smoky shadows. The living room was a charred junkyard. In the hallway a smashed AutoSentry lay in pieces near a horribly mutilated man who feebly gestured at them with an automatic pistol, its slide kicked back showing it was out of ammo. Lyons used his Ingram to end the misery of the dying soldier, while his teammates secured the foyer. Fed by the breeze from the broken fireplace, the library was an inferno, the walls of books burning out of control and thick smoke going up the staircase.

Since their target was in the cellar, Blancanales threw a proximity mine onto the next landing while Schwarz flipped an incendiary stick on the stairs to stop anybody from coming down. As the thermite charge briefly blazed, the trio rejoined their team leader and swept deeper into the building.

Chattering AK-47 assault rifles fired from the dining room, and Lyons used the Atchisson on some guards who had flipped over the dining table as protection. The burst of fléchette rounds splintered the obstruction and hardforce alike. Falling into view, a legless woman raised a hand for mercy. The urge was strong to accept her surrender, but Lyons saw her uniform, thought of the Marine tortured to death and fired the Atchisson once more.

The smoke was getting thick, and the team pulled on breathing masks before proceeding. The rest of the wing seemed to be empty, but in the next wing they found a lot of rooms set up as barracks, the walls dotted with empty gun racks. There were also several dog bowls on the floor, along with leather leashes and collars.

"Unless these guys are really into S&M," Schwarz stated, "then there's about a dozen guard dogs here. Maybe more."

"And damn big ones from the size of the bowls," Blancanales grunted, adjusting his face mask. "Can't feed a Doberman from a teacup."

"Pit bulls!" Lyons shouted as a pack of the animals came charging silently around a corner.

He tried to swing the Atchisson around fast, but the lead

animal leaped and clenched his jaws onto the main barrel of the weapon trying to wrest it away. That was a Russian FSB trick. Who trained these animals? If he released the weapon, the dog would rip out his guts before he could draw the Ingram, and the other dogs were almost here.

As his teammates opened fire on the rest of the pack, Lyons fired the Atchisson. The rounds hit a blank wall, doing no damage to the animals, and while the roar had to have been deafening, the pit bull stubbornly stayed on the gun. Backing into a corner, he employed his weapon as a shield to deflect the other dogs as they arrived in a black wave.

Now the surviving beasts were upon the men and Blancanales knew the next few rounds in his weapon were HE grenades. At this range he'd only kill his own team if he fired. Reversing the chunky grenade launcher, he used its wooden stock to club the next dog to death. But then an animal grabbed his weapon and yanked it from his grip. As the next charged, Blancanales shoved a chair in its way and dived backward to roll over a bunk and come up with his Beretta shooting.

Dropping a spent clip, Schwarz reloaded and fired controlled bursts at the floor on every side. A pit bull tried for his barrel, and he blew its head off. Another clamped its jaw on the canvas bag holding his laptop and started dragging the man away from the wall where the other dogs could strike from every direction. Schwarz stitched the rest of the pack with the M-16, while red jaws snapping for his groin and wrists. The 5.56 mm tumblers did tremendous damage, but even though badly wounded and bleeding profusely, the dogs still struggled to reach the invaders and hold them captive to await the arrival of their masters.

Kicking a large female in the throat, Lyons rammed a stiff finger into the eye of the big male pit bull on his weapon and it released the barrel, howling in anguish. Now the Able Team leader used the autoshotgun with surgical precision, and the brave dogs were torn to pieces.

Leaving the slaughter of the barracks, the team continued to sweep the mansion. Every room was checked, every closet, but the building seemed deserted. There was only the crackle of the burning timbers and the thick waves of smoke forming a writhing blanket along the ceiling.

Reaching the kitchen, Lyons sharply whistled and gestured out the rear window. Several heavily armed brigade hardmen were running across the estate from the direction of the canal. Able Team assumed a triad at the window and waited until the gunners were close before emptying their assorted weapons. The enemy died never knowing what hit them, or from where.

Out of spare 30 mm rounds, Blancanales tossed aside the heavy X-18 launcher and swung around an M-16 assault rifle just as the top half of a Dutch door swung open and a gunner inside started shooting, then coughing from the smoky atmosphere. The team hit the floor and the stuttering line of 7.62 mm rounds shattered a line of plates. Then Able Team responded and didn't miss.

Checking inside the well-stocked pantry, Lyons found a locked door and blew off its hinges. Exposed was a wide set of stairs that offered an easy avenue to the basement. Warily the men pulled back out of sight.

"Too convenient, gotta be a trap," Lyons stated, thumbing fresh shells into the tubular magazine of his weapon. "We need to make another door."

"Nobody would have their headquarters right next to the main entrance," Blancanales stated, looking at the kitchen floor.

Schwarz nodded. "On it," he said, kneeling amid the spent brass and broken glass to yank open his munition bag. With practiced ease, he attached four Claymore mines facedown on the boards, forming in a yard-wide square. H set the timers on the quadruple charge, and Able Team retreated into the hallway.

There was a tremendous bang, as if the world's largest pistol had gone off, and they returned to find a splintery hole in the floor. There was a room below full of smashed electronic equipment, broken furniture mixing with human remains. It appeared to be some kind of a control room. One of the dead men wore a lieutenant's bars, but the others were privates and technicians wearing no rank insignia.

Holding a canister in his hand, Blancanales pulled an arming ring, then tossed down a smoke grenade. It bounced among the wreckage, spewing out volumes of thick green gas, and Lyons jumped down the short drop to land firing his weapon at the doorway. Hideous shrieks announced another kill.

Two thumps told of the rest of the team arriving, and Lyons took cover while Schwarz shoved his M-16 through the doorway and fired in a large circle. Voices shouted, but not in pain.

Then he moved out of the way, and his teammates fired at the walls on either side of the door. The plasterboard exploded into dust, and more men tumbled into view mortally wounded. Even as they fell, Lyons shoved through the office chair as a diversion and Able Team rushed into the basement of the mansion with weapons firing.

More soldiers were encountered and sent to hell. Schwarz used the 40 mm M-203 grenade launcher to clear the stairs of six operational AutoSentries while Lyons and Blancanales slaughtered three more pit bulls charging in their direction. The men placed their shots and removed the animals as swiftly and humanely as possible.

Now a thick and heavy silence ruled the basement, the only sounds coming from above, the crash of burning timbers and the occasional round of ammunition cooking off from the intense heat of the growing fire. Soon the mansion would start to collapse, blocking any possible exit. But the men cleared their minds of that and concentrated on the task at hand: find Cole and get the codes.

The air was becoming stifling even with their masks, and sweat poured off the commandos as they checked among the Peace Brigade corpses for Cole. The terrorists seemed to be using the standard rank insignia of the Army, and while Able Team found a lot of strips and chevrons, there wasn't a single oak leaf in the crowd.

Closed doors lined the smoky corridor, and the team was forced to check each and every one. This was the worst aspect of inside combat. There were a million places for a sniper to hide, and they had to move fast, as well as not miss any possible hiding place. One mistake could mean a bullet between the shoulders from behind.

Most of the rooms proved to be empty, but in an office they found a very busty woman stripped to her bra and panties in the act of changing from a Peace Brigade uniform into a civilian dress.

"Freeze!" Lyons said loudly in his best police voice, the Atchisson leading his advance into the room. "We only want the codes. Tell us where they are and you live."

But at the sight of the Stony Man warriors in the doorway, the woman hissed in anger and threw herself across a desk to grab for a G-11 caseless rifle. As she turned, the men pulled triggers and annihilated that section of the office.

"N-never stop...us..." she gurgled, staring hatefully at them. "Wh-what we do..." Then the woman trembled and went forever still.

"Goddamn it, Cole is using his own people as traps," Lyons growled, shoving in the last cartridges from his bandolier. With a shrug he dropped the leather belt from around his shoulder. "Let's find the bastard and end this now!"

Spreading out, the team tore through the basement unt

finding a door closed with roll-down steel shutters. There was no handle, lock or even a keypad in sight.

"We have a winner," Blancanales whispered, aiming at the door in case it suddenly started to open.

Lyons pointed downward, and, hitting the floor, Schwarz found a tiny crack set between the steel shutter and the concrete jamb. But that was enough. Pulling out his Army laptop, he wiped off some dog drool and started to reel out a fiber-optics cable to slide it under the barrier.

The screen of the laptop came alive with a low-angle view of the sealed room. Red light bulbs illuminated the darkness, masking the presence of any other heat sources, so he switched to ultraviolet and the monitor swirled into a black-and-white picture of a warehouse. Resting on pallets, military crates with odd writing on the side were stacked to the ceiling, and steel shelving sagged under the weight of MRE cartons, blankets and medical supplies. It was the supply dump the brigade planned to use to live through the years of starvation after the nuclear war.

But more importantly, behind a crude barricade of water barrels, six brigade gunners were hurrying to assemble a flamethrower. None of them wore night-vision goggles, and the darkness was hampering their efforts considerably.

"This is their headquarters," Blancanales said, looking at the computer screen. "Cole is somewhere in there."

"Can't see anybody wearing oak leaves."

"Then there's another room."

Lyons grunted at the pronouncement. That was also his read on the situation. "Probably expect us to blast it open and charge through the smoke," he growled, adjusting his mask.

"Sitting ducks for that M-1A hot-dog roaster," Schwarz stated, packing away the laptop.

"Not this time," Lyons snarled, and jacked the shells from the Atchisson and pocketed the rounds to reload with new cartridges looped into his gun belt. Only seven, but that hopefully was enough.

Leveling the autoweapon, the commando cut loose, fléchettes cut through the shutters as if they were plywood. Men screamed from the other side, more in shock than pain. Then Lyons went low, and his teammates shoved the muzzles of their weapons through the hole and raked the men behind the water barrels.

The gunners fell as they died, and the flamethrower went tumbling away. It hit the floor in a crash, and lay there with its preburner at the end of the muzzle still hissing a bright blue flame. A deadly spark waiting to ignite the pressurized fuel tank into a hellish firebomb at the slightest trace of a leak.

Quickly reaching through the hole, Lyons found the switch and the shutter rumbled upward only to jam immediately, the jagged strips of curled metal ringing the hole making it impossible for the shutters to retract properly. But the opening on the floor was just high enough for the team to crawl through and gain entrance.

Schwarz and Blancanales stood guard while Lyons turned off the preburner and closed the valves of the flamethrower. Keeping low, the men now moved from crate to crate, using what cover was available as they penetrated hard and fast into the heart of the enemy fortress. The storage room went on for hundreds of feet, extending almost to the canal before the rear wall came into view and a loud shot rang out. Just one, and nothing more.

"Go, go, go!" Lyons cursed, and led a charge through the maze of shelving until reaching a small alcove.

Bright fluorescent lights hung above a large metal desk, a gray-and-red-striped flag decorating the wall. A small pile of ashes was smoldering in a coffee mug, and sitting in a hard chair behind the desk was a heavily muscled man in his midfifties wearing gray military fatigues that fit as if the had been tailored. On the collar were gold oak leaves. A smoking .50-caliber Desert Eagle pistol lay on the floor near his dangling hand, and the rear of his head was a steaming crater, brains and blood splattered across the flag and cinder-block wall.

CHAPTER TWENTY

Strike Zone Alpha Zulu, Atlantic Ocean

The four Peace Brigade jump jets moved as nimbly as dragonflies, traveling sideways and backward along the deck of the cruise liner. The bizarre maneuver scrambled the targeting computers on the Hornets, but an F-18 pilot tried anyway and only churned the water with his machine gun. Then another launched its last two Sidewinders and managed to catch a Harrier with a lucky strike. The jet vanished in a corona of thunder, and the Hornet sharply banked to avoid flying through the roiling explosion.

Grim congratulations sounded over the radios of the Navy fighters, but it was false bravado. Slowly being left behind by the moving battle was a pool of flaming wreckage. A C-160 Hercules air-to-air tanker had arrived from the *Kitty Hawk* to refuel the Hornets, but the Harriers had effortlessly blown it out of the sky.

With only a few hundred pounds of fuel in his tanks, Grimaldi knew the F-18 Hornets were actually losing this fight. The Brigade pilots were playing it smart, keeping their birds right above the *Terra Nova* where the Hornets couldn't attack without endangering the American team on board.

From that position, the jump jets could freely use cannon and missiles at the Navy planes, forcing them to fly faster and do more maneuvers rapidly consuming their dwindling fuel supply. Soon the Navy jets would go dry and start to drop from the sky. Then the Hornets would "walk" over on their belly jets and murder the helpless pilots floating in the ocean. But there was no other choice. They had to keep up the pressure and give Phoenix Force the chance to get the codes.

Deep in his guts, Grimaldi already knew that when the warning light flashed on his board, he was hitting the afterburners and at full speed ramming into one of the fat Harriers. If he was going to take the long walk, then he wasn't going alone.

Dotting the air, tracer rounds yammered from the *Terra Nova* as the last Phalanx cannon robotically tracked the F-18s and completely ignored the Harriers. Spiraling through the chaff, the Navy Hornets streaked up from below the gunwale and strafed the forward deck with .50-caliber rounds, the impact throwing the dying men into the sea. Stingers and LAWs launched from everywhere on the cruise liner, there was a violent detonation and the wreckage of a third Hornet was added to the oily surface of the Atlantic.

Skimming low to try for the Phalanx again, Grimaldi was startled to see two foamy wakes cut the surface of the ocean, heading for the vulnerable side of the ship.

Pulling the joystick back hard, Grimaldi rode the pain of his ribs as he climbed out of the way of the torpedoes. That Navy submarine had have finally found them and was trying to help.

"Abort those fish!" he yelled into his throat mike, slapping off the decoder so his transmission went out clean over the open airwaves. "Abort, abort! Sub, do you read me? This is Admiral Stone, scrub those fish!"

But it was too late. The torpedoes hit, sweeping along the entire length of the speeding vessel, the eruptions throwing high water, and steel and fire. As the boiling water and smoke washed away from the hull of the cruise liner, Grimaldi could see there was virtually no damage to the hull, only deep scratches and a badly ruined paint job.

"Practice shots!" Grimaldi breathed, relaxing his grip on the joystick. Somehow the Farm had to still be on-line and sending help their way. The dummy torpedoes used in naval war games certainly sounded like the real thing, but couldn't sink a tugboat. However, to the brigade it had to have seemed like they got nuked. Probably thought their ship was sinking.

The speakers immediately burst into speech.

"…ny chance you'll talk now, Hornets?" a stern voice demanded. "This is Captain Maitlin of the USS *Connecticut* and—"

"Silence! The enemy have ears," Grimaldi snapped, reducing his speed to save fuel. "Switch to setting Ocean, Romeo, Charlie, X ray."

"Better?" the sub captain asked over the headphones, his voice crystal clear.

Since radio waves couldn't penetrate water, Grimaldi knew that the sub had to have an antenna sticking out of the ocean somewhere. But good luck trying to find a foot-long metal rod in the middle of the ocean.

"Thank you, Captain. Sig reg is Hammer of Thor."

"Blue Firestorm."

"Confirmed, sir. Your bona fides are accepted. I am Admiral Stone in command of this attack wing. You are forbidden to fire again at that ship!" Grimaldi ordered, keeping a watch on the radar for enemy missiles. "We have a, well, a Navy SEAL team on board the vessel trying to do a…rescue. Do not fire again."

"Roger, wilco, Hornet. Can we help in any way? I have my own SEAL team and BUDS ready to go."

An underwater demolition squad? It had to be a big boat Grimaldi knew every plane in the world, but was hazy on submersibles.

"Not at the moment, *Connecticut*. But it would be appreciated if you fished any of us out of the drink when we splash down. We are sans vermouth up here."

"Dry as a martini, eh? Roger, Admiral. We'll stand by and await your orders. Maitlin, out."

"Over and out," Grimaldi replied, returning to the battle. They now had the firepower to blow the stinking brigade ship to hell, but still could not seriously harm it.

Privately he hoped that McCarter was doing lot better inside the vessel than they were doing outside.

ON THE BRIDGE of the *Terra Nova,* the officers finally released their grips on stanchions and tables as the vibrations of the multiple torpedo strike began to ebb away.

"Christ! The hull must be blown apart," a brigade hardman cried, going white. "We gotta be sinking. Abandon ship!"

Standing near the men operating the Phalanx control board, Captain Urik Bayers turned and struck the trembling brigade gunner across the face with stinging force. The man staggered from the blow and backed into the navigation table of the great ship.

"Shut up," Bayers hissed in ill-constrained fury. "That was just a warning. But if they think it will scare us into submission, then they are bigger fools than our employers.

"Now get out of my sight before I blow your head off," Bayers commanded, a hand resting on his holstered side arm.

"Yes, sir," the man replied sullenly, turning away to hide his rage and shame as he left the room.

"Ahoy, bridge. Deck Ten to the bridge," a voice called from the ship intercom.

"Go, Ten," Lieutenant Gunther Danvers commanded, hitting a button. "How's the search going?"

Surrounded by plastic wrapping on the deck, the XO was

busy at a table unwrapping ammo blocks for the G-11 caseless rifles for easy access. The blocks would absorb the moisture from the air and become inert in a few hours, but within minutes this would all be over, and it wouldn't matter anymore.

The intercom crackled for a moment. "Sir, we can't find the paratroopers anywhere on the exposed decks. One escaped into an elevator shaft and disappeared, but the others had to have been blown overboard by the wind."

"Impossible," Bayers snapped. "That was a SeaHawk helicopter. Holds eleven men, maybe a few more if jammed in tight, but we counted only five chutes."

"So?" Danvers asked gruffly, ripping open a fresh box of sealed ammunition.

The captain sneered. "So the goddamn Pentagon wouldn't send only five unless they thought that was enough to stop us. There is no way such an elite team would fall overboard like drunks at a party."

"Five against a thousand?" Danvers snorted. "Ridiculous. Nobody is that good."

"Tell that to my brother," Bayers stated, with a touch of hatred thickening his voice. His younger brother had been murdered by Delta Force, or whoever they were, in Baltimore, and there was almost nothing he wanted more than to capture one of these special operatives alive to get revenge. But the cause was more important than personal feelings.

"No problem, sir," a man said, saluting with his G-11 rifle. "We'll stop them."

"Maybe," Bayers said with a scowl, and went to the communications board and punched a telephone number into a keypad. "Bridge to Launch Bay One. Dr. Tahrir, this is the captain. I'm sending extra troops to help you hold the facility. Continue sending up hunters until the very last moment. Do not stop under any circumstances. Is that clear?"

There was no reply.

Checking the circuits to make sure the connection was intact, Bayers tried again. "Dr. Tahrir, report!"

Silence.

"The launcher," Danvers snarled, slamming a fist onto the panel. "The paratroopers didn't go overboard, they dropped into the space cannon!"

"Then the doc is already dead," a man said in shock.

Just then, an F-18 streaked by the bridge, rattling the few windows still intact, the wind rushing through the broken frames to buffet the crew and send papers swirling.

"Or captured, which is much worse," Bayers said. That would put the command codes in jeopardy. Unacceptable.

"Are they mad?" a man asked.

"No, they're dead," Bayers replied, and started throwing switches. This would take a few minutes, but the people in the launch room had just made the last mistake of their lives.

As THE BANGING on the sealed hatch to the launch room continued, Manning walked closer to the door, his scowl deepening. That was starting to sound like Morse code. A few words came through, so reversing his MP-5, the warrior used the grip to knock back, and the banging rapidly answered.

"It's T.J.!" he exclaimed, removing the wrench holding the wheel lock in place. Quickly turning the handle, Manning undogged the hatch and Hawkins slipped inside just as a hail of bullets arrived. The slugs skipped off the front of the steel door to then ricocheted off the walls of the launch room.

Dropping to the floor, Hawkins fired back with his stolen AK-47, and Manning added the firepower of his MP-5 to the fray. Down the ship corridor, brigade gunners ducked around a corner and thrust out their weapons to blindly respond.

''Ready!'' Hawkins growled, grabbing a red canister from his belt and pulling the pin.

As Manning started moving the hatch, Hawkins lobbed the incendiary charge down the corridor. The oval door boomed closed just as the grenade cut loose, filling the passageway with searing flame. Using both hands to turn the wheel, Manning dogged the watertight hatch shut and cut off the screams of the burning men.

''Thanks for the assist,'' Hawkins said, removing the spent clip from the Kalashnikov and taking one from a dead hardman on the deck. Then he paused. ''These okay?''

''Died fast, no booby traps,'' Manning said, sliding the wrench back into position. Then he smiled and slapped the other man on the shoulder. ''Nice to have you back, buddy.''

The slight blow made Hawkins wince, although he tried to hide the fact.

''Where and how bad?'' Manning ordered, pulling out a med kit.

''Sprained ankle,'' Hawkins said, limping to a low wooden crate and sitting down to remove his combat boot.

Under the boot, the flesh was mottled, deathly pale with black-and-purple bruises. Neither made a comment that the injury was a lot worse than a mere sprain. Manning laid out the kit on the crate and prepared a tensor bandage and morphine shot.

Down below the catwalk, Encizo forced open a file cabinet and began using a digital camera to record the various structural blueprints and electrical schematics. The flowing script seemed to be Arabic in nature, at least it was definitely from the Middle East. Then he noticed the signature and date in the lower corner. Dr. G. Bull and the then minister of military defense, Saddam Hussein. My God, these were some of the original design plans for Project Babylon in

Iraq. How did the Peace Brigade get its hands on these documents?

Suddenly from across the room, there was a muffled explosion inside a wall and somebody began shrieking from an air vent, then abruptly ceased.

"Stay hard," McCarter warned, checking the other vents and hatches. "They must know what our aim is by now and will do anything to stop us from leaving here with the codes."

"Don't have them yet," James said, busily working at the top of a ladder leaning against a hunter.

The armored hull of a killer satellite had finally succumbed to the tools of the man and he was attaching wires to circuit boards, his Army laptop scrolling madly as he searched for the operational codes. Tokaido had written the search program, so he knew it would get the data they needed. But the longer it took, the greater was the danger of a retaliatory strike from the brigade.

The commando paused as a slight tremor shook the hunter, and then on the screen of the laptop an endless progression of binary codes began to scroll by at lightning speed.

"Incoming!" James shouted, and the Stony Man warrior threw himself off the satellite to land on the conveyor belt. The cushioned leather took most of the impact, but James still had the wind knocked out of himself and lay there stunned for a moment before crawling underneath the belt.

Trying to find the source of the danger, McCarter had only a split second to realize what was happening when the six hunters started hissing out tufts of white propellant gas, struggling to change directions in the heavy gravity of Earth. Then small ports irised wide on the hunters, the openings lined with the silvery spirals of magnetic coils of rail guns.

"The hunters are live!" McCarter cursed, firing from the

hip even as he raced to get behind the enormous column of the launch cannon.

The 9 mm rounds of his machine gun bounced off the black hull of the first two hunters, the misshapen slugs ricocheting away to rattle along the catwalk. Firing again, the Phoenix Force warrior peppered the first hunter, probing for the open section of hull James had been using. Exposed circuit boards shattered, and sparks flew from smashed relays and the machine went still. One down, five to go.

But the other hunters sluggishly rotated his way and responded in a series of bright flashes. There was a blur in the air and the metal wall near McCarter rippled in a series of plasma explosions from the supersonic plastic cubes. Inch-deep pits were gouged out of the steel wall, and the concussion of the multiple blasts forced him to stagger away, almost into the line of sight of the nearly stationary hunters.

From different locations, Phoenix Force attacked with a fusillade of rounds, Encizo blasting one with a 40 mm shell from the M-203 attached to his MP-5. Rocking on the conveyor belt from the explosion, the hunters hissed back, the walls and ceiling roiling with deafening plasma strikes. As the end satellite turned to race after the little Cuban, it abruptly ceased firing as the hunter alongside got dangerously in the way. The team used the brief pause to seek better protection and frantically reload.

Darting into view, Manning hit one with a thermite grenade, the searing fireball melting the black sphere from the top down, molten titanium and a weird gelatin pouring over the cracked ceramic to puddle on the deck. The hellish waves of heat crippled the hunter alongside, and it stopped attacking. But that was the last of the thermal charges, and there were still three hunters remaining.

Slamming in a fresh clip, McCarter thanked God that the damn things were designed to fight in space. The altitude jets moving the huge machines weren't very fast. It was the only reason Phoenix Force was still alive. Those rail guns could chew through the reactive armor of a battleship in seconds. But the brigade didn't want the machines to run wild in the heart of their vessel. He paused. The machines were designed to destroy other satellites. How could they target a man?

"The hunters are being operated by somebody," he whispered into his throat mike, reaching around the launcher to fire a brief burst. "It has video cameras and they can see us!"

"Not for long!" Encizo snarled.

The commando stood with his MP-5 and a brigade AK-47 to hose the ceiling, and the rest of the team soon followed his example. As the ceiling fixtures shattered, the launch room went dark. Almost instantly the hunters stopped firing, the altitude jets hissing short bursts as the machine rotated about trying to find out what was wrong.

Phoenix Force started to fire, the muzzle-flashes of their weapons strobing the darkness. The hunters sighed in reply, the walls and machinery exploding from the plasma explosions.

"Hold your fire on my command," James said from the darkness. "Ready, set, now."

The team stopped, and James stood from under the conveyor belt to slap wads of C-4 onto the dull black hull of a hunter, the mound of clayish material already primed with timing pencils. As the machine began to rotate toward him, James snapped off the timing pencil and rolled along underneath the conveyor belt, getting as far away as possible.

The thunderclap tore a gaping hole in the hunter, and the Phoenix Force warriors concentrated their 9 mm rounds on the weakest location. Soon the machine ceased to fight, but the last two hunters seemed to redouble their efforts and constantly jerked about, hissing nonstop in an effort to slay the intruders.

A control panel was blown apart, and Manning fell, glass daggers embedded in his flak jacket. Then McCarter swung out of cover and threw a big glob of C-4 that he had been warming in his palms at the nearest Hunter. It hit the hull and stayed in place, but the timing pencil fell out to bang harmlessly on the deck.

Shit! Drawing a Veri pistol from a shoulder holster, McCarter shot the flare gun at the hunter, the sizzling magnesium round striking the C-4 with enough force to cause detonation. The satellite was blown off the conveyor belt to land with a crash and rolled into the corner to land upside down. The altitude jets fiercely hissed trying to turn the machine until another 40 mm round hit and ripped the hull open, the ceramic armor peeling back in long smoking strips to expose the interior works. Thick goop dribbled out like transparent blood as Hawkins emptied a full clip of 7.62 mm hardball ammo into the thing. Bright sparks flying, the hunter went still.

"Gary, jam the radios!" McCarter ordered, reloading the Veri pistol with his only spare flare. The Navy signal device was supposed to have been used to announce a nuclear strike on the ship if that was the only way to stop any more launches, but that was no longer a danger.

"Already done," the man replied over the earpiece. "I expected the brigade to order the hunters to self-destruct if we started to win the battle."

Shooting the MP-5 in his right hand, the Veri pistol ready in his left, McCarter grunted in reply. If only they were able to record the incoming signal from the brigade, the team could then relay it to the Hornets outside and eventually to the hunters in orbit. But to receive the command, they would have to clear the airwaves, which would mean the hunters would explode, killing them in the process.

Facing only a single hunter, Phoenix Force alternated between shooting and warming C-4 to pitch at the machine in wet smacks. James tried throwing a timing pencil like one of his Japanese iron spikes, but the stick wasn't designed for such a tactic and it hit the hull an inch too low and shattered.

"Give me some light!" McCarter snapped from the stygian gloom, the flashes of the machine guns the only sources of illumination.

Switching on the laser of his Beretta, Hawkins placed a taut finger on the trigger, but didn't shoot. Moving the red dot along the hull of the hunter, he found a glob of C-4 and kept it there.

Perfect. Moving fast, McCarter aimed and pulled the trigger. The signal flare hit, and the hunter was ripped apart, debris clanging against the walls and ceiling.

"Thanks," McCarter said, tossing away the useless pistol and snapping on a flashlight.

The rest of Phoenix Force quickly did the same, and the bright white beams shone clearly on the massive hunters. In combat, the light would only have drawn immediate retaliatory fire from the deadly rail guns.

"Big mothers," Hawkins commented, hobbling closer in the dim light and working the bolt on his machine gun to clear a jam. Then he easily attached a flashlight to the barrel of his AK-47 with military gun tape. "Damn, half of these are junk. We're not going to recover any code sequences from this trash."

"Silence," James commanded into his throat mike.

Instantly the men froze and in the stillness they could hear hard pounding from both of the sealed hatchways on the catwalk. The brigade reserve gunners had arrived during the firefight. If Manning hadn't jammed the door, the team would have been caught in the cross fire and cut down.

"T.J., cover the catwalk. Rafe, Gary, rig the stairs with

Claymores. Cal get those bloody codes!" McCarter ordered, aiming his MP-5 at the doors. "Move with a purpose, people!"

The men flowed into action, James bypassing the hunters and going directly to the main control board of the facility. Removing rainbow-colored CD disks from the smashed board, he slipped them into the Army laptop and as each beeped, he tossed it aside and shoved in another.

"These are the maintenance codes," he reported, squinting to see in the glow of the computer screen. "No, no, yes! This one will open the hull for a prelaunch inspection."

"Whatever you're doing," McCarter commanded, drawing his Browning Hi-Power and jacking the slide, "don't waste time explaining it to me."

James nodded and raced across the littered battle zone to the least damaged hunter and used alligator clips to attach the laptop to the bare wiring. The internal batteries of the hunter were dead, so he went to the next. That one still had a trickle of power coursing through the system, and he used the laptop to force the hunter to disengage the locks and open every access port of the armored hull. Nothing useful could be seen, so he crawled underneath and found an inspection port. Slowing his speed to not make a mistake, James inserted probes and started hacking into the hard drive. This software was from Kurtzman and accessed through a legitimate port, the machine began to sluggishly download its files, the data processed slow because of the low voltage from the destroyed batteries. But there was nothing James could do about that. With precious seconds ticking away, the man ran a check on each file, finding only orbital navigational data and attack plans. "Come on, darling," he cajoled, "give it up, you bitch...."

Unexpectedly the pounding on the hatches stopped. Rigging a trip wire on the top step of the stairs, Encizo felt a wave of warmth come from the steel surface and he cursed as a dull red spot appeared on the metal. The spot became orange, then yellow and finally white. Molten steel began to dribble onto the deck as a cutting torch started to cut a line through around the immobile wheel lock.

"They're coming through," he whispered over the com link, carefully removing the arming pin from the Claymore. But there was only a squeal in return. Shit, the jamming field was stopping all transmissions.

Placing two fingers into his mouth, the commando whistled sharply, and the others turned to see the bright flame etching the hatch as it started on the downward curve to finish the circle. Suddenly another orange dot appeared at the second door, quickly brightening to a glaring white.

"Volley fire on my command," McCarter ordered briskly. "No grenades unless the hatchway is completely clear or else they'll just fall back down here toward us."

"Got it!" James stated, pulling a disk from the laptop. "I have the codes!"

McCarter turned. "Self-destruct?"

"No. The safety ident. If our satellites broadcast this, the hunters wouldn't be able to attack them anymore."

"Good enough." McCarter acknowledged, resting his weapon on a shoulder. "Okay, into the launcher! Gary, you're the last."

"Understood," the big Canadian said, smiling in the reflected glow of the flashlight on his weapon. "Lead the way."

Scrambling over the wreckage and corpses, Phoenix Force piled into the magnetic launcher, but Manning stayed in the open breech, both hands gripping the ferruled edge of the curved portal. Meanwhile, James was fiddling with the laptop and soon a sheet of paper extruded from the tiny built-in printer. The fax paper was shiny gray, but still readable in the beams of the flashlights.

Outside the space cannon, there sounded metallic crashes and gunfire.

"They're through, and coming down the stairs," Manning said, bracing a boot against the jamb for better leverage to close the door. "They found the Claymores and deactivated them."

"I don't care. Wait for it," McCarter said, his eyes moving across the fax paper trying to memorize the alphanumeric codes, but the sequence was much too long, almost a hundred different symbols. Damn brigade thought of everything. Well, almost.

"They're crossing the room," Manning said tersely.

"Just a few seconds more," McCarter urged, then bullets hit the launcher and one skipped inside. "Now, man, now!"

Manning yanked the portal shut, and as the magnetic coils of the launcher cut off the jamming field, the hunters erupted with titanic force. The entire vessel seemed to shake and something large hit the outside of the space cannon hard enough to dent the foot-thick barrel.

"Hoisted by their own petard." Encizo grinned. "Literally."

"Close enough for government work," Hawkins agreed with a pained expression.

"Uncle Jack, can you read me, over?" McCarter said into his throat mike. There was no reply. "Jack, respond!"

Damn, he had been hoping that by broadcasting straight up the barrel of the launcher, the portable radio would have sufficient power to reach the Hornets. Apparently not.

"T.J., use that Kalashnikov and get us out of here," he ordered.

Limping to the LGH bag, Hawkins unzipped the nylon pouch fast and laid the spool of knotted 11 mm rope between his boots. Then pulling out the bullet trap, he snugly inserted the device into the muzzle of his AK-47, attached the rope to the wire bridle, assuming a loose stance for the massive recoil, aimed at the sky and fired.

The LGH shot away and the grapnel instantly extended its six steel prongs, the bridle tugging the rope spool into action, the line trailing behind and then sailing over the rim of the space cannon. Hawkins tugged the line to make sure it was secure and passed it to McCarter. Removing the last of his weapons and supplies, the Stony Man warrior grabbed hold and started up the line as if it were a ladder. Minutes later he reached the top and hooked an arm over the rim, black smoke from the real funnel upwind blocking most of his view of the sky. There was no way of telling if the Hornets were still flying or if they had been shot down or ran out of fuel by now.

"Uncle Jack, this is Big Mac," McCarter said quickly, turning his head about to try to find the F-18 Super Hornet. "Can you hear us, over."

"Loud and clear, Mac," Grimaldi replied in his earpiece. "What the hell did you guys just do to the ship?"

"Gave the brigade a taste of its own medicine," McCarter replied, levering himself onto the rim and taking a seat. "Here are the ident codes for the hunters. Give them to your relay ship and have it race back to the *Hawk* and have the captain try to reach the Farm's satellite. That's our best bet."

A chance in hell was more like it, the pilot thought. "Roger on that, Mac. Go."

Sliding the paper from a fatigue blouse pocket, McCarter rattled off the alphanumeric string quickly, ignoring the arrival of another grappling hook only a yard away. Soon Encizo was alongside, clinging to the rim of the funnel. He nodded and started removing his heavy combat boots.

"The codes are on their way," Grimaldi said as a Hornet streaked through the smoke overhead. "Now get off that rust bucket and let us finish."

"Roger that, Uncle Jack. Give us thirty seconds, then clear the road for us."

"My pleasure, Mac."

"Over and out," McCarter said to the sky, then turned to Encizo who was assisting Hawkins onto the rim. "Let's go."

James and Manning soon joined the others, and the men rappelled down the climbing lines outside the funnel. Standing on the cold deck, they waited a moment until an F-18 Hornet appeared from the north and strafed the deck below them with cannon fire and machine guns. The brigade gunners not torn apart by the hellstorm ran for cover.

Instantly the Stony Man warriors slid down to the next deck, ran to the railing and simply dived straight over the side of the cruise liner and into the ocean.

They hit the water twenty feet from the craft and swam hard underwater, fighting the pull of the great ship's undertow. Once clear, they bobbed to the surface and drank in deep gulps of air. Safe!

But seconds later, the last Phalanx began ripping a stream of 20 mm shells at the swimming men. Diving again, they spread out to give the enemy gunner several targets and stayed out of sight for as long as possible until their lungs burned and they were forced to the open air again.

The first thing they saw were Harriers coming their way.

Instantly the Phalanx started yammering, but the rounds began to explode underwater as if striking something hard. A heartbeat later, the water between Phoenix Force and the *Terra Nova* began to rise in a swell that rapidly increased in height until the armored conning tower of the *Connecticut* broke the surface, the 20 mm rounds detonating as harmless as firecrackers on the hull metal. Caught away from the ship, the Harriers paused at the sudden invasion of a billion-dollar war machine.

"Uncle Jack, the team is free," McCarter shouted into

his radio. "Repeat, the ground zero is clear. Sink that mother!"

"Roger that, Phoenix One. My Navy pilots have been itching to hear that command. The second wing just arrived and is loaded for bear. Brace yourselves."

In a screaming dive, the Bravo wing of Hornets came from the sky, converging on the cruise liner with cannons ablaze. The Harriers angled to attack and were blown out of the sky on the first salvo. Now a barrage of Sidewinders and Hellfire missiles slammed into the vulnerable top deck and penetrated to explode somewhere inside the massive vessel.

Then the team felt a motion in the water, and a foamy wake appeared just below the surface and streaked away to arch around the burning craft. It struck the other side with a blast that threw shrapnel and flame so high it almost caught a Hornet passing by as it dropped a load of bombs on the bridge and forecastle.

With a clang sailors appeared on the conning tower and scrambled to get rubber rafts dispatched for Phoenix Force. Beyond the submarine, McCarter could see that the *Terra Nova* was already starting to list as the crumpled vessel began to take on water.

"Look," James said, an arm under Hawkins to help the wounded man stay afloat.

On the horizon a third wing of Hornets and Eagles streaked toward the brigade ship, along with another C-160 Hercules air tanker. The first wave of Hornets was already slipping into formation for emergency refueling.

Suddenly the second wing attacked and the air was full of missile contrails spiraling inward. Stitched from stem to stern, the sinking *Terra Nova* was hammered into pieces, flames writhing into the sky as the diesel fuel for the masive engines finally ignited, completing the destruction from the inside until the vessel was reduced to a roiling inferno of explosions and smoke.

"A Kodak moment if I ever saw one," Manning joked grimly, the saltwater stinging his countless small cuts and abrasions.

"David, think the Farm will get the codes in time to do anything?" Encizo asked, spitting water from his mouth.

"Sure hope so," McCarter replied, his hair plastered flat against his head. "If not, then our only hope is Able Team."

CHAPTER TWENTY-ONE

Peace Brigade Fortress

As the roar of the fire consuming the mansion got steadily louder, Able Team checked the pockets of the corpse and then the drawers of the desk, but there was no sign of a code book.

While Schwarz inspected the ashes in the tray with a microscope pen, Lyons carefully studied the corpse itself. The watch on the left wrist matched the pale skin underneath, the same with an ornate ring on the right hand. Moving to the slack face of death, the big ex-cop checked the mouth for powder burns, then examined the collar, fingering the rank insignia of the warm corpse.

"It's Cole, all right," he said, making a fleeting gesture in sign language that relayed the message he was lying. The gold oak leaves on the collar were brand-new, just recently sewn into a blouse that was worn before. No way was this the commander of the Peace Brigade.

"So the coward took his own life rather than be captured," Schwarz growled, shaking his M-16 in rage. He had no idea what Lyons was planning, so he would just go along with whatever the man said and stay ready for trouble.

"Only thing we can do now is level this place," Blancanales stated, trying his utmost to sound natural.

"Agreed. Sergeant, give me the C-5 gelinite," Lyons ordered, reaching for the laptop. If Cole had hidden video cameras in the outer corridor, this ruse wouldn't work, but it was all he could think up. The prey had gone to ground and they needed to flush the tall grass. It was time to make the terrorists come to them.

"Here, Commander," Schwarz said, slipping the strap off a shoulder and passing over the computer. He knew that there actually was such a compound as C-5, but nobody used the stuff because it was much too unstable.

Lyons reached inside the bag and turned the built-in speaker volume to maximum, then switched the machine on with a large beep.

"Lieutenant, how long for us to reach safe distance?" Lyons asked, fiddling about with nothing inside the cushioned bag.

"Roughly three minutes to get to the canal, sir," Blancanales replied grimly. "The water should protect us from the blast."

Gently Lyons laid the processing computer on the metal desk. "I'll give us two minutes," he said. "You two start running right now. Once this arming mechanism is set, there's no turning it off."

Turning, his teammates started to race away when they heard the sigh of working hydraulics. Spinning with their weapons leveled, they saw a large section of the cinderblock wall disengage and swing away on disguised hinges.

"Kill them!" a gruff voice commanded from within. "Disarm that bomb!"

Firing brand-new AK-47 rifles, Peace Brigade gunners rushed from the secret room. Blancanales and Schwarz ducked behind a pallet of oddly numbered wooden crates and sprayed the opening with their M-16/M-203 combos. The mix of hardball and tumbler ammo made the enemy gunners jerk about, but none fell. More damn NATO body armor!

Behind the desk, Lyons moved fast and grabbed the beeping laptop to use as a shield. Incredibly the titanium computer was torn from his grip by a tracer round from the stuttering Kalashnikovs. That caught the Stony Man warrior by surprise. Jesus! If it had been real C-5 the mansion and everybody in it would have been vaporized.

"It's gonna blow!" Lyons shouted. As the enemy reacted, he swung up the Atchisson and ripped a full magazine at the brigade hardmen. The multiple impacts of the .33 shotgun pellets slammed them backward into the exposed room, two of them missing faces.

The enemy was still reeling as Able Team breached the doorway, firing steadily. Instantly Lyons saw a middle-aged man across the room. He was in neatly pressed military fatigues with shiny gold oak leaves on his collar, and was furiously ripping pages from a small book and tossing them into a flaming trash can. Behind him a small safe set into the wall stood open and empty.

The codes! Diving to the floor, Lyons blasted the can to pieces with the last round in the Atchisson, the impact shoving it into the corner and throwing hot ashes everywhere.

"Protect me!" Major Cole ordered, stuffing the rest of the small leather book in his mouth and chewing frantically.

The brigade gunners dropped to one knee and formed a firing line between the Stony Man team and their commander.

Blancanales could see the resolution in their faces to accept death to buy their commander the time he needed to destroy the codes, so he took the most desperate gamble of his life and threw away the M-16/M-203 and clutched his ear with the com link inserted.

"Oh my God!" he gasped, reeling. "It's happened! We're too late. New York and Washington have been nuked!"

"No," Schwarz whispered, dropping his own weapon. It

landed with a loud clatter that seemed to fill the small room. "Jesus Christ, the fools did it. The war has started!"

"The end of the world," Lyons cried out in anguish, ripping off his radio and casting it away. "The idiots! The fucking idiots. Damn them all to hell!"

Startled by these actions, the brigade gunners almost fired at the unarmed men, then beamed smiles at the wonderful news. Major Cole spit the now useless papers out of his mouth.

"Yes!" He laughed triumphantly. "We did it. We've won!"

Brandishing their weapons, the rest of the Peace Brigade started cheering, and from the floor Lyons fanned the line of hardmen with his Ingram machine pistol, catching each man underneath the jaw. The lifeless bodies flew backward and hit the wall.

Instantly realizing he had been tricked, Cole clawed for his side arm, and Blancanales and Schwarz both fired their handguns. The rogue major dropped to the floor, bleeding from the arms and legs.

"Damn you..." he growled, blood dribbling from his mouth.

Stepping over the fallen man, Lyons kicked the major's pistol away, then retrieved the partially chewed leather book from the desk.

"You are a fool, Major. Only amateurs would have bought that trick," Lyons said, thumbing through the damp pages. "You spent too much time torturing people and forgot to learn how to actually fight. Bad mistake."

"Never celebrate until the enemy is dead or disarmed," Blancanales added coldly, retrieving his weapon from the floor.

His face deathly pale, a furious Cole tried to speak again and could only rasp a low guttural noise. His chest was rising and falling rapidly, the pool underneath his body spreading quickly.

"Well?" Schwarz demanded, checking his own M-16/M-203 combo. The fall hadn't damaged the machine gun, but he worked the bolt to cycle through a live round just to make sure.

"Yeah, this is it," Lyons stated, folding back the leather cover to display a page of alphanumeric sequences.

"The ident codes?" Blancanales asked hopefully.

Lyons scowled slightly. "No. Those he burned already. But we have the self-destruct command."

"Good enough. Let's go."

"N-never leave..." Cole gurgled from the floor, and clawed a bloody hand under the desk to pull a Ruger .357 revolver. "I w-will not allow..."

In a smooth motion the Able Team commandos lowered their weapons and fired, filling the room with sound and fury. Wildly shaking from the multiple impacts, the supreme commander of the Peace Brigade still managed to fire his handgun but only hit the ceiling. Then he went limp and released the weapon.

"Bastard died a hell of a lot easier than many others today," Schwarz said, clearing the desk with a sweep of his arm, then removing his com link to quickly assemble a small folding-dish antenna. He angled it about, then hit the transmit switch.

"Stony One, this is Able Three, come in," he said, boosting the power to maximum. "Come in, Stony One. Please, respond."

There was only static.

"No good." He cursed, yanking the power cable loose. "We're too damn far away."

"And the big shortwave in the van is gone." Lyons scowled fiercely. "Plus we blew the radio room here."

Damnation, there was no time to drive back to Virginia.

The last links in the defense net could break at any moment and the war would start for real.

"What's involved in boosting a signal to reach the Farm?" Blancanales demanded, glancing about to see if there was anything useful in the room around them. But there was only the dead and the tools of death in sight.

"Raw power and height," Schwarz stated, patting the equipment pouch at his belt. "The rest I have on me."

Timbers crashed on the ground floor, shaking the room and making the corpses tremble in a gross pantomime of life.

"There's got to be something we can use," Lyons growled, then narrowed his eyes. "Didn't we pass a radio station coming here?"

"Better hope it's FM," Schwarz said, starting out of the room and into the warehouse. The smoke from the fire above was flowing from the air vents as thick as a muddy river.

"If not?" Blancanales asked.

"Then kiss your ass goodbye," Lyons stated.

As Able Team rushed from the burning mansion, several Peace Brigade gunners lurched from the smoking rubble clumsily firing weapons. But the wounded men were slow and inaccurate, and never got a second chance to try to stop the determined Stony Man warriors from leaving.

Outside, the estate was a shambles, but the garage was still partially standing. There had been several police cars parked in the building, but two were smashed from falling debris, two had every tire flat, and the fifth was missing its window and hood.

By hot-wiring the vehicle, Lyons got the engine to turn over and the team creaked away from the battlefield, slowly building speed with the rattling vehicle trailing oil and gas. Concentrating on the task at hand, the men tried not to think about the millions of innocent lives resting on the outcome of this desperate race.

Stony Man Farm, Virginia

AT THE EXTREME northern perimeter of the Farm, Madison DeForest was strolling along the foot trail in a lush peach orchard, trying to get the feel of the land on her new assignment. The past twenty-four hours had been a whirlwind of activity as she was contacted by a man named Buck Greene and recruited into a covert special operations group. Greene's bona fides had been verified by someone she had been told to contact in the Justice Department, and she had signed on for an undetermined length of time.

She snorted in amusement. So the three men had been members of an elite antiterrorist team. No wonder the Morlocks had gotten their butts kicked so hard, so fast.

Reaching up to pull an early peach from a leafy tree, the woman sniffed the fruit purely out of habit of buying groceries at stores for all her life, then gave it a squeeze and tucked the fruit into a loose pocket of her overalls. Although they called her a blacksuit, she was dressed as a damn farmhand and heavily armed.

Kicking some twigs off the dirt path, DeForest wandered along studying the lay of the land, trying to file away the contours in case of trouble. Something big was going on here; that much was obvious. If the ex-cop didn't know better, she would have sworn Barbara Price and the others were preparing for a major fight. But the defensives at this Farm were incredible! Hidden missile banks, land mines, not to mention an army of fellow blacksuits. How could any terrorist organization ever muster the resources to attack this military hardsite?

The earphone of her radio crackled softly.

Eh? Fiddling with the volume, DeForest listened intently and vaguely heard a familiar voice.

"...have the ident code..." the big blonde from the Pennsylvania war games shouted, his words rising and falling wildly. "Police are here to ar...us. We're stalling as... est...can. Must get...to Bear or...kira!" Now the man rattled off a long stream of letters and numbers, repeated the sequence, then started again.

The woman wasn't sure what was going on here, but fifteen years on the street taught a smart cop to follow her guts. Without any paper to use, she pushed up a sleeve and wrote on her skin the numbers and letters of what sounded like a launch code for missiles.

She was already walking through the orchard when the transmission started to repeat for a fifth time and then abruptly stopped. Damn. For a fleeting instant, it occurred to her that this might only be an initiation to razz the newest member on the base. But she would take the chance of looking foolish. The big blond man had saved a lot of cops, and she'd follow his request even if it was only a joke to embarrass her.

"Alert! Red alert!" DeForest shouted into her portable radio, her long legs sending the woman flashing through the orchard as she headed for the main building of the Farm.

"What is it?" Chief Greene snapped over her earpiece. "We got company coming?"

DeForest leaped over a picturesque fallen log and started racing along the wide-open fallow field for the distant buildings. Other blacksuits turned from their jobs to watch the Philadelphia beauty pelt by with a face grim as death. Several openly pulled their weapons and took cover facing the northern peach orchard to stop whatever was chasing her.

"Incoming from...ah, Ironman!" she shouted, suddenly recalling his code name. Yes, that was it. "He says Able has the ident codes!"

There came the squealing of a high-frequency receiver scanning for a broadcast.

"Damn it, I can't find anything!" Greene snarled over some static. "What channel are they on?"

"Standard morning band," she said, cresting a swell in the field. "You'll...never find them, sir. He went off the air."

"Did you hear the codes?" the chief of security demanded, stepping out of the tractor barn and starting toward the running woman.

DeForest raised an inky arm. "Wrote them down!"

"Thank God!" Greene cried, doing something to his belt radio. His model was larger than hers and sported a compact aerial for much greater range.

Panting slightly, DeForest nodded at the man and started for the main building, but he stopped her with a raised hand.

"No time for that," he said, then spoke into the radio. "Communications? Patch me through to the Bear and I mean right now! This is a Zulu Five emergency."

There was a squeal of changing frequencies from the Kenwood radio.

"Computer Room," a new voice said. "What the hell is this Zulu Five shit, Greene. Is the Farm under attack?"

"Shut up and listen," the chief ordered brusquely, then he thrust the radio into Madison's hands. "Tell them!"

Quickly the cop gave a condensed version of what had just happened in the orchard.

"But how the hell...the crazy bastards must have commandeered a civilian radio station," the man called Bear said in amazement. She recognized his voice from her brief orientation meeting yesterday. "Christ, I think this is real and not a trick of the brigade. Akira, what's our status?"

A young male voice replied, "The hunters have found our satellite and are converging for a kill."

"Alert," an older woman calmly announced. "We have

been hit. Our comsat is badly damaged and starting to go off-line.''

"The codes!" Kurtzman thundered over the radio.

DeForest read the sequence off her arm.

"Got it!" the young man cried.

"Broadcast it now!" Kurtzman commanded. "Full EM spectrum!"

"Too late! Our comsat is gone!"

"Use the SETI array!" Price barked. "Widest aperture of transmission, maximum power. Blanket the sky!"

Waves of static crackled over the handset while Greene and DeForest stood there in the grassy field listening to the end of the world.

"Wait a second," Kurtzman said, then was quiet for another minute.

"A hunter just detonated!" the young man shouted in triumph.

"From a missile attack?" Kurtzman demanded hotly. "Or did the self-destruct codes work?"

"Mount Palomer Observatory says there are no visible missile exhausts in space. The hunters are doing it to themselves."

"Then we've won?"

"Bet your ass, we did."

Wild cheering rose from the small speaker and continued without any sign of stopping.

"Well done, Buck," Price said, her voice thick with emotion. "Tell Able Team they did it! The hunters are blowing themselves apart across the world."

"I'll be sure to tell them when I see them, Barbara," the chief of security replied, looking at the clear blue sky above.

For the first time in a day, the man allowed himself to relax and took a deep breath. Nothing could be seen happening, but in his mind's eye the dark of space was filled with fiery detonations as the massive hunter-killers exploded with pyrotechnic fury. They had stopped the brigade with only seconds to go, but that was enough. The Farm had beaten the bastards.

Then Greene turned to the new recruit still standing anxiously nearby. The woman had no idea what she had just done, but it was her instinct that just saved America from nuclear annihilation.

"Maddy DeForest, right?" Greene said, taking the radio back and slipping it into the cushioned pouch on his gun belt.

"Madison, yes, sir," she replied patiently.

Grunting acknowledgment, Greene looked the blacksuit over, then pounded her on the shoulder. "Good goddamn job there, De."

"Mostly just luck, sir," DeForest said honestly. "I was in the right place at the right time."

"Kid, being lucky is just as important as being smart in our line of work." The man nodded to himself as if making a decision. "You got guts and smarts. The rest I can teach you. As of right now, you are off foot patrols. I have needed a replacement topkick for a long time, and I am offering the post to you. Interested?"

A promotion already? What had just happened here today? "I'm honored, Chief," DeForest replied hesitantly. "If you think I can handle the job, that is."

Green snorted in amusement. "You won't feel so goddamn honored when you hear what the KGB did to my last XO."

"The Russian KGB, sir?" DeForest scowled, not sure if he had heard that right.

"Soviet KGB," he corrected. "Big difference. Come on, have a few things to tell you about what really goes on round here."

Arching an eyebrow, the ex-cop followed after the grizzled veteran, her expression of disbelief getting constantly igger the more he talked.

EPILOGUE

Dining Room, Main Building, the Farm

There was a clatter of dishes and the smell of frying bacon from the direction of the kitchen as Barbara Price and Hal Brognola sat at an empty table in the main dining room and watched a TV monitor suspended in the corner.

With billowing clouds, there was a long sustained thunder of chemical fire and the space shuttle *Discovery* launched from Cape Canaveral carrying a ten-ton cargo of replacement satellites.

Reaching for a remote, Price turned off the television and leaned forward resting on her arms. She was beyond tired, and starting to get her second wind. But the woman knew that tonight she would sleep like a log.

"There she goes," Brognola said, pouring more sugar into his mug of coffee. The tantalizing smells from the kitchen were a knife in his stomach, but patience was the habit learned working in Washington D.C. "The national-defense net will be back on-line by nightfall, and the telecommunications network should be functional again by dawn tomorrow."

Price gave a shaky laugh. "If somebody had gone for a long camping trip in the Rockies, they'd come back on Friday and never know that anything happened."

"That's our job," Brognola said, sipping the brew.

"How is Able Team?" she asked.

The big Fed scowled, more at the coffee than anything else. If he didn't know better, the man would swear that Kurtzman was teaching the staff how to make coffee. Damn stuff got worse every time.

"Well, the local PD isn't thrilled by the cover story of a Justice Department undercover operation," Brognola said. "But they'll play ball and set them free in a few hours."

"Akira says he can destroy the record of their arrest, and the computer records of their fingerprints will be altered once the team is set loose," she added, settling back in the chair.

"Good. Phoenix Force is still on board the USS *Connecticut* and will arrive at Norfolk by tomorrow. But I think we should leave them in Liberty Town for a few days of R&R."

"Accepted. Did you hear that Buck is talking about making DeForest his second?" Price said, glancing at the closed door to security HQ across the room. The two were still in conference after six hours, the office strewed with maps and blueprints of the base.

"Well, he's thinking about it," Cowboy Kissinger corrected, ambling over from the kitchen with a serving tray full of covered dishes.

Placing the plastic tray on the table, he removed the lids to display a wealth of scrambled eggs, bacon, assorted tasty sundries and a small mountain of steaming golden waffles, the chef's specialty. "Buck has made no final decision on her yet. She's the newbie here. Doesn't even know where we keep the directional bearing grease."

Helping himself to the eggs and bacon, Brognola snorted a laugh. Oh, no, not that old gag again. Every Navy plebe was hit with the gag. A directional bearing was the course that a ship was traveling, not a machine part. But it took some of the newbies days to figure that out.

"It's right next to the left-handed wrenches, isn't it?" Price commented dryly, pouring maple syrup over some waffles. The rising steam smelled like ambrosia. How long had it been since her last meal, twelve hours, twenty? She had lost count in the crisis. How did that old saw go— soldiers lived off fear and adrenaline, the command staff lived off coffee and chewed fingernails? True words, indeed.

"Exactly." Kissinger grinned, eagerly placing out small dishes of hot white grits. "It's the only way we can control the snipes."

Price and Brognola stared at the heaps of boiled corn pone as if it were about to attack them, when the door to the room burst open and Carmen Delahunt walked in holding a thick stack of papers.

"We have a problem," she announced in greeting, offering Brognola and Price duplicate sheets. "The parent company that owns, or rather owned, the *Terra Nova* has a local bank to handle payroll, rent and such. But other than that, there doesn't seem to be any other bank accounts, checking, savings, nothing at all. As far as I can discern, Major Sebastian Cole put a hand into his pocket and pulled out millions in cash from nowhere."

"Maybe he looted the South African national treasury before he left the country?" Kissinger offered, reading over Brognola's shoulder. As the big Fed finished the first sheet, he passed it to the weapons master and started on the next.

Using stiff fingers to brush back her wild profusion of red hair, Delahunt frowned. "Those accounts are in order. Any pilfering was handled long ago."

"Then the brigade had a secret backer?" Price suggested.

"So it would appear," Kurtzman rumbled as he joined them. "And there's worse news."

"Tell me," she ordered.

"Hunt and I went over the digital photos that Able Team took of the supply crates in the brigade warehouse and what

Phoenix Force recorded of the tools and equipment panels on board the *Terra Nova*. A lot of the labels and manufacturing stamps had been painted over or scraped off, but there were still numerous snatches of flowing Arabic writing at both locations. Books, maps, schematics, ammo brass, you name it.''

"Damn. Okay, which regional Arab language is it?'' Brognola demanded, folding his hands. "Who was behind the attack?''

"All of them,'' Kurtzman replied.

"Coffee?'' Kissinger said, offering a mug.

Sniffing the aroma, Kurtzman curled a lip at the weak brew and passed. "Anyway, there are eight different variations I can find here,'' the computer wizard said, taking a paper napkin from a dispenser and cleaning his hands. "So either the brigade was so incredibly clever that, in case they failed, they faked various idiomatic subtongues to hide the real source of their supplies, or...'' He left the sentence hanging.

"Or they all helped Cole,'' Price said thoughtfully. "Every terrorist organization from each Arab nation.'' So a unified terrorist organization had finally been formed. This was a nightmare come to life.

"Are we sure about this?'' she demanded curtly.

Kurtzman shrugged. "As sure as we can be of anything in the usual chaos of the Middle East. But I believe that we have interpreted the data correctly.''

"We need confirmation. Have the Peace Brigade survivors been questioned?'' Brognola asked.

"There were none,'' Price replied, sighing. "Those not killed in direct action, soon took their own lives rather than be captured alive.''

Scowling, Kissinger loosened the strap on his shoulder holster. A UN of terrorists. Even if the Arabs were in charge, the IRA and the German terrorists, the Asian Dawn, hell, every loony out there might be members. With that level of combined resources and contacts, the freedom-loving nation was in for major trouble. This satellite thing looked like the opening shot of a new war for world domination.

"This information must be reported to the President immediately," Brognola said, rising from his chair. "I want a helicopter on the landing field in ten minutes. My God, think of it! A Pan-Arabian cartel with unlimited funds and a serious intent to destroy the United States."

"That's also our assessment of the situation," Delahunt agreed.

"An entire enemy organization and we don't even know its name," Price said, pushing aside the plate of food, her appetite gone. "Much less anything else. We'll just have to see what unfolds. And hope to God we're ready."

"They're called Unity," Mack Bolan stated grimly, standing in the hallway entrance of the dining room. "And we'll be ready."

James Axler

OUTLANDERS®

PRODIGAL CHALICE

The warriors, who dare to expose the deadly truth of mankind's destiny, discover a new gateway in Central America—one that could lead them deeper into the conspiracy that has doomed Earth. Here they encounter a most unusual baron struggling to control the vast oil resources of the region. Uncertain if this charismatic leader is friend or foe, Kane is lured into a search for an ancient relic of mythic proportions that may promise a better future…or plunge humanity back into the dark ages.

In the Outlands,
the shocking truth is humanity's last hope.